Aharon Megged

The Flying Camel and the Golden Hump

TRANSLATED FROM THE HEBREW BY

Vivian Eden

The Toby Press

The Flying Camel and the Golden Hump
First English Language Edition, 2007

The Toby Press LLC
POB 8531, New Milford, CT 06776-8531, USA
& POB 2455, London W1A 5WY, England
www.tobypress.com

Originally published in Hebrew as
Ha-Gamal Ha-Meofef Ve-Dabeshet Ha-Zahav.

Translations of the works of Rabelais are adapted from François Rabelais, *Five Books of the Lives, Heroic Deeds and Sayings of Gargantua and His Son Pantagruel,* trans. Sir Thomas Urquhart and Peter le Motteux, first published in 1653 and 1694.

References to "Le Clercq" refer to *The Complete Works of Rabelais, The Five Books of Gargantua and Pantagruel,* trans. Jacques Le Clercq, New York: Random House, 1936.

ISBN 978 1 59264 196 3, *paperback*

A CIP catalogue record for this title is available from the British Library.

Printed and bound in the United States.

The Flying Camel and the Golden Hump

Contents

Superfluous Introduction

I am writing this book against my will. It is a nuisance to me, a hindrance, caught, you might say, like a bone in my throat. I had been writing—with great exaltation—quite a different book, about which I shall perhaps say a few words later on, but a certain incident, petty, annoying—like the fall of a sparrow's droppings on your head as you walk down the street lost in thought, or the ring of a telephone in the midst of frenzied lovemaking—interrupted my writing, paralyzing me. It thrust the twenty-two and a half pages of densely written manuscript, abashed, insulted, open-mouthed in the middle of an unfinished sentence ("the dining-room was like a temple of splendor, and light was sown in his eyes, but when he saw her at the set Passover table, beneath the bronze bird, and the pallor of death on her face...") into my drawer to wait for this storm to pass, if it ever does, and forced me to cease from work. And to begin.

This book, that is.

If against his will, asks the reader, what then is the reason for this piece of work? Yes, that is a question. But in order to answer, one would need to explain the motives for writing in general! What is it that drives a man—yes, sometimes even against his will!—to pluck events still in the fullness of their gorgeous bloom from the field of life and lay them on the paper, horizontally, in straight lines; to pick them and press them between two covers until they dry up and shrivel like desiccated figs; to flatten them into sentences, words, letters, insubstantial things—and at the same time to delude himself that he is breathing a new soul, more elevated, more noble, into what Nature, with neither pride or pretension, had created; that he is, as it were, transmuting the "earthly clay" to pure gold. All this, and a great deal more, must be explained, but I haven't the least desire to do so, nor am I qualified, so I shall leave this matter to literary scholars or researchers who are more knowledgeable about this than we authors are. I will, instead, chronicle what happened, which is easy for me even if it arouses doubts.

But if the introduction is superfluous, as the author claims, why then, asks the reader, is he writing it? Yes, I see in my mind's eye the industrious reviewer—a clever and experienced craftsman, who does his master's bidding—coming to the editor of the newspaper's literary supplement to receive his quota of books, and the latter hands him this one. He opens it, sniffs through it with his eyes and, like Balzac, who boasted that he didn't need to read a book to know its quality because he could judge it by its cover, he aims a rather sour look at his employer and says: "Don't you have a more likely possibility for me?" "Maybe you'll do it anyway?" wheedles the editor, having already tried two other pen-pushers, both of whom turned him down politely. Mr. Bookflayer, a degenerate descendent of Zoilus the Scourge, is uneasy about refusing so he opens the book again, skims ten lines on page 15, takes in another eight on page 75 and proves to his own satisfaction that his instincts, which he can always trust, have not led him astray this time either—no, this is not for him. A sort of baroque style, florid and coquettish, something a bit artificial, as well as old-fashioned...and what's it about anyway? The relations among neighbors in an apartment building...how banal, trite to the point of loathsomeness...not worth wiping a pen on, let alone whetting it. He is just about to lay the book back down on the desk, this time with an unambiguous smack: No! Let the editor find himself some other victim! Then suddenly, as he riffles backward through the book, he sees the heading "Superfluous Introduction"—and the spark of an exciting idea ignites within him: if the author is being smart with me, then I'll outsmart him, he thinks; and at that very moment he has a vision of his article, which would be no longer than thirty-five lines, at most forty—and unfurling there at the top of the column, venomous, witty, eye-catching, delightful, and right on target is the headline:

SUPERFLUOUS BOOK!

"Yes, alright," he says to the editor as he tucks the book under his arm.

And in this instance, which is extremely rare, our paths coincide. I agree with him: a superfluous book. Should he insist upon outsmarting me again, if only not to have to confront me as an equal, and in order to achieve for himself a place of honor on the roll of critics—a kingdom for a headline!—he has no choice but to call his review

STUPENDOUSLY SUPERFLUOUS!

Chapter one

Overture on the Staircase

The beginning was on the staircase, and not by chance, as will later become apparent.

It began thus:

Twilight of a June day—an early evening hour, dusky, when the light is still fading in the street, languorous from the heat and the dust, while indoors the shadows start to grapple along the walls. I go into the building, press the light switch, and before me I see, mounting the stairs—

I pause on the third stair: can it be? Can it be he?

Schatz?

I go up five more steps and reach the first landing. Meanwhile the stranger, who from the back so resembles Schatz, tall, erect, with a rigid forelock combed angularly back and up like the "Z" at the end of his name, continues to ascend without looking behind him, and arrives at the third landing, his hand on the curving banister, and doesn't stop. From the profile observed from below at an acute twenty-five degree angle I can tell that indeed—

Is he on his way to see me? Because he doesn't stop at either of the two doors on the second floor, and continues to climb confidently, like someone who is familiar with the place and knows where he's going—

But that's impossible!—I say to myself—if this is indeed Schatz it is impossible that he is on his way up to the apartment of the writer whose very existence he does not acknowledge, whose reality—as it were—he denies; it is impossible that he would decide to overcome his famous pride, take up his staff and bundle—like Rabbi Yehoshua who swallowed his pride and went to Rabban Gamliel—and come to beg forgiveness from me, beating his breast and saying, "I have wronged you, I have erred, I have thought ill—"

But just as I was saying this to myself—marveling, prepared to forgive him all his sins, to interrupt his apologies and say Stop, stop, to err is human; to arise from my chair and kiss his forehead, come in peace, happy is the generation that is blessed with men like you...just as I was saying this to myself, the automatic light on the staircase went out and darkness reigned. His hand—I sensed—felt along the marble walls to find the light switch. My hand—

And now, in the moment of darkness, permit me to take the opportunity to say a few words concerning this man, Schatz, who is about my age—forty years old or so—who is about my height, and the tools of whose trade are about the same as mine, though I plow with them lengthwise and he widthwise, so to speak; just a few words, because I am acquainted only with his nether side. With his back, that is. With the nape of his neck, really. Because as for his face... In principle, I should have been the one to have not greeted him in the street, because I was the insultee; in fact, it was he who walked right past me as if he hadn't seen me, his eyes fixed straight ahead, a stern, unforgiving look on his face, his stride bristling and decisive, expressing defiance and conceit... His face, therefore, I knew only *en passant*, like a wind blowing against mine, without allowing me to really look at it, a case of "thou shalt see my back parts; but my face shall not be seen," whereas the nape of his neck—

It was at a memorial gathering on the first anniversary of the death of a poet whom everybody—young and old alike—honored, particularly after his decease. The hall was full, and I, who had arrived late, found an empty seat in one of the back rows. I directed my attention—over many grey heads and fewer youthful ones—to the podium. A young professor was reading aloud from the manuscript of a disquisition thick with quotations and their interpretations. The sentences were long, convoluted and swarming with foreign terms, and I, too indolent to follow them and fathom their depths, allowed my gaze to wander over the assembled pates, both bald and hirsute, in search of familiar faces.

Here and there, amongst the eroded profiles of writers whose pasts lay before them sitting mustered together in their suits, shoulder to shoulder in the camaraderie of those who defend their territory against interlopers, I discovered a few fresher faces, a few more slender necks, a few defiant noses; I attempted to catch the eye of my friend Michael Hochhauser who sat at the far end of one of the front rows, but his attention was fixed on the podium and his expression was—as it so often is—a mask of deceptive innocence, like that of a schoolboy who hangs intently upon his teacher's every word in class, only to mock him cruelly and crudely during the break.

He who scans the distant horizon misses what is under his nose. And so, when I brought my gaze back from its wanderings over the auditorium in order to focus it again upon the lecturer, who continued to wend his way through the thicket of his exegesis, I saw before me, upright like a tree planted by rivers of seats, whose head also shall not wither, Schatz's straight back, my breath almost falling on his shoulders. From time to time, without turning his face away from the podium, he filtered a whispered word or two through his lips into the ear of the young woman sitting next to him. A purple fedora, wide-brimmed, crowned her long black hair, and by the smile that played on her lips I understood that those whispers were barbed remarks directed either at the speaker or at the speech. I could not take my eyes off the back of the neck in front of me. Framed by the sideburns cut in a straight horizontal line and the collar of his white shirt was an expanse of flesh sown with small pustules, scarlet as sin. Were they bedbug bites? Perhaps the barber's razor caused them as it passed over the nape of his neck? Maybe scabies? Mange? Herpes? Hives? Among the sores, on the pasty, irritated skin, short bristles of black hair sprouted; a patch of blush shone on either side of the gulley bisecting this bareness, as on a cheek that has just been slapped or rubbed hard and beneath this, near the collar, stretched a shallow cut. There was something chilling about the sight of this scratched and pitted bareness, and when I examined it and its signs—obtruding themselves right before my eyes, like the marks of writing on parchment—I thought that just as one can read character in the lines on the palm of a hand, one can read it in the spots on the napes of the stiff-necked.

A mere ten seconds passed in darkness. I, who lived there, was of course the first to locate the electric switch—on the second floor landing—and I pressed it to turn on the light.

Schatz—now that I had recalled the back of his neck I could no longer doubt that it was indeed he—kept going up the stairs.

To the fourth floor?—I stopped amazed at the door of my own apartment on the third floor—but on the fourth floor there is only one apartment, and it's been vacant and locked for about six months—ever since the death of its owner, Dr. Klausner the pharmacist. Maybe he got the street address wrong, and in another moment he'll come gliding back down the stairs.

I stood, clutching my doorknob, and listened.

A faint buzzing was heard from above. The door, the door of Klausner's apartment, which had been motionless for half a year, opened; it opened, and the pleasant voice of a woman said, "Good thing you're back—the sink..."—and the door closed.

I went in and flung myself into the armchair in my study. Impossible!—I said to myself. The devil can't be tormenting me like this! He? There? Upstairs? Rented? Bought? Living?

But that apartment—as all the tenants knew—wasn't up for sale or even for rent, because Dr. Klausner had left no heirs and the court had appointed a trustee for it.

I looked up at the ceiling and listened. Yes. I could hear footsteps going back and forth in the apartment, and there were even some inanimate squeals, as if furniture was being moved.

Impossible!—I repeated to myself—the devil has tricks no mortal can imagine, but in the field of literature?! It's inconceivable that he would think up an allegory like this, a literary critic living right above a writer, walking on his head, as it were. Especially a critic whose first book was a polemic against allegory!

And if it's true—I thought—then that's the end of me! Not one line more will get written in this room, with the critic's footsteps pounding over my head.

A disaster! A disaster!—my brow exuded perspiration—utter annihilation!

I held my breath. The gurgle of flushing water was heard, flowing in the toilet, swirling and streaming in a noisy rush down the pipe from him right past me, and from me on down to the sewer.

A disaster!—I sighed—every time he or his wife—his wife?—needs to clear their orifices, both great and small, I will be earwitness to the dropping of the effluvia and their subsequent descent through the channels in the walls of the building.

Is this a deliberate plot on the part of Schatz to accomplish by force what he has been unable to accomplish by omission? I wondered. Having realized that he could not stanch my flow by ignoring me, has he decided to try to do so by trampling me underfoot?

Or—

Maybe he just happens to be spending the night here?

Maybe they're distant relatives of the late Dr. Klausner and have come to prepare the apartment for rental?

Maybe they've come to take away his furniture?

And maybe I'm just hallucinating it all?

I stood up, I went out, I went downstairs to the apartment directly beneath mine and rang Victoria's doorbell.

"Has someone moved into Klausner's apartment?" I asked.

"Weren't you here this afternoon?" smiled Victoria, her face glowing as always.

"I just got home."

"Come on in," she opened the door wider for me, as her robe, strewn with flaming roses, revealed more of her generous bosom than it concealed.

I said I was pressed for time. Just came for a moment.

Victoria told me that all afternoon the building had been bursting with movers carrying chests, suitcases, bundles, books, lots of books...

"A professor, I heard," she said. "You'll have a neighbor of your own ilk."

"Of your own ilk..." Victoria's 'literary' expressions...

"But the apartment..." I mumbled. "The trustee..."

"It's the trustee who sold it to them," said Victoria. "Your face is clouded..."

"Clouded," she says...

"They look like nice people really...very quiet and discreet..."

I went back upstairs to my apartment. The dull echo of footsteps was heard above.

Tears came to my eyes.

With profound sorrow and longing I remembered the late Dr. Klausner.

Chapter two

A Few Words in Memory of Dr. Klausner

Dr. Klausner was an extraordinary man. He was like one of those Russian landowners in Chekhov upon whose faces rests the soft splendor of an autumn sunset; however, his great love was Dostoevsky. When he went up or down the stairs, his step was muffled, as if he were taking care not to be heard, not to disturb. In his apartment, where he had lived alone for the twelve years following the death of his wife, complete silence reigned. He'd meet me sometimes as I was leaving my apartment, or as I was going in, stop for a few moments, and ask me what was new in literature, whether any interesting books had been published, and as I answered him, he would smile sadly as if to say: Yes, but what's that worth compared to Dostoevsky? "Read *The Brothers Karamazov* again," he would advise when I'd finished speaking. "Do you remember that scene with Fyodor Pavlovich, how he ran down the street, drunk, screaming with joy when he found out that Adelaida, the mother of his young son Dmitri, had died in the attic? Brilliant, no? But ask yourself why it's brilliant! Because afterwards he wept! Wept and wept and wept!" Tears stood in his grey eyes. "The contrast!" He pointed his finger at me. Or another time: "That scene with Rogozhin, at the end of *The Idiot*... When Rogozhin brings Prince Myshkin to his home in the evening, opens the curtain in the room and shows him Nastasya lying dead on the bed, after he had killed her...and then—listen to how brilliant this is!—the two of them lie down together on the other bed and Myshkin caresses his face...the face of the murderer! ...It seems impossible, doesn't it? Unbelievable! What is this, a farce? Is the writer mad?—But it's the truth! Truth, truth, truth! Not naturalistic truth! Naturalistic truth is on the surface! But deep truth! Of what *could* happen! Only someone who understands the depths of the human soul could write like that."

Once, on the sidewalk, near the gate, he said to me: "Write tragedy!" and when I laughed he said: "You know why nobody writes tragedies any more? Because people are superficial nowadays. Two things are necessary for tragedy: depth, and great faith. Today, people aren't deep and they don't believe in anything, so they write comedies, and novels, sort of tepid...If people aren't prepared to die for something, for an idea, for a principle, for something very very dear to them—there's no tragedy, you understand? If there is nothing holy—then there is no tremendous exaltation and there is no tremendous fall either, you understand. In Dostoevsky..."

It seemed that his whole life he had read only Dostoevsky, over and over again, until he knew him almost by heart. But the first time I went to visit him I found in his library, next to Dostoevsky, Tolstoy, Chekhov, Gogol, Turgenev, Goethe, Homer, and alongside old editions of the poems of Tchernichovsky, Shneur, Frug, Herzl's diaries and the like, a whole row of the works of Agatha Christie, in English pocket editions. When I expressed my astonishment he said: "For me it's like chess. When my late wife was alive, we would play chess. Now before I fall asleep, I like..." But after a moment, he smiled and said: "Don't look down on Agatha Christie. It's not just crimes and detective puzzles. There is something else behind it: the dark side of life. Yes, like in Chesterton. It's not Dostoevsky, of course, but nevertheless…" I looked at his delicate face, light gathering in its wrinkles and glowing forth from his spectacles, and asked myself what attracted him to "the dark side"—was it curiosity to understand the "sin" which he had never known at first hand? Which he had known and overcome?

The living room was sort of a shrine in memory of his wife. Everything was left as it had been, apparently, when she was alive. The large, heavy table in the middle of the room was covered with a plush cloth upon which lay four pure white lace mats, one on each side, with a larger one in the center on which a greenish vase, tall and thin like a crane's neck, held three multicolored peacock feathers. On the antique buffet were arranged, in wonderful order, tiny, skillfully made silver spoons, and centered among them was a silver chariot harnessed to a troika. A small marble bust of Beethoven sat on the wing of the piano, and next to him a vase of immortal flowers; on the open keyboard cover rested a book of music: Brahms' Concerto no.2 for Piano, op. 83. In the corner, near the heavy curtain that covered the window overlooking the courtyard—through which peeped the uppermost branches of a parkinsonia tree—stood a carved round pedestal table, and on it the icon of his wife, Zoya, in her bridal veil. She was beautiful: the face of a gypsy princess. Black hair, bright, bold eyes, an easy immodest smile playing over the bow-shaped lips; the smile of a woman who is well aware of her power over men. In front of the portrait lay a hairbrush with an ivory handle, an ivory comb and a silver filigree *poudrier.*

"Remember, Man is a profound mystery! A mystery we shall never be able to solve completely," said Dr. Klausner as he stood between the curtain and the table where the portrait of his wife was displayed. Then he offered evidence from *The Idiot* of the unexpected enigmas in the soul of man by retelling the story that Prince Myshkin had told Rogozhin about the farmer who murdered his best friend who was staying with him at an inn in order to take his silver watch, and as he drew the knife across his friend's neck he raised his eyes to heaven, crossed himself, and begged, "Forgive me, my God, for Jesus' sake!" Klausner added: "Great literature is that which comprehends the paradox, you understand? The paradox that is inside every one of us."

He crossed over to the piano, and as he touched the corner of the music book, as if he were about to turn the page, he said: "Are you familiar with this Brahms concerto?—one of his happiest works. Full of joy. Particularly the last part, the rondo..." He nodded his head in time as he hummed the gaily trilling melody. "So look. That was my late wife's favorite piece: Every Saturday night she would play it. And she was a tragic figure. Truly tragic!..."

When the fights between me and my ex-wife, Lili Federman, got worse, her shrieks could be heard up at his place, of course. Lili was unrestrained in her fury, her voice was wildfire, and it was impossible to deflect her. The more I would try to calm her down by whispering "the neighbors, the neighbors..."—the more she would raise her voice in curses so vulgar that the walls blushed to hear them. In those days Klausner would walk past me and greet me only with a nod of his head, lowering his eyes, as though he were embarrassed for me, as if it were he who was in disgrace and not I. Late one night when I came home completely drunk and rang our doorbell, Lili refused to let me in. I couldn't find the keys in my pocket; I banged hard on the door and shouted, "Open up! If not I'll break..." and so on. A few neighbors woke up and cracked their doors open a bit to listen, not saying anything. But when I kept on pounding like that with my fist, and banging my head against the door, Klausner came down from his apartment in a polka-dot robe tied with a fringed sash, grasped my arm and said: "Come upstairs to my place."

"Sit, I'll make you coffee, calm down." He sat me down by the table in the small, spotless kitchen. When he sat down too, the two cups placed before us—and sips of the hot drink slightly cleared the fog in my head—he said: "Not by force... You won't achieve anything by force... Woman, you understand, is a delicate and complex creature...like a small gold watch...tiny wheels, an intricate mechanism...Have you seen how the watchmaker fixes them? With a magnifying glass, with a miniature screwdriver, with tweezers... Slightly larger tools, and he would just destroy..."

He looked at me with tired, smiling eyes and said: "Zoya and I, for example…forty-two years together… Everyone thought: a pair of lovebirds… But it wasn't like that… Complicated."

Then he told me how they had lived for ten years in a sort of *ménage à trois*. Zoya had fallen in love with a well-known painter, "a very good man," whom he also respected and admired. At first, when he found out about it, it was a great tragedy for him and he almost resolved to put an end to his life. He told Zoya that they must part, and he thought that immediately afterwards he would commit suicide. But Zoya was very attached to him, didn't want to give him up, and said that if he left her she would put an end to her life as well. So the three of them were together, the artist coming to the house very frequently. "He was an excellent chess player, and we would play once or twice a week. Most of the time he would beat me, but sometimes I…" He smiled tiredly. He managed to suppress his jealousy, even though it never ceased to smolder within…but later he discovered that the painter was "not such a good man" after all, because he had other women…and he felt as if this painter had betrayed not only Zoya, but also him… "There's a paradox for you. Life is full of paradoxes like that."

"The most important thing is that everything should be open," he said, "open and direct. When everything is open and direct, then you understand that it's human nature, full of contradictions, from God, you know, and you are also able to forgive, to reconcile."

Another time he told me about another "paradox." He had an older brother who had run away from Russia after the Revolution and immigrated to Belgium. In the thirties he went bankrupt and decided to come to Palestine to buy an orange grove. As he didn't have any money, he took a bank loan. Dr. Klausner was his guarantor, and signed all the notes. A year after the war broke out, the brother vanished. He went to Australia without leaving a trace. Dr. Klausner had to redeem all the notes with his own money. The grove made no profit during the war years, and he was forced to sell Zoya's jewelry to pay off the debts. Eight long years. Zoya would weep in the night. She said that if a brother could betray so easily, how could you trust anyone! Jackals, all of them! "And I too ... I was devoured by it! Not because I had to pay huge sums every month—and it was hard for us—but the despair… and rumors reached us that he had gotten rich there, in Australia, dealing in army surplus…And I wrote many many times and never got an answer… How is it possible? I thought, how could a man descend so low, to a sub-human level… But five years after the war I received a letter from a lawyer in Melbourne, telling that my brother had died, after a long illness, and in his will he had left me half his capital, a great deal more than all the debt I had paid off for him… So you see, you never need to lose all faith in mankind."

He was an odd pharmacist. He would worry about his customers' money, even if he didn't know them. When someone came in to buy some medicine for a cold, he would say, "Why waste your money? Either way it doesn't help much… and anyway, a cold isn't so bad, it clears the system…" Or he would plead with his customers to buy the cheaper, local medicine rather than the expensive imported one; or advise them to use a home remedy, like grandma's recipes…an extraordinary pharmacist, he was.

And the silence that always reigned upstairs!

Many people came to his funeral. Some of them were regular customers at the pharmacy, some of them were veteran residents of Tel Aviv. I helped carry the coffin. It was very light. As if there were a child's corpse inside it.

Chapter three

What Goes Down Must Come Up

In the morning I woke up—after the looped and windowed raggedness of turbulent sleep—feeling like a vagrant. This house is not my home. The apartment, which had been my castle, so to speak, has been breached. I am exposed, naked. May this not be your fate, good householders.

One never knows what calamities lie in wait, what obstacles will appear like the devil in one's path when all one wants to do is sit and write in peace. One has already managed, with great exertion, after days and nights of grunting and groaning, of straining the heart and stomach, to roll a heavy boulder of doubts and hesitations out of the path, and to set down the first sentence on the blank page. Now—so it seems—the pen will roll merrily along, light as a wheel—when all of a sudden…

About two years ago a single girl, dark and slender and sharp-eyed, lived in the building next door, her window opposite mine. She was a clerk at one of the gas companies, or so I believe, and every day when she came home from her job and set about the housework she would put a record on her turntable—and the songs of the Italian singer Roberto Fiori, bold and tempestuous with passionate love and despair, would swirl forth from her apartment into mine and make themselves at home with great gusts of feeling. Not only they, but also the voice of the neighbor as she accompanied them in a nostalgic outpouring while scrubbing the floor or washing the dishes— "*S'amor quel che sento… Amor a un cor, che non ode, ne vede…*" My hand was paralyzed. Couldn't even move the pen over a single line. I would go over to her place and beg her: Please play your lovesick Italian only for yourself, because I… She would look at me with an affectionate smile and say: Yes, yes, of course, you're right… But the next day, again: "*La mia donna cara…*" Heartbreaking, earthshaking, saturating the space of my room. Hours. And on Saturdays—from morning till night.

I capitulated. I hadn't the heart to spoil her small pleasures. Roberto Fiori was the sweet nightingale of her dreams, the repository of her unheard prayers; to the songs of his hot Latin love she languished, on their wings she flew over the Mediterranean to Florence, Naples, Sicily… I would sit down to write only after Roberto Fiori's storm had abated, late in the evening.

Then one day there came a knight of flesh and blood—from a moshav in the Lakhish District, according to the neighbors—and rescued her from her loneliness and longings, and me from Fiorentian love. An arthritic old couple, submissive and waning, came to live in her place.

A nuisance of that sort, which emanates from one person's property and prevents another from enjoying the use of his own, is only natural. But now, with this invasion of my very own house—

I lay there and stared at the ceiling, alert to the noises above me, and thought about what I could expect from this day forth. To come to terms with a situation in which a sort of demonic spirit wanders above my head day and night, and I hear its steps like Hamlet heard the footsteps of his father's ghost—this I cannot do. I'll never get used to it. A man might get used to situations to which he is sentenced by a higher authority—to live in prison, or even a concentration camp. But here—this is no irreversible decree! One of us has got to go! And it won't be me! Because I'm the resident and he's the trespasser, the invader! I have lived in this apartment for almost five years. It's been my property ever since my marriage to Lili Federman and even after my divorce from her. I am accustomed to it and it is accustomed to me, and within it float the letters of the last book I have written and the dreams of the books I have yet to write. And I'm accustomed to the neighbors, and they to me, and to Speiser's little store, and to the chinaberry tree out the window and to the dove who flaps her wings on the slats of the eastern sunblind every morning... By any measure of law and justice he has to get out, and if he doesn't do so of his own free will—

I lay there and plotted how I could make him get out. The law, I knew, would not come to my aid. And without the help of the law...there are precedents even for that: religiously observant people, for example, bothered by neighbors who desecrate the Sabbath, hound them until their lives are no longer worth living...

I got up to dress and went out onto the little closed balcony behind the kitchen to take my socks off the clothesline.

As I stuck my head out the window, a drop of cold water fell on my scalp.

I turned my face upwards and my eyes took in a brassiere on the line, and above it the head of a woman whose fingers were fastening it with clothespins.

Simultaneously another drop fell from above, from the tail of the brassiere's shoulder strap—this time on my left cheek—and the woman's head vanished.

I was in shock: the series of humiliations was already beginning on the morning of the first day! Waters of affliction from the bosom of Schatz's wife drop on my head, splatter on my face!

Like spit!

I went inside and put on my clothes. While I dressed, it suddenly hit me that—as opposed to what I had thought when I woke up—the apartment was not invaded but rather blockaded: the terrible problem was not so much staying in as getting out.

You see, my usual morning schedule goes like this: take the

garbage down to the bin in the courtyard and bring the newspaper up from my mailbox; go up to the roof to feed the rabbits; go down—after a light breakfast—to the street to go to the library.

And now at each of these stages I am liable to meet Schatz face to face.

So, a man's home, I thought, is no longer his castle, but his trap!

Directed by a sense of caution which had been aroused the moment the drop fell on my scalp, I opened the door just a crack, the pail of garbage in my hand, and listened. The coast was clear.

I hurried out and flowed down the steps. I emptied the pail into the bin. I stepped over to my letter box, opened it and extracted the newspaper. I went back up the steps slowly while perusing the headlines on the front page, agitated to read about a murder-suicide—"in romantic circumstances"—that had taken place the night before on the north side of town, only a few blocks away. As I paused for a moment on the landing of the first floor to read a few lines in the body of the sensational news item—exceedingly sensational because the crime, or the tragedy, had happened so close to where I live—I heard a door slam upstairs, and immediately skipping footsteps on the stairs.

As I raised my head—

Yes, it was he; coming down straight-backed, black briefcase in hand, light jacket, green face, sharp glance, prickly.

He walked right past me as if I weren't there.

Blood rushed to my face; unmitigated hutzpah! And in my own building!

I slid a look over the descending figure, receding and disappearing into the courtyard, and for a long moment I couldn't budge from the spot.

The nerve! As if he were the landlord! And I—a stranger seeking shelter!

As I entered my apartment, unable to calm down, I was ripped apart by the thought that the most humiliating aspect of it all was that he was going down the steps while I was going up, so that the disgrace was cast over me, as it were, from above! He looks down upon me, while I lift up mine eyes unto him—

This insult cries out for revenge, I said to myself.

It's a matter of honor, I said to myself.

It took me an hour before I was able to go out to feed the rabbits on the roof.

When I reached the landing of the fourth floor I tiptoed over to see what was written next to the doorbell.

Yes, the handsome, smooth ceramic plaque on which Dr. Klausner's name had been engraved in blue italic script had disappeared. In its place was a simple paper strip, and on it, in typewritten letters: NAOMI AND NAPHTALI SCHATZ.

The die, then, had been cast.

I turned away with a sigh and went up the five additional steps to the roof. As I opened the door that creaked on its hinges, I heard the sound of a door opening below me as well. I stopped and looked back down the stairs. Yes, it was the door of the invaded apartment, which had opened a crack. A shadowy figure peeped forth. The same head that had appeared for a moment over the bra hanging on the clothesline: smooth black hair, inquisitive eyes, a gleaming neck...that's all I managed to register, as the door closed almost immediately.

That was Naomi.

I went to the rabbit hutch, which was built on the roof directly above the late Dr. Klausner's apartment. I opened the sack of feed, stuck the spoon in and began to distribute the mixture into the mangers. The six does and the one male rabbit stood still in their small coops, their eyes like sparkling amethysts following my every move and the tips of their whiskers twitching impatiently.

Chapter four

Rabbits

No doubt the reader is wondering what possible business a man like myself, whose work is writing, has with rabbits; and he will ask himself—with mischievous suspicion—whether I haven't inserted this animal here—an animal that chews its cud but whose hoof is not cloven—as a symbol; a scrap thrown to the exegetes to sink their teeth into, chew, and ruminate over. Rabbits, they'll say, are not to be taken literally! A symbol of cowardice, of lack of courage, qualities the author wishes to decry; or perhaps they symbolize the fecund presence of "Nature" in the barren city, or if not its presence, then the yearning for it. In English, of course, *rabbits* is a conflation of *rabbis* and *habits*, and could signify the mingling of the sacred and the profane in daily life, whereas in French *lapin* or *lapine* is an anagram of *le pain*—bread—the deep symbolic significance of which is universal…

The truth is that the matter is very simple: I was given the rabbits by Shmaryahu Har-El, who has been my friend since high school.

Dr. Shmaryahu Har-El, who is a professor of biology, had a rabbit hutch at home, the tiny, soft inhabitants of which he had received (or taken) from the Biological Institute to amuse his wife and two daughters, and also to provide, perhaps, some delicious meals for his table. When he was preparing to depart for a sabbatical year at the University of Iowa, he planned to return what he had borrowed—or rather the third generation of what he had borrowed—to its owner, that is, to the Institute. Since I too had grown fond of the animals during my frequent visits to his home, and since it is not much trouble to take care of them, I asked Shmaryahu to leave them to me, and he did.

On the roof of my building, directly above the late Dr. Klausner's apartment, is a structure of two attached rooms. One of them is used for storing all kinds of junk and the other had served as a laundry room back in the days when washing machines were still uncommon, but no longer had a purpose. With the agreement of the tenants, I put the wire cages of the ten rabbits of the *Palander* strain into this room—which has a water tap, a large basin and a drain—and two weeks later seven remained, six females and a male.

Three died, apparently from the stress of adjusting to their new surroundings. I called the six females Amalia, Amira, Adina, Aliza, Atara and Ada, and the male—Zebulun. At first glance, all the girls looked alike, as they each had pure snow-white fur, but I soon learned to distinguish among them: Amalia always seemed to be working very hard, Amira was a bit tyrannical towards the other does, Adina was particularly delicate and lady-like, Aliza was much the jolliest of the lot, Atara had a tuft of fur that stood up between her ears like a little crown, and Ada always seemed to stand to the side of the action, observing events as they transpired. The longer I tended and observed them, the better I became attuned to their whims and moods. By the twitch of an eyelash, the wiggle of an ear, the quiver of a jaw, the shiver of a nostril or a whisker, the jiggle of a short, fringed tail, I could tell whether they were well or ill, satisfied or hungry, cheerful or glum, and whether the females were calm or in heat.

It's not much of a bother: twice a day I give them their rations. In the morning, a mixture of sorghum and cornflour, and in the evening, feed in the form of pellets, which I buy once a month from a supplier at Kikar Hamoshavot. And water in their troughs, of course. They are clean animals who do not move their bowels a great deal. Their droppings fall through the screened floor onto trays beneath their cages, which I empty once a week or more. When I notice that one of the females is in heat—which is easy to discern by the strong odor emanating from her private parts—I remove her from her own cage and place her in the one occupied by Zebulun, who does his duty with skill and dispatch, a matter of a few seconds. At this time, Ada is pregnant, her abdomen already swollen, and it is to be expected that in another ten or twelve days she will give birth.

The offspring are a problem. Rabbits are prolific, as everyone knows. Every three months they are likely to have six or seven babies in a single litter. During the half year they have been in my charge the population could have jumped to several dozens. Seven are enough for me. Any more than that, and one must devote oneself, spending two or three hours a day as a sort of keeper. After each litter, when the babies are weaned and standing on their feet, I collect them in a carton and present them to the Biological Institute. A sort of interest generated by the trust fund, which I dedicate to public service.

The time invested in caring for them yields a net gain of pleasure. Some people hang a parrot's cage in their rooms, others set up an aquarium with goldfish, and many raise cats and dogs to amuse them—animals who consume great quantities of scraps from the butcher shop, and who are sometimes dangerous nuisances, scratching and biting and frightening the guests. I have rabbits on the roof. When I tire of writing, encounter an obstacle that is difficult to surmount, or have a spell of boredom, I go up to the roof and into the rabbit hutch, seat myself on the bench, and follow the movements of Amalia or Amira, observing their short, springy hops over the sawdust surface, the peculiar twitches of their tiny responses to—apparently—smells or slight noises as they move this way and that, the spasms of their mouths as they chew and ruminate with endless attention, or the expressions of their eyes, which change from moment to moment: curiosity, wonder, expectation, longing for who knows what, perhaps also gratitude. There are all sorts of stereotypes about rabbits that fable-makers like Aesop, La Fontaine and Krilov have promoted: the rabbit is cowardly, pusillanimous, frightened by the sound of a falling leaf, mean-spirited about the troubles of weaker creatures, boastful about what it lacks, ungrateful. I still have a childhood memory of a nasty fable of Krilov's about the forest animals who hunted and killed the bear, and when they gathered to divide the spoils, the rabbit also came along to demand his share even though he had not taken part in the hunt—a well-known coward, he had stood off to the side—and the animals, in their great magnanimity, awarded him the tip of the bear's ear... This fable is a big lie from beginning to end, a sort of character assassination, which also bears witness to astounding ignorance. The rabbit is not in the least capable of demanding a share of the bear's flesh or fur! Firstly, because the rabbit is a vegetarian, and meat is an abomination unto him. Secondly, he demands nothing of his fellow creatures, especially those who are not of his own species, and he is never driven to grab. Thirdly, if he didn't take part in the hunt, it was not out of cowardice, but because of his lofty and noble moral principles! Anyone who observes rabbits, even for a short while, will immediately notice their good manners, their moderation, the spiritual serenity with which they conduct their lives, their modesty. And their long ears are not a sign of conceit, as La Fontaine tries to insinuate in his vile and mocking fable about a rabbit who imagines that his ears are antlers, but rather their defense system, a kind of radar that warns them of danger and sends commands to their feet; that is—the defense system of peace-loving creatures!

And thus it was that I would observe the seven rabbits on the roof, in the intermission between chapter and chapter, or in the midst of a sentence that had run aground, with interest, delight, and relative peace of mind, and learn that there is a life full of nuance and refinement outside the realm of mankind. Observation that offered an anti-anthropocentric moral, if I may say so.

Finally, I must mention that never—I emphasize: never!—did a single one of the other tenants in the building complain about the rabbits on the roof. *Au contraire*: from time to time the neighbors would come up to the hutch to enjoy the sight of them, clucking to the rabbits as if to babies, and some of them—in this respect Victoria particularly excelled—would even bring along vegetable scraps from their own kitchens.

I set the food out for the rabbits, went down to my apartment, grabbed a light breakfast, and headed for the French library to work on my translation of Rabelais.

Chapter five

The Hebraization of Rabelais

So what?—I said to myself as I sat in the French library, in the spot Marcelle had assigned me, surrounded by dictionaries and reference books—so what if Schatz lives in the same building as I do? Why should that bother me at all? If he ignores my existence, why can't I ignore his? Why can't I carry on with my work as if nothing has happened?

I said this to myself as I wracked my brains to find an apt Hebrew noun for Gargantua's *braguette* in Chapter 8, which expounds on the clothes sewn for the twenty-two-month-old giant; that is, for the item of haberdashery that, like the fig leaf, covered his *membre naturel*—a furnishing for which our modest forefathers in the ghettoes of Rome, Frankfurt and Amsterdam had no need and for which, therefore, they had no name. Sixteen ells and a quarter of fabric—so it states in this chapter—were required to cover that noble organ of Gargantua's, which was like "the horn of plenty, ever gallant, succulent, juicy, ever flourishing, fructifying, full of liqueurs, full of flowers, full of fruits, full of all manner of delights, a pleasure to the eyes." How then shall I translate this *braguette* in a way that will be precise, charming and euphonious?—*sakeshach*, from "testicle" and "sack"?—but "sack" is too limp; *zmamzayin*, from "prick" and "muzzle"?—a vulgar combination; *nadanevar*, from "organ" and "scabbard"?—too hard to pronounce. Maybe *kisevar*, "organpocket." Is it a compact word, easy, "natural" sounding? And how shall I find another Hebrew word for the *membre* itself—so necessary here—after I've already called it *zokfan* (erector), *zokran* (thrustor), *hadran* (invader), *pokekan* (corker), *naknikon* (little sausage), *hotter* (pointer), *tzitz* (shoot), *nitzan* (bud), and even the biblically resonant *migdal-oz* (tower of strength), the prophetic *makel-shaked* (almond-rod) and *ezion gever*, that tree-of-man? Rabelais has no less than thirty-eight pet names for that insatiable organ with which man is endowed!

And on this occasion, more than at any other time during my hours in the library, I cursed the day I had taken upon myself this back-breaking task through which I am creeping at the petty pace of ten lines a day, a rate at which it will take me another twelve years to finish.

That damned "Peter Principle"! A man achieves success at a certain level, fairly low—and they kick him upstairs to a higher level where he's too small for the mantle he has to wear! Gargantuan! I once did a translation of a frivolous play by Felicien Marceau, a bedroom farce, in which I had some tricks using biblical expressions with bawdy intent, like: "rod and staff," "cup runneth over," "behold the upright," "in the evening it flourisheth; in the morning it withereth," and "leviathan to play therein." A dignitary from the Institute for Classical Translations was there on opening night, and was very impressed by my translation, laughing aloud during the whole play. After the final curtain he came up to me and asked whether I would be prepared to translate *Gargantua et Pantagruel*. I was flattered. I needed the money after my divorce from Lili Federman. I said, modestly, that I would think it over for a few days. When he phoned me a week later I said yes, because I hadn't the guts to refuse.

A man makes mistakes in his life. This translation is a forced march over a rocky road. Wandering through gorges and crevices.

Climbing steep and jagged mountains. You stumble or fall at every step. Every third word is booby-trapped. To translate Rabelais you must know medieval French, Renaissance French, Provencal French, Norman French; you must understand and feel the argot of inns, of marketplaces, of whores and thugs, of priests and scholars; it is essential to have Latin, Greek, German, Italian, Arabic, Hebrew—a few Hebrew words and phrases, some correct and some garbled, are scattered through these Five Books!—Basque; you have to know theology, law and jurisprudence, medicine, philosophy, astrology, all the natural sciences, all trades and all crafts. And in order to translate into Hebrew this archaic, multilayered and nuanced language (which employs archaic spelling too), you have to know Biblical, Mishnaic, Midrashic, Rabbinic, Piyyutic and Enlightenment Hebrew extremely well, and you must also be familiar with all the terms which have been coined in recent times. Where, then, is the language hero potent enough to invent Hebrew names for the one hundred and eleven games in the twentieth chapter of Book I? How shall he prevail over the translation of the names of the card games alone?

Au flux *au lansquenet*
A la prime *au cocu*

and so on and so on and so forth?

Translators often refer back to the work of their colleagues in other languages. I, too, tried to make use of Le Clercq's 1936 translation, only to discover rather quickly that it tripped me up. Wherever Rabelais is bouncy, light and charming, Le Clercq drags his feet heavily as though they were in chains. He goes on at unnecessary length, complicates things, patches—with a coarse thread—his interpretations and explanations onto the body of the text, tries to demonstrate that he is cleverer than his master and adds clumsy jokes of his own. Right from the opening verses "To the Readers," at the very beginning of Book I, I could see what a hamfisted journeyman's job he had done: Rabelais has seventy-one words in ten lines, and he—eighty-three words in eleven lines! What Rabelais puts with such simplicity in the first line:

A mis lecteurs qui ce livre lisez

Le Clercq translates:

Dear friends and readers who may scan these tomes

and the last line in the original, which has become proverbial because it takes wing so easily—

Pour ce que rire est le propre de l'homme

that is: "Because nothing suits mankind as well as laughter" (or "Since it is laughter which, indeed, is man")—becomes in Le Clercq's translation a sort of serious philosophical proposition utterly lacking in charm:

For laughter is the essence of mankind

Or in Chapter 5 of the first book, which is in its entirety a wild and noisy drunken spree, full of one or two word shouts, where the revelers in the original call out:

Tire!
Baille!
Tourne!
Brouille!

That is: Pour! Fetch! Fill! Mix!—Le Clercq translates:

Draw my wine, boy!
Give me my glass!
Fill mine up!
Water in mine, please!

No, God forbid that I should refer to a translation like this one!

Yet the Hebrew of the translation must be as rich as the language of the original! Plenteous, effervescent, overflowing at times, sometimes rollicking and riotous, but withal scholarly, replete with connotations from both classical and demotic strata of the language. Does Hebrew have intricately linked tirades of verbs, nouns and modifiers from all fields of the material and spiritual world, like the ones found in Rabelais?—There are, of course, the rolls of blessings and curses in Deuteronomy, and the collections of names for instruments, materials, objects, garments, plagues and diseases in the Bible in the chapters on the construction of the Ark of the Covenant, the Menorah, the sacrifices and the offerings, the purifications and the abominations, the building of the Temple and so forth; and in the Mishnah one can find hundreds of terms—the flavor of which is appropriately archaic, esoteric—for tools and trades, sacred and profane occupations, weights and measures, bodily functions and bed linen, as well as fantasies and exaggerations in matters ranging from fleas' eggs to unicorns' horns—but what about subsequent strata, later ones, as we are dealing here with the sixteenth century?

I turn, therefore, to the poets of the Golden Age; and more than to them, to Manuello Romano, whose works, though he antedated Rabelais by about two hundred years, are permeated with the free spirit of a Hebrew Renaissance, just as Rabelais' work is permeated by the spirit of the French Renaissance. In his satires—his "Book of Desire," "Songs of Saints and Lamentations," "The Song of Trades," "The Book of Wine," and so on—one can find the joyful and exuberant plenitude of elaborate expressions, full of nuances and connotations, bubbling with puns and conceits, winks and stings, wit and jest, rhymes and roguishness, scatology and jokes like one finds in *Gargantua and Pantagruel.* There alone, where the Hebrew language—which otherwise largely lamented and wept and groaned—threw off its chains and gave rein to its spirit, might we find lines like these which resemble the description of Rabelaisian revelers:

> One blurts out his secret thoughts,
> one vomits up his soul and farts,
> one drips water between his thighs

and shits right in the public eye,
one rises up from among the group,
strips off his clothes and prances nude...

So here I sit in the French library breaking my head over how to find a suitable way to say *l'exiture de la braguette*: "the bulge of the *kisever*"? "The convexity of the *kisever*"? "The protuberance of the *kisever*"?—I root around through the heap of Aramaic words in my memory in the hope that my salvation will spring from that esoteric language, giving a voluptuous swell of ancient music to the sentence...spice it up...I think maybe I'll stick the "*parmashtak*" in here, a word I found once by chance in the Mishnah for a male organ one cubit long.

Whence my excellent French?—asks the reader; after all, it is a less common language than English among the current generation of Israelis, or than Russian among the previous one!

Ah, but whence my excellent Hebrew?—I was already thirteen years old when I emigrated to Israel.

So, a few shreds of *curriculum vitae.*

Chapter six

A Brief "Life"

I was born in Cernauti, or Czernowitz, as we called it, on June 22—the longest day of the year—1940. Six days before the Red Army entered the city.

Family legend has it that the first time my mother saw my tiny hands resting on her breast they looked so lovely to her that she cried out in amazement: "*Mon Dieu, quelles mains!*"

When my father, who stood beside her, heard the words "*quelles mains*" he said: "So we'll call him Kalman!"—and thus I received my name, which has accompanied me for better and for worse until this very day.

My father, Israel Korngold, a Zionist since his youth, who as the owner of a shoe business in the town center was also considered "bourgeois"—was arrested together with several dozen other Zionist activists about two weeks after Soviet rule was established in our city. Fortunately, his interrogator was a Jewish Communist with whom he had studied at the Hebrew "Tarbut" high school, and he obtained his release after five days. His shop was confiscated, and he became its head clerk.

When I was exactly one year old the massive German attack on the Soviet occupied areas began, and two weeks later the Red Army retreated from Czernowitz and was replaced by Antonescu's reign of terror. Harsh decrees and persecutions followed in rapid succession, and more than half the Jews were sent to labor camps in Transdnistria, where they died of hunger and torture.

Once again luck was on my father's side, and because of connections he had with Popovici the mayor, he was able to get an "essential-worker's certificate" as a shoemaker, and allowed to remain in the city. Thus we were all saved.

Three rooms of our large apartment were confiscated as billets for officers of the Romanian Army and we lived in the other two, together with a Jewish dentist who had been evicted from her house in the choicest part of town. She was a stern-faced woman, tall, skeletal and masculine, and my mother spoke French with her.

Pre-war Czernowitz was a half-Jewish city, and most of its Jews were well-educated people who viewed it as a branch of Vienna, Berlin or Paris. My mother saw it as a branch of Paris. She knew six languages: German, Romanian, Russian, French, Yiddish and a little Hebrew, but French she loved most of all. Before her marriage she had wanted to be an actress or an opera singer and because she had not been able to fulfill this dream, she invested all her dramatic talent into speaking French. The dentist was a gift from God and when she chattered with her in the beloved language it seemed as though my mother forgot the war, the troubles, the scarcities and the crowding. She would accompany her speech with a pursing of the lips, a twinkling of the eyes and various small, charming gestures. Her voice would become sweet, melodious, bird-like, and sometimes she would even rise as she spoke and walk around the room as though she were moving around on stage. I would watch her with wonder, my eyes veiled with longing, following the movements of her lips and hands, devouring the shapely words issuing from her mouth. My mother was a beautiful woman, with a sunny face and fair hair, and I was in love with her. Naturally I was in love with French too.

My father's greatest love was Hebrew. He was an incurable

optimist—a foolish optimist I would say today, when I remember his end. Even when the Iron Guards went wild in the streets, beating up wearers of the yellow star and dragging them onto trucks to ship them off to forced labor camps, he would come home late at night, exhausted and hungry after twelve hours of work in the shoe factory, and do his best to cheer us up. His favorite phrase—this my mother told me—was: "It can't get any worse." Meaning: from now on it's got to get better. Even when the house was emptied of its finest objects, which we were forced to sell for a measure of barley or a glass of milk—first my mother's piano, then the silver utensils and the crystal goblets, and finally my wonderful rocking-horse with the long flaxen tail—he managed to keep up his good spirits, and a smile—though somewhat constricted—would play under his short yellow mustache. In the evenings—this I remember quite clearly—he would read to my mother, who held me in her lap, from a large, vowel-pointed Hebrew book: Bialik's biblical tales, *Vayehi Hayom*.

My father was proud of his book collection: he had rare books from the period of the Enlightenment on, volumes of *Hashiloach, Hatzfirah, Luach-Ahiassaf, Revivim, Lashon Vesefer*. Until the war broke out he would receive books in the mail from Palestine—the poems of Rachel, Shlonsky, Fichman, novels by Ya'ari-Poleskin, Avigdor Hame'iri, Kabak, Zarchi, Agnon. I still have many of them in the storeroom next to the rabbit hutch on the roof.

I wouldn't say that I was the Child Prodigy of Czernowitz, and that by the time I was three years old I knew pages of Gemara by heart, but when I was four—at that point the Russians had come back into the city and it had been annexed to the Ukrainian Republic—I already knew how to read the Hebrew alphabet on the first page of the prayerbook, and by the time I was five I could read Lewin-Kipnis' poems for children, which my father taught me.

Under the new regime my father got a post as an accountant for a leather-goods factory. He wanted to leave the city, which had become packed with refugees from all the surrounding areas, and find a way for us to get to the Land of Israel, but my mother held him back, hoping to realize her old dream by getting accepted to the new

People's Theater. So we stayed in Czernowitz for another four years, without her wish coming true.

When I was nine we moved to Bucharest. My mother's brother, Stefan Kaminsky, was a member of the Central Committee of the Romanian Communist Party, and when Gheorghiu-Dej took power, he became the Vice Minister for Trade and Industry. A broad-shouldered man with an elegant suit and a wide, self-assured smile, he organized us a two-and-a-half-room apartment in a baroque building on March Sixth Avenue, which still had a few pieces of antique furniture left behind by the previous residents, who had been either evicted or exiled; for my father he arranged a respectable position as an inspector of light industry. I was put into a well-connected school, where the children of high officials and party members studied. For a third language, one could choose English or French, and I chose French, of course.

I remember my five years in Bucharest as good years. We didn't lack for food, I excelled at school, and in the evenings I would lose myself in novels by Jules Verne, Hector Malot and Flaubert. Even then, I had discovered literary tendencies in myself. For my own pleasure I translated Francis Jammes' poems and *Le fin du capitaine Harvey* by Victor Hugo from French to Romanian, and wrote a farcical story about a glued-on horse tail, modeled after *Un nez gelé* by Alexandre Dumas.

My mother, who despaired of being an actress or an opera singer, took up spiritualism. Every Tuesday evening, when my father was away from home at meetings he was obliged to attend, several wives of high officials would gather at our house and hold séances directed by my mother. The "spirit" that appeared from the world beyond spoke mostly French, and the letters that the cup floating above the Ouija board selected would also combine themselves into French words. I would peek into these séances surreptitiously, through the keyhole, and was enchanted both by the French, which in this context became a sort of "mystery language," and by the "spirit world," which enflamed my imagination.

My father's "mystery language" was Hebrew, with which he

kept faith in secret. Of his large collection, only about fifty books remained. He had brought them with him with devoted exertion, and he would read from them, over and over again, in his free time. Without much desire to do so, but out of respect for his dedication, for two hours every Sunday I studied with him this ancient and esoteric language, which aroused in me utopian, though skeptical, visions of a "sun-blessed land" somewhere in the East. From my first textbook, an old and torn volume of *Hebrew Style* missing the first and last pages, I still remember by heart the poem "I have a garden and a well have I," the second stanza of A.D. Lifschitz's "Lullaby": "First I'll tell you my beloved / Hebrew that you are / Your name reveals you Israel / The tree from which you're carved" and lines from a poem by Sarah Shapira: "For dew and rain my tears will fall / Zion, thy hills / Neither fire nor sun our blood will redden / Zion thy skies." Gradually I succumbed to the magic of this language, like the magic of rare birds in the zoo, and the letters of the words sparkled at me, each one of them with its own shining light. Even today I can taste what I felt then as we read those poems... During classes at school, while the teacher wrote geometry theorems on the blackboard in Latin letters, I would amuse myself by writing and rhyming Hebrew words in my notebook.

If I had an erotic-Oedipal attitude towards French, as the psychologists would say in light of the foregoing revelations—then I had filial feelings towards Hebrew, as if to a paternal authority.

In the summer of 1953, when I was thirteen, with a Certificate for Excellence in Studies decorating my room, a great event took place in our city: The International Festival of the Peace Movement. The streets were decked with flags, flowers, slogans, huge pictures of Lenin, Stalin, Gheorghiu-Dej, the loudspeakers blared folksongs and revolutionary anthems from early in the morning until after midnight. About thirty thousand young people from seventy different nations inundated the city, which overflowed with their songs, dances, colorful costumes, laughter, joy. A spirit of freedom, brotherhood and gaiety swept over the city. Everybody hugged and kissed and exchanged greetings in every language and danced indefatigably in the squares and parks. My father got time off from work so he could participate, like thousands of other officials and workers, in the parades and rallies. My mother and I stood on the balcony of our apartment, on the third floor, and waved to the masses marching down the avenue in wide, orderly ranks, chanting in a great chorus "*Pace si Prietenie*"—"Peace and Friendship"—and singing with all their might. We saw my father waving to us with the sheaf of red gladiolas in his hand, and we blew him kisses. When he came home in the evening, tired but happy, the scent of flowers on his clothes, he announced to us, with tears of joy, that a delegation had also arrived from Israel.

The entire ten days of the festival my father was in a state of exaltation. He did not miss a single appearance of the Israeli delegation. He would run—dragging me along—from one end of town to the other, from the Youth Palace to the Culture Park, from The 23rd of August Stadium to the Floreasca Palace, from Stalin Park to the Cismigiu gardens, and on and on. Tears glittered in his eyes as he watched the youths and maidens in their embroidered shirts, flexible of torso and light of foot, flashing across the stage in shepherds' dances, or pioneers' dances or Yemenite dances, singing Hebrew songs to the accompaniment of drums and tambourines. His lips would move, following the words they sang, and from time to time he would breathe very deeply so as not to burst into tears. At the end of the performance he would rush backstage, squeeze over to the dancers and singers, press their hands and mutter a few words in Hebrew so laden with emotion that they were strangled in his throat. "They are from the Valley of Jezreel, from Ein-Harod, from Nahalal..." he would whisper as he held onto my hand, and I would look at the suntanned, mustached laughing boys and the long-haired, almond-eyed girls, whose smiles were modest, but at the same time full of the noble pride of a high caste, exclusive, and I thought to myself that all of them are happy, they come from a land of joy, and even if I ever get to that land, I'll never reach their level—I'll always be prevented from getting close to them or touching the hand of one of those willowy, proud-necked girls.

When my father found out that there was also a writer in the delegation, a young writer whose stories he had happened to read in an anthology that had reached him through mysterious channels—two stories about some fishermen's kibbutz, if I remember correctly—he could not rest until he had found him When he found him, he held him and would not let him go. He would not leave him until he had brought him around to our house.

My mother received him with great ceremony, served him delicacies, plum wine, fine salami, and showed him her class picture with Bernitsky the teacher, who had immigrated to Palestine two years before the war broke out. My father sat before him full of admiration and asked him questions about life in Israel, about Tel Aviv, Jerusalem, Netanya, about Ben Gurion and Sneh and Kolodny, and for news of writers like Fichman, Melzer, Orland and others whose names he knew. I understood everything my father asked, though of what the writer answered I understood but little, especially since he spoke in a low voice. He was a man of about thirty, long-nosed, curly haired, with a sad expression, and I looked at him and wondered whether he was sad because writers are generally sad. He was the first writer I had ever met. My father laid his hand on my shoulder and declared; "He already reads Hebrew!" and the writer smiled at me and said; "Perhaps one day he'll also write Hebrew..."

He did not know what he had prophesied. But when I came to him about twelve years later with my first story, so that he could publish it in the journal he edited, he didn't remember me. When I reminded him, and he smiled kindly on me—even then the story sat there for several weeks without him reading it or giving me a reply.

My poor, innocent father! He had no idea that his love of Hebrew was a minefield for him! He did not imagine—in his euphoria—that he was under surveillance. When the revels ended, when the streets emptied all at once—like rivers in the desert—of the youthful joy which had flowed through them for ten whole days and nights; when the songs and dances and pageants melted into thin air and the city returned to its usual grayness—they knocked on our door one night, and he was summoned for interrogation. He was under arrest for five days. My mother ran back and forth, in shock, between offices, and turned for help to her brother, Stefan Kaminsky, who received her coldly. He could tell her only that her husband was accused of having contact with a foreign agent, and that there was nothing he could do about it. The Israeli writer—so he said—was neither a singer nor a dancer, neither an athlete nor a basketball player, and he had been sent to spy and incite rebellion against the government. No trial was held for my father, and he was transferred to prison. My mother begged to visit him but was not permitted to do so. We ate our savings and sold the antique chest and the piano that didn't even belong to us. Only after four long months did Stefan Kaminsky come to see us and announce that he had managed to arrange a pardon for my father, on condition that we leave the country within forty-eight hours.

Via Trieste we arrived, penniless, in Haifa. There we were met by Elkanah, my father's brother.

Elkanah, who had immigrated to Palestine in 1933, was two years older than my father, but he was unmarried. He was of middling height, and an incomprehensible expression of amazement was always spread over his wide, fair and large-eyed face. He had a diamond polishing workshop in Netanya, and my father, once he had learned the craft of polishing, started work there.

My mother spoke French with the Algerian-born neighbor in the housing development where the Jewish Agency had assigned us an apartment.

At school I was the only Romanian in my class. My rolling "rrrrr" and the somewhat florid Hebrew I spoke attracted the mockery of my classmates, and even the teachers who read my compositions said my language was "too literary" and "not alive." I was fairly lonely, and alienated from my surroundings, but my height and my looks—to which the girls were not indifferent—combined with a feeling of as yet unrevealed destiny, implanted within me a certain pride, which protected me from depression.

I graduated with honors.

During the third year of my military service—in the Artillery Corps—my father was murdered by thieves who hit him over the head as he was locking the door of the diamond polishing workshop, where he was, by then, my uncle's full partner.

It was on the eve of Passover, and his blood spattered the doorpost.

Elkanah, who felt guilty about my father's death, sent me at his expense to Lyon, France, to specialize in French Literature.

I spent two years at the University of Lyon; two tempestuous years throbbing with events that affected my future. There I fell in love with one of the local students, a Catholic—Yvette was her name—a wonderfully delicate girl with a nearly transparent olive complexion, a high forehead, and fine, discriminating senses, who left me in the end, and whom I could not banish from my heart for years afterwards. It was there that I made my first attempts to write stories.

When I returned to Israel, I found my mother married to a rich vineyard-owner from Zikhron Ya'akov, her elder by ten years. From the verandah of their lovely villa, which stood at the crest of the Carmel range, she looked down over the fish pools of the plain and the sea, over the green tangles of reeds and the flying herons, as in a dreamy torpor she dropped powdery cubes of Turkish delight from the dish before her into her mouth. "*Mon Dieu, quels cheveux*!" she cried as she saw me when I came there for the first time and my hair was long.

I rented a small room in Tel Aviv, on a roof, which was exposed to the broiling sun in summer and to the cold in winter.

When I was twenty-four, my first story, "The Outcast", was published.

Five years later my book *Green Windows* was published, and six years after that, *Butterflies. The Flying Camel of the Golden Hump* came out a year and a half ago.

Five years ago I married Lili Federman, and two years later I divorced her. But that's another story.

Chapter seven

Woman on the Roof

The Romanian writer Mihail Sadoveanu (one of whose stories, the hero of which is Jewish, is called "Kalman," and I suspect that my father named me after him, and not as the family legend relates) tells of a humble farmer named Pompiliu who, whenever he went out into the village street, would stick close to the sides of the houses and the fences, hiding from time to time in some alley or lane, all in order to avoid meeting the head of the village, Dimitrie Tatarescu. Tatrescu had borrowed eighty lei long before, and Pompiliu avoided him so that he would not have to remind him of the debt.

Schatz didn't owe me a thing, and I am not a humble peasant; but every morning, when I had to go up to the roof to feed the rabbits, I would first open the door about a hand's breadth, listen, turn my head and peek out, listen again to make sure that the door upstairs wasn't opening as well—all in order to avoid running into my oppressor. Only when I was convinced there was no cause for concern would I quickly climb the stairs two at a time up to the fourth floor, and from there to the roof.

On the tenth day of the invasion, when I opened the door to the roof, I discovered, in broad daylight, before my very eyes—

standing there next to the clothesline upon which the expanse of a double sheet hung flapping in the gentle breeze—the woman who had moved in upstairs, whose shadowy profile I had previously seen but a few times. As she hung up a pair of men's purple underpants, using two clothespins, she smiled and sent a "Good morning!" my way. I took two steps toward her and returned her greeting. She clipped two additional clothespins at the two extremities of a second pair of underpants, blue, also men's, and said: "You are Kalman Keren. I'm Naomi Schatz, the upstairs neighbor."

A broad, open smile, expressing friendliness—if my senses did not deceive me—was on her tanned face, which was framed by the straight lines of her black hair.

"I hope these clotheslines are for all the tenants in the building,"—she bent over the laundry basket with her face turned toward me.

"Yes yes, certainly! You have the right to use them!" I hastened to say. And pointing to the open door of the rabbit hutch, I added that I'd only come up for a few moments to feed the rabbits.

"Oh, they're yours!" she smiled as she hung up a third pair of underpants, neon yellow, next to the other two. "We've been asking ourselves whose they were..."

That familial plural—"we've been asking," "ourselves"—the language of one mind, one covenant, one bed—embarrassed me for a moment; emphasized the unexpectedness of her free, simple, unimpeded remark. "Have you and your husband been bothered by them?" I said, tasting bitterness on the tip of my tongue as I uttered the word 'husband'.

"Not at all!" she laughed above the clothesline, between the blue underpants and the yellow ones.

The sight of the three pairs of underpants hanging there next to one another, their psychedelic colors gleaming in the morning light, amused me. My first meeting with my new neighbor, my introductory meeting, as it were, was once again not face to face, but face to rear. If the light of his face was denied me, at least his rear was revealed, without his knowledge. Here he was before me with his privates in public, with his pants down, as they say, in his *kisever*, to borrow an item of dress from Rabelais; if this neatly pressed, buttoned-up and starched critic were to know that I was standing here getting a close look at his colorful unmentionables hanging out—

As I write these lines, a philosophical consideration occurs to me, which I shall not spare the reader, concerning "revelation and concealment": Bialik, in his famous essay "Revelation and Concealment in Language," wrote that "no word contains the complete negation of any question, but what does it contain?—Its concealment," and he discusses the great difference between masters of the art of prose and masters of the art of poetry. But what about critics, about whom he said nothing? So, the major difference between the writer and the critic is, in my opinion, that the writer, the more he conceals himself—hides himself, adopts disguises, wears different masks, plays different characters—the more he reveals and exposes about himself; whereas the critic, the more he reveals—of other people, of course, of writers who are his "raw material"—the more he conceals himself. In short: he always takes good care to appear in public fully dressed: business suit, starched collar, necktie…

See what profound thoughts can be stimulated by the sight of underpants hanging on a clothesline!

"I hope we haven't been disturbing you!" She lifted her tanned arms to spread a second sheet along the clothesline, and the two tufts of auburn hair in her armpits glowed before my eyes.

"No, not at all…"

And how could I tell her—her, the woman standing here before me, naked of limb, caressed by the sun, like a peasant laundress, in a black singlet and a red skirt, and smiling—that I haven't been able to write a single line since the day they pitched their tent above my head? Or complain to her about the breadcrumbs that land on the balcony off my kitchen when she shakes out her tablecloth over the edge of her own balcony—crumbs from Schatz's table?

"You work at home, don't you?"

"Yes…that is, but not in the morning…"

And nonetheless it is strange—I thought—that this

sour-looking professor, whose monkish face is never graced by a smile, should wear beneath his ascetic garments underpants of blue, yellow, crimson…

"I've read your book," she smiled at me over the sheet as white as the driven snow, "*The Flying Camel and…*"

"*Of the Golden Hump*," I helped her out.

"Very nice!" she said.

"Very nice"…Whenever a compliment like that bounces off my eardrums I want to dam up the speaker's mouth with a handful of dust and never see him again…but here, now, from the mouth of that man's wife…doesn't he share his hatred of me with her?—I wondered—or maybe he doesn't share anything above his underpanted loins with her…

"Thanks," I said, and to avoid further embarrassment I said I had to go feed the rabbits.

"May I see them?" She moved in front of the clothesline.

"Of course."

We entered the dimness of the rabbit hutch, which smelled sourly of sorghum, rotting grass and droppings. The rabbits' noses twitched with excitement and impatience. "How come you raise rabbits?" she said.

As I scooped feed from the barrel and scattered it among the troughs I told her how I came to have the rabbits and how I take care of them.

"The first night we didn't know what it was," said Naomi. "We heard noises above us and thought maybe it was burglars on the roof… Poor things, they don't get any sun here…" She squatted on her haunches, and with a piece of straw in her hand she tickled the whiskers of one of the does.

I too hunkered down on my haunches, next to her, and told her the names of all the does: Amalia, Adina, Aliza… and the signs by which to identify them. This amused her very much. She said it was like in Agnon, in "Edo and Ennam", where the names of the characters all begin with the same letter. Gamzu, Ginnat, Greiffenbach, Gmulah… "Someday the literary critics will come up with elaborate interpretations of your rabbits' names..." she smiled at me. I said that the lives of rabbits, unlike the lives of characters in literature, are so short that they will die before the critics ever manage to come up with an interpretation of them. "And this is the only male; his name is Zebulun"—I pointed at the male rabbit, set apart in his own cage, where he nosed agitatedly in the fodder before him. She looked at him thoughtfully, smiling, and then laughed and said: "A real allegory! Like in Agnon's story 'The Pledge of Faith', with Reichnitz's six daughters who are the six days of the week, and Ehrlich's daughter who is the Sabbath! Beautiful! All those females whose names begin with 'A', and one male rabbit named Zebulun... Some critic could have a wonderful time with that..."

"I see you know your Agnon very well," I said.

"I studied a bit of literature at university," she said modestly.

Ah!—I said to myself—so you were Schatz's student, and he taught you a few things after school.

The odor of sweat from under her arms mixed rather headily with the sour smell of the rabbits' food and excretions. Under her black singlet played the breasts of an adolescent girl, and the hem of the red skirt tenting over her knees and thighs brushed against her two-strapped sandals. Her elbow—tanned, rounded and adorned with a dimple—was so close to my own elbow, nearly touching it, that for a brief moment, in this sun-warmed dimness, opposite the rabbits quietly twitching in their straw, I was seized by a strong desire—emanating from the stimulated, starved imagination of a man who has been celibate for several months—to clasp her neck, to stifle her mouth with kisses, to lay her down on this concrete floor, to lift up her wide skirt—

"It's sort of fun to take care of rabbits," I said.

"Rrrrabbits," she imitated my rolling 'R' sounds. "You're from Rrrromania, aren't you?"

"Born in Cernowicz," I said. "Before the war it was Romania; now it's the Ukraine."

"'*Shibukin*'... what does *shibukin* mean?"

"*Shibukin*?" I asked.

"In your book. There were a lot of words that I had to look up in the dictionary…"

I apologized and told her that I had learned Hebrew while I was still in the Diaspora, from my father, whose Hebrew, like an antique store, was inhabited by rare, obsolete words. I said I knew that my written language was too "literary." "Divorce," I said, "in Aramaic."

"I thought you were older, when I read the book." She blushed.

"Yes?" I laughed.

"On the first day, when we moved in, I saw you going up the steps. That's Kalman Keren? I said to myself…"

"Disappointed?"

"On the contrary!" she laughed, and her blush intensified.

I tickled Zebulun's nose with the piece of straw I had in my hand and I said: "And you—you're Israeli born, of course."

"In Ein-Harod." She tickled, with a straw, Ada's protruding lip.

Like the pricking of a thorn in my heart. My mind went black. That schitzy Schatz, that urban book-rat, that thick-skinned pedant, that dry-faced Savonarola—not only has he attained the rank of professor, a cap and gown, the decorations of the Order of the Black Garter—but he has also attained the luscious pick of the Israeli crop—Ein-Harod!—and plucked, like a scoundrel, the blooming lily of the valley in order to dry it in his room, pressed between crumbling parchments.

Ein-Harod!… Not that I'd been there, and been impressed, and envious…but the name…the name itself… I immediately recalled those hours I sat with my father in the Floreasca Palace watching—enchanted, yes, enchanted—the long-haired girls dancing on the stage, sheaves of wheat in their hands, or laurel wreaths on their heads, light-footed, their dresses floating, their long arms harvesting the standing grain for the harvest festival or gathering grapes for the vintage festival or raising up offerings for the festival of the first fruits, accompanied by flutes, tambourines and cymbals, heroic young men lifting them gracefully and twirling with them, and all of them forming circles and chains, leaping and drumming and singing, and my father, with tears in his eyes, whispering: "They are from Ein-Harod, from Degania, from the founding kibbutz settlements…" and afterwards, backstage, when I felt such yearning, accompanied by the certainty that I would never be able to get near them, to touch one of those girls…

When I was writing *The Flying Camel* I traveled the length and breadth of the land to collect impressions and scenes, but I didn't stop off at Ein-Harod. I rode past it, sending my gaze out over the hill from the bus window, allowing my imagination to fly over it with the hot wind, and deciding in my heart not to alight at the bus stop, not to walk up the tree-shaded road leading to the houses and the lawns—so as not to defile a pure, virgin memory…

"Did you grow up there?" I asked, feeling small.

"Until I was nine. Then my parents separated and I moved to the city with my mother… I'm really a city girl." She stood up and straightened her back, stretching after her extended crouching.

"Yes, it's time to go." I stood up beside her.

"I'd like to photograph them." She glanced towards the rabbits.

"Please do!…It's your…hobby, then, photography?"

"A quarter of my living…" she laughed.

And she told me that she worked part time, three hours a day, in the afternoon, at the office of some graphic artists who among other things, design book jackets and illustrations, mostly for children's books. She thought that pictures of the rabbits could be used to illustrate a book that was due to be published soon.

"Please do!" I said. "I never thought those rabbits would ever appear in books! At long last they'll be of some use! Literary, at least!"

"By the way," she said as we went out onto the whitewashed roof where the blinding light battered our eyes, "the jacket of your book was very effective. It's good they didn't have a drawing of a flying camel, which would have been so literal, but a chess board with two rooks casting long shadows, to convey the atmosphere of the book… that is, its formal values…"

As I walked to the French library conflicting feelings raced through my heart. On the one hand—joy, joy at this surprising welcome which came to me when I hadn't been in the least prepared for it; I had got myself—no, I hadn't got myself, there was found for me—an ally in the enemy's nest. A sort of agent planted in his headquarters. On the other hand—heart-wrenching sorrow. Because, after all, this songbird—this nightingale of charm and understanding, and younger than he by at least seven years, maybe more—is a prisoner in the cage of the blue-faced braggart. Is she not his, after all? Did she not talk in the first person plural about the two of them?

But aside from that, she herself…

Obviously, that particular morning I didn't manage to translate a single line of Rabelais.

Chapter eight

The Flying Camel of the Golden Hump

According to the conventions of the well-made novel, where the wheels of the plot roll along the tracks of cause and effect, whether lubricated by psychological-internal logic or pushed helpfully in the right direction by the gentle, elegant hand of an imaginative writer who is sensitive to the needs of the readers and lays before them tasty morsels, it would seem that henceforth there ought to be a clandestine love affair between the hero—the writer of these lines—and Schatz's wife, conducted in the privacy of Schatz's own room during the morning hours when he is out of the house lecturing in an air-conditioned hall about the implicit connections in complex texts, while not the slightest suspicion clouds his sharp, clear mind; or in the hero's room, on the third floor; or in the hot rabbit hutch, which emits such aphrodisiac odors. A torrid, illicit affair, full of gripping descriptions of intertwined bodies enflamed with passion, breaking apart with deep sighs of fulfillment and release, and so on and so forth; an affair the deeper meaning of which would symbolize, simultaneously, both the intercourse between the Diaspora-born and the Israeli-born, and the revenge of the writer on the critic. Since this book is not a well-made novel, but rather a description of things as they were, things that actually happened, the reader will have to be patient. In the real world the chronological order of events is not always congruent with the ways meanings emerge from one another.

"The revenge of the writer on the critic" … But the perplexed reader—or the one who is irritated and impatient—asks: What revenge? Why? What is the meaning of the enmity between them? What has the critic done to the writer, or the writer to the critic, to cause this hostility that stirs such deep desire for revenge?

A complete and unambiguous answer to this question is beyond me. Even today (and despite Naomi's explanations, several weeks after the encounter on the roof, which will be related further along in this book), I cannot understand why, when I walked past Schatz two weeks after the publication of *The Flying Camel of the Golden Hump*, he did not condescend to acknowledge me, even though he knew me and recognized me, but continued to walk straight on, nose in the air, proud and rancorous, as if I had sinned against him; and why, about two months later, he crossed the street to the opposite sidewalk (and was almost run over by the wheels of a car that braked with an alarming shriek), when he saw me coming towards him; and why, in this very building, as I went up the stairs, or down them—

But first I should relate, if only briefly, what this book of mine is, *The Flying Camel of the Golden Hump.*

So, the story of the flying camel has its biographical origin—like the origin of my name—in a family joke. My mother told it even back in Bucharest to guests who came to our home, as they sat with steaming cups of tea and the dishes of strawberry *confiture* she had prepared with her own hands before them:

When Elkanah, my father's brother, arrived in Palestine in 1933, he went to look for work in Netanya. Three days after he got there he was sent by the Labor Exchange to load a cart of sand on the seashore. He stood there and copied the actions of the cart driver: he dug the shovel into the pile of flowing, golden sand and heaved it into the cart. Dug and heaved, dug and heaved. As he was unaccustomed to the work, rivers of perspiration rolled down his face and blisters bloomed on his hands. Every time he paused to wipe the sweat off his brow, the carter would shove him and prod him to continue. Suddenly he saw a string of camels driven by an Arab moving along the moist seashore. Through the open mouths of the sacks loaded on the humps of the camels—the first camels he had seen in the Holy Land—he saw the coarse sand glittering with bits of seashells and his eyes lit up. The gleam of the seashells looked like gold to him. He rested the shovel and cried out in wonder: "*Oy Gold!*" The carter gave him a withering look and said, in Yiddish: "Listen Korn-gold, if it's gold you want—fly away to the camels!" and fired him on the spot. What did Elkanah do? He went and sold the gold watch he had brought out of Romania with him, a bar mitzvah present, and bought a camel with the proceeds. On this camel he would haul coarse sand from the seashore to the new buildings going up in the burgeoning settlement. He did so well that eventually the money he accumulated was enough to establish a diamond polishing shop, from which he got rich. Thus the camel brought him both luck and gold.

This story, which I heard when I was still a child, stuck in my mind and wouldn't leave it. I would fantasize about it—see my uncle leading a camel loaded with gold, or riding on it—and it would change shape again and again, until finally it turned into the story I began to write more than three years ago: *The Flying Camel of the Golden Hump*

The hero of the story is Kinka, a somewhat naïve man of twenty-five, who immigrated to Palestine in 1889 with a group of pioneers from Romania. As they went from Jaffa to Rishon LeZion, Kinka straggled behind the group, until he found himself wandering alone in the sands. When he tired of walking, he lay down and slept under a broom tree. And when he awoke, behold, a camel knelt before his eyes. He understood that a miracle had been done unto him—and he arose and mounted the camel. The moment he sat down, the camel unfurled two wings that had been hidden in the folds of its hump, lifted into the air and carried its rider far away into the vastness of the Negev. There it landed in the middle of a Bedouin encampment, and upon the spot where it landed it knelt and would not get up. The Bedouin gathered around, and when they found before them an odd young man, a "Moskuby," dressed in European clothes with a straw hat on his head, who didn't know their language and to whom the land was strange, they wanted to take the camel from this stranger and send him to hell. But the camel refused to rise from its kneeling position. They beat it, they kicked it, they pulled it, they shouted at it—and still it refused to rise. They commanded Kinka to make it get up. And lo, the moment he pulled on the rein, the camel arose and obeyed him. When the Bedouin saw that, they understood this was no ordinary camel, but a spirit. They begged Kinka to stay with them and did him great honor. For three years Kinka lived with the Bedouin, worked with them on his camel, plowed and threshed, hauled and loaded, learned their language and their customs, and became as one of them. Until one morning—it was the camel that sensed the danger lying in wait for the life of its master, for the son of the sheik plotted to take his life, because of Fatima's love for him—when Kinka mounted the saddle to ride, the camel again spread its hidden wings, rose up, up, up in the air, wheeled like an eagle, devoured the distances, and landed with him on the threshing floor at Yavniel. Five years Kinka spent in Yavniel with his camel—

But I shan't retell the whole story here, which spreads over two hundred and seventy-three pages, the length and breadth of the country, and eighty years, during which Kinka gets no older but remains the same young man of twenty-five. I shall present here only a synopsis of the ending of the story, so that those who have not read it (and their numbers are few, because the book was a best-seller and came out in several editions) will understand what follows:

In 1969 Kinka is working with his camel removing rocks from an archeological dig in the area of Hebron, where remnants of a synagogue from the period of the Second Temple have been excavated. One day he discovers a cache of golden coins under one of the stones. He does not withstand the temptation, takes the coins and stashes them in the camel's hump. For years this hump had served as a kind of savings bank, and every time he had received a golden coin from his brother in America, he had slipped it inside through a slot he had made. The coins had always been few, and light in weight, but now they are many in number and heavy in weight, and they fill the entire space inside the hump. When Kinka mounts the camel and presses it to rise, it refuses. This is the first time in eighty years that such a thing had happened to Kinka. He scolds the camel, argues with it, wheedles it, pleads with it—and when all this doesn't help, he raises his stick and whacks it. Thrice he whacks the camel, on its thighs, on its ribs and on its neck. On the third whack the camel lets loose a terrifying snort, accompanied by a rolling neigh of fury, pain and torment that shakes the surrounding hills, gets up onto its feet, and, spreading its wings once more, rises very slowly into the air and carries its rider towards Jerusalem. It circles the Temple Mount and lands right on top of the Golden Dome. With the impact, Kinka tumbles out of the saddle, rolls over along the Temple square a number of times, until he comes to a halt at the foot of the Western Wall. He screams "*Gold!*" but the people praying at the Wall think they hear "*Gewald!*" They run towards the bleeding man, but find him dead.

What hasn't been written about this book, which gave me meteoric publicity on the Israeli literary horizon? It has been compared to Mendele Mocher Seforim's story, "The Mare", and to the chapters on Balak the dog in Agnon's *Days Gone By*, to Voltaire's *Candide* and his *Zadig*, to *Gulliver's Travels* and *Don Quixote*… The critics wrote that it is a fabulous amalgam of Hebrew and Arabic folk legends. They mentioned Balaam's ass and Al-Buraq, Mohammed's flying horse, who, according to one of the legends, transported him down from Heaven to the foot of the Western Wall. One Dr. Amnon Bar-Am—who, as I discovered later, is a professor of anthropology at the Hebrew University—went to the trouble of doing a thorough study of the folkloristic elements in this picaresque novel, from which I learned some things I hadn't known before, for example: that the story of Yokheved from Tiberias, who lost her mind for the love of Kinka and who was buried, after her suicide, in a Muslim cemetery—which appears on pages 72–75 of the novel—is nothing but a variant of a story that was told among the Jews of Ramleh in the time of the

Caliph Hisham (eighth century) about the daughter of the Karaite Rabbi Avraham ben Ya'acov, who fell in love with the son of the military governor of the city, drowned herself in a deep well, and was also buried in a Muslim cemetery; or that the line Kinka repeats several times—"Whatever a man does, he does for himself"—has its source in a tale of Ya'acov Yosef of Polonnoye, the author of *The Chronicles of Ya'acov Yosef* (who heard it from the Ba'al Shem Tov), about a poor man, a beggar, who would mutter to everyone who gave him a coin, "Whatever a man does he does for himself," and he said it to the king, who got furious and commanded his servants to give the man a chicken force-fed with a deadly poison, and so on.

One critic, given to onomastics, devoted half her article to examining the sources and significances of the name Kinka (as she was unaware that Kinka was my Uncle Elkanah's nickname within the family). Firstly—she discovered—the 'K' of Kinka is the first letter of both my given name and my surname, and its doubling bears witness to my complete identification with the character. Secondly—she said—Kinka is derived from κυνικοί the Greek Dog Sect, in other languages called the 'Cynics', who originally preached abstention from passions and pleasures and made do with little, and who in a later period degenerated into complete disregard for all moral values—to a "cynical attitude"—which is also the line along which the hero of my story developed, from modesty and innocence to cynicism. And thirdly—and this discovery was an amazing revelation, a piece of news that made me begin to believe that some mysterious power was directing my writing!—'Keynuqa'a' was the name of a Jewish clan in the Arabian city of Medina in Mohammed's time, and they were goldsmiths! In the year 624—she cited primary texts—a quarrel broke out in the city's bazaar between the men of Keynuqa'a and the Muslims, and the Jews retreated to their strongholds only to surrender after sixteen days of siege. Once they agreed to give over their arms they were allowed to leave, and they wandered to Edrai on the East Bank of the Jordan. And Kinka, too—she wrote—clashes with the Muslim Arabs at various stages of his life, lives among them and flees from them, negotiates with them and defends himself from them, and his relations with them, like the relations of the men of Keynuqa'a, are ambivalent!

Another critic, who writes in a psychologizing manner, analyzed the book according to all its concealed levels, discussing the realistic and surrealistic elements in it, the real and the imaginary, and came up with two astonishing conclusions. Firstly, that Kinka is homosexual, and the evidence for this is the distance he keeps between himself and the women who fall in love with him, his excessive fondness for Bedouin youths and his strange, tragic relations—disguised as a relationship of intellectual and political closeness—with the Haganah commander (later commander of an armored division in the Israel Defense Forces) Emmanuel Broshi, which lasts for twenty-five years. Secondly, that the camel in the book—"the ship of the desert"—is an archetypal symbol of Kinka's spiritual and social condition: loneliness, subversion and alienation, bearing a "hump" of indebtedness and guilt that is impossible to get rid of; that the "gold" in the hump symbolizes the longing for happiness, the yearning for erotic satisfaction, and that therefore it "stands to reason" that the act of thrusting the gold into the hump through a hole that he has pierced in it is a symbolic act of homosexual intercourse.

A paper by Hephzibah Givati called "The Significance of the Bird in the Novel *The Flying Camel*" was more than 3,000 words long, while the episode in the book about the bird who lands on the camel's hump, accompanies Kinka on his way and sings him songs in Yiddish is a mere 600 words!

The most magnificent work of all was produced by the critic Shomron Shavit, who entitled his long article (eleven pages in a journal!) "The End of the Zionist Dream?" In his opinion, the whole book is nothing but an allegory of "the rise and fall of Zionism." The flying camel is the utopian dream, soaring on the wings of imagination, to return to the Land of the Fathers, the Land of the East; the dream, like the camel, lands on the earth of clotted reality and is forced to contend with it. It lands and takes off, takes off and lands. Kinka's wanderings, riding on the camel, leading it, working with it, for eighty years, throughout the land as he stops at various places that are stations in the fulfillment of Zionism, symbolize Zionism's fluctuations between its exalted aims and the exigencies of reality (the title of this section of the paper is "The Exalted and the Exigent"). The golden coins deposited in the camel's hump symbolize the start of the decay of Zionism through materialism and the desire for gain (title: "From Zionism to Cynicism") and the hiding of the treasure trove in the hump symbolizes the total corruption of the Zionist ideal following the conquests and the lustful greediness in the wake of the Six Day War. The heavy gold "sinks the ship of the desert" the way excess cargo capsizes a ship at sea (title: "Capitalism Capsizes"); and the inevitable result is that the camel returns to its origins, lands on the dome of the Muslim mosque and shakes off the rider who betrayed his dream; the latter rolls to the place where ultra-Orthodox Jews wearing caftans and prayer-shawls are praying, Jews for whom the Land of Israel is the Holy Land and not the accursed Zionist state, which has no hope. In the final section of the article ("Kinka's Consciousness"), Shavit scrutinizes Kinka's consciousness and examines his attitudes towards the reality through which he travels. Comparing him to Don Quixote, to Candide and to Fielding's Joseph Andrews, he observes that in contrast to those three picaresque heroes, Kinka is an "uninvolved observer (*un observateur désengagé*)," but his lack of involvement expresses "passive resistance" (here he digresses at length to discuss the meaning of another of Kinka's sayings: "Only that which a man does not have can never be taken from him"); this passivity is "paradoxically endowed with extraordinary power, which disturbs the reader's complacency and arouses him anew to examine all the common assumptions of our society."

Twenty-eight articles were written about this book of mine in the six months after it was published.

But Schatz—not a word!

The same Schatz who greeted every new Hebrew novel as it came on the market, either with exaggerated praise and obsequious compliments or with scornful spite—wrote not a word!

No, not a word!

Even Professor J.N. Schuster, who so rarely descends from the

Parnassus of his pure research to the lowly plain of "literary small fry" as he calls it, broke his aristocratic silence and published a major article about the book in his quarterly journal.

Schuster's article was more interesting than any of the articles that appeared before or after it because it dealt not with the contents of the novel but with its unique characteristics with respect to language, style and semantics.

This profound and virtuoso article, in which the number of bibliographical footnotes alone reached fifty-six, raised the value of my stock in academic circles, which had been chilly and reserved about my three books, including the last. In the first three pages of the article he discussed the "enormous associative and connotative load" of the novel's title, particularly the phrase 'Golden Hump'. The word 'hump', he noted, appears only once in the Bible, in Isaiah 30:6, "And their treasures upon the humps of camels," and it is in the context of "the land of trouble and anguish," "the viper and the flying serpent," so that it arouses in the reader, even before he gets to the story itself, "repulsive" associations about the land and its fate. Professor Schuster then analyzes the "phonetic dissonance" between the Hebrew words for 'hump' and 'gold' and demonstrates that the collocation of the two words creates a "connotative harmony of contrasts." He also notes certain etymological connections between the two lexical items.

For the next seven pages the article deals with a single type of punctuation mark: the semi-colon(;). Professor Schuster found—something which I myself had never noticed—that the distributive frequency of the semi-colon in my book is three and a half times greater than its average frequency in the Hebrew literature of the last generation: an average of twelve on every page! To this fact—statistic, as it were—he attributes extremely important suggestive significance, indicative of the attitude of the narrator towards his own text: just as the preponderance of ellipses (...) in a text bears witness to the intense emotional involvement of the narrator (see Brenner, for example), and just as the paucity of exclamation points, question marks and commas bears witness to a sacramental-ironic attitude towards the text (see Agnon, for example)—so the high frequency of semi-colons in my work (and he brings many examples of this from my book) bears witness to the intention of the narrator to pose as a "detached observer" of facts and events; a pose which "multiplies the ironic power of an apparently narrative-functional-emotionally-neutral text," as he put it. He calls this type of punctuation "distributive indifferentiation," a coinage that subsequently achieved great currency in the critical marketplace.

The third part of the article includes a graphic representation of the development of the novel. With the help of three curves drawn from point A (which stands for the beginning of the novel) to point B (which stands for its end), he demonstrates that the novel's development is wave-parabolic; that is, a wave consisting of reversing parabolas, the foci of which are located at the stages of the hero's cognitive development and the vertices of which are tangent to the axes of objective reality. The sequence of events in this story as well as the direction of that sequence may, according to Schuster, be found in a simple formula expressing the relationship between focus and vertex, that is, between internal and external mutations. That formula is:

$$y^2 = \frac{2px}{\beta}$$

where y is Kinka, x is Israeli reality, p is the distance between them and β is the attitude of the narrator. Professor Schuster proves that the wave-parabolic development of the story is neither random nor arbitrary, but is correlative, rather, to the shape of the camel's hump, to the shape of the undulating sand dunes described in the book, and to the trajectory of a bullet, which symbolizes the combative character of the *Yishuv* and the State.

The last part of the article follows a single metaphor which, according to Professor Schuster, is woven as a *leitmotif* throughout the novel from beginning to end: the metaphor of the stone. He cites the entire opening sentence of the novel ("Kinka straggled behind; when he noticed that the distance between himself and the group ahead had increased, he asked himself why and recalled that he had stumbled over a slippery stone lying in his path; and only at this moment did he become conscious that the two middle toes in his left shoe hurt him"), as well as the closing sentence ("His bloody brow was turned towards the Wall; but his right ear rested, crushed, on the smooth stone, as if listening for the sound of approaching footsteps"), and notes that between the two the word 'stone' in its singular and plural forms appears no fewer than 128 times. Enumerating about a dozen of these stones (the stone thrown at Kinka by an Arab youth in Jenin; the stone that tumbles down to his feet in the quarry at Gilboa; the stone upon which he and Pessia sit at Hanita; the stone that injures the camel's knee at Kadesh Barnea; the stone under which he finds the treasure trove of coins; and others) and examining closely the semantic characteristics of 'stone' in its textual and associative contexts, he shows how this stone is transmuted, in its significance, from a prophetic "stone of stumbling" (Isaiah 8:14) in the opening sentence to the proverbial "rolling stone" in Chapter Three and then to "millstone," "cornerstone," "touchstone" and so on until the implied significance of "foundation stone" (in the Mosque of Omar episode), and of "the stone shall cry out of the wall" (Habbakuk 2:11) in the final scene. That is to say (and these are his very words) the stone is transmuted from literal object to metonymy, from metonymy to metaphor, and from metaphor to symbol.

Thus spake Professor J.N. Schuster, but Schatz—not a word!

About eight months after the book was published, and the waves of criticism had abated, and I, so to speak, was resting on my laurels—my eyes were rudely torn open one Friday morning by the headline in one of the literary supplements: "CAMEL CUD," signed with a name I had neither heard of nor seen in any of the newspapers, Shulamith Nahor.

The article was written in vulgar language and a boastful tone, sneering and hostile: this Shulamith could not understand all the fuss about the novel, all the praises heaped upon it by "dubious scholars" and the popularity it had achieved among the reading public. She herself "didn't give a damn" (her very words!). She had been thoroughly bored reading it, and had found it hard to finish. The book revealed nothing new to her, neither with respect to content nor with respect to form, and the "truths" it expressed were banalities. In short, the camel doesn't fly and the hump holds no gold, and the whole book is nothing but "a camel sitting around in the stony rubbish of a wasteland, masticating straw and regurgitating its cud."

For three days that article banished the sleep from my eyes, and for four days the lunch from my mouth. I went not forth from my house, nor did I wish to see the face of any man. I asked myself who this Shulamith Nahor was, and whence the great enmity burning in her broadside against me. The name is a pseudonym, I said to myself, but it couldn't be Schatz hiding behind it, because the whole thing just wasn't his style at all!

No. It was not Schatz. Only two weeks later did I discover that Shulamith Nahor—no pseudonym—was his student, second year in the Department of Hebrew Literature.

I was still recovering from this blow, comforting myself with all the encomiums showered on me by our best critics, with the dozens of readers' letters I had received, all of them very admiring, and with the certitude that this slut, Shulamith Nahor, who without a doubt is not just Schatz's student but also his mistress—that's what I told myself—is not worth my wasting the most fleeting thought upon, and who's going to remember her name, anyway—when a second blow rained down upon me: an article entitled "THE GOLDEN CAMEL OF KEREN."

And the author (once more of the female gender)—none other than Dr. Elisheva Tal-Blumfeld!

Unlike the previous review, this article (the ironic name of which was intended to echo "The Golden Ass of Apuleius"...) was written in a serious, analytical tone and dealt with aspects of the book itself: its content, its style, its images, and most of all, its protagonists. I shall not repeat what she said; I shall say only that in summing up her detailed analysis Ms. Tal-Blumfeld arrived at the conclusion that what the other critics—admiringly and respectfully—had called "influences"' were in truth "imitations": of *The Tin Drum, One Hundred Years of Solitude, Zadig, Tristram Shandy* by Laurence Sterne (a book I had never even read), and *The Golden Ass* by Apuleius; but, that unlike *The Golden Ass*, my book lacked "authentic coherence" and suffered from a "hump of eclectic imitations."

This blow pained me infinitely more than the first, not only because the article was knowledgeably and authoritatively written, and not only because Dr. Tal-Blumfeld was a reputable critic who had taught many good graduate students and had written the famous book *The Real and the Non-Real in Literature*—but primarily because I had believed that she was a friend of mine. I had met her on three or four occasions when we had conversed pleasantly and wittily, like two people who understood each other well, and once, as we sat together in a small café I even had a feeling—from the flirtatious way she was speaking, her laughter and her signaling looks—that she was trying to tempt me into a romantic adventure (even though I am younger than she by ten years, at least. Maybe even because of that). And now, all of a sudden... from her, of all people... It was as if I had been betrayed.

I swallowed the insult and overcame the inward bitterness this unexpected blow had left me. But ten days after the article appeared I could no longer maintain the proud silence that was devouring me from within, and I called her. I told her that I had read her edifying article with great interest, but that one thing in it had rather surprised me: how could I have imitated a book I had never read, i.e., *Tristram Shandy*?

"You never read it?" she said, embarrassed. "I was certain... it's a classic... and in two of your chapters the resemblance is absolutely amazing!" And when I assured her yet again that I hadn't read it, she said, "I truly am sorry! I'll publish an apology at once, next week!" And she added in a somewhat intimate voice, as if between old friends: "Were you hurt? By the article?" (The nerve!—I thought—She wants the best of both worlds: she knifes me in the back to win the glory of the critic, and then she insinuates her hot little palm into my hand to win the affection of the criticized!)

"Not at all," I laughed, "but I was a bit puzzled that you sort of accused me of stealing..."

"Stealing?!" she cried, in her clear, amiable voice. "What nonsense! I wrote 'imitations,' but all great literature is full of imitations. Fielding imitated Richardson, Smollet imitated La Sage, Defoe imitated Cervantes... How many writers imitated and still do imitate Cervantes? And isn't *The Travels of Benjamin the Third* an imitation of Don Quixote? And *Tristram Shandy* itself? You're in very good company! I didn't think you'd be hurt by it!" I told her it was beyond my comprehension how a single book, like *The Flying Camel*, could be an imitation of so many books that are so different from each another. "That's what's so original about it!" she laughed in her limpid, bell-like voice. "And by the way, I read it straight through in a single sitting and in many places I even burst out laughing. How long did it take you to write it?" I asked her why she hadn't bothered to mention in her article that she had "enjoyed" it. "But that was mentioned in thirty other articles!" she laughed. I said that as I was reading her article, I felt that she had been influenced by Schatz's opinions. "Schatz?!" she cried. "That inflated turkey? I'm not speaking to him. I barely say hello to him when we pass each other in the halls. How can anyone stand that cock of shit!"

"Cock," she said, instead of "crock."

When the third edition of the book came out, I was interviewed, an interview that spread over three pages of the newspaper. Here are a few excerpts from it:

No, better not.

Chapter nine

Stolen Waters

For eight days after my meeting with Naomi—a meeting that was pregnant with promise, or so it seemed to me—I didn't encounter her face to face. Twice I heard her steps on the staircase. I rushed to the spy-hole in the door and peeping through it, my eye registered first her flowered head-scarf, then the shopping basket dangling from her arm, and then her back as she descended—but I never saw her face to face. Every day I expected her to ring the doorbell, appear camera in hand, and ask again to photograph the rabbits, but she never appeared and, disappointed as well as a bit resentful, I thought: Schatz has forbidden her to see me after she told him about our meeting.

It goes without saying that during those days I didn't add a single sentence to page 23 of my book (about which I shall have something to say further along), the bottom half of which was completely blank, as it had been before the invasion. In the evenings I would now hear above my head not only steps and creaks, but also the rat-a-tat-tat of my learned neighbor's typewriter, an unbelievably industrious sprinting rat-a-tat-tat, emitted in bursts, almost without pause, with a ping at the transitions from line to line, after which it would continue to sprint. The unflagging professor's window was open to the evening air, and his desk stood next to the window; my window too, one story down, was open because of the heat, and my desk stood next to the window as well. The aggressive sounds that came forth from beneath the keys of the pounder above would flit about like bats beating on my windowpanes…

I would sit in my chair, tight-lipped, tense, my face burning with impotent rage at being held hostage in my own room, a prisoner of writing, my hands tied—and forced to listen to the bell of the typewriter chariot jingling at regular intervals Every jingle—another row of words strings itself across the industrious typist's white page. I would count the lines, line by line, line by line, and whenever the typing ceased for a brief moment (now the gears of his brain are turning!—I said to myself) I knew: this is not the final word! Oh no! This studious all-night partier will neither slumber nor sleep. The moment he completes a page, he pulls it from the machine, inserts a new one, and on and on flows the Jordan of his sentences…

How could I sit at my desk and write when I couldn't even return his machine-gun fire in kind, for I, the child, apparently, of a different era, still plow my field with an out-dated, primitive instrument called 'pen' and move oh-so-slowly along the furrow, like a Romanian farmer walking behind a yoke of oxen! How could I write when I felt that if I were to lay a sentence down on the paper its image would be reflected, inverted, like in a *camera obscura*—or distorted, like in a concave mirror—on the page in production in that upper room! Or it would be registered by the mechanized brain of the man sitting above me! How could I—with the rat-a-tat of the typewriter pelting like hailstones on my head, on my ears, deafening my thoughts, distracting me, driving me to decode—according to what? by the rhythm? by the number of strokes?—which words are being notched into place? And how could I ask what he is writing up there, damn it, at this very moment?!

Here, perhaps, I should say something about Naphtali Schatz's theories, as set forth in his two books—spaced three years apart—the one, *Against Allegory* and the other, *The Three-Mirrored Chamber.*

Against Allegory was Schatz's maiden book, and its appearance four years ago earned him high status among the younger generation of critics. At first glance, it might seem that to come out strongly against allegory in the 1970s is the equivalent of slaughtering a cow that has dropped dead long ago, leaving only a few pungent picked-over remains lying about in the field. Since Orwell, who has written any allegories? But the big innovation in Schatz's book was that he subsumed under the category of "Allegory" such great works as Tolstoy's *Resurrection*, Kafka's "Metamorphosis", "The Bear" by Faulkner, *The Plague* by Camus, *The Tin Drum* by Günter Grass, and therefore—after a close and detailed analysis—he discredited them! Schatz's central contention in this book was supported by well-based evidence that bore witness to his familiarity with world literature in its various periods. He argued, with the acuity and enthusiasm of a polemicist or a sharp lawyer, against Chesterton's famous assertion that "Every great literature has always been allegorical." His thesis is this: any work of literature which serves—whether by the intention of the author or not by his intention—as the illustration of an idea, as well as any work of literature which lures its readers into "drawing a moral" from it, undermines itself by destroying its own aesthetic autonomy, without which literature has no existence as an independent authentic art. As I said, this was his maiden book, the first fruit of his intellect, and the unripenesses in it could have set many healthy teeth on edge; however, since it was a youthful "*J'accuse,*" insubordinate and rebellious, which not only smashed, with judiciously placed kicks, a number of revered icons in the temple of world literature, but also slew about a score of Hebrew writers, leaving them like corpses on the field of battle, it won him many true believers among the younger generation, who—stalks still green and fresh and upright—had only just sprouted forth from the Israeli earth.

(I must note, incidentally, that my name was not mentioned at all in this book, although a few critics detected "allegorical elements" in my first two books.)

The Three-Mirrored Chamber (which was published about a year after my book *The Flying Camel of the Golden Hump*), was, in some ways, the continuation and development of *Against Allegory*.

However, it was much longer than its predecessor (286 pages as opposed to 155), more mature and more complex. Schatz's main thesis in this book[I] is: the test of an "absolute" work of literature is whether its text is hermetic and enclosed within a significant structure that is like a chamber with three mirrors. "Mirrors can never be used as windows," writes Schatz, and thus the hermetic text is one that does not look outside itself and is not transparent with respect to the external world, but rather is turned inwards on itself, autarchic. The "chamber" in which the text takes place is described as constructed of three mirrors: two of them opposite each other on facing walls and the third on the ceiling. The two facing each other create the "double irony": the text, which purports to be an adaptation of the materials of reality to linguistic qualities but which is, rather, a composition independent of external reality (like a musical composition) is reflected in both mirrors at once—that is, its reflection is multiplied infinitely (and this is the meaning of the "irony" in the work); the upper mirror reflects what is happening in the opposing mirrors, from different angles, and expresses the reflection of the text in the consciousness of the anonymous reader, whose unspecified presence also constitutes part of the hermetic work. In an "absolute" text of this sort—says Schatz—the writer does not solicit any specific, extra-textual meaning, nor does he dictate any such meaning, but every one of his readers is its echo, and every reading is an adventure in the infinite possibilities of comprehension. After Schatz summarizes the theories of I.A. Richards, William Empson, Roland Barthes and Roman Jakobson about reality-literature-reader relationships and refutes their assumptions with admirable virtuosity, he analyzes at length two works that he presents as classics of "absolute literature," which support his thesis: Borges' "The Library of Babel" and Agnon's "Edo and Ennam".

The second part of the book examines a large number of works of world literature in general and Hebrew literature in particular

---

I Which is also an antithesis to Stendhal's well-known statement that the novel is a mirror that goes along the King's Road and reflects what it sees on both sides.

with the intent to distinguish between the "autonomous" and the "extrinsic" elements in them. This is not the place to present even a brief summary of these analyses. I shall only say that he coined a new concept called 'reductive sub-treasurability', which has since become common currency among critics, who sprinkle it like caraway seeds over the loaves of a great many articles; and that following some caprice—which I don't understand—he arranged the works under discussion in series of threes and fours (sort of along the prophet Amos's lines of "For three transgressions of...and for four I will not turn away the punishment thereof...") and in alphabetical order by author. Thus he discusses, for example, Borges, Böll, and Bellow, and the fourth wheel is some Hebrew writer whose name begins with 'B'; or: Gogol, Grass, Gombrowicz—and some Israeli writer beginning with 'G'; or Kleist, Kafka, Kundera—and one of our own beginning with 'K'; and so on.

Here I must mention that my own name begins with 'K' not once, but twice. Yet despite the fact that any unprejudiced and non-hostile reader of my last book would have put me in as a link—however modest—in the 'K' sequence, my name was not even mentioned once in this book.

Anyway, those are the two books Naphtali Schatz wrote, in addition to an endless stream of articles in newspapers and journals about contemporary literature, all of them sharp and witty, some of them excelling in their depth and others in their authoritativeness, some malicious and others benevolent, depending on the specific identities of the respective victims and beneficiaries.

It comes as no surprise, then, that—as I sat in my chair, prevented from doing my own writing by the nuisance that had worked its way into my home and settled into my life, and by the barrage of typewriter strokes hailing down on me from above—I would ask myself, my eyes rolling heavenward, where the unsheathed talons of this cultural vulture might land now.

Let me get back to chronological order.

For eight days, as I said, after our meeting on the roof, I didn't see

Naomi. When I came home from the French library on the ninth day, upon entering the building I was greeted by a thin stream of water trickling down the steps, snaking like a sidewinder along the bottom of the balustrade. When I reached my own landing I found that the water had formed a small puddle where the tile floor is a bit concave, and the overflow had already arrived at my doorstep. The source of the water was from above, so I went upstairs to see if someone had turned on the tap in the rabbit hutch and had forgotten to turn it off. When I got to the fourth floor, I saw that the water was flowing out from under Schatz's door. Knowing that he himself was never home at this time of day, I rang the doorbell, and then rang it a second time, but nobody answered. Naomi had already gone to work. I put my ear to the door, and the sound of flowing water, burbling and gurgling, was heard within. I stood there and wondered what I should do. The two of them wouldn't get home until about six o'clock, and in the meantime the water would flood the staircase and penetrate my own apartment.

I went downstairs to consult Victoria—the unofficial *concierge* of the building who monitors its goings-on—and rang her doorbell. She wasn't home either. I went back up to my own floor, and saw that indeed the water had risen. When I opened my door, it was tonguing my entrance hall and in another moment it would lick my woolen carpet.

If *mater artium necessitas* and need is father to the deed—then lack is the spur of memory. As I stood there watching the tongue of water lapping closer and closer to the carpet—which I hastened to roll up—I remembered that I had in my possession, somewhere, a key to the apartment upstairs. It had been given to me by the late Dr. Klausner himself. As he had spent most of the day at his pharmacy, and as he trusted me completely, he gave me a key to use in case the gas man came while he was out, or the electrician, or the handyman, or in case, God forbid, anything happened to him, because he wasn't in the best of health. I ransacked the drawers of the kitchen cabinet and found the key.

To enter or not to enter?—that was the question. A Talmudic

question: What is the law regarding a man who enters his neighbor's premises without the owner's permission but with the intention of preventing flood damage? If it is a matter of saving a life—plainly: it is permitted. And if it is a matter of water which by its nature spreads and is likely to damage property...

For a few minutes I pondered this point of law, and then I said to myself: if Schatz trespasses on me every evening through the window and causes me immeasurable damage—I, who will trespass on his property just this once, and through the door, in order to prevent damage...

I opened the door with the key and went in. The entry-hall was covered with a thin layer of water and estuaries of it had penetrated the living room, soaking the carpet and wetting books that were on the floor. Walking on the tips of my shoes, I followed the sound of rushing water and arrived at the bathroom. The bathtub tap was open and in the water that overflowed the sides floated items of colorful, transparent laundry. I shut the tap, and hastened back to dry land.

So this is the Kingdom of Schatz! I said as I stood in the doorway of the living room.

What a contrast between the way the apartment looks now and the way it looked in the days of its previous owner, Dr. Klausner of blessed memory! Back then the place was pervaded by a sort of eternal serenity, every object in the place that seemed to have been intended for it since the days of Creation, each piece of furniture without a suspicion of dust, each embroidered cloth without a wrinkle, with an aura of quiet nobility, rich with memories, radiating from it all—but now agitation, confusion and mess reigned: books and pamphlets, newspapers and notebooks were strewn about the room. Some stood or lay, crowded together or widely spaced, on shelves that lined two walls from floor to ceiling, others were jumbled in no particular order on every available surface: the two tables—the desk by the window and the low tea table in the middle of the room, the two chairs against the wall, the leather armchair, even the floor, which was flooded by the toenail-deep water. On a high stool next to the bookcase sat a tall stack of journals, and I, out of curiosity, baptized my soles and stepped over to see them. From the top down they were:

British Journal of Aesthetics, No. 17, 1963
Virginia Quarterly Review, No. 2, 1970
L'arc, No. 26
Modern Fiction Studies, VII, Vol. I
Bulletin of Bibliography, XXIX, No.5
Georges Poulet: *Etudes sur le temps humain*
Kenyon Review, No. 3, 1973
Revue d'Art Dramatique, 1968
The Journal of Aesthetics and Art Criticism, 1975
Esprit, 1963
Review of Comparative Literature, XVIII, No. 3
Journal of the Linguistic Circle of New York, Vol. I
Memoirs and Proceedings of the Manchester Literary and Philosophical Society, Vol. 104, No. 61-62

Leaning against the wall, near the bookshelves, was a pile of Hebrew newspapers, waist-high, of which the bottom-most were yellowed with age. In the corner, at the foot of the desk, lay three books, and my eye took in what was embossed on their spines: *The Complete Works of M.J. Berdichevsky*. The water was beginning to lap at their bindings, and I—reflexively, you might say—rushed over, skipping on the toes of my sodden shoes, to save them from certain destruction. I picked them up from the floor and put them on the desk.

As I set them down a piece of paper fell out of one of the books, fluttered to the floor and got wet. I pulled it out of the water. It was an anlysis of Berdichevsky's famous "Kalonymos and Naomi".

As I set the soiled paper, upon which the writing had blurred, beside the typewriter—my enemy and my adversary, which bombards me every evening, which grinds up the guts of the many books in the room to turn them into article-sausage—upon a neat stack of paper, the title on the uppermost page caught my eye: "The Key to a Possible Hebrew Aesthetic". I was automatically drawn to read what was typed below:

> The question of the existence of differential linguistic aesthetics, like the question of the existence of differential linguistic poetics, has been of concern to researchers such as R.L. Jenkins[1] and P.M. Speigel[2] when confronted with deviant literary models transmitted from one natural language to another through suggestive synchronization. The question we will examine here is whether semantic and phonetic analyses of Hebrew texts written in different periods will reveal a coherent aesthetic regularity that will enable…

I stood there spellbound, amazed, faced with this treasure house of knowledge that had revealed itself to me, like the one in Aladdin's cave, unexpectedly—

On the other side of the typewriter stood a picture in a wooden frame, which I recognized at once: Bakunin! The wide beard, like Marx's, the hair down to the shoulders, the eyes radiating intelligence! And beneath it, in Russian, "Mikhail Alexandrovitch Bakunin." What's he got to do with Bakunin?—I wondered—Has he been possessed by one of Dostoevsky's "demons"? Is he plotting a revolution?

As I raised my head, the bedroom sprang into view, with its door wide open.

The wide double bed was unmade. A thin pink blanket was crumpled up in one corner, as if it had been kicked there. On one of the pillows lay a short blue nightgown sprigged with tiny yellow flowers, which looked like an eight-year-old girl's party dress. On the second pillow were flung a pair of purple-striped pajama bottoms, which cascaded down from the bed to the floor. In the midst of this arena tumbled the wildly disarranged pages of some English newspaper—*The New York Review of Books*? *The Times Literary Supplement*?—which had been abandoned in the midst of being read. On the white dressing table stood a round concave mirror, in which was reflected, crookedly, the image of the rectangular mirror of the clothes closet across from it.

On the wall to the right of the bed hung an enormous poster of *The Taming of the Shrew*, and on the wall to its left an enormous poster of *Pygmalion*; and I asked myself whether Naphtali Schatz saw himself as a Petruchio who teaches a lesson to his stubborn Katherine, or as a Professor Higgins who trains his wild rural Naomi Doolittle.

I headed for the door.

Before I left I surveyed the living room once again. It looked to me like Faust's study after Mephistopheles had stolen in secretly and turned the place upside down with his tricksy capriciousness.

At 6:15 I heard the footsteps of my two neighbors going up the stairs. They stopped for a moment next to my apartment and uttered a few words of astonishment at the sight of the puddle on the tiles of the landing, continued on up and unlocked the door to their own apartment.

From above, the shocked cries of the two of them reached my ears. How? Where? Oh my God!...the sound of urgent running; and as the door closed on them—a cacophony of screams and splashes, squishes and squeals. The sentence fragments that flew into my window brought word of a quarrel that had arisen between them: "Off! All of them! Yes, also in the bathtub... Come see... yourself..."—I heard Naomi's angry voice; and his, stern and accusatory: "...Not by themselves, they didn't...kindly explain...no miracle...act of God?..." and her voice, from another corner of the apartment, defending herself fiercely: "I would have heard... No, no, I didn't leave...yes, I'm sure! Before I went out!" And again his voice, pursuing her: "Who filled it?...From below?! Ground water?!" And a moment later, in reply to a line that escaped me: "Burst? Here? Under the floor?! What kind of nonsense is that!..." And finally, as if both had despaired of solving the mystery—of how water flows into rooms when all the taps are closed—their cries were stilled and only the sounds of furniture being moved and dripping water being mopped and wrung out were heard.

I had resolved to reveal the solution of the riddle to Naomi when she spoke to me on the staircase or in the courtyard, but the following day, when I came home in the evening, I heard banging sounds from above, and when I lifted mine eyes unto the fourth floor, I saw a strange man in a work apron standing by the open door, hammer and screwdriver in hand, installing a new lock for my suspicion-tormented neighbors.

Three days later, at three in the afternoon, I saw a bunch of keys dangling from the keyhole of the Schatzian mailbox when I emptied mine. I stood and debated with myself: Take them out? Leave them?...But out of the sense of good citizenship with which I am so indelibly imbued I said to myself that it wouldn't be fair to leave the keys just hanging there, having been forgotten, out of absentmindedness, by the professor or his wife, because incidents of housebreaking and burglary are so common in our city, and any passing punk could just pull them out, walk up to the apartment on the fourth floor, go right in and empty it of all its valuables. I therefore took the bunch of keys out of the keyhole, and, knowing that Schatz is never home at this time of day, said: I'll return these to Naomi's hands—a virtuous act which may be rewarded.

I went up and rang the doorbell. There was no answer. That meant Naomi had already gone out and that there was nobody home. I wavered as to what to do next, but some inner demon incited me. I opened the door and went in. I laid the keys down on "The Key to a Possible Hebrew Aesthetic", under the picture of Bakunin—and walked out.

At half past five, I heard from my room Schatz's confident vigorous footsteps going up the stairs, stopping in front of his door. Then I heard the indistinct buzz of the doorbell, another buzz, and a third. Another moment or two of silence and afterwards—like gravel rolling off a cliff—the rapid pitter-pat of footsteps hurrying down the stairs. About a quarter of an hour passed, and again the ascending footsteps were heard, pugnacious and energetic. And again the doorbell, three times. And then—once more the rapid descent.

An hour later—footsteps again, this time of four feet, two of them light and two of them heavy, climbing up the stairs. The door above opened with the turn of a key and slammed.

Only fragments of the ensuing discourse between husband and wife reached my attentive ears, but I was able to gather that the winds of mystery had penetrated through cracks that had appeared in the walls of Schatz's rational-hermetic citadel: he remembers quite clearly—without a shadow of doubt!—that he had his keys on him. Even remembers that he opened the mailbox with them but that there were no letters inside... If that's the case, so how?...No, he never ever leaves them on his desk!...—But you don't believe that one object can be in two places at the same time...—That, more or less, was Naomi's argument, and I heard, if I'm not mistaken, the names of Einstein and Newton offered in evidence; even "the fourth dimension" was invoked.

Ha, mysteries of the universe! The supernatural, the extrasensory, which today, at the end of the twentieth-century are dancing like demons—flying saucers, creatures from outer space—throughout our enlightened world, exactly as they did in the dark middle ages; they break into locked apartments as into open brains eaten with doubts in the era of Newtonian physics; they lure learned professors, confused adolescents, seekers of God, foolish virgins, into speculations about that which is above them, the Transcendental...

But afterwards—did my ears deceive me?—I also heard Freud's name enter the discussion: losing a key... slip... subconscious forgetfulness... what does all this imply?

Only the devil knows.

Chapter ten

Apartment Building

I should have begun this book with a description of the apartment building in which I live, 39 Avigdor Street, Tel Aviv. Ever since my youth I have had enormous respect for writers like Victor Hugo, Dickens, and Balzac, who, before they throw themselves into the twists and tempests of their plot, take their readers by the hand and lead them calmly to the place where it all happens; like elderly tour guides they explain to them very slowly, detail by detail, at length and with great thoroughness—sometimes wearying but nonetheless worthy—what they are seeing: the quarter of the city, the streets, the house, its rooms, their inhabitants, moving in a circuit from the perimeter to the center. Balzac, in *Le père Goriot*, for example—a book I remember from when I was thirteen—devotes his first twelve or fifteen pages to a description of the boarding-house of Mme. Vauquer in the Rue Neuve-Sainte-Geneviève, between the Latin Quarter and the Faubourg Saint-Marceau, in the area "between the hills of Montmartre and the heights of Montrouge"; as he steers the reader through this *quartier*, he renders the alleys and the gutters, the crumbling old houses and the elegant homes interspersed among them, the cobblestones and the colors of the walls, and when he leads the reader into the boarding-house itself, he shows him, patiently and at length, all of the rooms on each of its three stories, and everything inside them—each piece of furniture, every object, every dish, every picture on the walls, every stove in a corner, every oilcloth on a table (a very grim picture, as you may remember, smelling of rot, miserliness and malevolence); then he describes the wretched mistress of the boarding-house and every one of her thirteen tenants; only at the end of those fifteen pages does he get to old Goriot himself, the hero of his story.

This system has one great advantage: the reader—though he may lose patience from time to time at the number of details heaped upon him before any action whatsoever has taken place—knows from the start exactly where he is. Once he gets swept away by the plot he doesn't need to waste his imagination wandering hither and thither around town—sometimes around the world—in order to find out where the author has arbitrarily set him down. This is in contrast to most of the books that have come out over the past few decades (the egocentric authors of which are not considerate of their readers), in which frequently only when you arrive at page 58 do you realize, to your surprise, that you are in San Francisco and not in West Berlin, as you had initially supposed.

So, even though I have already reached page 80 of this book of mine—a book that is swelling gradually but inexorably like a fetus in an unwanted pregnancy—it is still not too late to describe the building where I live, where this tale of the tense relations between the third and fourth floors—as well as the staircase—takes place; tensions that at certain moments seemed to me powerful enough to crack the walls of the building. Thus, I really must offer this description at once, because about two weeks after the events related above there was a meeting of all the tenants, and the reader needs to know who they are.

(By the way, even Proust, who unlike the three aforementioned authors is a modern writer by anyone's reckoning, opens *Le temps retrouvé* with a detailed description of the setting: the hall, the bedroom, the wallpaper, the paintings on the walls, the view from the window…).

I shall begin with the street. Avigdor is a small, quiet street in the old northern section of town, that is, in the neighborhood bordered to the south by the longitudinal line between the government office complex and the sea, and to the north by the Yarkon River. The buildings on this street are three or four stories high, and were built before the founding of the state. Thus, most of the people living in them are elderly immigrants from Europe, and the trees in front of the buildings—ficus, chinaberry, Poinciana, mulberry, palm—are taller than the telephone poles, their tops entangled with the high tension cables. These entanglements are dangerous, and every fall workers from the electric company or the municipality come around to saw off the uppermost branches, which are liable to break the cables, or to fall heavily on the cars parked by the curb when storms wrench them off.

The residents of the street are, for the most part, acquainted with one another, if not by name then by face, and when they walk past one another they nod their heads or raise their eyebrows in greeting. Some of them have dogs, which they walk in the morning hours or at twilight. Mr. Gutman, for example, a short bald man in khaki shorts, leads his twin poodles to Zachariah Park at exactly six o'clock every morning, holding their leashes in one hand while the other cradles to his ear a transistor radio broadcasting "How goodly are thy tents, O Jacob" and the first newscast of the day; Mrs. Danziger, whose hairy, long-whiskered schnauzer trails after her as evening falls, stops at every second step to wait for him as he urinates on a wall or sniffs the droppings of one of his own kind while she mutters repressive things to him in German. Every day residents of the street meet one another at Speiser's store, which is sort of a neighborhood club, or the equivalent of the village well in ancient times. While Speiser—an inquisitive conversation-loving man, who has known his customers for many years and is familiar with what happens in their homes—weighs the piece of cheese, or the thinly-sliced sausage, he tells you about who is in trouble with the income tax people, who has quarreled with his neighbor, who has gone abroad and whose daughter has divorced her husband. Thus, two days after Schatz invaded our quiet street and our building, Speiser interrogated me about who he was and what he does; and four days later he asked me—while figuring out how much I owed him—if the professor was so badly off that his wife has to buy on credit, because she asked to pay only once a month, on the fifth.

Now I shall describe the building in which I live, number 39, floor by floor.

In the small garden at the front of the house, bounded by jasmine bushes, grow two tall palm trees with serrated trunks and balding crowns of five or six bright leaves. In the middle of the lawn between them rises a dense colony of cacti growing on a slope of limestone veiled with lichen, which Hedva Porat, from the second floor, tends with great devotion.

On the ground floor, opposite the wide lobby, three steps down, is Dr. Bzhizovski's dental clinic. When its door opens, the odor of ether and iodine floats out and expands to fill the air above the staircase. This clinic—which to my great sorrow I too need to visit from time to time—its furnishings, and its instruments are at least forty years old. Beside the clumsy white drill apparatus, now yellowed with age, stands a cuspidor that continuously emits a slight stink, as from a sewer of stagnant water; whenever the thin jet of water relentlessly sprayed into it in irregular, nerve-wracking hisses suddenly gains strength, it spurts out a suspicious kind of foam. The probes arranged in a row on the marble slab, which is also yellowed and stained, are all snub-toothed, bent-toothed, and blunt-toothed, and as they feel around in the crevices of sick teeth they emit nauseating squeaks. The pincers are crude as handymen's wrenches. The patient's chair groans and wheezes as it is raised or lowered by a pedal press. Dr. Bzhizovski is stingy as Harpagon, and around the necks of those unfortunate enough to find themselves under his guillotine, he hangs soiled rectangles of wrapping paper, which he uses several times apiece. Anyone who thumbs through the magazines in his waiting room finds himself going back several years in time to Watergate, to violent confrontations with the Bader-Meinhoff gang, to Idi Amin's boastful harangues and to the Vietnam War.

On the first floor, in the apartment directly above his clinic, live Dr. Bzhizovski and his wife. Although they both immigrated to Israel in 1937, they still speak Polish to one another. The Hebrew he speaks is Polish in intonation and androgynous in grammar. The Hebrew she speaks consists entirely of about a hundred polite words. "Hallo Meester Keren"—she says to me—"Today steps no vash?" and her intention is to complain that the Arab cleaning man hasn't washed the staircase.

Whenever Mrs. Bzhizovski—a woman wide of shoulder and chest and short of neck—steps out her door, even in the morning hours of a weekday, she looks as if she is going to a concert: her blonde wig—which makes her look ten years younger—sports two round, flat symmetrical curls stuck to her temples on either side; a layer of yellowish powder gilds her face; fresh perfume enwraps her and sweeps behind her like the train of a gown, lingering on the staircase for a long while after she leaves, so it is always possible to know whether she has gone out or is At Home. Above the tower of her bosom, an artificial flower the color of a withered rose adorns her dress. The pleasant smile with which she greets her neighbors has something in it of nobility nodding graciously to the common folk. Every Saturday evening a large, Polish-speaking group gathers in their apartment for a card game that lasts until after midnight.

Opposite this apartment lives Mr. Menachem Ben-Ze'ev. Ben-Ze'ev is about sixty years old, the manager of a branch of the United Mizrahi Bank, and a Talmudist. In the past, when he was younger, he was the principal of a state religious school in Holon and a teacher of Bible and literature; he still keeps up with the literary supplements to the newspapers and reads books by young writers as well as by veterans. When he runs into me by his door or the entrance to our building, he makes me linger for long conversations in which he is the one who does most of the talking and I am the one who keeps quiet. Most of what he has to say revolves around errors that he finds in articles or books. "You have of course read A.'s article on Spinoza in *Haaretz*," he tells me. "A man with pretensions to familiarity with the sources, how can he write that Spinoza was influenced by Rabbi

Hasdai Karkash about the three fundamentals of faith!? Terrible ignorance! First of all, Karkash postulated six fundamentals of faith, and it was only Rabbi Joseph Albo who postulated three: the existence of God, the Law from Mount Sinai, reward and punishment. Secondly, Spinoza doesn't have three fundamentals, and it was from Ibn Gabirol that he got the notion about God's will…" or (grabbing me by the lapel of my shirt): "Listen, tell your friend, the honorable writer M., that he should learn Hebrew before he writes any novels, and the first thing he should learn is to tell the difference between the Bible and the Talmud when he quotes a well-known phrase…"

About my own books he never said a word, and I would ask myself whether his silence meant that he hadn't read them, that he had nothing to say about them, or that he had a bad opinion of them; but once he said something to me about Schatz, which penetrated my bones like a soothing balm. "I read *The Three-Mirrored Chamber*"—he straightened the skullcap on his balding head, and an ironic smile glittered in his eyes and shone on his round face—"He's not nearly as clever as he thinks he is, and what he has written is more noise than news. The whole business of trifurcation can be found in the Midrash Tanhuma, where Rabbi Yehoshua the son of Rabbi Nehemia says that everything is trifurcated: the Torah is trifurcated, the Mishnah is trifurcated, prayer is trifurcated, holiness is trifurcated, Israel is trifurcated, and even the pander is trifurcated… If so, Schatz also becomes a pimp of criticism…and as for what he writes about mirrors—vanity of vanities! There is but one looking glass! If it is polished—the Holy Spirit reigns! If it is filthy, no cleverness in the world will help!" And one day, about three weeks after Schatz had settled into our building, he whispered to me: "Tell me, that professor who lives up there, above you, did some tragedy happened to him, or is he mourning the destruction of the Temple? He walks right past me, doesn't greet me, sour-faced… Even if he is very strict about observing mourning, he should have known that the *Shulkhan Arukh* says, 'If someone who doesn't know he is in mourning greets him, he must reply…'"

I have seen his wife but a few times. She is a tall, pretty woman with a sad expression, quiet and modest, and because she is sickly, she is mostly confined to her home. They have two married sons, both of them successful lawyers.

Above the Ben-Ze'ev apartment live Victoria and Albert Azoulai.

Albert is a police officer, a lieutenant or sergeant, and is away from home most the day and night. He is a courteous man, resolute and reserved—if I can judge by his appearance as he passes me on the staircase. His salt-and-pepper hair is cropped short, and his mustache is narrow, business-like, not flamboyant. His voice is scratchy, restrained and never escapes out the door or the window.

Victoria—Tiberias-born and tenth generation in this country—deserves a chapter of her own, both by virtue of her colorful attributes, and by virtue of my rather intricate relationship with her.

At the moment I will say only this: Victoria is an abundant woman: of abundant good will, abundant passion, abundant laughter, abundant song. She is an excellent cook, which is advertised by the smells wafting up from her kitchen to my apartment—smells of stews and fried fish, roast meats, spices, smells of soups and baked goods. Her clear voice floats up to my window as well, as she overflows with nostalgic songs of the early period of Israeli history, like "I Wish I Were a Bird" or "Land of My Love" or "Come Back to Me", and when her voice climbs very high, in a crescendo, like in "The Land of Israel Is Beautiful, the Land of Israel Blooms"—the leaves on the trees in two courtyards tremble and the birds flee from the treetops. More than any of the other residents, she has taken the building in hand, and keeps an eye on what goes on in it. She also has, of course, a "dark side", which all characters—even "folksy" characters—must have if they aren't to be one—or two—dimensional, but this side of her will be revealed later on, when I talk about the relationship between us.

Across from Victoria's apartment lives Hedva Porat.

Hedva—everybody calls her by her first name alone—is a kindergarten teacher. A woman of about fifty-five, her dark hair is sprinkled with strands of grey, and her playful eyes are yellowed with sadness. In the corner of her beautifully sculpted mouth are tiny wrinkles. I heard her life story from Victoria: when she was young she was a member of a kibbutz in the Negev, and there she married a young man who was one of its founders. About a year later they moved from the kibbutz to the city. The young man, whose conscience was never completely at ease about leaving the kibbutz, and who didn't even like the work he'd found as a minor clerk in a government office, one day simply upped and left both Tel Aviv and his young wife. He never told her where he'd gone and he never returned. "Abandoned her," said Victoria. A few years later, she "fell for this painter, poor thing, a man with no conscience—the way only an artist can be—who got her pregnant. She had a son by him, and he didn't want to know anything about it, the bastard." She raised the son—Yaron, "a wonderful boy"—alone, and during his army service he was killed in a helicopter accident in Sinai. Despite all that has happened to her, she manages to keep her spirits up, devotes herself to her work in the kindergarten, of which she is the director, and tends the cactus patch in the front garden.

"I told her: grow gladiolas! They grow beautifully here! They're cheerful! No, she just wants cactuses! Cactuses with thorns! She pricks herself, you understand?" Victoria's eyes sparkled as she told me about Hedva.

"Have you noticed that she blinks when she talks? Why does she blink?—Everything that happens to a person gets written in the eyes like letters in a book. The eyelids are shades that open and close to the light. And she, she tries to hide the letters from the light."

Victoria sees the world through portents and omens. She once told me that Hedva's birth sign was Cancer, and that Cancers are strengthened by suffering, and have a lot of dignity.

Whenever I encounter Hedva, her face lights up and she graces me with a smile that has something intimate about it, as if she has known me for many years, or as if she wants to confess her innermost soul to me. I, for some reason, feel warmly towards her too, maybe because I know what has happened to her. "She's a subject for a great novel!" Victoria told me once.

On the third floor, above the Azoulais, is my apartment.

This two-and-a-half-room apartment was purchased before my marriage to Lili Federman through the joint efforts of her parents and Nuriel Jacobson, my mother's husband from Zikhron Ya'acov. Just before our divorce, about three years ago, Nuriel—who was much happier about the divorce than he had been about the marriage—paid the Federmans more than the half they had invested in the apartment, thus obtaining it for me so I could "write without having to worry about anything." Lili, whose bohemianism expressed itself largely in her clothes—long dresses that had swept through all the bazaars between New Delhi and Addis Abeba—had taken the trouble to ensure that the atmosphere of the apartment was "bohemian" as well. She had exchanged the basic furniture we had received as wedding gifts for decorative objects of no great utility: puffy leather cushions in place of an upholstered armchair, a rustic wooden bench instead of a soft couch, a Japanese lantern instead of a simple hanging lamp, an old chest that doubled as a table, brass dishes from the flea market, rugs made out of patches of cloth, and in the bedroom—red woolen curtains, which she had made out of Arab saddlebags she found in the old city of Jerusalem and a shabby green bedspread with a kitschy picture of a belly dancer in the shade of a coconut tree. The only thing I didn't let her touch was my study. Its furnishings remained modest and functional: a desk, a chair, an armchair and a bookcase. When she moved out she didn't want to take anything with her except for her personal belongings, and I didn't have the energy, or the will, to spend time on interior design—so the decor of the apartment has stayed as it was.

In this apartment I wrote *The Flying Camel of the Golden Hump.* In this apartment I am now not writing my new book, about which I shall say something further along.

In the apartment opposite me lives a strange, lonely, bitter man named Heinz Hirsch. Although we live right across from one another, I see him only at rare intervals. He leaves very early in the morning and rides his bicycle out to the beehives he tends among the citrus groves of the Sharon, from which he earns his living, returning home in the evening. He is an educated man, knowledgeable about German and English literature—as I have found out in the few remarks we have exchanged—quiet and quick to anger. Sometimes when one of the radios or televisions in our neighborhood is playing at very high volume I hear his shout flying out the window, propelled by terrifying anger, like that of an imprisoned, wounded animal bursting out of its cage: "QUIET PLEASE!!!" It's hard to blame him for that: he had a peculiar son, maybe a genius or maybe deranged, whom he loved very much, and one day, a number of years ago—after the youngster was thrown out of the army because of a doubtful case of breach of discipline—he left home and disappeared.

Above me, as you know, is Schatz's dwelling.

There is also another apartment on the fourth floor, but nobody lives there. Once—or so Victoria told me—before I moved into this building, a sailor lived there, one of the founders of the Israeli Navy, later a captain in the merchant marine, who stopped by very infrequently, for a night or two, when he was ashore. For about ten years he hasn't been seen in the building. Rumor has it that he jumped ship in one of the oriental ports, where he married a wealthy Filipina. Another rumor has it that he joined a research expedition to the South Pole where he died of cold and hunger. Because he wasn't married and had no children no one has ever come to claim the apartment.

On the roof—the rabbit hutch. Clotheslines. Next to the rabbit hutch is another small locked room, which is used to store all kinds of junk, and where I keep the few books I inherited from my father. Old books, through the yellowed pages of which the worms have tunneled winding passages.

Chapter eleven

Intermezzo

One morning, at about ten—was it a week after the flood? Ten days?—when I went up to the roof to feed the rabbits, I stopped at the threshold, astounded, dumbfounded, wide-eyed, unable to breathe, red-faced, blinded:

On a grey blanket, spread out on the white roof, in its southwest corner, lying supine, eyes closed—

Yes, she. She and none other!

Unbelievable!

Stark naked—except for a narrow strip of bikini around her hips—abandoned to the sun, the light, the birds of the heavens.

Nailed to my place, afraid to bat an eyelash or breathe, I couldn't take my gaze off her:

Oh, this couldn't happen, even in my dreams. In my wildest imaginings—as they say—I couldn't invent such a thing!

I stood there stricken with wonder at the sight of this brilliant spectacle, like Moses at the sight of the burning bush—no, like David at the sight of Bathsheba, "who was very beautiful to look upon," bathing on the roof!

The two ripe figs of her breasts—flattened, swelling around

their nipples—shone in their glory on the bronze of the buoyant-skinned body. Two strips of pallor which stretched away from them to the arches of her shoulders indicated the boundaries of the absent bra. The basin of her belly was concave, relaxed, and in its center—winking, as if hinting in invitation, the eye of her navel, with its fold like an eyelid. Her knees were raised, and spread slightly apart, thus revealing to the ecstatic beholder all the charm and loveliness of the legs, from the arched soles and delightful ankles, to the heights of the rounded kneecaps, down the billows of the perfect thighs with the dimples and concavities in their soft, caressable recesses unto the hidden places of the groin in the shadow of her secrets. Her head rested on a blue towel, flat on the blanket, and her hair spread out in a wide fan.

Rays of sunlight skittered across her closed eyelids, which seemed to tremble as they soaked up the light. Her arms lay by her sides, and the tangled bushes of her armpits were like the nests of birds that in another moment would fly out over the lush field of her glowing bosom.

I was captivated, mesmerized, couldn't move from the spot. My gaze floated down from the face to the neck, rested on the glorious chest, dipped into the strawberries of the nipples, caressed the bowl of the belly, the radiant zone of her hips, slid over the dips of the velvet thighs, probed the secrets between the slightly spread legs as if intending to open a locked garden, a fountain sealed—

Until a movement of hers, as she began to turn over onto her belly, chased me back down the stairs.

Chapter twelve

My Life with Lili

As I've already deviated from my path and moved, as if distracted, from the Tractate on Damages to the Tractate on Women, I shall no longer be able to avoid saying something about the period of my marriage to Lili Federman.

My life with Lili was a double mistake: through a mistake I married her and through a mistake I divorced her.

I first met her in a small café-theater, one evening when an experimental actors' group was performing Jean Genet's *The Maids*. The audience of about twenty-thirty people was divided between those who sat on stools around the low tables and those who sat on a large straw mat on the floor. My friend Michael Hochhauser and I sat at one of the tables sipping beer, and even before the performance began, I noticed a girl trying to catch my eye. She was sitting on the mat, her long legs folded to one side, and between her fingers dangled a cigarette in a long holder. On her head she wore a blue beret set at an angle over her long blonde hair, and in its navel blossomed a red flower. This beret, combined with the cigarette in the long holder—from which she inhaled smoke now and then and sent it straight up from lips rounded into a perfect O—lent her an original appearance of an outmoded young woman trying to look like a Viennese *femme fatale* from the beginning of the century. From time to time she directed a look at me, which would linger for a few seconds, quiet, unembarrassed, smiling a bit, as if asking who I was, or aren't I the one who… I moved my face close to my friend Michael and asked him who the girl over there on the left, with the beret, was. "You don't know Lili Federman?" he smiled. "Ah, so that's her?" I said, as if it were shameful not to have recognized such a famous name. For some reason—and to this very day I don't understand what it was that so confused my judgment, or blinded it—I was convinced at that moment that she was famous because she was the daughter of the well-known Federman, the one who owns all those hotels, one of the richest men in Israel.

The performance of *The Maids* began, the characters moved and spoke in the circle of light on the floor in front of us, and I, all my attention was on that girl—twenty-four-years old, maybe twenty-five—whose long legs were crossed beneath her, in her one hand the cigarette holder, in her other an ash-tray—her arms were long, too—and her gaze concentrated on the performance before her, taking in, it seemed, every gesture and every syllable. As I looked at her like this, from the side, only occasionally looking at Claire and Solange plotting to poison their mistress, I decided that I was in love with her.

The reader wonders: decided that he was in love? Yes!—I say, both from my personal experience and on general principles—it is indeed possible! A man can bring himself to be in love! Can say to himself, I am in love! And fan a tiny spark that ignites within him until it bursts into flame, or at least smolders. It all depends on circumstance. On the individual's situation at a specific time, under given conditions. I should explain my situation at that particular time, in those particular circumstances.

I was then in the midst of a "hot spell" of writing: a cycle of stories I later entitled *Butterflies*. And at the same time, I was in bad shape. My first book, *Green Windows*, published six years earlier, had earned some guarded praise with its appearance (one of the critics, who mentioned that I was "a new immigrant from Romania"—

although by that time I had already been in Sabra-land for fourteen years—wrote: "Kalman Keren's *Green Windows* confronts us with an unfamiliar incarnation of life in our country; its kernel of consciousness, alternately calm and careening, is that of alienated youth, standing outside our human carnival, segregated by a barrier of opaque windows from those within, absorbed in themselves and their futilities ...") but was quickly forgotten. I was working four nights a week as a proofreader for a newspaper, and I lived in a tiny room on a roof on Hirschberg Street. All I wanted to do was to devote myself to writing, so that I could write four or five hours a day. But I couldn't find those hours. I would wake up at about nine or ten o'clock, and by then the room had become so hot from the sun embracing it on all sides, that when I sat down at the table, the perspiration would soil my hand. In the evenings, when the shadow of the house next door alleviated some of the accumulated heat, Michael Hochhauser would come around and stay for an hour or two. And even though Michael is my friend, my only friend, I suspected him of coming around so much in order to keep me from my writing. Because he tends to be malevolent in petty ways—this has its roots in envy, even towards his friends. In short, I would write only about an hour or two a day, and what with one thing and another, the ship of my art had run aground. But as I sat in the dim smoke-filled café, slowly sipping the beer, half hearing Genet's sentences in a Hebrew that blunted their sting and castrated their passions, and sending glances, clouded with alcohol fumes, at the girl sitting there on the left, my fantasies were accompanied by the thought that I could, without much effort, after a little courting, have her. Get friendly with her, and then marry her. And that would solve all my problems: I wouldn't have to work at night any more. In fact, I wouldn't have to work for my living at all. The days and the nights would all be my own—I could write six, seven, ten hours a day. In other words, I would be provided for by my rich father-in-law, Mr. Federman-of-the-hotels.

The sensitive reader, who respects literature and its creators, is probably turning up his nose: such materialism on the part of a writer? Such cynicism?! To marry a woman for her money?! But let him page through the biographies of writers! Of the great authors he most admires—including the Jewish ones—how many of them married wealthy women in order to free themselves from the need to earn their bread! Just so they could sit and write without having to worry. Shall I list them here? Ho, the address book by my telephone wouldn't hold them all! It is they who reaped all the glory, of course, and the world has forgotten the women who supported them, petted them, bowed to all their caprices, padded their pride, supported their delusions of grandeur, suffered from their persecution complexes, scattered gold at their feet! No, I—in my fantasy games—was a legitimate link in this "anti-romantic" literary chain. And maybe "romantic" after all—for they sacrificed Love for their Art!

When the performance was over, after the weak applause, my friend Michael, who hadn't missed my attempts to catch Lili Federman's eye, and whose manners had never been terribly subtle, called over to her loudly to come and sit at our table. When she came and sat down with us, he said: "Meet Kalman Keren—he's dying to meet you." Lili supported her chin in the palms of her hands, elbows leaning on the table, looked straight into my eyes, smiled, and said: "*Green Windows*?"

And instantly she captured my heart! Instantly I was prepared to kiss her! Because who, how many people in this whole country, had read *Green Windows*, or had even heard of it? Yes, at that moment I was prepared to stretch forth my hand to her neck, bring her face close to mine and kiss her!

And I must say at once: Lili Federman was not beautiful. More precisely, she wasn't even pretty. This, which I hadn't noticed from afar in the dim light and in my fantasy visions, became clear to me now, when her face was just a few inches away from mine. Her blue eyes were watery, and her eyelids were surrounded by a corolla of redness that looked like an infection. Her lips were pale and thin. On her light-colored cheeks were a few pockmarks, like remnants of some skin disease. In addition—which I discovered later, when she stood up—her chest was flat. Only her button-like nipples caused a minimal protrusion in the upper part of the long white dress that came down to her ankles. But all these flaws were covered by the charm; charm was in her intelligent smile, charm in the naughtily angled beret on her thin, shoulder-length hair, charm in her long fingers, and the most charming charm of all was her lack of embarrassment: she was not ashamed of herself, and unlike girls who are conscious of their lack of beauty, she didn't try to hide her face, nor did she camouflage it with cosmetics. It was as if she said: this is how God created me, and if He wasn't ashamed of His work, I have nothing to be ashamed of either!

Lili asked my opinion of the performance, and I, who had absorbed sideways only bits of it, only a few sentences that had grated on my ear in their inaccuracy, said that the translation had castrated Genet, had blunted both his nuance and his grossness, and that what he had written in prickly thieves language had become limp and impotent. "In the original," I said, "Claire says, about all mistresses: 'You are our perverted mirrors, our disgusting anus, our shame, our excrement…' and here they said: 'You are our crooked mirrors, our dirty rears, our garbage…'"—"You know French?" Lily looked at me curiously, interestedly, with restrained surprise. At this point, Michael became my advocate, a pander at my service, and said that I was almost a Frenchman by birth, French-Romanian, like Ionesco, that I had finished the Sorbonne with honors, that I had translated Rimbaud and Apollinaire, Voltaire and Molière, Malot and Malraux… I cut him off and said modestly that I had spent two years in Lyon and knew Genet very well in the original. "Do you like Genet?" she asked, and the smile never left her face. "Would you like a Benedictine?" I said.

My friend Michael, who is covetous and miserly in matters of literature, is very generous in matters of women. He got up and left in order to leave us by ourselves.

At a late hour, after I had bestowed upon her about half of what I knew about Genet, and had entertained her with stories from his *Thief's Journal* about his friend Stilletano, the thief, pimp and drug-pusher, I walked her to the nearby taxi station. As we approached it, she said: "Have you written anything else besides *Green Windows*?" I said I was in the midst of writing my second book, which would be a collection of stories. Suddenly a spark of heroism ignited within me and I said: "Are you ready to hear one of them?"—"Now?" she laughed. "Yes, if it's not too late for you… I live not far from here…" She hesitated for a moment, but all at once she too was swept up in that same spirit of adventurousness, and she said: "Yes! Why not?"

I made coffee for the two of us. I sat on the bed, Lili on a stool opposite me, and read her the first story in the *Butterflies* sequence, the story of a comic character, a Jewish insect-collector from Budapest, who comes to the Jezreel Valley in the nineteen-twenties in search of the rare winged beetle *Pterygota*. As all around him the Jewish pioneers are laboring at draining the swamps, he hunts mosquitoes, grasshoppers, cicadas, dragonflies and antlions, classifying them and pinning them into his collection box. The industrious swamp drainers are so enchanted with this that they get distracted from their work; in the evenings they crowd into his tent and feast their eyes on his collection, and in the mornings one of them might lay down his shovel or his pick and join him in the pursuit of some pink-winged grasshopper. This goes on, until the head of the work gang throws him out and everything returns to normal. Lili laughed a great deal, and then looked serious, and when I finished reading, she said just one word: "Beautiful!" which to me was worth ten articles of critical praise.

When she stood up, I did as well, and kissed her. Lili returned a kiss on my mouth, which was not like my kiss—a kiss of thanks—but lasted a great deal longer than I had imagined. And even before I had disengaged my lips from hers, she had begun to take off her long, priestess's dress. In another moment, without my having gotten ready for it, without my having expected it at all—she stood there naked before me.

Ha, our *prima noctis*!

Yes, our first night of lovemaking was a complete fiasco.

Despite all my efforts—hugs, embraces, caresses and kisses, at first standing up and with the light on, and then on the bed in darkness—my sentinel remained at ease and did not agree to come to attention. Even though she, too, tried all her best tricks to rouse my lust unto desire—my lust desired not. All my heroism deserted me. Was it the sight of that flat chest with its two pink, shallow nipples in the lamplight that deterred me? Or her repressive height, taller than mine? Or the purposeful haste with which she proceeded, to which I was not accustomed?

Such is the crime and such is its punishment! I said to myself as I lay there next to Lili, embarrassed, defeated and limp, with my head between her nipples as she smoothed my hair to comfort me—thou desireth not the daughter, but the father's gold and silver, and for that thou art punished! For gold and silver are cold and have no soul, and will not return the love of he who desires them, but will vanquish him, and cut off his horn. Since thou hast desired to support thy hope upon a staff of bent reed—thy strength shall be as a bent reed!

When Eos, the goddess of Dawn, stretched her rosy fingers through the window of my room on the roof and stroked Federman's daughter's mound of Venus, spilling golden splendor over her triangular lawn of hair—she got up, put on her white dress, leaned over and kissed me on the mouth, smiled and left.

Oh loveless night! Oh disappointing dawn!

I went around all day as if I were sick, like a man with a fever. My own failure glorified the charm of Lili's assets for me. In my imagination she was seventy times more beautiful than she had been at night, face to face, chest to chest. Before my eyes floated the blue beret with the red blossom, the long amber cigarette-holder, her serpentine limbs, the fine filaments of her golden hair... How could I have lost her? How could I have lost her, when she *wanted me*?!—I suffered the tortures of Tantalus: even her father's golden apples were almost within my reach, and I plucked them not!

No, I couldn't come to terms with this shameful failure, I must try one more time!—I said—Just one more time!

Every evening—or more precisely, every night, as it was nearly midnight when I left the newspaper office—I haunted that tiny, dim café-theater, hoping to find her there. One week later, on Saturday night, as I sat at the table—there she was coming in the door, tall, smiling… She immediately came over and sat down next to me, unembarrassed, unembarrassing, an old friend. After about a quarter of an hour, it was she who—to my great surprise and delight!—suggested that I read her another story from *Butterflies.*

Once more we sat in my room. I set a bottle of wine and two goblets on the table. When I finished reading she said: "Wonderful!"

I got up and kissed her. I turned off the light. I took off her dress and laid her down on my bed. When I closed my eyes and thrust my tongue in her mouth I conjured up—as I had decided to do a few days earlier—the image of Louise, Louise the passion of my last three months in Lyon, after my separation from Yvette, soft-limbed Louise, lively and lovely Louise, Louise with whom I partook of such delights. Every time I imagine those nights with her—my passion kindles and swells. And if I were not wary about plays on words—which everyone knows is the lowest form of literary humor—I would say to myself: If thy member thou wouldst please, please remember Louise…

We partook of delight. Both of us.

I lay there, tranquil, next to her, and happy days glowed before me: a spacious apartment, flooded with light, on the seventh floor of one of the luxury buildings uptown; from the wide window in my book-lined study I can see the boulevard down below and the blue of the sea in the distance; in the morning I sit down at my mind-broadening desk and write, and write, and write, for six, seven hours… the maid is busy in the kitchen… In the evening, in the salon, tumblers of whiskey on the rocks in our hands…

Ha, the pranks of Puck, who anoints the eyelids of sleepers and blinds the eyes of the wise! But… was that Puck?

Not a week passed—a week of love and delight, meetings by daylight and meetings by night, lovemaking in which Lili was intensely active—before I discovered the bitter truth:

Lili's father was not the famous Federman, the Federman with the hotels, the Federman with all the property, but rather one Mendel Federman, a man of the people, a health insurance clerk, a decent man indeed, a veteran member of the Labor Federation, but not in the least wealthy.

Lili herself—which I had known earlier without attributing much importance to it, because I had said to myself: yes, they all do that, the rich girls, to demonstrate their independence or to rebel against their parents—earned her living as a salesgirl in Steimatzky's bookstore.

The dream slipped through my fingers like a ghost.

But I couldn't turn back. Lili clung to me. Her long arms clung to me. Her legs too. I spoke love. And above all—her intelligent praise of my stories! Her admiration for them! Just as a compliment to a woman on her beauty flows like dew onto her soul—so does a compliment to a writer on his stories.

In the autumn of that same year the wedding took place, in the Engineer's Hall, to the great joy of humble Mr. Federman and his wife—she was their only daughter, and they loved her, and had worried that they wouldn't find a husband for her—and to the dissatisfaction of my mother and her husband Nuriel Jacobson, who did not like the awkward, bleary-eyed bride, and who were doubtful and suspicious of her bohemian ways. My friend Michael, his portion of chicken on the plate before him and his fourth glass of 777 Cognac sliding down his gullet—said: "You have no idea how lucky you are, Korngold!" (he always insisted on calling me by my non-Hebraized name, despite my protests). "Do you realize what it means for a writer to have a wife in Steimatzky's Books? A dream come true! You'll be an incredible best-seller!"

Mendel Federman withdrew all his savings from the bank, Nuriel Jacobson donated his share, unwillingly, and thus the two-and-a-half-room apartment at 39 Avigdor Street was bought and furnished.

We lived under the same roof for two years, as man and wife. When I look back and think…

But here I must stop and return to the delineation of the dramatic plot going on between the third and fourth floors—mostly on the staircase—for the reader is no doubt more impatient to know how it develops than he is enthusiastic to peek through the keyhole into the rooms of a family that in any case broke up some time ago.

Later on, if there is a hiatus of some sort, I will say a few words about those two years, and about the divorce, which, like the marriage, was based on a mistake.

Chapter thirteen

The Tenants' Meeting

The tenants' meeting was called for Tuesday evening in Victoria Azoulai's apartment, and two items were on the agenda: A. Increasing the monthly maintenance payments; B. Tarring the roof. The meeting was scheduled for 8:30, but began only at 9:15.

By 8:40 the following tenants had already gathered in Victoria's living-room—Dr. Bzhizovski and his wife, Mr. Menachem Ben-Ze'ev and his wife, Hedva Porat, Victoria and myself. Victoria apologized for the absence of her husband, who was working the night shift, and said that we didn't have to wait for Heinz Hirsch because he never came to tenants' meetings anyway, but that when she had seen him that morning he had promised her that he would accept any decisions that were made. So we sat around in armchairs and on the green plush sofa, we tasted the sweets that the hostess had set out for us in crystal dishes and silver salvers as well as the almonds and peanuts she had set out in the large copper bowl, and we awaited the arrival of Schatz and his wife. Victoria's living room is a feast for the eyes and even just sitting there doing nothing is not boring: Persian carpets cover the floor from wall to wall, two carved Damascus tables inlaid with ivory stand in corners, on the antique sideboard of walnut wood various copper objects are arranged—a menorah, candlesticks, perfume flasks; and decorating the walls—a tapestry portraying the Rambam, a picture of the tomb of Rabbi Meir Ba'al HaNess with a splendiferously bearded Jew at its entrance and family photographs, among them Albert in his police uniform.

Mr. Ben Ze'ev said: "Since Mr. Schatz works at the University, we should allow him his *akademische Viertel* and permit him to be fifteen minutes late." Mrs. Bzhizovski, who was formally dressed, as always, in a brown dress with a white lace collar and a crimson rose rippling from the battlements of her bosom, said: "Mister Schatz is Professor?" Her perfumes filled the room. Victoria said: "A famous professor! A great honor for our house!"—"I doesn't read Hebrew, so I doesn't know this, sorry!" laughed Mrs. Bzhizovski apologetically, as she looked at each of us in turn.

"You really must learn," Victoria admonished her. "You can't really live here without knowing the language. Life is in the power of the tongue, as the good book says!" "Mine life already finish so!" laughed Mrs. Bzhizovski. Her husband looked at his watch, tapped the dial with his finger, and said: "Shall we begin?"— "Let's give them another five minutes," said Hedva Porat. "They're new tenants, after all!"

Mr. Ben Ze'ev told an edifying story about tardiness: the tale of a Jerusalem scholar, a ritual scribe, who was always late for afternoon prayers. Since he was the necessary tenth man for the prayer quorum, they couldn't begin the service until he arrived. When they asked him why he was late, he didn't explain but said only that he was occupied with the mitzvot. They all wondered what divine commandment so concerned him that he was always late for prayers, until one day, when they pressed him, he revealed that he worked at copying and decorating the biblical verses on parchments for mezuzot. As he worked at ornamenting the letters, his heart was distracted by the beauty of them, and he was tempted by sinful thoughts. The words themselves and even the names of each letter he decorated reminded him of erotic passages in The Song of Songs. Therefore, he resolved that each time he finished writing a mezuzah, he would write out the biblical verses a second time for himself, plain and unadorned, and read them, and in this fashion he would direct his consciousness back to his holy task of writing and overcome the Evil Inclination. "It looks as though our professor is late for this very reason," smiled Mr. Ben-Ze'ev as he looked in my direction. "First he decorates the letters and the Evil Inclination takes over, and then he goes back and writes them out plain and unadorned..."

"A beautiful story with a good moral," said Victoria, "but if we're talking about commandments I must mention that the professor has broken one: his maintenance fees for the past month haven't been paid yet!"

"Absent-minded, like all professors!" said Hedva.

"Perhaps Mr. Keren would be so kind as to remind him..." Mr. Ben Ze'ev sent another smile in my direction.

But at that very moment the doorbell rang, and into the apartment walked Naphtali and Naomi Schatz.

Victoria introduced the other tenants by name, one by one. When she reached me, Schatz's glance skipped right over, as if scorched. When she got to Mr. Ben-Ze'ev, the latter said: "I read your article about Musil. It's not as you claimed: Musil didn't attend the military academy in Vienna, but the one in Eisenstadt, the city of Baron Esterhazy and Akiva Eiger."

"You're wrong," argued Schatz, blinking angrily. "It was Vienna."

"Look it up," laughed Ben-Ze'ev.

Schatz gave him a severe look, and seated himself in the empty chair beside Mrs. Bzhizovski. Naomi sat on the sofa and helped herself to a handful of peanuts from the bowl.

"Shall we begin?" Victoria surveyed the circle of those present. Assuming a bright, formal expression she said: "First of all, I would like to welcome our new tenants. We are greatly honored. I've heard, and also read, that Professor Schatz is one of our most important experts in the field of literature, and has written some famous books and many articles... Our building, I might say, is filling with wisdom... We have an important author, and now a great scholar... May the Muse shine upon him in our house...and may his life among us be a blessing to all concerned!"

Schatz, who sat straightbacked in his chair with his hands clasped on his knees, had his gaze fixed on her face, and didn't blink an eyelash, didn't smile, didn't thank her for her greeting.

"And now to item number one on our agenda." Victoria's face donned a businesslike expression. "As you all know, the cost of cleaning materials and labor has gone up in the past year..."

Schatz's gaze circled around the assembled faces, and when he got to me, he hastened to look away and stared rather at the portrait of Maimonides on the wall, to his right. This was my first opportunity to study him close up, not en passant but en face, "large as life," as they say.

Does a man's face reveal his inner life? Schatz's face looked like Doge Lorenzo's in the Bellini painting: something between an ascetic monk and a ruler who hides his passions under a mask of piety. What is the fire, cold as frost, hidden in his bones, which enflames him to embark upon Crusades against the infidels? And who are the infidels?—I considered the severe, angular lines of his face.

"No steps vash and more money?" said Mrs. Bzhizovski. "I not understands!"

"Ask your husband," said Victoria, "how much a filling cost last year and how much it costs now. More than twice as much, isn't that so, Dr. Bzhizovski?

"We pay income tax, business tax, and value added tax," expostulated Bzhizovski. "The Arab who cleans here doesn't pay any of that! Why do we have to give him more?"

Hedva said: "But he has to support a family... These days to support a family..."

"Arabs has ewrysing, ewrysing, so..." laughed Mrs. Bzhizovski.

As I glanced over at Naomi she also glanced over at me and our eyes met for a moment. She sat slightly hunched over, her hair falling on either side of her face, and her eyes, nose and mouth peeking out as if from behind a parted curtain. As my glance fell on the two soft breasts under her knitted chartreuse singlet, I couldn't help but ask myself whether they had tanned a lot or a little since my eyes had shone upon them. Had she sunbathed again on the roof? When? At what hours? Had she felt the rays of my gaze exploring her nakedness and decided not to go back there? Had Schatz forbidden it? Ach, the horrid Herod of Ein Harod! I crushed a sigh of envy in my chest.

Mrs. Ben-Ze'ev was saying: "Let us be reasonable! After all, we're not the ones who determine the laws of economics, and if wages are going up all over the country…"

No, I'll skip over the details of this discussion. A writer who attempts to describe a tenants' meeting—or a party, soldiers' talk, or a Friday night get-together in somebody's living room—is exposing himself to the dangers of floundering about in the shallow waters of a low, simplistic, lame naturalism, which partakes more of imitation than of creativity; that kind of realism—according to several important critics—had plagued Israeli writing two and three generations ago, and only in the past twenty years or so have we shaken it off like a duck shaking the waters of a swamp off its feathers and taken wing to fly far and wide. I shall not, therefore, set foot in this quagmire, and will say only that the motion to raise the monthly maintenance fees by fifty percent, was passed by a majority of seven to four and that Victoria immediately moved on to the second item on the agenda: tarring the roof.

And here I must—yes, despite the preceding observations—describe in some detail the discussion that ensued concerning the roof, because it touches directly upon the drama that is the subject of this superfluous book.

Immediately after Victoria presented the problem—tarring the roof before winter sets in, at the cost of 3,000 Israeli Lira to be shouldered equally by all the tenants—Schatz requested the floor, to everyone's astonishment, and was granted it. Thus spake Schatz:

"Before we begin to consider the tarring of the roof—a very important matter in and of itself, I am sure—I would like to raise another problem concerning the roof which, in my opinion, is no less urgent. Above my apartment—I might say directly above my head—there is a hutch of hares. Those hares—a dozen or more, I haven't counted them—eat, shit, if you'll excuse me, stink, copulate, thump and disturb my peace and quiet, night and day. Especially night. In this context I ask two questions: A., is this with the knowledge and concurrence of all the tenants? And B., does such use of an outbuilding for agricultural purposes—stable, chicken-coop, rabbit hutch, they're all the same in principle—on the roof of an urban structure constitute a flagrant contravention of the Tenants' Protection Law?"

Although Schatz spoke with frigid conviction and conveyed a readiness, though restrained, for battle, his words brought smiles to the faces of Ben-Ze'ev and Hedva. The others looked questioningly back and forth from Schatz to me, from me to Schatz. Victoria turned to me and said: "Since the hutch belongs to Mr. Keren, perhaps he would be so kind as to reply..."

There I stood face to face with my enemy, out in the open. He had declared war on me. And if on one front it had been a silent war, he had now opened a second front with a heavy bombardment. His contention in the matter of the hutch was so insolent, so false, so malicious, that I was almost at a loss for words to refute it. Perhaps I would have kept silent and allowed others to speak in my stead had I not been encouraged by the sight of Naomi, who sat with her head bowed, her eyes lowered, as though embarrassed, and who for a brief moment—while they were all waiting in suspense to hear what would issue forth from my mouth—looked up at me from the depths of her face.

"I should like to begin by drawing the speaker's attention to a number of errors," I said, trying to suppress my wrath. "First of all, not hares but rabbits. Anyone who works with words ought to know the difference. Secondly, not a dozen but seven, six females and one male. Thirdly, they do not copulate, because the male is kept separately from the females, alone in a cage, and rabbits do not practice telecoitus, that is, long-distance sexual intercourse. Fourthly, they never thump—at most they rustle. Fifthly, even if they do have a distinctive odor, it could not be said that they stink, and anyway the odor gets wafted away by the wind and does not descend into the building. As for the concurrence of the tenants—not one of them has ever complained. And with respect to the Tenants Protection Law—if no tenant is attacked, then there is nothing to protect him from. Finally, in contradistinction to that law, there is also the Animal Protection Law."

Hedva addressed Schatz in her warm, cheerful voice. "I don't see what the issue is! They're sweet, quiet animals who don't bother anyone..."

Schatz gave her a chilling look: "Madame, it is not you who lives under the hare shit..."

"Rabbit," corrected Hedva.

"It is not you who has to listen to their nightly orgies!"

"Orgies?" Hedva looked at him wide-eyed and laughed.

Victoria looked around at the assembly as if she couldn't believe her ears.

"I work until very late at night, madam, and you must agree that it is my legal right, as the owner of Apartment 8 on the fourth floor, to demand that no animal—whether or not it has cloven hooves and chews its cud, whether it's a hare or a rabbit, an ass or a camel with wings—no animal disturb either my sleep or my work!"

"Camel with wings"—this serpent has spewed out his poison!

Naomi, I saw, had covered her face with her hands.

"Mr. Schatz!" Victoria leapt to my defense. "Or rather, Professor Schatz. You are new in this building. Before you, Dr. Klausner lived in Apartment 8, a very refined gentleman, very cultured, not young—he was more than seventy years old, may he rest in peace, before he left us forever. Not only did he never complain about the rabbits, but he was very fond of them, and he would go up and feed them scraps from his kitchen with his own hands..."

"Pardon me, Mrs...."

"Azoulai."

"...this whole sad story about dear old Dr. Klausner is completely irrelevant to the matter under discussion. The hares are a nuisance! To me and to no one else! Period. And the roof is the common property of all the tenants, as far as I know. If there is anyone here for whom raising hares is a hobby—or profession—that's fine. But not at my expense!"

"Look," said Hedva, making an attempt, doomed from its inception, to influence him by being nice. "All of us here really like those rabbits. That's a fact. A little nature corner on the roof..."

"I very much respect your love of nature, madam," Schatz interrupted her impatiently. "But anyone who is looking for nature will, I am sure, find it in greater abundance, greater variety, and derive greater benefit from it in the Galilee or in the Negev. Don't you think so?"

"I am think Mister Professor is right," said Mrs. Bzhizovski. "Must be animals on roof? Animals is dirt!"

Mrs. Ben-Ze'ev said quietly: "Mrs. Bzhizovski, if we're discussing dirt, then a great deal more dirt is brought into the building by all the people who come to the clinic downstairs. At any rate more than those poor little rabbits bring sitting quietly up on the roof where nobody sees or hears them."

"I beg your pardon, Mrs. Ben-Ze'ev," Dr. Bzhizovski angled his insulted face at her. "My patients are all decent, cultivated, clean individuals. Everyone knows that. And if a cigarette butt gets dropped by accident on the staircase, or a scrap of paper, my assistant cleans it up at once. There's no need to talk like that, please."

"This is not to the point, ladies and gentlemen!" said Victoria. "Professor Schatz has raised a question here..."

Mr. Ben-Ze'ev, who had been sitting there looking highly amused during the entire discussion, fingering the skullcap on his head from time to time, as though to make sure it was still there, turned to the company and said:

"Gentlemen, the matter of the rabbits on the roof and whether they disturb or do not disturb the sleep of the tenant who dwells beneath them, and the matter of their owner's legal obligation, whether he is required to get rid of them or not required to—is not a new problem. The Talmud has already dealt with it! 'In apt quotation,' as they say, we may find our salvation, and resolve the present dilemma by analogy. In Tractate Baba Kama, chapter two, there is a discussion of a dog and a goat that jump off the top of a roof and break vessels in the courtyard. Whose vessels? A neighbor's. And it says in the Mishnah that the owners—of the dog and the goat, that is—must pay for the damages. Then the Talmud comes along and clarifies that if they jumped, he is liable, but if they fell he is not liable. Why is he not liable? Because anything that happens by mischance rather than by malfeasance, that is, by error rather than by forcible intent, is not liable. This case can be applied to our problem: the rabbits do not customarily cause damage, and if they do cause any damage to a tenant beneath them, through a noise that they make, for example, that would not be malfeasance, but mischance, like the dog or the goat falling off the roof. Therefore, their owner is not liable, and is required neither to pay damages nor to remove them from the roof."

Schatz, who displayed intensifying signs of impatience during Ben-Ze'ev's disquisition, was barely able to suppress his fury:

"I am not as familiar with the Talmud as Mr.... but as I do not follow religious law in any matter whatever, I am certainly not going to see myself as bound by it in this matter either! Thank God, this country still is not a theocracy—and I hope that it never will be. I demand my rights according to the civil law that prevails here, and it is my right not to be disturbed in my own apartment. Therefore I'm telling you explicitly and in no uncertain terms: if it is not decided here tonight to get this nuisance off the roof—a nuisance that sorely injures my ability to work—I will turn to the law. And until then—that is, until such time as the law is applied to the transgressor—I will not be prepared to pay a single cent towards the maintenance of this building!"

"Mr. Schatz!" cried Victoria, shocked.

A clamor of protest arose, with this one talking to that one, and that one to this one, and everyone all at once, and from amidst this general hubbub I took the floor and said:

"Ladies and gentlemen, in a democratic state there is equality before the law. If the tenant from Apartment 8 turns to the law for help, let it be known that I, too, shall turn to the law. Because if the rabbits injure his ability to work, as he claims, then he himself not only injures my ability to work, but completely paralyzes it! Every evening, until midnight, sometimes even until two A.M., his typewriter rattles away above my head with such a stupefying storm, with such aggressive annoyance and such pitiless persistence that I can't write even a single line. The very law which requires—if it so requires—the removal of the rabbits from the hutch, will by the same token demand the removal of the tenant who lives upstairs from me from his apartment!!"

"Sssssssso!" Schatz opened his eyes wide in a face that had gone white as chalk, and this was the first time he had ever addressed me directly—"I injure your ability to work!" and spreading his hands, he turned once again to the assembled tenants. "I am terribly sorry, ladies and gentlemen, very sorry indeed! Hebrew literature has suffered a great loss!" And again directly to me: "But if so, why don't you choose a different apartment? The city is big—you are free to choose! Writing is my profession, and there is no law that has the power to prevent me from practicing my profession! And if I disturb you by not ceasing to practice my profession—a consummation for which you no doubt most devoutly wish—then be my guest and leave!"

"Professor Schatz!" cried Victoria. "You forget that Mr. Keren has lived in this building for more than five years, and you, if you'll forgive me…"

"Madam!" Schatz cut her off. "Of you I ask only one thing at this time. To put my motion to a vote! I have the right to demand that, haven't I?"

Victoria was at a loss. She turned to the assembly as if to ask what to do next, and the tenants all looked at one another until Hedva said rebelliously: "Put it to a vote, then! Why not?"

In favor of the motion "to obligate Mr. Keren to remove the rabbits from the roof" were two votes: Schatz and Mrs. Bzhizovski. The motion fell.

Schatz arose, straightened up, and with eyes aflame with fury said, "Thank you, ladies and gentlemen," turned to the door and walked out.

Naomi stayed in her seat, hunched over, her two hands on her blazing cheeks, her eyes bright.

Only after a silence of three whole minutes was discussion renewed—in a heavy atmosphere—about the tarring of the roof.

As we went out, Naomi passed in front of me in silence and went up the stairs. I waited outside my apartment until I heard the door slam upstairs.

I sat down in my armchair and tilted my ear to catch what was going on above my head.

There was complete silence. Even the tintinnabulation of the typewriter was still.

Chapter fourteen

My Friend Michael

From the moment Schatz had invaded my home and became stuck like a thorn in my flesh, my head had been so full of plots to get rid of him—if not from the building then at least from my head—that I had almost forgotten the existence of my friend Michael Hochhauser. But after the tenants' meeting, still seething from Schatz's insolence and villainous threats, with fragments of his barbed sentences—"agricultural enterprise on the roof", "camel with wings", "loss to Hebrew literature"—spinning endlessly around and around my brain like a broken record, I felt an urgent need to share my troubles with another soul. And no soul is closer to me than my friend Michael.

I phoned his house several times but got no reply. I rang in the morning, in the evening, even late at night, and there was no answer. Anxiety stole into my heart; I worried that something might have happened to him. About two months earlier, his book of poems, *I Said No*, had been published, and after a book of his comes out he invariably enters a state of deep crisis. Sick. In body and in spirit. Unrecognizable. He babbles incomprehensibly and at great length a mixed stream of abuse—directed at the state, his friends, Jews in general, literature as a whole—and self-denigration, along the lines of who-am-I-I-am-nothing-but-a-dead-dog; he buys all the Friday newspapers, combs them hungrily from beginning to end to find some fragment of a line about himself and about his book, and when he doesn't find any he throws them down as though they were disgusting creepy crawly things; he suspects every person who does not congratulate him of being his enemy and plotting to wipe him out, and he is no less suspicious of anyone who does praise him; he locks himself up in his room, or, alternatively, prowls the streets like Diogenes, searching with his lantern for the one man in a thousand in a corrupt city; he goes into bars and stays till after midnight drinking and acting up, falling all over tourists, particularly women, and pouring his heart out to them, sometimes getting in fights until he's thrown out into the street… As I sat in my room, the telephone receiver to my ear, hearing only the futile ringing echo—anxiety, as I said, stole into my heart. I tried to recall whether any critical articles had appeared, for that would be cause for despair, for losing control, for hating the whole world, and above all—for excessive drinking. Maybe he got sick, I thought, and was taken to the hospital. Maybe he fell down the stairs and broke all his bones. Maybe—no, he wouldn't try to commit suicide, I decided. He had once confessed to me that he was afflicted with a "God complex," and a person with a complex like that would never kill himself. I myself, in any case, was not guilty of having caused him to suffer. I admit that I am not always entirely frank when I praise friends' books; sometimes I do it just so as not to make them unhappy, or in order to maintain good relations over the long run. But this time, I really had been perfectly frank when I told him that I liked *I Said No*. Very much! Very very much! In this book, in my humble opinion, his violence, rebelliousness, and aggressive vulgarity have been distilled to a delicate refinement, an airy transparency, laden with grief, that he had been unable to achieve in any of his earlier books:

I said no

in your eyes I saw

in my eyes images

of my dead father

kissing my lips

your pallid lips

no

I said

no

wilting

on my face.

That same tone of resignation, tinged with not a little self-destructiveness, wafts like a gentle breeze at the twilight of an unbearably hot day through most of the sixty-eight poems in the book.

So the next day at noon when I left the French library, I decided that instead of going home (home, I say…is this house still my home, with that gasbag Schatz's gasses infecting its passages?), I would go see what had happened to Michael.

Yes, to my relief, to my delight, he was at home. Alive.

He opened the door for me, the eternal cigarette between his fingers, pale, and did not answer my greeting. He led me into his room, flopped into an armchair, took a drag and muttered indifferently: "What's new?"

"Is your telephone out of order or what?" I sat down in the chair by the desk. In the typewriter glowed a piece of white paper with several jewel-like lines upon it. "I tried maybe twenty times…"

"I disconnected it." He flicked the cigarette over the ashtray on the corner of the table.

"Disconnected?!"

With a long, pale face—perhaps I'd better say with a face purified by suffering, for a sort of martyric beauty shone forth from its pallor and from the long hair flowing down to his shoulders—he said he was fed up with the twenty-four-hours-a-day expectation of telephone calls from the thirty-two addressees to whom he had sent his book. Not a single phone call! Not even just to thank him! To confirm that the book had arrived! Elementary civility, no? He's not expecting anyone to say anything positive, no! He gave up on that long ago, because he understands the human soul! The narrowness of vision, the narrowness of mind, the envy! But a word of thanks!... So, in order to protect his nerves, he had disconnected the telephone. So much for expectations.

I gave him a piece of my mind. I got angry. I said he was a spoiled, paranoid megalomaniac. Less than two months had gone by since the book had come out, only about a month had gone by, probably, since his "addressees" had received it in the mail—what did he expect? A book of poems is not read like a mystery story. People who relate to it seriously keep it around for days, weeks—read a poem, think about it, read it over again to see if they have understood it, read another poem...

A disdainful smile snaked over his face as he looked at me. "I'm asking myself whether you're being naive, or hypocritical. Because I know you aren't naive, then you must be a hypocrite!"

I smiled. I am accustomed to his attacks, which he regrets afterwards. We were silent. From the sheet of paper in the typewriter, towards which my glance strayed for a moment, I culled the line "From all that garbage you publish, which is a disgrace to read, not just to print..." After lighting a second cigarette from the tail of the first, and crushing the butt into the ashtray, he asked:

"You really don't realize what's going on?"

And now he proceeded to enlighten me as to what had been happening all around him: a conspiracy of silence. They had decided to slay him with silence. To eliminate him. He has plenty of evidence supporting this. When I tried to protest that it was just his fevered imagination he cut me off, and in a long tirade he added up, one by one—like a criminal investigator—the clues and the footprints all leading, like clear rivulets into a swamp, to the scene of the crime and its perpetrators: not a single line about the book had appeared in any of the newspapers, nor had there been any reviews; he had not been asked to speak on either of the literary programs on the radio; when *Tabernacle* had finally printed one of the poems from the book—after a delay of three months, well after the book itself had come out—it appeared *on page 17 in the lower left-hand corner*, so that it was nearly impossible to see! In the table of contents for that issue, his name hadn't appeared at all! He was included in "and others"! And I should pay attention to the amazing phenomenon that for the past year and a half, his name has always been included with "and others"—it was as if he had been excised from the population registry! Reuven Reisner, who had written a survey of developments in Israeli poetry over the past five years, had mentioned him "with all the kids," in a sentence crowded with a dozen minor names; in another article in which—wonder of wonders!—his name was indeed mentioned, and even accompanied by several lines of discussion, it was said that he was "affiliated with" the "Sshockk!" group! "Affiliated!"—why, he had been one of its three founders! In the book stores—he had been to them all—*I Said No* was not displayed in a single show window; it could be found on the shelves in only three stores—three!—and even there it was off-handedly squeezed in with dozens of other poetry books, among them volumes written by people whose names had been completely forgotten for the past forty years; only one hundred and sixty copies—he had verified this with the publisher—had been distributed to the stores, and only fifty-eight had been sold thus far, two months after the book had come out! And "the final nail in his coffin": on the announcement of the appearance of the book they had printed "by Michael Hochhaus" instead of Hochhauser! They had cut off his leg! "They just brandished an ax at me and cut off my leg!" he screamed.

"Oh!" I cried impatiently. "You're not going to tell me that the typesetter and the proofreader are partners to this fantastic conspiracy you're imagining?"

"You're an idiot, Korngold!" he shouted at me. "Only a stupid, unintelligent, insensitive, blind man wouldn't see that all these things are connected! That none of them were accidents! That there is a hidden hand directing it all! How can you not understand that they have plotted to wipe me out! Intentionally! Maliciously! Viciously! Mercilessly!" Tears glittered in his eyes.

"They" meant the two literary cliques. I lowered my eyes and kept quiet. There was no point in arguing with him any more. He was bleeding. He sat folded over in the armchair, his long arms hugging one another, as if to defend his body, and his long legs crossed beneath him, as if to avoid any contact with the world… I pitied him.

Here I should briefly detain the reader, as well as the flow of the story, in order to serve as a guide for the perplexed with respect to the times, to elucidate that not all of my friend Michael's fears and sufferings were engendered by the sick imagination of a man whose troubles have driven him mad.

The two major cliques tumbling around in the belly of Israeli literature, each clasping the other's heel and fighting for primacy, are "Sshockk!"—of which Michael Hochhauser had indeed been one of the founding fathers—and "Nevermore".

(The common reader, untutored in the details of the history of modern literature, will of course wonder what connection there could possibly be between an English name like "Nevermore" and a group of Hebrew-Israeli writers, most of whom are native-born. So, the answer may be found in the memoirs of one of its founders, which were published some time ago in *Epoch*. When the seven original members gathered in his apartment and discussed a name for the group, one of them suggested that it be called *Mereddor*, a conflation of the Hebrew words for 'revolt'—*mered*— and 'generation'—*dor*—to express their revolt against the previous generation. The others objected and said that their rivals would make fun of the name, playing on the French *merde*, which means excrement. They suggested the name Ad-Eyn-Dor, 'till-no-generation', from Jabotinsky's translation of Poe's "The Raven". There was opposition to this as well, because Jabotinsky was a despised Revisionist reactionary. As

"The Raven" had been mentioned, the original English of *Ad-Eyn-Dor*, 'Nevermore', came up, and its literal meaning of 'not the same again' seemed aptly to express the spirit of the group: things will never be the same again! And as for the foreignness, the non-Hebrewness of the name—so much the better!).

The two cliques are engaged in an endless struggle. It is endless because it is mindless: there's no telling what the difference is between them, except that each has its own prophets and sons of prophets, all of whom prophesy in a similar style. But where shall wisdom be found and where is the place of understanding? Who understands the difference between the "Greens" and the "Blues" in Byzantium, between the Guelphs and the Ghibellines in Florence, between the donkey cult and the elephant cult in Washington, between the hassidim of Gur and the hassidim of Vizhnitz in Bnei Brak? The passion for existence of cults and parties, their passion to immortalize themselves—that alone is their raison d'être. In any case, Sshockk! and Nevermore—even though there are three additional groups, poverty-stricken and barely audible, alongside them—have cast their nets over the field of literature from horizon to horizon: journals and literary supplements, publishers and the universities, radio and television, cultural centers and the clubs. Evil and bitter is the fate of he who belongs neither to one group nor to the other: he is forced to beg at thresholds, to knock on closed doors, to lower his head, to bend his knee, to flatter, to grasp at the hem of X's garment or at the sleeve of Y's robe; only he who is powerful of pen, of foot and of elbow can beat himself a path outside their stockade.

(I myself, by the way, whether because I arrived in the corridors of literature late and from afar, and missed the hour of the dawning of the two above-mentioned groups, or because I am by nature a loner, stand apart from their hustle and bustle, stride alone along the narrow path my feet have trod. And if I have arrived at the place where I have arrived without the aid or support of either side, it is because of grace emerging from chaos.)

But to get back to my friend Michael: not only was he one of the pioneers and founders of Sshockk!, as recounted above, but he was also in the vanguard of its battles, fighting its wars at the gates. You could say that he was the evangelist of Sshockk! He and his style of revolt, he and his unruly, stormy, rebellious spirit! It was he who shattered the altars, he who expelled the money-changers from the temple grounds: the bootlickers, the corrupt and degenerate writers who had won places of honor by the eastern wall not by right of their talents and their virtues, but by right of their connections upstairs, by being stewards for the politicians, their servants, their spokesmen, their mouthpieces! "Let us clear out this stink of corpses," he had written then, at the beginning of his career, in the early days of Sshockk!, "so there will be fresh air to breathe!"

But it was precisely that stormy temperament of his—the very same temperament that had raised him to the high places of the group and to glory—which brought him low: he quarreled with them all. With the members of his group and with the members of Nevermore, with his admirers and with his rivals—he quarreled and quibbled with them over issues great and small. Mostly small. Did the reason for his complete alienation from the group a year and a half ago lie in a feud with the editor of Sshockk! over the fact that his poems had appeared on page ten rather than on page one? Or did it lie in his fury at one of the critics in the group who had written that Michael had been influenced by e.e. cummings? In any case, since then—or so he claims—he has been excommunicated and shunned. So even though it is hard to believe that the typesetter and the proofreader were agents of his enemies, or that all thirty-two of his "addressees" (next to the list of whose names he had drawn two columns—"Reply" and "No Reply"—as he showed me on a piece of paper he took out of the drawer) had received orders from above not to acknowledge the receipt of his book, there was nevertheless a grain of truth in his bitter complaint: three or four supplements and journals had ceased to print him, three or four critics had ceased to mention him.

"I'm leaving the country." The sentence dropped from his mouth after a lengthy silence.

I burst out laughing. "Where to?"

"I'm leaving," he reiterated. "'The land eateth up the inhabitants thereof.'"

Just as mourning becomes Electra, suffering becomes Michael. His face grows more beautiful. With his flaring nostrils and his blue eyes glittering with cold fire, with the pallor of his cheeks as noble as the pallor of the first morning light—he resembled a "poet-prophet" in whom the zeal of a saint and the innocence of a child have combined.

"Yes," I grinned. "The people here eat one another alive."

"It's impossible to live here. Believe me, Korngold, it's impossible to live. Too crowded. Everyone is always trying to knock the other guy over the edge, to make a little space for himself. Joyce escaped from Ireland for the same reason. Vogel was here for a couple of months and fled. I can't stand it. They make life miserable."

After more silence, he erupted in flames again:

"They're a Mafia! Believe me, they're a Mafia. They've got a contract out on my head! They've plotted to wipe me out."

"Plotted?" I said.

"Yes, plotted!"

And he went on to say that he had "reliable information" to the effect that the week after his book had come out, on Friday afternoon, at their regular café—they had decided that this time they would finish him off. They divided up the work: this one would speak against him on the radio, that one would write about him, someone else would spread a rumor that five of his poems were plagiarized... In another week or two—"You wait and see"—three devastating reviews would come out, in three different newspapers. He had reliable information, he said. The mere fact that he was still alive, still writing, bringing out another book, after they had declared him a non-person—that's what annoyed them so much. So this time they decided to eliminate him once and for all, so that he wouldn't rise again. He's leaving the country!—he repeated, decisively.

I kept quiet. Glancing again at the page in the typewriter, I took in another line: "For eight whole years you licked, with your slippery tongue, the stinking ass of that creeping hypocrite..."

Suddenly, in a soft, plaintive voice, like that of a child begging forgiveness, he said: "Tell me, is it really such a bad book, *I Said No*?"

"What are you talking about?!" I cried out from where I was sitting. "It's a marvelous book! It's..." I cast about for a more accurate adjective, more significant, but the words of the poems swirled like a mist before my eyes, like a swarm of midges, and I lost my head among them. So six or seven times I repeated "Marvelous! Marvelous!"

A pale smile paused on his face, skeptical, unbelieving. Then, with a pained expression, he said:

"How many books like it have come out in the past twenty years? And look how..."

"Yes, it's a terrible injustice," I said, "but just ignore them. Nothing stands in the way of the truth!"

"Life is short, Kalman! Life is short!"

I kept quiet.

With trembling fingers he drew another cigarette out of the packet and lighting it, he said, "And what's new by you? How's the book coming along?"

I laughed. I said I hadn't written a word. I told him about the new neighbor, right over my head.

"Him?!" he cried. "In your building? A tragedy! A veritable holocaust!"

But after a moment he smiled and said:

"Well, maybe not... Who is rich? It is written: He who has his privy inside the house, near the table! You used to have an in-house bookseller, now you have an in-house critic. What have you got to complain about?"

I told him all about the pressure I was under. About the nerve-wracking tension between the two floors. About the tenants' meeting and about his attack on my rabbits.

I noticed that as he listened to what I was saying, a smile spread across his face. As if he were amused by some plan slowly weaving itself in his mind. When I was done, he blew a jet of smoke up towards the ceiling, and said, slowly, the way Sherlock Holmes would speak to Dr. Watson:

"Tell me, why not break his bones?"

I looked at him, equally amused.

"Physically, you mean?"

"Why not? For a long time I've thought about breaking his bones in some dark alley. Never had the opportunity, though. Now that he lives right in your building..."

A conspiratorial smile, sweet revenge, spread across my face, too. I recalled that the enmity between Michael and Schatz ran very much deeper than the hatred between me and Schatz, which had nothing to do with anything in particular. Schatz had been one of the first supporters of Sshockk!, but then, for some unclear reason, he went over to Nevermore. Afterwards—again for some unclear reason—he abandoned that group as well and like Ba'al Peor set himself up in a high place that looketh down on the desert, whence he spake his parables, both blessings and curses, unto all the camp. Michael cannot forgive Schatz the review of his previous book, where Schatz declared that Hochhauser had in fact written only one good book, his first, and that since then he had continuously degenerated, "trapped, like a spider, in the web of dry words he has spun around himself, without discrimination, without self-control, without serious aesthetic consideration, in a strange and meaningless idiosyncratic mixture of supposedly enraged spittle and empty rantings in the Futurist mode of the early part of this century... An eclectic mish-mash which is nothing but pure plagiarism." And he predicted Hochhauser's speedy demise.

"Look, it's pretty simple now." Michael flickered his eye in a wink from *The Godfather*. "You spy on him, find out what time he leaves, what time he comes home... then one night, in the courtyard or on the staircase..."

"Don't be ridiculous!"

"Ridiculous? He's a leech, a bloodsucker, a parasite! They used to stand parasites up by the wall and shoot them down. And if you can't shoot—just break their bones!"

"So you think you'll shut him up that way, huh?"

"You don't know his type... They're big cowards! But even if I don't shut him up... Listen, he spilled my blood! Actually spilled my blood! And why should a murderer come out clean, unpunished, go free—like a victor!—and go on spilling blood?! If the police don't do anything, if its total anarchy, then we have to take the law into our own hands! That's perfectly clear!"

"That's a weakling's reaction," I said.

"Weak?!" he screamed. "You don't have any blood in your veins, Korngold, that's why you talk like that! You're degenerate!... You'd better realize that the passion to redeem one's honor is one of the healthiest, noblest, most beautiful feelings that Nature has bestowed on Mankind! But our decayed, castrated, impotent society has tossed it, in the name of Culture—Culture!—onto the rubbish heap of supposedly primitive values. And for two years my desecrated honor has been crying out for revenge! It will not be silent! And shitface Schatz, that man of no conscience...that worm..."

"Physical revenge?" I repeated.

"Blood for blood!" he said. "Blood for blood!"

"What will you do to him? Knock him down? You can't keep a critic down..."

He gave me a conspiratorial look, and then said:

"I'll be coming around to see you one of these days."

"Bring a stick with you," I said.

Chapter fifteen

Caveat Lector

In a country as small as our own, the reader of any book having a public dimension to it tends to see it as a roman á clef. That is to say, he reads it as if the names of the characters in the book are not their real names, but rather masks covering up other, well-known names. Upon reading 'Schatz', for example, his stimulated imagination, thirsting for scandal, begins to survey the landscape; his fingers, as it were, page enthusiastically through the *Who's Who*, searching for the literary critic whose name begins with 'Sch' or ends with 'z' who is the real person whose identity is disguised by 'Schatz'. Similarly, someone reading 'Michael Hochhauser' is immediately driven by the mass curiosity to dive between the lines of all the newspapers and books he has ever read, seen on some occasion, or heard about, searching for the name of a poet that resembles 'Michael'—Daniel or Gabriel, or maybe Raphael—or a surname related to 'Hochhauser'—Althauser? Weishauser? Eisenhauser? Hochberger? Hochmann? Hochheimer? It goes without saying that such a reader immediately links Klausner the pharmacist to the famous Herr Doktor Professor Josef Klausner, may he rest in peace, whom the writer, so it seems, misses.

Alternatively, the reader leaps not on names but on incidents or episodes with which he is familiar from real life, and says: Ah ha! That's what the writer was really talking about! But in order to disguise it he changed things a bit here and there, elaborated this and simplified that, painted it yellow instead of green, observed it from the north side instead of from the south, pencilled in composite sketches of this one and that one, all just in order to lead me astray...but he hasn't managed to fool me, because, after all, our country is a small one and we dwell among our own People.

This tendency is foolish and perverse, in my opinion. It displaces the queenly crown from Literature's fair brow and degrades her into a lowly, gossiping servant. Indeed, as opposed to the notion Schatz expresses in his book *Against Allegory*, I believe that Literature, even when it takes its raw materials from life, is Parable. It has been said in the Talmud that "Job was never born and never existed, but was a parable"—and to this I say: "Job was born and Job existed, and nonetheless was a parable." In other words, it makes no difference whether or not there ever was a man named Job, because from the moment he entered the pages of the book, he became a parable, and the reader must reason inductively from the particular to the general.

And furthermore: it is not important whether there is a living man named Schatz or not, or whether this Schatz is really Schatz and not Katz or Batz in disguise. From the moment he is here—he lives and is a parable.

Therefore my advice to you, dear reader, is this: do not allow your heart to be tempted by the crude, gossiping urge to ask who's who. Remember that all this really happened, even if it is a parable. Remember, reader, that this is true, as we return to the plot to see what is new.

Chapter sixteen

A Woman Alone

If my own flesh dwindled after the tenants' meeting, my rabbits grew plumper. My female neighbors, in order to express solidarity with me and disgust and protest towards my enemy, would come up to the roof at various times of day bearing scraps from their tables and kitchens, which they would shake into the feeding troughs. The rabbits never had it so good.

Even Mrs. Bzhizovski—despite the fact that it suited neither her dignity nor her dress to climb roofwards with bowls of peelings and leftovers—found it necessary to express her apologies to me. Standing at the courtyard gate, particles of her powder floating up my nostrils, she told me that I oughtn't take her vote in favor of Schatz's motion as anything *persönlich* against me. She, as a woman of *Kultur*, had been educated from her youth to show respect to academics, and if the Professor says that the animals upstairs disturb him from writing his *dysertacjas*, why then the *dysertacjas* are more important than the animals, no? But she has nothing at all against my animals; on the contrary, she wishes them well.

It was Mr. Ben-Ze'ev's delicate, sickly wife, rather than he, who went up to the roof, even though she had been suffering from dizzy spells for the past few months. He stopped me at the entrance to the building instead, and expressed his solidarity with my struggle against the persecutor of rabbits by making mention for the first time of my book *The Flying Camel of the Golden Hump*—mention which indicated that he had indeed read it: "By the way, about the 'winged camel' with which the wicked professor taunted you—not a nice taunt! Doesn't redound to his glory!—I don't know whether you yourself are aware that a flying camel is mentioned in the Mishnah. In Tractate Nedarim it says: What is a false oath? An oath about something impossible, as, for example, 'if I didn't see a camel flying in the air, ' or 'if I didn't see a serpent resembling the beam of an oil press,' and so forth. And the Rambam, in his philosophical essay explaining induction, gives the example of a man who swears he saw a single camel floating through the air, and then another man comes along and swears he saw three camels floating through the air, and if it is possible—he says—that the first man is telling the truth, it is possible that the second man is telling the truth as well, because if the camel-Form caused this beast to float through the air, it causes the whole species to do so, and therefore a quality of the particular is a quality of the general."

I was astonished and said that I hadn't ever read those things, neither in the Mishnah nor in Maimonides.

"That you haven't read them—that isn't good!" he said. "A Hebrew writer must be familiar with the traditional sources. But that it was a camel you wrote about, rather than any other animal—that's a good sign! A sign of truth! And if two people, or more, aim at the same thing without knowing of one another—they aim at the truth! And in this case, they are aiming at the archetype deep in the human subconscious! Jung has already written what he had to say. And with respect to the taunts of the honored professor—don't pay any attention to them. In Proverbs it is written: 'It is the glory of God to conceal a thing, but the glory of kings is to search out a matter.' If the critic is king—or a slave who would be king—the writer, relative to him, as it were, is God. Let him search things out, and you go your own way and conceal things."

I thanked him, and said that I myself had had similar thoughts in the matter of "the revealed and the concealed."

The next day, when I went up to the roof earlier than usual, I found Hedva standing at the hutch poking cabbage leaves into the cages.

"Look at how they're stuffing themselves!" She regarded them happily. "It's such a pleasure to see an appetite like that!"

Like locusts the rabbits devoured leaf after leaf.

"Have you been subpoenaed to appear in court yet?" she smiled.

"No, not yet," I laughed.

Then she said, blinking: "Sometimes I think: there's so much wrongdoing and disrespect in our society… Why? What for?…I mean this country is drenched with pain! Wars, and fears… And people make each other's lives miserable…"

I remembered what Victoria had told me about her.

"In literature as well. I read what they're writing these days. Of course not everything. But it's cynical, mocking…"

"Mocking?" I echoed.

"Look, it's possible to take the saddest things and turn them into a satire if you want to…"

"It depends how…"

"With talent! Even with talent! But that's not what I'm looking for in literature! I'm not looking for talent!"

"Other things are written. Different people write different…" I said.

"I know! There are also all kinds of personal fantasies…but not the *pain*! The pain!"

"It's not exactly like that," I mumbled, and scattered the feed into the troughs.

"I mean, literature is a very human thing. It deals with matters of the soul."

"Yes, yes…"

We stood and watched the rabbits noisily masticating their fodder.

Hedva said: "For a long time I've been meaning to ask you… is there, in your opinion, any connection between literature and morality?"

I bent down to the manger and stirred the fodder in it, and when Adina, who was pregnant, approached I said: "And what's your opinion, Adina? Is there a connection between literature and morality, or isn't there?

"It's a controversial question," I said as I stood back up.

"Yes, I know. I was interested in what your opinion was," she blinked.

I poured water into the drinking bowls and invited her over to my apartment for a cup of coffee.

She was on vacation from the kindergarten and I didn't at all feel like going to the library. Hedva hadn't visited the apartment even once since Lili left, and now, as she sat in the living room looking around her, she was surprised that everything had stayed as it had been. She asked what Lili was doing and where she was. I told her that as far as I knew she was in Akron, Ohio, married to a rich Jewish contractor, the mother of a son, and "living happily ever after."

"That's nice!" She lit herself a cigarette.

I went out to the kitchen.

"What's bothering you about art and morality?" I set the cup of coffee down in front of her.

"It's been bothering me for years."

She gazed once more at the pictures on the wall, looking around.

"Look, if I were to tell you what I've been through…"

I am frequently astonished by the passionate desire of people "whom there were none to praise / And very few to love" to tell their life-stories to a writer, hoping—whether or not they say so outright—that he will put it into a book. "Oh, if you only knew what has happened to me!"—I often hear—"You could write a whole novel about it!" Or "If only I had the talent to write! I have so much to tell! But as soon as I pick up a pen and sit down to write—not a single sentence comes out. The words just fail me…" What is this passion,

I ask myself, just as I asked to no avail in the short introduction to this book that you hold in your hand. What is this illusion? It is as if the moment that experiences are turned into letters, are set down on paper, they acquire eternal life. Transcendence. Importance. Nobility. But in fact frequently the opposite happens: lives rich in event, full of stormy emotions, loves, hates, heart-rending quarrels, illness, separation, divorce, shocking tragedies—when they are written down they shrink and wither between the covers, or seem dull and disgusting… If the events actually happened already, and there is nothing to invent—why write them down? Why make a copy, when the copy is inevitably paler than the original?

So when Hedva recounted her painful history with the painter she'd loved (her story took about two hours to tell, and the second cup of coffee that I served her got cold without her even touching it), I felt, even though she didn't say so explicitly, that she was inwardly nursing the hope that I would write about it some time, or maybe use it as raw material for a sort of *Madame Bovary*, or a small-scale *Anna Karenina*…

"About a year ago they interviewed him on the radio, late at night," she lowered her eyes to the ashtray as she crushed the tail of her cigarette out. "The interview lasted for maybe an hour. I lay in bed and listened. He has this kind of smooth voice, all butter and honey…a modest man, 'hid among the stuff' like young Saul…" She looked up at me with a smile of unmitigated bitterness. "The interviewer asks him how come he has never had an exhibition at the Israel Museum, and he answers: It's really not important to me, I'm not a pushy person who elbows his way into things… The interviewer asks him what books he reads, and he answers that his favorite writer is Mauriac, because Mauriac understands what suffering is, and pity… God!—I thought—He talks about suffering! About pity! And if I were to reveal what I know about him…

"But he's a respected artist. Shows in Paris. He's famous!" she exclaimed three or four times during the course of her story, and the bitterness etched itself into the wrinkles at the corners of her mouth.

"Does this interest you at all?" A hesitant smile trembled on her lips.

"Yes! Tell me about it," I said enthusiastically.

"I wasn't used to drinking, you understand?" a slight moan tinged her laughter. "And really that whole way of life was quite strange to me."

Her story with the artist, E., began like this:

One summer evening, a few years after her young husband had left her, her neighbor—"Gerda by name, a frivolous, adulterous woman"—took Hedva to an opening of an exhibition by the artist, who was an acquaintance of hers. The gallery was packed with invited guests, bohemians, friends, collectors… The painter—she said—was "a man of seductive appearance," if I took her meaning. Of middle height, with graying but youthful wavy hair, fluid movements, and eyes that were "lustful and cunning, frankly seductive." Later that night he invited his friends to a party on his roof, and Gerda dragged Hedva along.

Hedva wasn't acquainted with any of the many guests, and when Gerda vanished with a splendidly dressed man she'd managed to bag, she found refuge by the drinks table. Because she was not accustomed to drinking, her second glass of hard liquor ("Nobody spoke to me, you understand? So what could I do?") made her to feel sick. A fog thickened inside her head, her legs became heavy, and she thought she was going to faint. The artist, who happened to be walking by, noticed how pale she had turned, asked what was wrong, took her arm and led her down to his apartment, which was just beneath the roof-garden. He tended her like a real gentleman. He reassured her, walked her to the bathroom, where she "vomited her heart out"—to her great embarrassment—and afterwards he brought her into his studio where he ordered her to lie down and not get up again until she felt better.

She fell asleep, and was awakened by the sound of loud music and people dancing on the roof. She got up and tried to steal quietly out of the house, so no one would notice her, but met the painter at the threshold. He blocked her way, asked how she felt, and begged her to come up and join the dancers. When she refused, he invited her to come to his home whenever she wanted, to see his paintings. She thanked him, and when she tried once again to cross the threshold, he put his hands on her shoulders, drew her face close to his, whispered "This pallor suits you"—and planted a kiss on her mouth.

"That kiss of grace killed me," she blew a jet of smoke towards the ceiling, and smiled.

"Does this interest you?" she asked again, after a silence.

The very next night she went to his house, sat in his studio, listened, enchanted, to his explanations of his pictures. She gazed, entranced, at his expressive, sensual face, at the playful sparkle of his green eyes… A heartbreaker, sure of his conquests.

And she slept there, in his bed.

And in the following days she went around like a sleepwalker. "Yes, a sleepwalker. There isn't any other word to describe it." During work hours, at the kindergarten, she was impatient for their date in the evening. She admired his paintings, his talent. She was excited by his tenderness towards her. He was an artist and a lover…

(Am I hearing a sigh in the silent pauses that fragment her speech? Or the strangled whisper of the embers of a strong love, which have not been extinguished under the ash of resentment?)

But she swiftly discovered that she was not the only one who visited his studio. She met them: young women and women who were not-so-young. The jealousy fanned her love. Intoxicated her. Pushed her to do crazy, foolish things. Like the night she rang his doorbell without getting an answer. She knew there was a woman in there with him—there was a pinkish light in the window, from the small table lamp—nevertheless she rang again and again, stubbornly, aggressively, until she forced him to open the door, and he, wearing only his trousers, apologized—ridiculous!—and said that he'd explain it to her tomorrow. "Oh, don't ask what stupid things I did back then… I want to sink through the floor whenever I remember them…"

"How old are you?" She angled her gaze at me from below, as she crushed out yet another cigarette in the ashtray.

Close to forty, I said.

She looked at me affectionately, and smiled.

The more she saw him, the more she discovered the ugly side beneath his friendly and considerate surface: his boundless self-love, his pathological miserliness—he never, ever took her out to a café or restaurant, and he never once gave her a single gift…

"Look, it's funny to mention it…maybe petty…but now and then we would come back from some party in a taxi…and when it was time to pay…always, but always, he would discover that he didn't have any money in his wallet, and he would ask me to pay, he would return the money later…and he always forgot about it, of course…"

She discovered his habit of lying, about great things and small, obvious, absurd, tasteless lies, from which he mostly derived no great benefit; and his complete disregard for other people's feelings—

"You can't begin to imagine what he was capable of doing! It was really hopeless! You could have death throes right in front of his very eyes and he wouldn't even notice. His skin was so thick that no tears, no pleading, nothing could penetrate."

Once, in the winter, when she came down with a bad case of the flu, she phoned and dared to ask him to come over and take her electric heater for repairs. And he promised to do so. He didn't, of course. But he never called to apologize, or to ask how she was feeling. And during those whole two weeks he did not come to visit her even once! And when she recovered—the lies he invented to excuse his non-appearance! The lies! "And yet… and yet—how can I tell you this?…He lied with such charm…with such 'innocence'…that all I could do was laugh… Charm in a man makes up for a lot of crimes! Any woman could fall for that one."

Five months later…

"Maybe I should stop now."

For about five minutes she smoked in silence. She looked again at the walls around her, and was silent.

Five months later she was pregnant.

When she told him, he demanded that she have an abortion.

When she refused, he said that he would not acknowledge his paternity of the child.

And demanded hurtfully that she never come see him again.

"In fact I hate artists," her lips trembled.

"Not you," she smiled through the smoke that brought tears to her eyes.

And she took a handkerchief to dry them.

"I phoned him from the hospital. I said: You have a son. Do you want to see him? He slammed down the receiver."

Yaron met him, for the first time, when he was eleven years old.

"I'll tell you about it some time, if you have time.

"But he's a very successful artist! One of his pictures, I read recently, sold for five thousand dollars, in an auction."

Now, as I read what I have written, I say to myself: what a sentimental melodrama this is. Sentimental and banal, flattened out on paper. But when Hedva told it—sending about a dozen cigarettes up in smoke, pausing from time to time when the waves of memory breaking over her washed the words out of her mouth, her voice cracking, then getting stronger and back on track—I had listened spellbound to her words, and thought: her story is a one-time event, utterly unique, because every person's life is utterly unique, and everything that happens to them is utterly unique, unrepeatable. It is only writing, that copies life, that renders "banal" that which could never possibly be banal! And as for me… No, I won't make a "story" out of this, no "novel". And I won't be so foolish as to copy quivering life onto paper so that its vital soul evaporates! I, I am able to write only things from my imagination, things that never were…

Thus say I, who am now writing this book that is all about things that really happened… So how very right the readers will be if they shake their heads and say it is indeed "superfluous"!

Chapter seventeen

The Tale of a Black Cat

Like most people, I cling to a number of superstitions. A dream in which the sun shines above my head but casts no shadow at my feet is a bad omen, leaving me in a state of anxiety the whole of the next day. Whenever I encounter a distorted reflection of my own face in a windowpane—either because the glass is flawed or because a shadow has fallen upon it—I become afraid that I will fall ill. An insect that comes into the room—particularly if it flies in through the window and scurries about on the floor as if intoxicated—is a messenger of the netherworld, the incarnation of a demon, or of a sinful soul. If the pen falls from my hand as I begin to write it is an omen that nothing that I write on that day will turn out well. And whenever a black cat crosses my path I am compelled—and no attempt to deter myself will help—to take three steps backwards before I walk on, in order to neutralize the curse of the Evil Eye. So as not to appear ridiculous to passersby, as I step backwards I fix my eyes on a treetop or high window, as if I'm interested in something that had caught my eye.

The power of Reason to counter these beliefs is negligible.

Among the books that my father of blessed memory left me, I found an old, worm-eaten volume published during the Enlightenment, in 1866, called *The Key.* In very Baroque language, the author, the highly literate Rabbi Moses Aaron Shatzkes of Karlin, explicates Talmudic legends and aphorisms through logic and common sense, in order, as he puts it, "to release the enchained message from the manacles of metaphor, and from the prison-house of riddles, the solution..." One of his exegeses has to do with dogs. In Tractate Baba Kama it is written: "Dogs wail, and the Angel of Death comes into town; dogs play, Elijah the Prophet comes into town." Shatzkes—the enlightened rabbi for whom superstition is despicable—asserts that "the Angel of Death" refers either to the fire of revolt kindling amongst the people, or else to foreign wars, and that the "dogs" are the preservers of the city, "the guardians of the gates from the king's forces," who in the language of the metaphor are called 'dogs'. He offers support for this interpretation from the saying: "A man shall not live in a place where no horse neighs and no dog barks"'—that is to say, in a town where there is no cavalry and no corps of guards. When I read this rational exegesis I said: "Shatzkes, Shatzkes, what do you know about the complexities of Being? You perceive only what is on the surface and have no feeling at all for the quaking that traverses the depths, from one end of the universe to the other, which even the dogs can sense."

The superstition about black cats was transmitted to me by Aunt Sophia, my Uncle Stefan Kaminski's wife. Sophia—even though she was a Communist, a Party member, a modern and educated woman whose elegant clothes aroused envy as she walked through the streets of Bucharest—was possessed by about a hundred superstitions, and at every step she would spit and mutter charms against the Evil Eye. A mirror that falls to the floor and breaks, strands of hair entangled in a knot, a rope tied in a noose, a stopped clock, spilled wine, a corpse in a dream, the number thirteen, and of course: a black cat. When she walked me to school and a black cat crossed our path, she would pull me by the arm to a sharp halt, stand at attention for a second or two, take three steps backward pulling me along with her, and stand at attention once more, this time with her eyes closed, as if whispering an incantation. Only upon the completion of this ritual would we continue on our way. On a snowy day, when the black creature running across the white surface brought to mind a devil defiantly polluting the purity of nature, this ritual took twice as long. I was late for school more than once on account of this.

Aunt Sophia, I am sure, would never have agreed to take up residence in the building where I live, 39 Avigdor Street, because 39 is three times 13.

Furthermore, this house is surrounded by cats, on the street and in the courtyard. Black, white, grey, black-and-white, and they multiply. You empty your trash into the rubbish bin and all of a sudden, like a genie from a bottle, a cat leaps out in front of your face, scares the living daylights out of you, swerves and runs away. You go up the stairs, and there in the corner of the first or second landing you suddenly discover a newborn kitten crouching, wrinkled and frightened, mewing in pleading little chirps that are enough to break your heart. You step out of the building onto the street—and one of them hurls itself, for some unknown reason, at the foot of one of the trees in the courtyard, and feverishly begins to dig and burrow. And at night—the wails of passion, the wails of hunger, body and soul, the wails of existential despair, the wails of longing and yearning, the wails of the world's pain.

One night a year ago or more, as I sat writing at this table, I heard faint wails outside my study, at the threshold of my door. Wails as if for mercy begging, crying like a human cries, like a small abandoned child. I paused a moment in my writing, paused and listened for a while. To the wails there now were added nails that scratched, or claws that scrabbled, at the bottom of my door. A hungry cat, I then conjectured, seeking food here at my door. A cat just scratching at my door… Still I sat there in my place, hoping it would go away, thinking it would soon despair and scratch upon a neighbor's door. But at its task the cat persisted, paused and wailed, howled, desisted, whined, insisted, exploiting all its repertoire. First its voice was thin and sweet, then it groaned from deep within, then weak and weary it continued to implore. Though on the creature I took pity,

I, hard-hearted, kept on sitting; didn't rise to let it in, didn't bring it cream or milk. Thus I pondered as I sat there: "Why me? What on earth has brought this cat here, and not to someone else's door? Why not Victoria's or Hedva's? Why not to Heinz across the hall? If I feed it something this time, it will come here every midnight, whine and scratch upon my door, interrupt my concentration so I will not write at all..." Soon there was blissful silence: all at once the cat went quiet, scratched no longer on my door. Must have gone off down the stairs. Yet all that night, despite the silence, sleep chose not to grace my eyelids as I tossed upon my bed, wracked by conscience, fears, regret. "Cat!" I cried, "My God hath sent thee, as a test to try my soul! Art thou not an incarnation of a departed human soul, a child, perhaps, or some relation, seeking mercy at my door? Oh sin devoid of expiation, thy pleas for mercy to ignore! Cat, tell me—tell me!—what damnation awaits my soul forevermore?" Thus cried I, and I, agnostic, a rational man and nothing more...

But the case of my Aunt Sophia proves that even someone who is a devotee of Marxism—a very rationalistic theory, everyone agrees—is not immune to superstition.

And this is what happened to me the day after my encounter with Hedva, when she told me her life story.

Leaving the house in the evening to visit Michael, as I turned from the gate to the sidewalk, a black cat crossed my path as it ran from one side of the street to the other. But at the very same instant, I saw—not twenty paces away from me—Schatz, walking towards me, briefcase in hand, approaching the building. I stopped dead still, not knowing what to do: to walk forward was impossible—I certainly wasn't about to tempt Satan! But I wasn't about to take three steps backward either—I certainly didn't want to do anything that would make me look ridiculous in front of Schatz. To turn back and walk in the opposite direction—that wouldn't break the curse of the Evil Eye. To stay where I was and wait until he walked past me—stupid, embarrassing. And anyway I would be forced to greet him. Or—which was worse—not to greet him. All this passed through my mind in that brief instant when I halted at the juxtaposed sights of the passing cat and the approaching Schatz. But to my great amazement—and good luck!—he also stopped dead. For the proverbial instant he stood there and hesitated, as though measuring the distance remaining between him and me, and immediately he set his briefcase down on the stone wall and opened it, as if he were looking for something. I managed to catch a glimpse of his hand rummaging among the papers, and I hastened to seize the opportunity which had befallen me like a miracle: I bent over, as if to tie a shoelace that had come undone, and while doing so I took three tiny steps backwards, heel alongside toe. When I stood up, I saw Schatz stepping backwards, his eyes raised to the window of the third floor of the house across the street, as though he had noticed something there that had aroused his curiosity. I rushed across the street and around the corner.

I never made it to Michael's place that day.

Chapter eighteen

Inadvertent Conversation

When I entered Speiser's store, I saw Naomi inside. We exchanged greetings and smiled at one another. As she had to wait until Mrs. Ehrlich finished her order, she turned to me and asked me how I was and what I was writing these days. I said that I was translating Rabelais. "Rabelais? From French?" she cried, astonished. Yes, from French, I smiled. "That must be awfully difficult!" She looked at me with surprise and a trace of pity. Yes—I said, it's difficult, but I take great pleasure in the actual work of translation. "Yes...yes..." She looked at me affirmatively, and asked me where my French was from. I told her: from Romania, and then I had two years of advanced study in France. "I read *Gargantua* in English," she said, "or at any rate a few chapters of it... It's impossible to read all of *Gargantua.*" "Not to mention *Pantagruel*!" I said. "No, not to mention *Pantagruel...*" she giggled. "And *Panurge* as well," I said. "Yes, and *Panurge* as well," she laughed. Then we laughed in unison, like two people who understand each other. "And you're going to translate all that?! It's enough work for years!" She made a sour face, as though she felt sorry for me.

Meanwhile, Mrs. Ehrlich had paid for her purchases and Mr. Speiser said: "What will you have today, Mrs. Schatz?"

I stood there and waited my turn. I saw that Naomi's shoulder blades, the color of which had previously been blush apricot, had now turned brown as plums, and her arms and neck had also darkened. A sort of flickering heat wave radiated from her face. I asked myself where it was that she had gotten so tanned. On the roof? When? During the hours I was sitting like a Jesuit scholiast over the heavy dictionaries in the French library? At the beach? When? And at the sight of the little tufts of hair peeping out of her armpits, I was momentarily dazzled by the splendid, breathtaking vision of her body supine under the bright morning sky: two small sunwheels radiating forth from the burnished tan…

Naomi asked for brown sugar, two packages of pumpernickel bread, two jars of strawberry jam, two hundred grams of Roquefort cheese…; He doesn't have any Roquefort at the moment, Mr. Speiser said, but he has some Beit-Yitzhak gruyère, very good, he would recommend it…; —Beit-Yitzhak gruyère? Naomi hesitated. —Taste some. Speiser offered her a thin sliver of cheese on a piece of transparent paper, and she, with thumb and forefinger, lifted it and brought it to her mouth, tasted it on the tip of her tongue, her tanned face signaled satisfaction, said yes… —Alright, that'll be fine…a hundred grams of sliced Polish sausage, but the real thing, not like last time… one jar of Beit Hashitta brand black olives, the Maccabi beers…what else?—she tried to remember, running her glance along the shelves, over canned goods, the jars, the packets, something wild in her green eyes, her shining hair…— Two sticks of butter, a large bottle of soda water… Have I forgotten anything? …Yes, sardines, five tins, Minerva please…; —What about Porthos, Mrs. Schatz? Just came in today—Speiser offered—also from Portugal, very good mackerels…; —My husband is addicted to Minerva, smiled Naomi.

Addicted to Minerva!—I inwardly cried—five tins!

I saw him in my mind's eye, sitting by the kitchen table, a tin of sardines open before him, and he, with his fork, greedily devouring from within it the little pickled fish drenched in oil, the little flat fish, all silvery, the crowded ones and the entangled ones, the crude ones and the scumbled ones, dipping each bite in the greenish oil, dropping it into his mouth, chewing, sucking, blinking… Oh, how could she stand it! And the smell emanating from his mouth after he had swallowed this whole stinking mess of fish…

"Four hundred seventy-five *lira* and two *agorot,*" Speiser announced after he had counted the purchases and totted up their prices on the calculating machine. "Cash or credit today, Mrs. Schatz?"

"Add it to my account, please," said Naomi, and she promised to pay everything she owed on the sixth of the month, because her husband gets his salary on the fifth.

As she gathered her purchases into her basket, I asked for and received: a loaf of bread, two yoghurts and Canaan white cheese.

I was about to leave, but when I saw the two shopping bags Naomi was holding, one heavy and one light, I stretched my hand out towards the heavy one and said: "Let me help you."

"No! No!" she protested. But I stood my ground and seized the handles, and she gave in and let me carry it.

We walked along together, and Naomi called my attention to the jasmine growing in the hedges along the sidewalk. She stopped for a moment, and plucked a small white blossom, inhaled its fragrance with great pleasure, and said that in the Galilee, in the area of Nahal Keziv, there is a lot of wild jasmine but it has no fragrance at all. This, the cultivated jasmine, originally came from India. I admitted I was a complete ignoramus about flowers. "You're missing a lot," she said, and added that—aside from being beautiful—plants were as rich and interesting a world as the world of animals.

"I thought you would come take pictures of the rabbits," I said.

"Oh, yes," she said. "I wanted to, but my company didn't agree. They said there was already a rabbit on the cover of *Watership Down,* so they sent me off to photograph mountain goats."

"Mountain goats?" I asked. "Where did you find mountain goats?"

"At Ein Gedi!" she laughed, and told me that she had spent three wonderful days in the environs of Ein Gedi, photographing gorgeous mountain goats on the cliffs of Nahal Arugot, Nahal Hever, and Nahal David.

"Is that where you got so tanned?" I glanced admiringly at her arms and shoulders.

"It was terribly hot!"—she said—"But it was gorgeous!" This young guy went along with her, "a child of the desert" from the field school, guiding her to the depths of the meandering wadis, and they found leopard tracks, and they discovered rare plants, fossils millions of years old... Do I know what a "storm-wheel" is?—No, I don't know. A cyclone? A whirlwind? No! she laughed, that's what everyone thinks, but a "storm-wheel" is a kind of desert thistle, wheel-like...and they found saltgrass, and inkberry. I said that as for me, I had spent my whole life in cities, both abroad and in Israel, and I envied her having grown up with all those things, flora and fauna, ever since she was a baby. Does she miss the kibbutz?—No, she said, she doesn't miss it. She had a hard time there as a child. The communal education system is a disaster, in her opinion.

"Disaster?" I echoed.

"Who's that woman?" she whispered instead of answering, as Mrs. Grossmeyer walked past us, and I greeted her with a nod.

"A cellist. In the Chamber Orchestra," I said.

"She's very impressive. I've seen her a couple of times and I said to myself: she must be some kind of artist."

Mrs. Grossmeyer, who resides at number 37 on our street, is indeed an impressive woman: erect, silver-blue hair flowing on either side of her pale face, blue eyes, an expression of imposing serenity.

I returned to my question about why the communal education system is a "disaster" in her opinion.

"Like plant nurseries," she laughed.

Then she said:

"When I was two years old, I nearly choked to death. The nursery teacher hated my mother, so when I refused to eat my semolina porridge, she would force the spoon into my mouth so hard that..."

I laughed. "Truly a disaster!" I said.

"No, I'm exaggerating," she said a few steps later.

But she misses the landscape. The landscape of the Jezreel Valley.

Very much.

As we approached our building, she said: "By the way, I'm sorry about what happened at the tenants' meeting."

I glanced at her sideways and said she had a twig of tamarisk dangling from her hair.

"Really?" She passed her hand over her head.

I set down the shopping bag and with two fingers I removed the flexible twig from her hair and dropped it earthwards.

"Thanks," she blushed.

"Well, you didn't say anything," I said as we continued walking. "You didn't vote..."

"You've got to understand him," she said. "He works hard. Works nights. Till two sometimes."

"Yes, I know."

"Every little sound disturbs him. A sort of inward irritability..."

"Yes, he looks a bit irritable..."

"Which is why he quarrels with so many people..."

"So many?"

"As you well know! There are lots of people who really *hate* him!"

"Personally?"

"Alright, in general people hate critics..." she giggled, and added that he's more hated than the rest because he never compromises. He's sharp, incisive, direct and when from time to time she tries to tell him that he has to soften the tone of his writing a bit, he replies that he would rather be considered a bastard than obsequious and hypocritical.

"Maybe he's right..." I said.

"In some ways they're unfair to him. People he writes against take what he says as a personal insult, but he has nothing against them, personally..."

"What's important to him is the issue at hand!" I said.

"Precisely!" She slanted me a laughing look.

Going up the path to the building, she said quietly: "Don't suppose that he has an easy life..."

"I can imagine..." I said.

When we came to the first landing she added: "He never had. Even as a child."

"Yes. That makes a difference. Always."

On the stairs to the third floor, she said:

"He had to fight hard to get to where he is. Even at the university."

"Oh, it's ghastly there! A jungle!"

And on the stairs to the fourth floor:

"If it weren't for his talent..."

"Brilliant!" I said as we stood before her door.

Again she threw a look at me, and burst out laughing.

"What are you laughing at?"

"Nothing..." she smiled, and thanked me for being her porter.

I went downstairs to my apartment, and as I put the groceries into the refrigerator I said to myself: She's a prisoner! A bird in a cage! A gazelle in a pen! What is she doing there, in the house of that bluebeard scholar?!

Later, as I sat in my room, I still felt a hot breeze from the sirocco in her face, from her searing voice. I saw her skipping over the boulders among the vineyards of Ein Gedi, and she looked to me like Shulamith, Tsip, Shosh, Ruthi, Reena, Shula, Batya, Bathsheba... a girl from the Independence Festival songs, songs from the days I never experienced, that I would never be able to touch... *Bathsheba, Bathsheba, this song is for you... Shoshana, Shoshana, Shoshana, the moon's carried upon a cloud... Tsip Tsip Tsipi, don't say another word... Listen, Itsik, what is it Reena... We'll remember you Ruthi Rutha as well as your laughter that chimed…* yes, one of those who danced there on the stage, in those distant days in Bucharest, barefoot beauties adorned with wheaten sheaves:

> I went down to the
> GARden of nuts
> To see the fruits of the vaa-lley,
> To see whether the vine flourished,
> and the pom-UH-granates BUD.

Chapter nineteen

Under Her Wing

Twice following my separation from Lili, Victoria Azoulai attempted to seduce me, and both times I withstood the attempt. Not because I am righteous as Joseph, or a hero like Tolstoy's Father Sergei, but—I must admit—out of fear. I am a coward… If Victoria's husband had been a dentist, a grocer, a bank manager or even a professor—I might have yielded to the temptation. After all, the writer is like any other man, especially when he lives alone, and when his flesh thickens, his spirit sickens. However, when the husband is a police officer… I have always had qualms about government officials. Even when dealing with minor clerks—in the Income Tax Bureau, the Population Registry Office, or the Rabbinate—I quake at the knees, stutter, forget what I had wanted to say, can't find the right responses. And of course, policemen. All the more so a detective or chief inspector like Albert Azoulai, who to me seems a mysterious figure, closed, silent, arousing respect and awe.

The first time was about three months after Lili left the apartment. Late in the morning, as I sat and wrote—at the time I was translating a play by Georges Feydeau, commissioned by one of the theatres (a play, by the way, that was never performed, although I did get paid for my work)—Victoria rang my doorbell. When I opened it, she asked—blushing, which was unusual for her—if I could help her for a few minutes. She was doing a thorough housecleaning, and if it wasn't too much trouble for me—

I remember her gaze, when she made this request. It wasn't her customary expression: her eyes glittered, and they held a look of demand, of promise...and I, though I did not know what awaited me, was flooded by a wave of warmth.

How could I refuse when her generosity to me has always been boundless? If I ran out of matches, I would go down and get some from her. Sometimes I'd even borrow an egg.

Of course, I said. Gladly! I followed her down to her apartment and we entered the kitchen. A tall folding ladder stood in the middle of the room, and about twenty china plates with gold rims were arranged in two rows on the table.

"All I'd like you to do is..." said Victoria, and she explained what she wanted: she would climb up on the ladder to bring the plates down from the top shelf of the cupboard, and I would take them from her and set them on the table.

It was as simple as could be, but she spoke breathily, blushing, unsmiling, as if she had an ulterior motive.

As she climbed the ladder, she asked me to keep hold of it to make sure she wouldn't fall. And when I looked up, I couldn't prevent my naughty eyes from climbing up her calves to the open mouth of her short dress, which rose as she lifted her arms up to reach the plates. Gazing thus, holding my breath, "I saw the light at the end of the tunnel," as they say. Because, throbbing, I discovered the shadowy sparkle from the secret bush that is between the two shores, which nearly dazzled me and stiffened the organ of my loins, as Rabelais would have said.

Victoria, holding five plates, bent over me—and as she bent over, there slid towards me her two overflowing haystacks, pure as milk, that is, her blessing from above, "the hidden light in the whiteness of the bodice," in the words of the poet Moshe Zacuto—and put them—the plates, I mean—in my hands. I took them with trembling arms and set them on the table.

Once again I held on to the ladder, and once again my venerating eyes worshipped the revelation of the Mystery. But this time, instead of leaning over to me, Victoria paused at the top of the ladder, plates in hand, eyes lowered towards me, veiled, expectant. Expecting what? I knew: expecting me to pass my hand along her leg, from her leg to her thigh, if not higher, to the unlocked garden, to the fountain unsealed.

My hand was paralyzed. It clutched the ladder and didn't let go. Disappointed, Victoria leant towards me once more and handed me the plates.

Twice more she handed plates down to me, three at a time, and as she informed me that there weren't any more and that she was coming down, she fell from the ladder onto my neck, as though she had slipped, and encircled me with her arms. As she hung there fluttering a moment, I set her down on the floor. For a long moment she stood pressed against me, her arms about my neck, her sparkling gaze raised towards me—and the slightest forward movement on my part—and I was as winded and excited as she—would have sufficed to adhere us to one another with passionate enthusiasm.

But through my brain the following consideration flashed like lightning: what if the door were to open this very second… and Albert, armed with his pistol, stood at the entrance to the kitchen…the fire of vengeance burning in his eyes… I gently pried her off me.

Turbulent and red-faced, I left her apartment without saying a word.

That was her first attempt. But here I must immediately note that Victoria is not a lewd and lascivious woman. Not in the least. If her passions get the better of her from time to time and incite her to light-headed actions—it cannot be explained other than by the fact that she is endowed with an abundance of love, love for everyone who has not done her ill, for everyone she wishes well. This love, which overflows its banks, she longs to bestow, and for the most part she hasn't upon whom to bestow it: her husband, whose obligation it is to fulfill her, is at home only rarely, sometimes during the day and sometimes at night, and you never know when. Her eldest daughter, the married one, lives far away, in Naharia. Her older son is a career officer in the army, and he too visits only on rare occasions. Her younger son has wandered off to Canada. If at times—though rarely, and this, too, is to her credit—she wishes to bestow some of her bounty upon me, it is only because I happen to be in her immediate vicinity and she likes me. Should this be thought sinful?

At any rate, following the incident related above, whenever we ran into one another on the staircase or in the courtyard, we would exchange a few words as if nothing had happened; and if Victoria treated me with the same cheerful naturalness as always, without any embarrassment, why it's just another sign of her innocence.

The second incident took place about a year ago, and it bears some relation to literature.

More than once Victoria had hinted to me, as if casually, very modestly, that she too writes. "Some time when you have a free evening, perhaps you would be kind enough to hear a few pages from the fruit of my pen. I'd very much like to know if it's worth anything," she told me.

It was in fact because she didn't pester me, and because she only mentioned this two or three times, widely separated, that I felt myself obligated to grant her request. So one afternoon, I told her that I would have time for her that evening.

That evening was like a holiday for her, and as for a holiday she adorned herself. She wore a long dress, citron-colored, printed with roses; her raven-black hair shone as if it had just been washed, and a red rose was stuck in it, on the left side. On the Damascus table, inlaid with ivory, stood a noble-necked decanter in which red wine sparkled and around it were arranged plates of sweets and biscuits. On the buffet stood a vase of red carnations.

With a charming gesture and a slight bow, and she asked me to sit down on the sofa, and with a charming gesture she poured some of the cherry wine into the two silver goblets—antiques, she said, family heirlooms from the time of Rabbi Haim Abulafia. She clinked her glass to mine, and drank but the tiniest little sip. "Shall I bring the fruit of my pen?" she said; and with that, she rose, smoothed her dress, and taking tiny steps, festive and proud, holding her small body at its full height, she stepped into the next room.

She returned not with a notebook, but with an album covered in blue velvet. And sitting beside me, she lay it in front of us, a gift from her aunt that she had received on the occasion of her bat mitzvah. "I shall read you just a short chapter." She opened the album and turned its pages slowly, page after page. The paper was thick, and the letters in her rounded hand, naive and precise, glistened upon it like strings of precious stones. The corners of the pages, sometimes in the upper margin and sometimes in the lower, were adorned with tiny, colorful illuminations: an olive branch, an anemone, a boat, waves on the Sea of Galilee, the dome of a holy tomb. I asked Victoria if she knew how to draw as well, and she laughed and said: "Sins of my youth." When she reached the middle of the album, she placed her hand on the page and said: "I shall read the chapter about grandmother's courtyard."

Here are the contents of that chapter, as well as I can recall them—a chapter that experienced taxonomists would classify as 'folkloristic literature', and about which the pedants among them would be more specific and add: 'folkloristic-romantic' or 'folkloristic-naive':

To the large courtyard in Tiberias, surrounded by walls of basalt, would flock, at all hours of the day, Jews and Arabs, Ashkenazim and Sephardim, sellers and buyers, donkeys and camels—and Grandmother Sarina's eye kept track of them all, and she dealt haughtily with them. Grandfather, Haham Eliyahu, was busy with Torah, and he spent most of his time at the synagogue, at the tomb of Rabbi Meir Baal Ha-Ness, dealing with charitable matters, or bathing in the mineral springs. Often, he would go to Safed, Ein-Zeytim and Meron, to prostrate himself upon the tombs of the sages. Grandmother Sarina—who "halted on her thigh," but whose walk was forceful and energetic as she dragged along her crippled leg and her heavy body—was the one who managed all the negotiations in the courtyard: with the Arab grain merchants, who would come from

Jenin, or from Irbid on the other side of the Jordan, and unload sacks of wheat, barley and millet, and with the Jewish buyers, who would come from the city itself, or from the settlements in the Galilee, from Ayelet Hashahar and Kfar Giladi, and load the grain onto vans and trucks. In the warm summer evenings, when the light breeze off the Sea of Galilee gave some relief from the hot and dusty desert wind, the whole family, grandmother and grandfather, the children and the grandchildren, would gather in the courtyard under the venerable fig-tree, sipping coffee, cracking watermelon or sunflower seeds, and Grandmother Sarina would spin her tales, of things that had happened in the days of the Turks, in the days of the great plague, in the days of the first world war, tales of Beduin from Horon and of soldiers from the Arab Legion and the Foreign Legion, of horsemen and highwaymen, of the pioneers who had come over from Russia, and of miracles that had happened to the ill and the lame, who were cured by prostrating themselves on the graves of the sages. Neighbors and acquaintances from the nearby streets came to hear Grandmother Sarina's stories too.

Sarina's granddaughter, fifteen-year-old Rachel, child of Abulafia the baker, would thirstily drink in her grandmother's stories. And one evening, she noticed one of those present in the circle of listeners, a youth of sixteen or seventeen, "with hair black as a raven's wing, eyes two smoldering coals and a cloud of grief hovering over his face," as Victoria had written. When she asked her aunt who he was, she whispered that he was the nephew of Pinhas Abutbul, the grocer from the market lane, and he came from Tel Aviv, but she didn't know his name. That whole evening Rachel couldn't tear her eyes away from him, "although she knew it was not nice for a girl of good family to gaze upon the face of a youth, because of what people would say". The youth came back the following evening, and the one after that, and sat and listened to the stories, "his face secretive and melancholic", and Rachel began to feel that "the fires of love were kindling in her bosom." She did not know his name or what he did, but one night as she lay in her bed, "tortured by the pangs of love," she heard her father whispering to her mother, in the next room, that

Pinhas Abutbul's nephew was hiding from the British here, as he was a member of the Irgun, and that his real name was not Ben-Ami, but Nissim. "Her heart throbbed within her until she thought she would faint." The following evening, when she once again saw "Ben-Ami" in her grandmother's courtyard, knowing that he was "one of the heroes fighting for the liberation of our people," she vowed in her heart that "only unto him would she sanctify her maidenhood," and if it were not God's will to have him take notice of her, she would marry no other man, and die a virgin's death.

But her parents had already promised her to Eliyahu, the son of the customs officer Yitzhak Almoslino, who went off every day to his work at the police station in Rosh Pina. Rachel had no special feelings towards Eliyahu, although he was a handsome youth, tall and an outstanding athlete in the Maccabi Club. The engagement party was to take place in two weeks, and she, in despair, turned for help to Sarina, and revealed her secret to her. Grandmother Sarina, who loved her granddaughter very much, said: "My child, do as your parents command. Ben-Ami is like the falcon that soars one day among the cliffs of the Arbel, and the next among the cliffs of the Golan, while Eliyahu is like the date palm growing in the courtyard of our house, and no wind shall move him from his place." Rachel, weeping copiously, declared she would never marry the son of "an official of the wicked government that is crushing our people." She said she didn't love him. She said that it was better for her to die than to marry him. When her father learnt of her refusal, he scolded her, argued with her, and said that if she didn't plight her troth to Eliyahu, she would bring disgrace to the whole family and break her mother's heart.

The day of the betrothal ceremony arrived, and lo! the town buzzed with the news that Nissim, the nephew of Pinhas Abutbul, had been killed by the British. The police had ambushed him in the outskirts of Safed. They tried to apprehend him and when he attempted to escape, they shot and killed him.

Deep mourning enveloped the Jews of the town. The ceremony was postponed. Rachel wept for her beloved, and would not be comforted.

A year later Rachel was wed to Eliyahu. But her wounded heart never recovered.

With her dainty pink handkerchief Victoria blotted the beads of sweat from her face, fixed her gaze upon me, and awaited my utterance.

"Very nice!" I said.

Indeed, I was charmed by the picture of this world, which was foreign to me, suffused with the color of its time, which was equally foreign to me, a picture that glowed with the grace of naiveté.

"You're just saying that!" she said.

"No, in all sincerity—very nice!"

"The style is alright?" she asked.

"Absolutely right!" I said, and added that in my opinion, two things are most essential in any story: first of all that it be truthful…

"Everything here is true!" she interrupted me. "Believe me that everything I've told you here is exactly the way it was! Word for word! I didn't make up a thing from my own imagination!"

"…And secondly," I added, swallowing, "the writer must be faithful to himself, must *be* himself!"

"It is I!" laughed Victoria. "That girl is I! I just changed the names! For reasons maybe you can understand! It's allowed in a story, I think…"

"Yes, of course it's allowed!"

"Do you think…" she raised her hopeful gaze to me "…do you think they would publish a story like this? I thought maybe I could send it to a newspaper…"

"Maybe… It's worth trying…"

"But I'm embarrassed…" she laughed like a shy little girl and lowered her head between her shoulders. "What would my children say…my husband… I mean…"

"They would be proud of you!" I said.

"You think so?"

"Yes," I declared, and praised her discriminating eye, offering as example two descriptions in her story: the one, a portrayal of the grandmother's face, "crooked to one side" from the effort of dragging the crippled leg behind her, and the other…

I noticed that as I spoke she fixed her gaze not on my eyes but on my lips, as though she weren't listening to my words, but watching them. Suddenly, in the middle of what I was saying, she cried, "I'm so happy!" in an outburst of strong feeling, flung her arms about my neck and pressed a kiss to my mouth. She moved her face back from me, and with eyes shining she repeated: "I'm so, so happy!"

I saw the change that had come over her face, which now held the same expression as that other time: tempestuous and dark. She was breathing rapidly. She was waiting, I knew, waiting and anticipating, but like that other time, I had the same vision: the door could open…suddenly… Albert, his sword at his side…

"I've got to go…" I stood up.

Victoria walked me to the door, thanked me a thousand times, and as I left she said: "Forgive me, I was so excited…"

Two days after I had met Naomi in Speiser's store, as I was heading home up the stairs late in the evening, just as I reached the second-floor landing, Victoria's door opened a little—she had heard my footsteps, apparently—and standing in her doorway, wrapped in a blue flannel robe, she said:

"Do you have time to step in for a few minutes?"

I went in, sat down on the sofa, and, sitting down beside me she said secretively, "I wanted to consult with you. With regard to Professor N."

"N.?"

"His name is Naphtali, isn't it?"

"Yes. What about Professor N.?" I laughed.

"He isn't paying!" Her eyes sprayed shrapnel. "It's been two months already that he hasn't paid!"

I thought a while, and said: "There are municipal by-laws for co-operative buildings."

"I know that there are municipal by-laws for co-operative buildings. And he knows it too! What can we do? Take him to court?"

Yes, I knew we couldn't take him to court. Undoubtedly he himself was preparing a case against us. Against me.

I asked if there weren't some way to apply sanctions to a recalcitrant tenant.

"Sanctions?" smiled Victoria. "What sanctions? Should we tell the Arab not to clean the staircase near his apartment? Tell the gardener not to water his share of the garden? Mrs. Bzhizovski is rebelling, she says she'll also stop paying! And now Mr. Hirsch is threatening not to pay as well. Where will it end?"

"Look, Victoria," I said. "If you were to request me to remove the rabbits from the roof…"

"Absolutely not!" Her gaze shone on me. "What can you be thinking of? To submit to tyranny?"

"What do you suggest?"

"I thought…" with her hand she adjusted the lapels of her robe, which revealed two bright mountains and a valley, "maybe you could have a word with his wife… I saw that the two of you were friendly…"

"Me?" I cried, as if burned. "Absolutely not! About a thing like this?"

Victoria looked at me, as though trying to discover the reason for my panicked reluctance, and then said:

"However you please."

"Sorry," I said.

She kept on looking at me, gazing straight into my eyes, and said: "You're a Gemini, no?"

"Yes," I answered, surprised. "June. How could you tell?"

(Actually I was born on the cusp between Gemini and Cancer.)

"Everything is written in your eyes," she uttered mysteriously.

Mysteriousness makes me anxious. All my fears rush like ants out of their holes and crawl all over my body. What was lying in ambush for me? Illness? Failures?

"What else is written in them?"

Victoria read my eyes as if she were reading a crystal ball, tea leaves, tarot cards.

"Why are you so distant?"

"From whom?"

"In general…"

"What do you see?"

"You are at a crossroads," she said.

Which frightened me: the truth.

"Between what and what?"

Victoria plunged into the depths of my eyes.

"On the one hand… I see a large chamber… full of light… like a palace… and in it a long table, set for a banquet…"

God!—I cried within, like one bedazzled—she's a sorceress! A seer! A witch! Why, it's the hall I described in the twenty-three pages of the book I had begun to write!

"And on the other hand…" I asked, fearfully.

"On the other hand…an alley, at the end of the alley a tall tree and in it a bird's nest. A black bird."

I stared at her like one in shock. What is the alley? Who is the black bird?

"Which must I choose?" I asked, trembling.

"Shall a man choose a black bird when a chamber filled with light lies before him?" She smiled at me with brilliant eyes.

I did not take my gaze from her eyes. If she has the gift of looking into the unknown—I said to myself—and the power to see the future, she must tell me plainly: Shall I continue the book I began, or not? Will I succeed, or not?

"Will I succeed?" I asked.

"Give me your hand," she said.

I extended my hand to her. She grasped it, set it down on her thigh (the margins of the robe had spread open, and the thigh was naked and warm), and read my palm. Passing her fingertip along the criss-crossing lines, she said:

"These little ones are the obstacles in your path. Your doubts. Geminis always have a lot of doubts. Everything is double for them.

And you are double, too. You are yourself and you are also not yourself. Someone else. And those two crosses, they're the temptations. The crossroads, like I told you when I looked in your eyes. But the line of destiny, you see, overcomes them and ascends the hill of the moon. You are very sensual, I see. It gets as far as this summit surrounded by a halo. This is the halo of glory. You will have tremendous success!" She pressed my hand warmly against her thigh.

I was so grateful to her that I put my other hand on top of her hand, and I, too, pressed warmly on her thigh.

At the same moment the portals of the blue robe flew apart, like the opening of the gates of Eden, and all the hidden glories flowed towards me, leapt upon me, as she fell on my neck, pressed herself against me, and embraced me.

No, this time I could no longer withstand the temptation. Can a man take fire in his bosom, and his clothes not be burned?

All my fears melted, evaporated. What do I care about the police? What do I care about a husband's revenge—"For the goodman is not at home, he is gone a long journey"—encircled by those burning arms, pressed against this blazing bosom of Potiphar's wife—

And only because I do not wish to sully my pen—which might have been alright in the case of a book like *Gargantua and Pantagruel,* the author of which chose to devote it to drunkards and fools, but not in the case of a work dedicated to the most elevated spheres of Literature—shall I refrain from describing the impassioned scene which ensued on Victoria Azoulai's green plush sofa.

Especially since the portrait of Maimonides gazed down upon us from the wall.

Chapter twenty

Verse Epistle

The following morning I found an envelope in my mailbox, in which there was a sheet of pink paper with these lines of verse upon it:

When Mr. "N" arrived
We greeted him with a smile:
Intelligent, learned and wise,
And trustworthy-looking besides.

For all of us deeply respect
A trained, diligent intellect,
At university lecturing adept,
Who writes great critical texts.

But barely a fortnight went by
Till we saw we'd been wrong, and sighed:
The man is two-faced and sly,
Hating animals and humans alike.

He's really conceited and proud
Having thrown true learning out,
For in the Bible are written these words:
Be humble and trust in the Lord.

He won't speak to us common folk,
With "peasants" he won't get too close.
He holds himself rigid as an oak,
A peacock who looks down his nose.
And if this wasn't all bad enough,
His manners are terrible stuff:
The Professor so "fine" and aloof
Wants the rabbits removed from the roof!

The Tenants' By-Laws he defies,
And the maintenance fees he denies,
Though my language may not be alright,
I must say he's a big "Parasite"!

So listen Professor, oh list!
You'd better take heed now of this:
If our rules you don't cease to resist—
We will soon spit you out of our midst!

By Victoria Azoulai

Chapter twenty-one

Dream

When I woke up, I remembered the dream:

I am lying in a dim cave near Tiberias, on bat droppings. And suddenly at its entrance, through which the light of day was breaking, a maiden in a long white dress appears, with an unfurled scroll in her hand. I rise slightly and attempt to read what is written on the scroll, but see to my amazement that all the letters are eyes. Eyes glittering like fire. I am afraid to stand up, but the maiden standing before me smiles and says: "Come, wingèd Elisha." I know that it's Lili, and I'm surprised that she calls me "wingèd Elisha," because she knows me. I get up, wanting to approach her, but at that very moment I hear a voice shrieking above my head in Aramaic: "Genius, genius, were I not so abashed…" I look up and see that it is an owl perched on a protrusion of the rockface who was shrieking. I blurt out: "What?" And he hoots: "*Dictum sapienti sat est.*" And laughs. I become alarmed and ask myself what he was saying. Was he bringing me citations from Maimonides' *Guide for the Perplexed*? The owl laughs again and hoots: "The dove's wing and the whore's thing!" and at the same moment the maiden drops the scroll to the ground, approaches me with arms outstretched, and as she touches my shoulders she says in a soft and lilting voice: "My beloved from Romania, come to Degania." I say: "Lili, but you..." and she says, "Why dost thou call me Lili, for I am Naomi..."

I replay this dream over and over, and I say to myself: this is a dream about falling. I fell to the second floor, instead of rising to the fourth. I fell into a dim cave near Tiberias, instead of climbing to the beautiful vistas of Degania. I fell into the trap set for me by the serving maid, instead of rising to the majestic dwelling of the Queen.

Chapter twenty-two

My Life with Lili (2)

When I look back at the two years of my marriage to Lili Federman, I see a sort of arid, rocky plain swept from time to time by tempestuous thunderstorms. Indeed, those two years unfolded between long, thunderous silences, and short, even more thunderous quarrels.

Although, as I have already related, the dizzying vision of happiness that had turned my head quickly revealed itself to be a false enchantment—as though I had wakened to find Leah rather than Rachel at my side—one good thing, at least, did come out of that marriage: I quit my job as a proofreader on the night shift at the newspaper, and my time was my own, to do with as I pleased. Though Lili's tiny salary from Steimatzky's bookstore was not enough to support us, I made enough from periodic translation jobs, on which I didn't waste more than two or three hours a day, to make up the difference. The remaining hours were devoted to my writing.

I wrote in the morning, I wrote at night. And this was the bitter root of the quarrels and strife between us. All I wanted was to write! To write! Lili's wants were...she wanted other things. Conflicting wants in a family bring about family disagreements, as the sexologists and sociologists have already discovered in their deep studies and have made public in their research reports.

During the first weeks of our marriage I would go at noontime to the bookstore and wait for Lili until she finished her work, in order to have lunch with her at one of the nearby cafés. But I quickly stopped doing that. Envy was what expelled me from there: I would walk up and down between the rows of books, picking up this book and that, pretending to browse through them, but my eye would always sidle over to have a look at what other people were browsing through...what they wanted to buy... And in despairing low spirits I took note of the bitter fact that not one single time—not one single time on any of those days that I went in there and stood in the store for half an hour or more!—did anyone ask for my book. And this, despite the fact that Lili had displayed *Green Windows* in a prominent, "preferred" place! My eye would count the number of copies of my book lying on the shelf, and with a breaking heart I would discover that their number was the same as it had been a week before, two weeks before—not one was gone. Oh, the sharp and poignant tortures of jealousy, which pricked my flesh like pins. I'd stand by the sales desk, a book open in my hands, and to my left or to my right would stand a girl—a student, or soldier, or teacher, or development town librarian, or (judging from her shorts and tanned legs) someone who had just come in from the Negev. She would open a book, another book, leaf through it, read, turn a page; pause there, a blush blooming in her cheek... Yes, my tracking, dissecting, envious gaze followed inquisitively—an inquisitiveness that was even "literary" to some extent—the expressions on the faces of those girls as they stood there like that, with their legs spread a bit apart, or with their legs crossed, and the book open before their eyes, near their faces; at one with it, making love with it—illicit love! As if the book hiding their faces drew a curtain between them and the public domain, and in this hidden corner they took as their own, they came into intimate union—which has a whiff of adultery about it, I would say, and it's no wonder that they blush!—with...with the author himself, it would seem! Yes, I will never forget the elation I felt—greater than any I had ever felt upon reading a rave review of one of my stories—when one day, as I walked along the beach, I noticed a long-legged woman with wet yellow hair stretched out on a lounge chair with a book opened in front of her eyes. I walked past her to see who she was, with her perfect Venus legs and lo! how my face brightened, how my heart palpitated, as before my eyes appeared the green letters on the white cover, *Green Windows*! I said to myself, conquering my swelling pride: if a beautiful girl like that reads my book at the beach…

But here, in this large shop, with its hundreds of books—not a one! "You should be proud of that," Lili consoled me on our way from Steimatzky's to the coffee house. "*Green Windows* wasn't meant to be a popular book! It's intended for an élite audience! It's esoteric! This just proves its quality!"

I laughed, I raged. I said that not only "cheap" books became best-sellers; so did "quality" books. I mentioned some great names. "It took them years until they became best-sellers!" Lili hooked her arm through mine. "You'll see, in another two or three years…"

I stopped coming to the store. Out of sight, out of mind, as they say. The blessing my friend Michael had bestowed upon me at the wedding reception—"Happy is the writer whose wife is a bookseller"—became a curse. For Lili's sales reports ("Today a teacher from Hertzliya came in and asked for your book"; "They called up from the Municipal High School in Bat Yam and asked if we had two copies"; "K., the Member of the Knesset, inquired about the book and promised to buy it") only served to remind me of how miserable my condition was. And instead of completely ignoring this matter, which is a terrible plague when you're in the middle of writing, it buzzed like a mosquito in my brain.

I also didn't go out much with Lili, and the reason for that—even though it's silly—was her height. My height is a meter 76, which is above average; but Lili's was one meter 83! Stork! Crane! Ostrich! Hugging her was like "going up to the palm tree… taking hold of the boughs thereof" and walking beside her meant walking in her shadow! When we walked together, I couldn't put my arm around her shoulder or her neck and if I put my arm around her waist, she would put her arm around my shoulders, and then I'd feel utterly ridiculous. And of course she always wore dresses that came down to her ankles, making her seem even taller than she was.

Ah, Lili's dresses. Her wardrobe. In the carved closet—the "antique" she had bought in the flea-market with Adam and Eve in the Garden of Eden engraved on its doors, two date palms and snakes twined around them—hung about thirty dresses, all of them long: plain white cotton dresses with no embroidery; black Bedouin dresses, battered and tattered, hippie dresses, laced at the waist and puffed at the cuff; dirndls, worn and shabby, torn and patched, polka-dot and paisley… I must admit that they all suited her well; her and the berets, blue, red, black and white that she wore angled across her head, with an insouciance that proclaimed a sort of self-mockery. I must admit that she attracted the attention of passersby in the street, or sitters-around in cafés, particularly when she went barefoot. But as far as I myself was concerned, it wasn't very pleasant. This wasn't how I had intended to become famous, as the consort of the crane "whose robe reacheth her ankles" as the Mishnah puts it.

Evenings I would sit in my study—the room in which I am sitting at this very moment—and write. Completing the surrealistic story sequence *Butterflies*. Lili would sit, her bare legs crossed in the lotus position, on the rug in the living room, or cradled in the puffy seating cushion, reading. Reading books in Hebrew, in English, that she would borrow from the store, and sometimes return, sometimes not. From "Modern Classics" to science fiction. The later it got, the more I sensed her impatience. Through the wall. She was jealous of the paper upon which I wrote, to which I granted the better part of my strength and valor. Through the wall I would sense how whilst her eyes bent over the book her ears were leaning towards me. Listening to the scratchings of my pen. Urging me to finish. At eleven-thirty or twelve she would get up and decide to go off to bed. To communicate her displeasure, her anger, her protest, she would set about making various noises: moving furniture, opening and slamming doors, banging aluminum and glass dishes and pans in the kitchen, running water in the sinks or the toilet. As I've mentioned, she had different wants than I did. To go out! To go out! To go out in the evenings to a club, a café, the theater, friends… I told her: Go out by yourself! I'm giving you permission!—She hadn't married me for that, she said. And when she blew up, she would accuse: "You're completely insensitive to other people! Horribly egocentric! I don't know how you can possibly write about human beings, when you're so absolutely out of touch with their feelings!" I wouldn't answer her. I would continue writing, redoubling my efforts to remain "out of touch". About six months after our wedding, she bought—with money that her father had given her—a television set. The set was a weapon of war. With a barrage from the television she would bombard my stronghold. Through the wall I would hear the quacking of the announcers, the chirping of the hit songs, the smashing, shooting and shouting of the police series, and the imbecilic laughter of the sitcoms. Pale, containing my fury so it would not burst its bounds, I would emerge from my room and request—in a calm manner that ate deeply into my spiritual reserves—that she turn down the volume. And with an ironic smile on her face, hinting of both schadenfreude and righteousness, she would step over to the set and turn it down about half-way. Back in my room, I could still hear it and I would try to calm down, concentrate, put myself "out of touch", write… Sometimes, when the noise got to be too much, I would get up, invade the living room, step straight up to the set and turn it off without saying a word. Then the volcano would erupt! The round earth's imagin'd corners trembled!

In retrospect I can't help but see that she did have something of a case. According to Exodus 21:10, a husband is legally responsible for his wife's "food, raiment, and duty of marriage." "Raiment" she took care of herself, expansively, and both of us took care of "food." As for her "duty of marriage," it was neglected, to tell the truth. I can't recall how many such "duties" per week Maimonides decrees as the obligation of a man whose trade is writing, but I—in whom sexual energy had been sublimated to spiritual energy, as the psychologists put it—limited myself to two: Tuesdays—about which it is twice written in Genesis "it was good"—and Saturday nights. Tuesday nights we would go out to a club, or the theater, or sometimes a movie—and then to bed; on Saturday nights we would go to visit friends—her friends, all of them—and when we came home, usually a little high, we would have ourselves a small orgy. But the lioness is not satisfied by crumbs. And because she was forced to bridle her passions, she became restless, edgy, angry.

So she did have a case. But behind her smiling, intelligent, pleasant facade—which sought to draw attention to itself even though she had not been blessed with beauty—was an overflowing cauldron of passions, of which the wildest and strongest was Envy. *Invidia*—in Latin. The second in the list of the seven deadly sins according to Catholic doctrine; those who commit it are doomed to Hell; and its primary offshoot is Suspicion.

Lili was envious and suspicious, and her envy and suspicion followed me around like bloodhounds sniffing my footprints. Things got so bad that not only would she interrogate me about every step I took outside the house, day or night, but she would also find some pretext to phone me from the bookstore every time I went to the French library to work on my translations, to make sure I was really there. This caused me a great deal of embarrassment, as the librarian had to leave her post at the desk and come over to call me to the phone. "Kalmi," I would hear Lili's caressing voice, free of any hint of suspicion. "Maybe you could stop at the store on your way home and pick up a few eggs. There isn't a single egg in the house…"— "Is it urgent?" I would whisper, so the librarian couldn't hear. "The shops are closed today in the afternoon, so if it's no bother for you…" Another day it would be that I mustn't forget to water the plants, or that I should draw some money from the bank, or that maybe I should get some tickets for a movie, or to tell me that she had gotten her period…

Jealousy caused suspicion, and suspicion led to wrath. *Ira* in Latin, the third of the seven deadly sins, the one of which it is said that it is "the pursuit of justice that has been perverted to the lust for revenge and ridicule." One day, about a year into our marriage, as I sat in the library looking in *Larousse* to find out the date of Diderot's meeting with Yekaterina the Great, Queen of Russia, I raised my eyes from the book, and there stood Lili before my eyes! She was in her "raggedy" dress, the faded blue one, with four square patches below the hips, front and back.

"Surprised?" She sat down in the chair next to mine. Yes, I was very surprised.

"Am I disturbing you?" She looked around the reading room.

"No... How come... In the middle of work..."

"I took off for half an hour. I'm sick of it." She took her long cigarette holder out of the pocket of her dress and fitted a cigarette into its end.

"Smoking's not allowed here," I whispered.

"It's no big deal," she said, and lit up. I pulled the cigarette out of the holder and squashed it into the saucer of paper-clips. She reddened. She looked around, directing her gaze at the people sitting reading books, rested it for a moment on the librarian by the central desk, got up and left without saying a word.

In the evening, as we sat down to eat, Lili said: "I see that my unexpected visit to the library totally embarrassed you!"

"Embarrassed?" I grinned.

"Totally upset your equilibrium!"

"Really? I didn't notice..."

Suddenly, without warning, her voice climbed to a high octave: "Don't you dare humiliate me in front of your Parisian whore! Ever!"

"What whore?" I asked, astounded.

"Don't you dare grab my cigarette from me in front of that fat whore just to show her how much you don't care about me! Walking all over me like that!"

I was so shocked that I was bereft of speech. I took the knife and commenced to slice the bread.

"Now I understand why you run off to the library so cheerfully! To screw that fat bitch who's so crazy about you, right?"

A pale smile played across my face. This Marcelle, the librarian, the "fat bitch," was the mother of three or four children and had a face like *la vache qui rit* and such bloated biceps that only a person dazzled by blinding jealousy could possibly imagine that I would take her in my arms.

"Right? Tell me! I'm asking you! Answer me!!!" shrieked Lili.

"Don't yell so much." I pointed the knife up at the ceiling, to indicate Dr. Klausner's apartment, where everything could be heard.

"MURRRderer!" she screamed. "You want to kill me with that knife! Cut my throat! So I won't bother you!"

"Stop shouting! Right now!" I grabbed her arm.

"If not—you'll kill me." She grabbed my other hand, the one holding the knife, and tried to force it away from me. "This is what you've been plotting all along. Murder!"

I set the knife down and left the house with a forceful slam of the door.

Lili opened the door and yelled in a voice that filled the entire stairwell: "Don't you dare come back! You hear? Killer!"

From that night on, I started leaving the house at night, very frequently. At about half past twelve, when I tired of writing, and Lili was already in bed, I would go down to the bar on the next street, sit there for an hour, an hour and a half, drink, and go home.

The neighbors—particularly Dr. Klausner—didn't get much sleep during that period of their lives. At two in the morning they would be awakened by screams.

Poor Lili! Now, as I write about her from a distance in time and space, I feel sorry for her. A person who cannot control her demons must herself be controlled by an evil demon. And she was controlled by an evil demon born of the deprivations Nature had visited upon her. Her excessive height, her pale lashes, the redness around her eyes, her somewhat wide mouth, her flat chest…a passionate temperament that was never satisfied… At the end of a quarrel she would moan like a little girl from her feelings of regret and self-despair. She would curl up on the sofa or on the rug, like a fetus in its mother's womb, and cry and cry…

Sometimes, when she calmed down a bit after a volcanic outburst like that, she would say with a bitter smile: "You're using this, right? In your next story. It's all material for you, isn't it?... Okay, it's okay with me. That's the inhuman side of you."

And she found some respite—from the clashes with me, with herself—in a new occupation: making rag dolls. In the evenings, as I sat in my room and wrote, she—when she got tired of reading—would sit on the floor, in the midst of a small ocean of different colored rags—scraps of fabric she would get from a seamstress who lived on our street—cut them with scissors, fold, baste, tie, sew... Those dolls were touching in appearance: they were all very tiny, and they were all like poor servants, submissive and sad. Their arms were always close to their body, as if tied to it, their shoulders were bent, they wore peasant kerchiefs on their heads, and their eyes—two short, angled stitches—looked like they were crying. Eventually she lined them up in rows on the sideboard, the windowsill, and hung a few of them up on the walls.

In the seventh month of the second year of our marriage Lili decided that I was in love with Ariella Klinger.

She decided that one day, at noontime, on her way home from Steimatzky's after she saw me sitting with Ariella in a café on Dizengoff Street.

She sat down beside us, ordered a large dish of ice cream, and from the moment she started licking it off the spoon until the moment she finished it, she didn't say a word. To Ariella's questions she answered "Yes" and "No" without further amplification.

After we rose to leave, when we were a few steps away from the café, she said: "You're in love with her, aren't you?" I laughed. I dispensed with Ariella in a few words of condescension and contempt. Lili didn't believe a single syllable.

Here I must say something about the poet Ariella Klinger. Although most readers of this book have probably read her work, or at least heard of her, I am sure that very few have actually seen her. She doesn't go out much in public. She does not belong to any of the literary cliques, and usually stays at home. I respect her poems, which have in them a certain demonic power, although I don't understand most of them; I respect her intelligence—something to which anyone who spends even half an hour in her company could bear witness; but I am incapable of falling in love with her.

The reason? Something affected, artificial—should I say "theatrical"?—in her movements, in the timbre of her voice... nuances...how can I describe it? For example, her hair is long and black, parted in the middle, falling in two cascades on either side of her face. The right cascade frequently conceals her right eye. And as she sat there opposite me, she would raise her right hand, in a slow, elegant, gesture, to draw the hair back away from her eye, the way one draws open a curtain, and at the same time she would toss her head upwards and sideways. I did not like this gesture. It was unpleasantly arrogant. It was as though it proclaimed: This is how I am! On purpose! Or, when she talks (in a low voice, husky from smoking) she accompanies her words with arching gestures of her open palms, her fingers spread wide apart; she passes her hand in front of her face, in slow circles, as if she were putting a spell on them, or on you, and sometimes she enlists her other hand, its fingers also spread wide apart, and with both of them she executes a *port de bras* as it's called in ballet—a gesture which sort of explained in a picturesque fashion what she wanted to say. These gestures turned me off. Or in the midst of speaking, for no apparent reason, she would change her husky, low voice, shimmering with secrets, to a clear and solemn alto, high and filled with pathos... Or when she got up from her chair, she'd give you a cold and penetrating look, very mysterious, as if to say: There are things, my friend, in heaven and earth more profound than the depths and darker than black night, but I know them, I know...and then she would take leave of you without saying good-bye, without a smile, moving off with proud steps towards "the garden of dark secrets..." Oh, how could I fall in love with a woman like that?

But Lili had decided I was in love with her, and no protests could budge her from her conviction.

And upon that rock, the ship of our marriage was wrecked, and swept away by stormy waves.

One night I returned home even later than usual, at half past three in the morning. In the bar where I was a "regular," I had met a tourist from France, who wrote about films for *L'Express*—a thin, delightful woman tanned by the sun of the Club Mediteranée. We drank, we talked about Goddard and Ajar and Jouvet and Genet, we drank some more, and joked, I about Lyon, she about Eilat, I walked her to the entrance of her hotel, we kissed like friends, we smiled at one another as if we knew that this encounter would lead to no more than a pleasant memory.

Lili had not gone to bed. The lights were on in the apartment, and she sat cross-legged on the rug in the living-room in her nightgown, a book lying open in front of her.

As I stood in the doorway of the room she said:

"Were you with Ariella?"

My head was spinning a bit. Both from the drink and from the encounter with the Frenchwoman, whose scent—a mixture of light perfume and the smell of the salt sea—remained with me.

"Yes!" I said boldly.

"You fucked her?" She looked at me with burning eyes.

I was shocked. I am not a puritan in matters of language—I've even translated several plays about adultery that were full of obscenities—but every time I hear a woman pronounce that explicit verb, my ears ring.

"Yes!" I said, after some hesitation.

Lili got up from where she was sitting and went into the bedroom. I fell into the armchair, awaiting a delayed eruption of the volcano.

About ten minutes later, Lili came out of the bedroom with her suitcase in her hand. She set the suitcase down by the front door, and with firm steps walked towards me and slapped me across the face four times with both hands, left, right, left, right, until my head buzzed.

Then I heard the door slam hard, a slam that shook the foundations of the universe.

And that was the end of our marriage. An end based on a mistake, just as its beginning had been based on a mistake.

Chapter twenty-three

Yvette

Yvette was so subtle that when she spoke about Mallarmé it would seem as though she were doing her nails. She knew the poems of Saint Jean de la Croix by heart. She was in love with him. And I was jealous.

But she studied biology. Because the study of literature was, in her opinion, "wasteful, if not corrupt."

She never let me "know" her in the Biblical sense. For seven months—almost the entire first academic year—we saw each other, and not even once. She guarded her purity from me. Because "to be too happy is to sin."

"Sin?" I would say between kisses.

"Yes. Sin, sin!"

On summer evenings we would climb the road that wound its way up the Fourvière, the mountain overlooking the old quarter of the city. We would sit on a bench in the pine grove at its summit and look down from above on the city, on the two rivers that cross it, the Rhône and the Saône, on the bridges, on the twinkling lights. Stars would fall and dissolve on their way to the river. Yvette would melt into my arms. The scent of her kisses was the scent of geraniums, and they tasted of hot blood. She was so fragile that I was very careful when I embraced her, for fear she might crumble. She loved me, and she loved God, and the saints, and the meditations of the spirit. She would lay her head upon my knees, and as I gently massaged her small, firm breasts, she would suddenly sit up and say: "But nevertheless, Pascal was not right about one thing: casuistry is not the purification of sin…"

Her father, who owned a shop for musical instruments in the center of town—"Berlioz"—was an enthusiastic supporter of the Jesuit Society.

Whenever we were locked in an intoxicating kiss, and I, unable to overcome my passions, would stroke her knee with my hand and gather courage to explore from the thigh up, beneath the hem of her dress—she would straighten up all at once, put her dress in order, and say, while smoothing back my hair, "Let us go inside, *mon amour*."

"Go inside" meant: into the church behind us, Notre Dame de Fourvière, upon the turret of which gleamed the Madonna adorned with a golden crown, looking out over the city spread below.

I would follow her, my one hand in my pocket to suppress my sinful passion so that it would not thrust itself into the field of vision of the Holy Virgin in the vault of the altar.

The vast church was empty at that hour. The dim light of crystal chandeliers and wax candles flickered in front of the altar. Gilded mosaic images of the evangelists and the saints looked down from the walls all around and from the huge dome of the ceiling. Yvette sat with her hands clasped in her lap and her eyes closed in heavenly peace. I lowered my head. I hated that church, the smell of incense and wax, the gilded haloes around the heads of the saints, one of which, I imagined, would shortly fly from its place and hover about the head of my beloved.

Once she told me that she had dreamt about my father:

She saw him running in a field, among red flowers, on "Mount Zion," alarmed, as if he were being pursued, and suddenly his strength gave out and he fell. He lay there on his back upon the carpet of red flowers, his mouth open as if to scream. But he was mute. At the edge of the field rose a very high crucifix, with a serpent wound around it. She wanted to tell him: Look up! Look up!—but she awakened.

Were it not for the snake, I would have thought she made up that dream. To hint that I should get rid of the barrier between us.

Her beauty was godly in my eyes. Her temples were so transparent that bluish veins were visible running through them. The amber clarity of twilight suffused her face, like the mysterious glow that penetrated the stained glass windows high in the cathedral. At the university, during lectures on Stendhal, I would imagine that I, like Julien Sorel, was climbing the ladder to her room, to her bed. My testicles ached.

At the end of the academic year, she told me that she was going to Normandy, that we would not see each other any more. "This is our fate, *mon amour,*" she said sadly.

We sat in Simone's small café, in the old quarter of the city, by the window. A thin rain sprinkled the cobbles of the street. We were alone in the café, and Yvette held my hand between her two—limp, pitying—hands, lying on the heavy, countrified wooden table. She gazed into my eyes with a yearning, consoling look, and was silent. That pure clarity radiating from her eyes was difficult to resist. I stretched my hand out to the thick book lying beside her elbow. I opened it in its middle, and on both pages were drawings of enlarged sea-algae cells. Sort of blurry ink-blots, blue, green and purple, surrounded by interlaced circles. With my finger I pointed out what was written at the bottom of the page: Symbiosis. Yvette smiled and shut the book without even looking at it. "You will forget," she said. "The strong sunlight of your country will erase it all." I looked away from her. Beyond the weeping window I could see the small square, with a well in its center, and the walls of the gloomy cathedral, Saint Jean-Baptiste. Two women walked arm in arm under one umbrella, skipping over the puddles. One of them slipped and stumbled on a stone, and her friend helped her up. They both laughed, and a small smile escaped me too. On the walls hung two busts of soldiers, and on wooden panels mottoes were engraved in burnt letters. Yvette said: "Next year… You will live again in the little room on the *rue*

Sala?" I said to her: "I dreamt about you last night." And I told her my dream:

Huge, two-dimensional fish—sort of colorful cardboard fish, with peculiar fins—slowly descended from the sky with small children riding on them. The fish and their riders floated downwards, and the fish, standing on their fins, arranged themselves in single file and were tied to one another. A little girl in a long white dress held a rope that came out of the mouth of the first fish and led the caravan. As the caravan approached me, I saw that the little girl was she. I called: Yvette! Yvette!—but the girl stepped proudly forward, looking straight ahead, and paid no attention to me. I gazed sadly after the departing caravan, until the girl's feet waded into the blue sea.

Tears shone in Yvette's eyes. Her two graceful hands pressed mine. She said: "I shall be devoured by longings."

"Shall we go?" I said.

Yvette gathered up her purse.

A very fine rain fell. I had an umbrella and she had a blue plastic coat with a hood. She linked her arm through mine and—just as they had so many times before—our footsteps rang out in two voices on the cobbles of the narrow street: the beat of my rhythmic steps, and the faster tapping of her sharp heels.

Until this very day, when I recall those two voices of our footsteps on the paving stones of the old quarter of Lyon, my heart flutters in my breast.

On either side were small shops, and in their windows were embroidered dresses, jewelry, religious objects, images and statues, antique clocks, books, flowers.

"Shall we go up?"

"Up" was the Fourvière. The pine grove, the bench, the church.

When we reached the *rue du Boeuf,* before the turn up to the mountain, I stopped. I said: "No."

I didn't want a farewell ceremony. No farewell ceremony before the statue of the holy virgin.

Her eyes opened wide in astonishment.

Her face was wet from the rain.

"I'll walk you to the bus," I said.

We retraced our steps. When we passed the jewelry store I stopped again. I walked back two steps and guided her inside.

I asked for a thin gold chain with a golden cross.

Yvette pulled me aside and whispered: "I don't want it. I won't take it. No."

"A parting gift," I said. "Permit me."

She looked at me for a long moment, then said: "Yes. But only with a fish."

The sales clerk rummaged in her boxes, looking for a chain with a fish pendant, but didn't find one.

Yvette looked from the clerk to me, from me to the clerk, and back at me.

Then, with a smile, tears glistening in her eyes, she placed a consoling hand on my sleeve, and said: "*Au revoir, mon cheri.*"

And walked out of the shop.

I watched her walk away, almost at a run, until she disappeared around the corner.

Thus we parted.

Chapter twenty-four

War of Attrition

From keystroke to keystroke and line to line Schatz's typewriter rats and tats above my head. Line, ping, another line, ping—the masterpiece of Hebrew aesthetics winds its way towards completion, industriously, perseveringly. It has already undoubtedly reached page three hundred—

I—my hand is paralyzed. Soon my right hand shall wither. The twenty-three pages of the book I had started lie there in the drawer, growing moldy, it seems. When I take them out, I gaze at them with great pity and am unable even to complete the sentence that has been stopped in its middle. Even when the typewriter is silent, I cannot write. If there is no voice—there is a seeing eye. Anything I write would be photographed by its lens—in inverted letters. If two songbirds will not sing on the same branch, as they say, then certainly two penbirds cannot live in the same house.

Every time I think about how he invaded my house and conquered it, how he silenced me in the midst of my labor—my blood boils. The hutzpah! The nerve! A stranger comes to dwell in the land, and possesses it.

For hours I would sit and plot strategies to make him go away, get out, leave the house forever. And when I couldn't come up with any plan, I would conjure up an accident for him. So many people get killed in car crashes in this country—I would tell myself—about a thousand a year. Why shouldn't he be one of them? Why should others perish—better and more honest than he, among them infants who have done ill to no man—and not he? Why is he so fortunate? Look, he's crossing the main road on his way home, striding along erect, briefcase in hand, eyes front, completely unaware of the car turning in swiftly and sharply from the left—for his mind is fully occupied with the next paragraph of his composition on Hebrew aesthetics, going over a sentence he has been thinking about for several hours already, for instance about the dialectic between the continuum of chronological time and semantic time—and all of a sudden… the awful scream…

Tears well in my eyes as I see him lying crushed, bleeding, on the asphalt. The black briefcase, torn from his hand, gapes open on the road, some distance from him, pages fluttering out of it. Hebrew aesthetics. Beaten and bloody. People run up and crowd around him. Two of them, who know what they are doing, take the initiative and bend to check if he is still alive. His eyes are open, but frozen. His face has gone grey. They adjust his shoulders. Open his shirt. One of them crouches over him, places mouth on mouth, knee on chest, tries to give artificial respiration. The wail of the approaching ambulances makes the air shudder…

Tears well up in my eyes. So young, so gifted, in his prime. Forty. Less. What prompted him to choose an apartment in this particular building? If he hadn't lived here, he wouldn't have crossed this busy street on his way home. He could have lived many years longer, written many more books…

They put him on a stretcher. Rigid. They slide him into the ambulance like a loaf of bread into an oven. He departs to the wail of the siren. Disappears.

Then the funeral. In the afternoon. A big crowd, shocked by the tragedy, gathers in the courtyard of the morgue. His students, the two cliques, no boundaries between them, all intermingling, stooped and mourning. All differences forgotten. What worth are quarrels and strife in the face of death? Stricken with sorrow they all whisper praise of the dead man. Hush. "Akiva Ben Mahalalel says: Look upon three things and thou will come not to sin. Know whence thou comest and whither thou goest, and before whom..." —Is that Naomi over there sobbing behind the black veil? I strangle on my own tears— "Justice goeth before him..." The black-garbed beadles walk ahead of the coffin.

At the graveside, after he is buried, I am asked to eulogize him. I, who was his neighbor, the person closest to him. Room beneath room. In a hoarse, choking voice, I speak: A genius is gone from our midst. A renaissance man. A researcher and critic of sharp mind and brilliant pen. A diligent, dedicated scholar who spent both night and day in research and writing, and knew no rest. His two books opened new horizons to our literature and changed its entire course. They gave us criteria to judge between the good and the bad, the excellent and the trivial. He was the conscience and the compass of our literature, the guardian standing watch and the teacher showing the way. It is difficult to imagine how writers of poetry and fiction could have written their books without this pillar of fire that went before them. It is difficult to imagine how readers of books could have understood what they read without this great light that illuminated for them not only the lines themselves, but also between the lines. Before his time this man is dead and his writing is broken off in the middle. He had yet another book...

The entire eulogy runs through my mind as I sit in my room and listen for sounds beyond the walls, above the ceiling. Yes, today the accident happened, I tell myself. Because it is silent in the apartment. Because it is already six-thirty and his tread has not yet been heard on the staircase. Tomorrow the funeral will take place. At three in the afternoon. Who will support Naomi as she walks behind the coffin? Has she brothers? Father and mother?

But at a quarter past seven I hear the familiar footsteps ascending. He has risen from the dead. And after them, the thumps of the opening and closing door. And at nine the machine is already firing away.

Or suicide, I say to myself on another day. Why shouldn't he commit suicide, for example? Is there nothing bothering him? Driving him to despair? Hasn't he any guilt feelings? Fears from which there is no escape? Paranoia? Hypochondria?... And if not in his personal life—doesn't he feel the hopelessness of the human condition? Or the Jewish condition, ours? After all, he's a thinking man, highly intelligent! And there's not a sensible and sensitive man in the world who isn't stricken from time to time by thoughts of suicide! Of course most people hang back, stop short of carrying them out—but there are easy ways, painless, forty sleeping pills, for example...

But no!—I castigate myself disparagingly. A person like him wouldn't commit suicide! He? Sensitive? He's got the hide of an elephant! Thick-skinned! Not a chance!

One evening, as I sat in my room, paralyzed, hatred swelling within me, furious, helpless, helpless against the machine firing barrage after barrage above my head, each letter embossed by it like the pecking of the beak of a bird of prey in my flesh, an idea flashed through my mind—

An eye for an eye. A tooth for a tooth. A barrage for a barrage.

I got up, went to the living-room, opened the telephone book, found the number of the late Dr. Klausner—

Yes. I know: not to my credit. Hooligans and thugs do that. But it's a matter of life and death for me! My right to write is at stake! No moralistic pussy-footing for me at such times of mortal peril!

I dialed the number. I heard the double barrage of rings. Brring-BRRING. Brring-BRRING. Someone picked up the receiver on the other end. It was Naomi's voice: "Hallo?" And again: "Hallo?" And then: "Who is it?"

I remained silent. I waited. The typewriter went silent too. It was eleven o'clock. I tried to visualize her. Was she in bed? In a transparent nightgown? The tanned shoulders glowing under the light of the small lamp?

The receiver was returned to its place. The typewriter continued its rat-tat.

So I missed. Upon the pretext of silencing the source of fire, I had hit an innocent civilian.

I waited five minutes. I dialed again.

Again the receiver was picked up. Again I heard Naomi's pleasant, tired voice : "Hallo... hallo...who is it?" I felt her breath on my face.

Again the typewriter went silent; and after the receiver was back in its cradle, it renewed its industrious racing.

I waited a quarter of an hour.

I said to myself: If I bombard every fifteen minutes—he has to stop. A person can't write if non-stop ringing cuts off his flow of thought.

When the receiver was picked up for the third time—after six or seven rounds of ringing—it was Schatz's angry voice on the telephone: "Hallo!... Hallo!... Who is that??!"

In the background Naomi's sleepy voice could be heard: "Somebody got the wrong number, apparently."

"Why doesn't he answer, if that's the case?" said Schatz. And into the mouthpiece of the receiver, angrily: "What number do you want?" And after waiting another minute he flung the receiver back into its resting place.

And went back to work. To his night shift. With redoubled zeal.

I don't know where Schatz served in the army, or if he ever served, but I myself was in the Artillery Corps. During the War of Attrition—the one that took so many lives on either side of the Suez Canal—when I was called to reserve duty I was sent to the "Mafreket" outpost. The shellings, both from our side and the Egyptians', were sporadic: never at set times, never at regular intervals, never during the course of an entire day, and never at the same targets. That was the most dumbfounding thing, the most frightening: the element of surprise, with respect to both time and place. Suddenly, at ten in the morning, or at three in the afternoon, the shell would explode with a tremendous bang, spraying great showers of sand and stones not ten meters from where you stood—if you were lucky—and for a moment you would be coated in dust, with your head, wearing its helmet, planted in the ground. Suddenly, at midnight, the bunker where you had lain for the night was shaken, and you were surprised to see a wall of concrete and earth collapsing completely, burying beneath itself several of your friends who are screaming and groaning among the ruins. Or, sometimes, for four hours straight the shells would whistle and hit and explode all around you and you could not raise your head from the trench into which you had fled by the skin of your teeth. And afterwards—no one knew why—two days of respite. All the guns were still.

I waited for about two hours. At 1:15 a.m. I dialed again.

I heard two bursts of ringing, and the receiver across the border was lifted. No one spoke, nor was it hung up.

For ten minutes or so I held the receiver to my ear, and then let it be.

When I debriefed myself on this experimental, truncated barrage, I came to the conclusion that although its results were limited, in general the "*Konzeptsia*"—to use a term that had been popular during the War of Attrition—had proven itself. If I kept it up, the annoyances would so disturb Schatz's "daily routine"—that is to say his writing, his output—that he would be forced to find a solution, whether temporary or permanent, beyond the boundaries of the apartment, which would become a trap for him; that is, unless he decided to disconnect the telephone altogether. The risk I took—that he would get on my trail—was minimal, because even if he were to say to himself that this was a calculated attack by someone who hated him, there are lots of people who hate him—as Naomi said in our conversation—and it was inconceivable that he would suspect that there was an enemy within. Within the building, that is.

The following evening I renewed the barrage. Five times I rang, between the hours of 9 p.m. and 1 a.m. The first two times Naomi answered. The third time Schatz answered and threatened: "I'm warning you! If you don't cut it out, I'll call the police!" But in the background I heard Naomi's voice: "Maybe it's out of order… It happened to my mother once…" The last two times, the receiver was not picked up at all, but since I kept my own receiver in my hand for five minutes each time, until I got tired of it, the rat-a-tat of the typewriter ceased for a full two times six—that is, twelve—minutes.

I said to myself: even if the pauses in the operation of the machine are short at the moment, if I persist in these annoyances, he'll lose his mind in the end. He won't be able to stand it.

On the third night, my first call was answered by Naomi. She asked softly: "Who is it?" and held onto the receiver. The typewriter stopped its noise. I too held onto the receiver... Only the light rustle—the atmosphere as it were, that always whispers in the earpiece, was heard, and beyond it I imagined I heard Naomi's breathing. I listened. I didn't think about Schatz, or about his typewriter, or about the desperate, grotesque battles I was undertaking. I stopped myself from whispering: Naomi... Listen to me... Get out of there... Get out of that prison... You will wither there...

It was she who hung up first.

When I called again I heard the busy signal. I tried four more times, the last of them at 2 a.m., and each time I got a busy signal. It seems they had caught on to the anonymous nuisance and had left the receiver off the hook.

I did not give up. On the fourth night, Naomi again answered my first call—this time at 10:30—again held on to the receiver, for a long moment. Why doesn't she hang up?—I wondered. Does she hope to hear the voice of the mystery man from the unseen end of the line? Will he convey an important message to her? Or perhaps she senses that it is I. It feels like a clandestine rendezvous between us. Without speech and without words. It is our souls that speak to one another. From afar I heard Schatz's voice: "Why don't you hang up? From the silence you won't be able to guess who it is..." She did not answer. I saw her smiling, listening with inquisitive pleasure to the light humming in the receiver. Is she sitting in the armchair? Lying down, her legs curled up, in bed, her head and arm on the pillow? "I told you," Schatz's voice was heard, "to hang up!" And, very muffled, after she had apparently covered the mouthpiece with her hand: "Do you want...whole evenings?... But..." and his voice from afar: "What call are you waiting for so late at night?" and the receiver was set down.

I called back just to feel her breath, her expectancy, her alert attention. But the receiver was lifted and hung back up at once; and when I called again, I was taunted by the busy signal.

When I returned to my battle station the following evening, I was no longer concerned with silencing the enemy position. That concern had been replaced by "forbidden games". The forbidden, secret games between me and Naomi. We had a covenant between us. A covenant of whispering silence. Waves of ether, flowing through the thin, concealed wire, are what transmit the secrets from me to her, from her to me, in a code that none save the two of us can decipher, in sessions, as the poet said, of sweet silent thought.

On the other end there was her anticipation. Expectancy, guessing. Gently the receiver was laid to rest. At once I dialed again, but was answered by the rapid, anxious busy signal.

And that whole evening I was prevented from renewing the connection.

I sat next to the stilled telephone and evaluated my position. "Debriefed" myself, as they say in the military: a man like Schatz, who has so many contacts with professors, teachers, students, who is a member of numerous committees, who negotiates with the editorial boards of newspapers and journals, and publishing houses—he can't possibly disconnect his telephone for whole evenings at a time. So what would he do? Would he call the police, as he threatened? Perhaps he has already filed a complaint about "nuisance calls"? Are the police able to pick up the trail of a stubborn nuisance?

I dialed 100, the police emergency number. I told the policewoman who answered my call that I've been annoyed by the telephone, for several evenings now, at various times, what should I do? —Report, sir, to the nearest police station and file a complaint, she said. Is there any chance they would be able to locate the nuisance caller?—I can't tell you, sir. They will get in touch with the telephone company, and will try, with its assistance, to identify the telephone from which the calls are being placed. Yes, they locate them sometimes.

I hung up and considered my next move. Yes, I was putting myself at risk. If I got caught, it would be a disgrace I could never shake. My shame would be known not only within the walls of the building, but would also be spread abroad. But Schatz hadn't gone to the police yet. If he had, he wouldn't have disconnected the phone, but would have kept me on the line as long as possible, maybe would even have spoken into the phone, spoken at length, to aid the police in locating me. I had to go on. There was a certain charm in this risk. In this provocation.

The next day, as I was opening my mailbox, Naomi came through the foyer and went to open her box. A wave of warmth swept over me, like after an evening of stolen lovemaking. Can she not tell from my face that it was I who had been sitting at the other end of the line? That it was I who had listened for long moments to her breathing?

I asked her what animals she had been photographing lately. "Dogs," she laughed. "City dogs. Poodles." Wasn't she planning any trips to the bosom of nature, to the countryside soon? Don't I wish! she said. She's sick of this city. What's so bad about it? I asked.—Ah! she sighed. And added: "There are nuts in this town." Nuts?— I wondered. "At two in the morning they call on the telephone, don't say who they are, don't answer. It's been like that for a few nights already. Just to drive a person crazy…" I stood there and commiserated. Did they suspect anyone in particular? "Naphtali has so many enemies," she smiled.

"Call the police!" I said.

"Yes, if it carries on, we'll have to do that, I'm afraid…"

That night I called once. At eleven. Two whole minutes our silence lingered.

I knew I would not continue.

I was defeated.

Schatz's typewriter kept up its industrious, insidious, incendiary rat-a-tat-tat.

Let him move to another apartment!—I hear the angry voice of the impatient reader—if he suffers so much, if he's "paralyzed" as he claims, why doesn't he move to a different building, instead of fighting ridiculous, hopeless wars?!

No, I absolutely could not do that!

First of all, it's a matter of honor. I was here first and he's the stranger in my midst! I have the rights of seniority and the rights of tenure. Why should I submit to this injustice and allow him to push me out?! Secondly, it's a matter of convenience. I am accustomed to my apartment, the building, the street, the trees, the neighbors, the cats, the grocer, the post office clerk, the laundry, the restaurant—why should I exchange them for another neighborhood where I don't know what awaits me? Thirdly, it's a matter of finances: moving to another apartment involves enormous expense—an agent's commission for selling this one, an agent's commission for buying the other one, Property Value Tax and all the other taxes, lawyers' fees for writing the contracts, fees for listing the transactions in the Land Registry, packing expenses, moving expenses, unpacking—why should I take all that upon myself, and where do I have the money for it?

Finally: what guarantee do I have that in the new building I wouldn't discover to my surprise, to my misfortune, above me or below me, in the apartment to my left or to my right—like one discovers a mouse or a rat in the pantry—some other rat-tat-tatting little critic? Who also fires away with tireless industry at his typewriter, from morning till night, or from night till morning? Who also radiates deadly stinking conceit all around him so it fills the staircase, the foyer and the courtyard? The odds that this could happen are fairly high: there are five universities in this country, and every year they release about five hundred critic cubs, who multiply like mice, gnawing at books and swallowing them, invading many buildings and nesting in apartments and holes…

I'm reminded of "*une anecdote*" that my mother used to read me back in Romania, when she drilled me in French:

A lodger at an inn asks the innkeeper to bring him something to eat, because he is hungry. The latter responds:

Il y a une souris dans le garde-manger. Que faut-il faire pour m'en débarrasser?

That is: There is a mouse in the pantry. What should be done to get rid of it?

Says the hungry lodger.

Fermez la porte et laissez la souris crever de faim!

Close the door and let the mouse starve to death!

Yes, like the mouse in the story, they too, the critics, will never starve to death. They will eat up all the delicacies in the pantry, and get fat.

Chapter twenty-five

The Ballad of the Empty Flat

The flat across from the critic's place is
Desolate, empty and bolted.
He stands and wonders in his own doorway
Whose is it? Does anyone own it?

Whene'er he faces that door all alone
So strangely our critic doth feel:
The sight of that threshold to no man's home
Makes him shiver from scalp to heel.

Its owner, a sailor, the rumor goes
Was lost at sea with his vessel.
Hath he no child? No kin? Who knows?
Is he a myth, perhaps, or a legend?

Sometimes he hurries past in great haste
And gets home all quaking inside.

When he sits down to write, think and erase,
The sailor's ghost slowly doth rise.

"Aroint thee hence thou spirit foul!"
The critic angrily cries.
"I cannot bear amorphous Doubt,
Nor thy shadowy presence abide!"

With a wave of his hand he chases the ghost
And the figure dissolves into air.
But sometimes at night, on the critic's way
  home
He meets the ghost right on the stairs.

This spirit blocks the critic's path
And voicelessly doth say:
"Thy probings have incurred my wrath!
The Truth thou shalt never assay!

"And if deepest secrets thou dar'st to probe
I'll pursue thee and take my revenge!"
Thus spake the ghost, breathing forth smoke
And vanished. A puzzle. The end.

Chapter twenty-six

Heinz Hollers

At six o'clock in the evening I was blasted from my chair by the sound of a terrible scream in the stairwell—"You'll pay, mister!!!"—and like an arrow from a bow I shot over to the peephole and screwed my eye to it.

The door of Heinz Hirsch's apartment was open. He stood on its threshold, pointing an accusing finger at Schatz, who stood pale and perplexed, briefcase in hand, on the landing between the two apartments.

"I don't know what you're talking about..." muttered Schatz.

"You'll find out!" roared Heinz. "You live in this building and you'll pay like any other tenant! Nobody else is obligated to clean up your dirt with their money! And I don't care whether you hate rabbits or love cats! We don't allow swine in here!"

"Sir, I don't know who you are..." mumbled Schatz.

"So now you'll know. Hirsch, *ja*? Beekeeper! Not professor! Beekeeper! A man who's never read a book in his life, *ja*? Not in English and not in German! But he's no parasite!!!" Heinz's voice rumbled through the entire building, so that all the neighbors' doors opened.

"Don't yell at me, alright?" Schatz took a step towards the stairs to the fourth floor.

"Don't you give us ultimatums!" Heinz crossed the threshold with his pointing finger leading the way. "And don't you threaten us! If I had been at that meeting, I would have thrown you out! Don't think that the fact that you're a professor gives you any special privileges. No special privileges! I've seen bigger professors than you in my life—and they were human beings."

"Tell it to the judge…" said Schatz with a feeble, pale smile as he stood on the stair.

"No judge! You'll pay! And today! Everything you owe!" Heinz called after him.

"And stop throwing cigarette butts in the hall!" Heinz's voice pursued Schatz as he went up the stairs without looking back.

"Professor! Literature!" Heinz slammed the door to his apartment, hard.

Chapter twenty-seven

Naomi Pays

The following morning, at a quarter to ten, just before I left for the library, my doorbell rang. When I opened the door—there stood Naomi.

"May I come in a moment?"

I showed her into my study, and she sat down on the edge of the armchair, like a neighbor who has dropped in for a visit.

"I'm not disturbing you?"

I wanted to tell her that her dropping in like this was a holiday to me. That she was like a ray of sunlight in the dullness of the room. I wanted to tell her that she found favor in my eyes, was beautiful in that sleeveless purple blouse with embroidery on the front, in her full, black skirt, beautiful in her sandals and the leather purse hanging from her shoulder, beautiful with her alert, green eyes and her brown face surrounded by its frame of black hair; that she looked to me like a young roe, like the gazelle of Ein Gedi…

"Listen… I heard the shouting last night, of that neighbor… Hirsch?"

"Yes, Heinz Hirsch."

"It doesn't matter whether he's right or not. Maybe he's right. At any rate, I'm sure he expressed the opinion of all the tenants in the building..."

"He exaggerated," I said. "He loses his temper. He exaggerated a little."

"Look," she opened the large leather purse hanging at her side. "I've brought the money and I want to give it to you."

"I'm not the treasurer..." I said.

"I know. Look..." She paused for a moment and looked at me like I was a conspirator worthy of trust. "Naphtali doesn't know about this. And he doesn't need to know about it... But I don't want there to be riots in this building because of us. I'd like to ask you to give this to Mrs. Azoulai"—she stretched five bills towards me—"and tell her..."

She thought for a moment.

"It doesn't matter what you tell her. Don't tell her anything. You got the money to cover Mr. Schatz's debt. Let her think whatever she wants."

I hesitated. I stammered: ""But the neighbors..."

"The neighbors won't have to add anything to what they pay."

"Not that..." I said, "but downstairs, in the entrance hall, there's a list. I'm sure you've seen it. Every tenant, after he's paid, they cross out his name. Cross him off. If your name doesn't get crossed off, the neighbors will keep thinking you haven't paid..."

"Let them cross it off. It doesn't matter. Naphtali never looks at that list." She laid the bills on the desk and put a book on top of them, so they wouldn't blow away.

"Alright?" she smiled.

I smiled.

"And forgive me for getting you involved in all this." She rose, and I rose with her. "I simply didn't have any alternative."

"That's okay," I said.

"Is this where you write?" She glanced around the room, at the bookshelves.

I couldn't say: No, this is the room where I *don't* write. For over two months now.

"Daumier?" Her gaze lingered on the drawing of Don Quixote, riding on a desiccated, starving Rosinante, all flesh and bones.

"Yes. Daumier."

"Like a hump." She pointed at the horse's protruding, skeletal back.

"A hollow hump," I noted.

"Yes," she laughed.

As I opened the door for her, I said: "If you ever need anything…"

She gave me a playful, twinkling smile, and turned to go down the stairs.

For a long time after that I sat in my study, flustered: Oh, Lily of the Valleys! My Dulcinea of Ein Harod!

Chapter twenty-eight

Ultimus Liber

The time has come for me to say something about the book I am not writing, for indeed the reader of this tale constantly asks himself—with justified skepticism: so this Schatz from the fourth floor is preventing our author from writing. What writing? What pearl of great price is lost to us when he doesn't write? And maybe he is pulling the wool over our eyes? Maybe his quiver is empty? And maybe it is better that he not write?

Alors, the idea I have been gestating for the past two years, inwardly elaborating and nourishing, nursing and nurturing, around which I have been weaving an extensive web in my imagination, is this:

To write the book to end all books. The *ultimus liber.* Something parallel to a "universal field theory" in physics. That is to say, a book after which it will be impossible to write any more books, for there will be nothing more to write. It will be both allegory and its interpretation. Thesis and antithesis. Signifier and signified. The deconstruction of itself and of literature per se. And it will include, to use Kant's phrase when he wrote his *Prolegomena to Any Future Metaphysic* (a title which in the original is no less than twelve words long: *Prolegomena zu einer jeden künftigen Metaphysik die als Wissenschaft wird auftreten können)*—all-possible-future-criticism-thereon-which-could-appear-whether–in-science-or-evaluation.

Ah, what insane ambition!—laughs the reader—what a megalomaniac goal!

But—let the reader take note:

Did not a similar dream of grandeur inspire Dante when he wrote *The Divine Comedy* in its three parts, which were intended to comprehend the universe and the fullness thereof, this world and the next, Paradise and Hell and all that lies between, earth and heaven and the celestial spheres, all crimes and all punishments, pure love and evil passions, past, present and future? Did not a similar idea stand before Goethe's eyes as he wrote *Faust*, in which Mephistopheles takes the weary scholar along with him on a "study tour", "to the narrow world, and then to the wide"? Or, if we approach our own day and age, did not Joyce play with the notion that it would no longer be possible to write books after *Finnegan's Wake*, because within it he had broken the bones of language and wrecked the ship of plot on the rocks, had contradicted as he constructed, and said everything that could be said about the world, thesis and antithesis in a single opus? Did not a similar vision drive the pen of Musil, whose Ulrich is "a man without qualities" who nonetheless includes within himself all possible human qualities, in whom many personalities inhere, who desires to "try everything and to have experienced everything," and whose story (of which I have read only the first 570 pages) is an ironic illumination of its time and simultaneously a supra-temporal philosophical treatise on existence and the universe?

Or what of Rabelais—whom I am now translating at a snail's pace?

In his preface to *Gargantua et Pantagruel* Rabelais compares his book to the 'Sileni'—those Greek apothecaries' boxes, to which Alcibiades, in the *Symposium*, compares Socrates—decorated on the outside with colorful, humorous pictures of musicians, satyrs, horned rabbits, saddled ducks, winged goats and the like, and filled with contents more valuable than gold: balm of Gilead, frankincense and myrrh, precious stones, ligure, agate and amethyst... Yes, Rabelais filled this book so that it would be all-embracing, which is why he called his heroes Pan-tagruel, Pan-urge, and so on—so that the book would include all branches of knowledge: the humanities and the natural sciences, theology and metaphysics, and all the vanities of this world, in France and in Rome and on all the imaginary islands—on the island of "Medamoti", on the Islands of "Tohu and Bohu", on the island of "Niphleseth", the island of "Ruach" (all of them Hebrew names, though garbled), and on the island of the Papefigues and the Papimanes, and so on and so forth. A book that is at one and the same time satire and encyclopedia, a parody of things and the things themselves, thesis and antithesis... Did not that farmer's son, physician and writer, believer and heretic, student and questioner, clown and blasphemer say to himself: now I am writing the one-and-only-book-that-is-beyond-comparison-and-that-supersedes-all-others?

Who can count the delusions of grandeur writers have had! Or their burning ambitions!

Flaubert, master craftsman of the detailed, complex and comprehensive plot, wrote to his mistress Louise Colet, when he was thirty-one and in the midst of writing *Madame Bovary,* that his dream was to write a book "about nothing"! "A book that would have almost no subject, or in which the subject would be almost invisible"! "The finest works," he wrote, "are those that contain the least matter."

And Faulkner—who goes on at such great length and gives such detailed descriptions in his stories—declared to cadets at West Point that his deepest desire was "to reduce all of his experience to a single word, if possible," "like the man who engraved the whole morning prayer on the head of a pin..."

Like clay in the hands of the potter—as he expands, he wishes to reduce.

Will it be thought sinful of me to hold such an ambitious aspiration—to write the book to end all books? An aspiration the value of which can be judged only by the success of its realization?

The book—which I had just begun to write, which doesn't even have a title yet, and which were it not for Schatz's cruel and brutal invasion of my territory would have been at least at its fiftieth page by now—was supposed to be more than a thousand pages long. Its plot—if I can use the term 'plot' for this tapestry of words that is an interlacing of a chronological sequence of events with the interpretation of that sequence, slices of life with philosophical musings, things-themselves and parodies of them, impartial reportage and satirical observation—all takes place during a single evening.

It is the eve of the Passover Seder. An evening on which twenty-two members of a family—not counting babies—from town and country, kibbutz and moshav, religious and non-religious, members of various professions holding various views, gather together at a house in Jerusalem to feast at the table of the aged patriarch, Amram Hacohen, who had come to the Land of Israel as a child, at the turn of the century. The book was to contain four parts and fourteen chapters, like the fourteen chapters of the Passover Haggadah. The chapters of the first part were *Kadesh, Urhatz, Karpas, Yahatz*—'Sanctification', 'Washing', 'Greens' and 'Splitting'; the second part was to consist of *Maggid, Rahtza, Motzi matza*—'Narration', 'Ablutions', 'Benediction on Matza'; in Part Three the chapters were to be *Maror, Korech, Shulhan Orech*—'Bitter Herbs', 'Combination', 'Laid Table'; and in the fourth and final part the chapters were to be *Tzafun, Barech, Hallel, Nirtza*—'The Concealed', 'Grace', 'Praise', 'Songs'. Each chapter was to differ from its fellows not only with respect to its contents—the events recounted therein—but also with respect to its spirit, its composition and its style. If the chapter 'Sanctification', for example, was to open in a thin and mysterious tone, with the whispering of the Ari's incantation "I will prepare the meal of the King on High" and the raising of the first glass, continuing in an idyllic and festive timbre to reveal the identities of the characters—then in the chapter 'Narration', which opens the second part, the complex, tension-filled relationships between the members of the family are revealed, and it is written as a tempestuous, though restrained, drama, in which fragments of the text of the Haggadah crash into segments of the most secret, emotion-filled private thoughts of the characters, a clash that shatters all the rules of composition; and if in the chapter 'Laid Table' the atmosphere is one of gay relaxation, in which the jokes people tell conceal and reveal old grudges and repressed intentions, written in a "pop" style—then the chapter 'Songs', which deviates from the ceremoniousness of the Seder, opens with almost frivolous exuberance, derived from the refreshing nature of the old, well-known songs, like "Who Knows One?" and "One Kid, One Kid", and ends in an atmosphere of profound introspection directed at reconciliation and the mending of the rents in the family fabric, in a style approaching that of a philosophical treatise.

These fourteen chapters, in which "real" time is but seven hours, will not only spin out the complex, interlaced relationships of the twenty-two members of the family—including in-depth probings of the consciousness and subconscious of each and every one of the them—but will also burst the bounds of the family circle through associative ramblings and the medium of the Haggadah's text, to the expanses of the history of the Jewish People and the mazes of universal human myths, like those of Blood and Fire, Sacrifice of the Firstborn, Redemption through Purification by Water, the Appearance of the Angel at Midnight, and so on. Into the narrative, or discursive, text, will be woven not only passages from the canonical Haggadah, but also fragments of earlier versions, as well as ancient interpretations, including poems and exegeses of The Song of Songs, from which will emanate the erotic motif in the plot.

Like the chameleon, which changes color as it crawls from place to place, the book will change its colors as it moves from one kind of material to another. When the plot squeezes into the kitchen—in the chapter 'Praise'—and the three women washing dishes begin to gossip, it will become a kind of "maids' novel"; in the scene in which the hidden Afikoman is discovered, its concealment and the search for it will constitute a sort of thriller; the 'Combination' chapter will be formulated like a science fiction story; when the jolly hour of 'Songs' rolls around, it will don a clown's mask and be written as a wild farce, and so on. The whole story will be a colorful mosaic of different styles, different genres, and parodies of them all.

And in the midst of all this exuberant color, which changes

from moment to moment, from chapter to chapter—there is one person—the central protagonist of the story—planted at the corner of the table, silent and observing. He is a young man, who had emigrated from Hungary only a few weeks earlier, having escaped illegally. Everything that happens around the table is strange and wonderful to him. He takes in every utterance, every movement, and with his sensitive responsiveness he feels the "deep flow" beneath the surface of all that is said and done by those present, as well as the deep, mythical meanings in the text of the Haggadah and the ritual acts that accompany it. He sees, and hears, and as he experiences what is going on all around him, he relives his own life, which has known much suffering and many reversals of fortune. He faints for a long moment—without any of the people around the table noticing—when the grandfather sprinkles the drops of wine in "blood and fire and pillars of smoke"; he is gripped by terrible anxiety when the door opens during "Pour out thy wrath"; he has a mystical, apocalyptic vision as the voices ring out in the singing of "O, bring near the day that is neither day nor night". At this Seder, it is he who is the Paschal lamb, he who is the sacrificial offering.

Why is this book different from all other books—asks the reader, like the child at the Seder—when there are other books, equally broad in scope, which also contain within them parodic, satirical and allegorical elements, streams of consciousness and so forth? Why is it so different that the writer can presume to see it as the *Ultimus Liber*?

Alors, the uniqueness of this book lies in the fact that it includes within itself—whether through the dialogue of the characters, the musings of the central protagonist, or the direct or indirect comments of the author—every possible interpretation of itself, leaving no room for any further exegesis. In its "self-awareness" and self-interpretation—it contradicts itself. Not only itself, but the literary act itself.

I have so lengthily described the contents and format of the book that has not yet been written in order to make it absolutely clear that Schatz's continuous and disturbing noise above my head did not simply interrupt the production of some mere sociological tale in the mode of the previous generation of Israeli writers, or a pretentious and self-aggrandizing *avant garde* verbal paste job in the mode of the "new wave"—but the creation of a piece of art that is the work of a lifetime. It interrupted the writing of a book of a thousand pages and more, of a kind that almost certainly has never been written before, and, were it to come to fruition, would never be written thereafter either.

Chapter twenty-nine

A Terrible Thing That Happened in Our Town

On a Friday, about two weeks after my chance meeting with Naomi by the mailboxes, one of the newspapers carried an article signed by Naphtali Schatz that landed like a stink bomb on the bustling literary street of the city, an article worthy of the epithet: base brutality; an article about which could be said, like about the incident of the concubine at Gibeah: wantonness has been committed in Israel.

The article, which took up almost a whole page of the newspaper, and to which its author had given the title "Wild Asses' Bray and Donkeys' Dung", was about Michael Hochhauser's book, *I Said No*.

Before I discuss this libelous essay, I must address a few words to the common reader who usually skips over the literary supplements to the daily newspapers, the one to whose attention and into whose hands such publications do not generally come, and who therefore is not party to the mysteries of the vigorous, vivacious, ebullient and effervescent literary life lived in our Hebrew homeland:

Beatings and kickings, blows and snipings, stabbings and muggings are everyday occurrences in our teeming literary quarter; what in the jargon of the crime reports is called "settling of accounts" is common practice there. Not a week passes in which four or five corpses of writers and poets aren't found spread-eagled and bleeding on the sidewalk, with severe head or chest injuries, struggling to get back up on their feet with the last remnants of their strength while no one offers first aid or help. The fear of two or three assassins, armed with clubs and switchblades, has fallen like a shadow over the entire quarter, and anyone whom they have spared, even if he is a sensitive soul, even if he is merciful and kind, hides behind lock and key, afraid to go out in the street until the storm is over. A person from another neighborhood wandering by chance into this quarter would stand petrified like a man in shock. He would not understand the meaning of the unearthly vision unfolding before his eyes: what is driving those thugs to lash out in all directions without regard to law or order? What demon eggs them on to such bloodthirsty cruelty, to such murderousness? Is it hunger for power?—But what power is here, and over whom? Is it because the quarter is too crowded, and they want to eliminate its population, thin it out, until only they are left alive?—But how and from whom will they earn their living when at long last they are alone? Then perhaps they want to "cleanse" the quarter of what they consider "undesirable" elements, leaving only themselves and their protégés, who would have to purchase safety with "protection money"? But what kind of "cleansing" would this be, when it breeds violence, and the progeny of violence is—violence? It is a mystery—the astounded outsider will say—a mystery with no explanation, save the passions of the human heart!

I have offered this preface to indicate that despite the routineness of the wild scene described above, an article like the one penned by Schatz that Friday had not appeared in the Hebrew press, to the best of my knowledge, since the brutal pieces by Abraham Uri Kovner in the nineteenth century—he was that critic, who, as you know, was caught counterfeiting and embezzling, was convicted and exiled to Siberia, and ended up becoming an apostate. Just consider the title itself—"Wild Asses' Bray and Donkeys' Dung"—not only is its vile hostility intended to wipe out its victim completely, but it also abuses the child of his spirit by basely and gratuitously perverting lines that had been written in all innocence from within profound spiritual agony. The words "bray" and "dung" were lifted (and intentionally taken out of context) from one of the strongest and most painful poems in the book, the opening lines of which are:

> i cannot bray
>
> holyholyholy
>
> but ding dong dung
>
> is sung
>
> by my eyes
>
> and the flies on my glasses
>
> buzz the mourner's kaddish

What has Schatz wrought? He has taken "dung" from the haunting thematic assonance dung/sung/buzz/but, castrated "glasses" to "asses", and brewed a vile potion to poison the poet.

And it is the same throughout the article. He perverts and distorts lines, inverts their meanings, rapes them according to his volition, breaks them and couples together fragments from here and from there that have no connection between them—all in order to make their author look ridiculous, to dangle him before the readers' eyes for them to mock!

"If there was anyone who still deluded himself, following the first two books by Mister Hochhauser"—Schatz opens his article (throughout which he always refers to the poet as "Mister Hochhauser")—"that the writer has some 'message' for the reader, with respect either to intellectual content or any formal innovation, this pretentious book, *I Said No*—the very title of which is supposedly intended to demonstrate rebelliousness, a sort of demonstrative muscle-flexing on the part of a spoiled child who has decided to 'shock the bourgeoisie' (of the sort which in any case had rolled over and died at the beginning of this century)—comes along and proves conclusively that all the posturings of angst-ridden significance, all the verbal acrobatics and psychedelic tricks are powerless to conceal his fundamental spiritual hollowness and emotional emptiness, which gape forth from every limping line and every squinting verse of this wretched, pitiful book."

Shall I go on and quote more? No, this critic, diseased with hatred, does not merit the repetition of his words, which are so full of internal contradictions, intentional distortions, unsupported assertions, unproven conclusions and gratuitous insults—all of which "are powerless to conceal" the malevolence and lack of intellectual honesty behind them. I will cite, then, but a small selection of the expressions sown thickly throughout this libel, which bear witness to the self-righteous delicacy of the author's soul: "A thin and limited associative universe," "a shallow imitation of Auden's *Epigones* by a poet who has long since ceased to be relevant," "hollow expressions lifted from banal recipes of the imitative poetry kitchens of the experimental New York and San Francisco quarterlies," vain self-glorification in synthetic verses," "counterfeited experiences," "ornamental decorativeness prompted by commercial pandering to a snobbish sub-cultured audience," "utterly foul blather," "complete lack of musical sense," "addiction to metaphorical clichés which every first-year student recognizes from the introductory course," "next to these stinking daubs, even a less than mediocre poet like Ya'akov Gruber is a genius," "banal shallowness leading to yawning boredom," "wise-guy technical tricksterism," "moralistic foaming at the mouth totally devoid of integrity," "an undisguised come-on to young girls in high heels looking for gift books in tune with the times," "aggressive mutterings constituting an artificial substitute for authentic emotional expression," "vulgar poses on the part of a main-street exhibitionist" and so on and so forth.

And the way it ended!

"In the presence of this literary flatulence, which bears witness to the depths to which a poetaster of negligible ability who is out of touch with all real experience can sink, the reader cannot help but ask himself why the paper upon which these vanities are printed is condemned to such punishment and forced to be sacrificed to the personal and social frustrations of Little Mister Hochhauser, who for some reason has declared himself to be a poet."

I read the article on Friday afternoon, in my study, and my blood boiled. Such wickedness—I said to myself—cannot be left unavenged!

And every one of those insults and injuries—I grabbed my head in my hands—had been typed right above my skull, within range of my very own ears! On the evenings I had sat here and plotted how to silence the offensive machine, which in my innocence I had assumed to be engaged in the creation and production of weighty research—deeper than the sea, and complex as a Leibniz treatise—into the vast reaches of Hebrew aesthetics.

Three times in succession I read this article from beginning to end, trying to find some grains of truth hidden between the lines, something that might lend a smidgen of credibility to such a vicious attack—for it couldn't be possible that its author is totally in the wrong!—but I found none.

And when I pictured Michael reading this article—which had almost certainly come into his hands, and if it hadn't, his "friends" would let him know about it soon enough, bringing "comfort" before the blow fell—I thought: What will he do now? What will he do when he reads the review denouncing him before a hundred thousand, two hundred thousand, readers all over the country as a good-for-nothing, cheat, thief, charlatan, ass-licker, forger, bloated wind and stinking drip? The title alone could cause its victim to have a heart attack when he first sees it. Why, a person could commit suicide after reading such smears, against which he has no way to defend himself! Would he indeed pack up and leave the country, as he had threatened to do?

Or would he swallow the bitter pill and say, Vanity of vanities, all is vanity, tomorrow this too will pass?

I sat and pondered whether I should go see him, or call him, perhaps, but what would I say to him? Would I carol the usual comforting banalities, like—Don't take any notice… Who does that son of a bitch think he is anyway… Trust your own abilities…

And I decided it would be best to say nothing at all, because anything I could say would just sow salt in his wound.

But by evening I could not stand my own silence any longer, and I called. His phone had not been disconnected.

"Yes?" I heard his voice, indifferent, cold.

"Look, Michael, I read the review, of course…"

Silence.

"If I were to tell you that it's an outrage…"

"Listen here, Korngold," he cut me off. "If you have anything to say to me, don't whisper it in my ear. Shout! Shout it in the streets! Publish it in five columns! I just don't need to hear any whispers!"

"Look, Michael, you know that I…"

"But you won't do it!" He interrupted my mumblings. "You won't shout, you won't write, you won't lift a finger, because you're chicken! A fawning coward like the rest of them! And the only thing that matters to you is to save your own skin!"

"My skin? But I…"

"Yes! You! You!" he screamed, so that the receiver trembled by my ear. "You sit there under the feet of that asshole just dreaming that maybe—just maybe!—when he shakes his tablecloth out the window, you'll catch a few of the crumbs!"

"If you're going to talk like that…" I said weakly, as the demeaning picture of the crumbs falling on me from above, on the porch off the kitchen, on the first day Schatz came to live here rose before my eyes.

"I'm talking like that because it's the truth! The whole lot of you are a bunch of hypocrites and ass-lickers, egocentrics in love with yourselves, and even if you saw a man gasping for breath right before your very eyes, not a one of you would lift a finger to help him. At least I've saved my skin!—That's all that counts! That's all that counts!!!"

And he slammed down the phone.

I didn't leave the house. When I heard Schatz's footsteps above my head, walking from place to place, from corner to corner, I said to myself: That arch-assassin is walking around, right above my head, not two meters distant from me—free! And what do I do?—I see injustice and play dumb! Stand right in the blood-puddle and ignore it! Does not my silence make me an accessory to the crime?

But on the other hand—I defended myself from the accusations—how would Michael have acted had it been I who was the victim? I mean, he's also "egocentric and in love with himself"—never once has he come to the defense of a friend…and he, he's got a sharp and violent pen, while I—I've never written a review in my life. I'm not equipped for it. I stammer and limp like a cripple whenever I attempt polemics! Ridiculous.

And when I thought about how this incident between Michael and me…

(Oh, Naomi!—My heart takes pity on her when I hear those dull footsteps above—how can you breathe that same air, saturated with poison, viperous poison!)

When I thought about how this incident could cut off the ties between us—forever!—I became very sad: who else is as close to me as Michael? Have I another friend beside him?

Back in the days when everyone saw me as an interloper, a stranger, a "Romanian" just arrived, a *homo novis* walking on land that was not his own—he opened his home to me! And later his paper!

I decided to go see him, to work it out face-to-face. Openly. I would suggest to him—I decided—that the two of us would write the response to the review together, and I would sign it.

At nightfall, I went out and walked over to his place.

I rang the doorbell, I knocked—no one answered.

When I went home—

From some distance away I saw a small knot of people gathered at the entrance to the courtyard.

When I got closer, I found all the tenants there, and two or three neighbors from the building next door, talking excitedly.

I asked what had happened.

Professor Schatz had been attacked on the stairs and was injured, they said.

What?—I cried, alarmed, the blood draining from my face—When?!

About fifteen minutes ago—they said—an ambulance came and took him to the hospital.

Oh no, it's impossible!—I cried inwardly—It's not possible that he really…

"I heard a person skrimming, skrimming…" said Mrs. Bzhizovski. "I did not know vot… I have gone down steps, I have see za Professor lying… Blut here and here… Za clinic of my husband was shutted, he is not in home, I take vatter from za home and spill on him… He doesn't spik, only opens eyes… After zat Mrs. Azoulai telephone to embulance, come tek him to feerst-ed stetion."

"He tumbled down the stairs," said Victoria, red-faced. "I'm quite sure of it. He was attacked on the staircase, apparently, on his way home, and tumbled down, and then he broke his arm. When I got to him, he lay on the floor, white as a sheet, holding on to his elbow and just groaning in pain: My arm…my arm…"

"Zere vas blut also, Meesis Azoulai!" said Mrs. Bzhizovski.

"That was from the fall, apparently. He hurt his face and arms, but I don't think it's serious."

I tried to replay the event in my imagination: Michael decides to go up and take his revenge upon his enemy. As he enters the building, he sees Schatz going up the stairs. He catches up with him on the first-floor landing. Raises his voice. Castigates. Schatz's silence makes him even angrier and he slaps his face. Schatz defends himself, tries to hit back. Michael, the stronger of the two, grabs his arm and forces him to the floor. Schatz tumbles down…

Unbelievable!—I thought—Unbelievable!

The women, excited, offered various suggestions as to the identity of the attacker and the reason for the attack. Mrs. Ben-

Ze'ev posited that maybe it was a burglar who intended to break into one of the apartments, and when he encountered the tenant he hit him in an attempt to flee. Mrs. Bzhizovski fanned a glimmer of suspicion about Heinz Hirsch. "Two veeks ago," she smirked, "he hollered at him zo... I tinked Mister Schatz vill hev an apoplexia!" Everyone defended him, however, saying that although Hirsch was quick to anger, he had never raised a hand to anyone. Hedva offered the hypothesis that perhaps it was a student who wanted to get even with the professor, who had failed him on his exams. Such things have happened. Victoria related that when she had gone up to his wife, to tell her what had happened, she had muttered, on her way down the stairs, "I knew it, I knew it..."

Mr. Ben-Ze'ev took my elbow and led me a little aside.

"You have of course read the invective against Hochhauser that the madman published?" He smiled at me. "Do you think perhaps that the poet..."

"Attacked him?" I said. "I don't believe it! He will certainly give him what he deserves some time, but not like that. He has a pen! No less sharp than Schatz's!"

"Do you know him?" He gave me a skeptical and amused look.

"I know him well! He is a poet of great refinement, very sensitive..."

"A refined poet and a refined man aren't necessarily one and the same," chuckled Ben-Ze'ev. "I used to know a very refined poet, whose name I won't mention, who gave the critic Ya'akov Rabinowitz a black eye. As the Book of Proverbs says, 'the wringing of the nose bringeth forth blood'!"

While we spoke a police car came down the street and pulled up beside us.

Two policemen emerged from it. One of them went up to Victoria, shook her hand, and said: "What's up, Mrs. Azoulai? What's been happening here?"

Excited, her face glowing, Victoria led the policemen to the entrance of the building. "Here, here's where I found him lying." She showed them the tiles at the foot of the stairs, where a bloodstain glistened like a mark of shame. "The attacker knocked him down the stairs, apparently. Or maybe he fell down by himself. It seems he passed out from the fall."

The policemen measured the floor with their eyes, then the height of the staircase. The one who knew Victoria said: "I understand he's a new tenant in your building."

"Three months," said Victoria.

"Anybody here know him personally?" He surveyed those present with his eyes.

All eyes turned toward me.

"You?" asked the policeman.

"A bit."

"Could we go into your apartment for a moment?"

"Please."

When we had gone up three steps, the policeman turned back and said: "You can come with us, Mrs. Azoulai."

Victoria accompanied us happily, leaving the rest of the tenants, disappointed, downstairs.

I opened two bottles of beer and poured some for the two policemen, Victoria, and myself.

"You say that you know him?" The policeman set his glass down on the table after having gulped down more than half of it, and surveyed the appearance of the room.

"A bit."

"Tell me please: does he have any enemies that you know of?"

I hesitated. I recalled the police column in the daily newspapers, which every so often reports that so-and-so, who was attacked, or robbed, or whose car was vandalized, had declared to the investigating officer that he did not know who might have done it. He has no enemies at all!

"I don't know of any particular enemies," I said. "But Mr. Schatz is a professor. In the academic world there are always intrigues, jealousies, competition…"

The policeman grinned.

"In the academic world, as you call it, this is the way they solve problems?"

I felt uncomfortable. His question had the tone of a rebuke.

"There's anger, there's hatred…these can sometimes drive a man out of his mind," I said. "Maybe he stood in the way of someone at the university, or caused him to be fired…"

"And whoever it was jumped him in revenge?" said the policeman skeptically.

"It's possible… He didn't say anything to you himself? Didn't see who attacked him?"

"He said it was dark on the staircase."

"He didn't say whether he suspected anyone?"

"He said he didn't know. He hasn't any enemies, he said."

Victoria smiled.

"Does he have any items of value in his home? Jewelry, diamonds?"

"As far as I know, no. Not unless books are 'items of value'…"

"There are book thieves, too," laughed the second policeman.

"But they don't mug for them!" I laughed. The investigation is 'turning a corner', I said to myself comfortably.

"Anything can happen these days! You'd be surprised!"

"Is he on good terms with the neighbors?" The investigating officer addressed his question to Victoria.

"Good terms?" snorted Victoria. "He's got all of them mad at him. He didn't want to pay his maintenance fees. He's a difficult person! Not very nice at all!"

"If our rules you don't cease to resist / We will soon spit you out of our midst." I recollected the hot-tempered Victoria's naive verses.

"Anyone threaten him?"

"The tenants?" said Victoria. "People yelled at him. Yes. But no one threatened! This building is a decent one! Twenty-five years and nothing ever happened here! Excepting Albert we never saw any police here." She laughed. "And I don't see much of him, either!"

The two policemen laughed with her.

The investigating officer emptied the remaining beer in the glass into his gullet.

"So you don't know either," he turned back to me, "of anyone who threatened him, or tried to annoy him…"

Like Raskolnikov, who goes back to old Ivanovna's house after having murdered her, I found myself drawn back to the scene of my crime.

"I know that they harassed him…on the telephone…"

"Threatened?" The policeman latched onto my words, as if they were the end of the thread that was going to lead him to the tracks of the criminal.

"I don't know if they threatened… His wife just told me that they would call him up, at different times at night…"

"And she didn't say whether they suspected anyone?"

"No. She just said a lot of people hated him."

"A lot…" The policeman regarded me speculatively.

Then he got up and said:

"Good. We'll make do with that for now. Thank you very much Mr.…"

"Keren."

"By the way, what do you do? Academic?"

"Mr. Keren is a writer!" cried Victoria. "A famous writer! Shame on the police force if you've never heard of him!"

"We are honored!" smiled the investigating officer.

"I've seen you on television, I think…" said the second policeman.

"You must be mistaken. I've never appeared on television."

""I must be mixing you up…"

"Any messages for Albert, Mrs. Azoulai?" asked the investigating officer.

"Tell him to bring home a watermelon!" laughed Victoria. "Every day he promises, and every day he forgets!"

After they had gone out, Victoria said, pointing her finger straight up: "The rabbits must be very happy!"

And as she stood on the threshold, bathing me in a dark and excited glance: "His wife…she has black birds in her eyes!"

Chapter thirty

Surprise Visit

I sat alone in my room, after Victoria's exit, and thought about what had happened. I took no delight in the misfortune of my upstairs neighbor. For what sort of misfortune was this—it was not for this sort of misfortune that had I been praying... Moreover, I was pained for Michael. If it had indeed been he who had sent his enemy flying down the steps, then he himself had fallen even lower, lower than low, and he was now the loser. A man should not be taken to task when he is in a state of misery, especially when his name and reputation have been publicly besmirched. Nonetheless, he ought to have restrained himself and known that this was not the way either to redeem his honor or to take his revenge. Schatz would walk about now even more upright than before: the victim of crude, physical violence! And his scar—should a scar remain—would be worn with pride as a decoration honoring his prowess in that righteous battle in which he had exhibited conspicuous courage. And as for me...if indeed he were in need of hospitalization, I would be granted a few days of cease-fire. But what then? The machine upstairs would rat-tat-tat again, produce some other "invective"—as Ben Ze'ev put it—without me knowing about whom, and his presence, his constant presence in this building, with only a thin layer of poured concrete separating the soles of his shoes from my skull...

At eleven o'clock I was startled by the sound of the doorbell ringing.

It was Naomi—to my great surprise.

"I saw your light on, so I decided you hadn't gone to sleep yet... Am I disturbing you?"

I asked her if she would like something to drink. Yes—she said—she really needed something. Strong coffee, if I had any. And we sat down in the small kitchen, by the table.

"You've heard what happened, of course."

"Yes," I said. "How is he?"

"Broken arm. He'll have to stay in the hospital for a few days."

At least he managed to break one of his many bones, I thought to myself, recalling what Michael had said to me at his place.

"Serious?"

"They'll put a cast on him. The problem is that it's his right hand. He won't be able to write for a few weeks, at least."

"A few *weeks*?!"

"So it seems. Tomorrow they'll take x-rays. To see if any internal organs have been injured."

"From the fall?"

"He fell down five or six steps. And the problem is that he has a kidney condition. Since he was a child. They call it 'cystic kidney'," she smiled.

"Is it a serious condition?"

"No. Problems in the urinary tract from time to time. Anuria, they call it," she smiled again. "He had an operation, years ago. Now after the fall...who knows?"

"Yes..." I sighed.

"You've probably guessed who did it."

The kettle whistled. I jumped up and started to make the coffee. I set the cups down before us, and Naomi said:

"Of course you read the article yesterday."

"Yes, I read it."

"So you can imagine."

I took a few sips and said:

"He said so?"

"He didn't say a thing. The neighbors told me they heard cries on the staircase."

"The police were here. They asked me whether I knew if he had any enemies…"

"What did you say?"

"I said that a man like him, a university professor maybe…"

Naomi took a few quiet swallows of her coffee.

"The funniest thing is…" she smiled, "…is that he thinks I'm his enemy too now."

I looked at her in wonder.

"Yesterday, when I read the review in the newspaper—he never shows me anything before it's published—I said to him: I'm afraid you're going to pay for this… I meant, of course, that someone would get on to him…write nasty things… Just now, in the hospital, when he felt a bit better—he had terrible pains in his arm—he said to me: You wished this on me… I wished it…"

"Ridiculous."

"A partner in the crime…"

"Oh come on!" I laughed.

I brought a plate of cookies, and said:

"You didn't like the review…"

"It's awful—just awful! If I were in that poet's shoes… I don't know what I would do…"

"Get even?"

She put both hands on her face and mumbled "Why did he have to write like that? Why why why…"

"Yes…a review like that… I don't think that since Kovner's day…"

"Who?"

"There was this critic, in Russia, in the nineteenth century, Abraham Uri Kovner. Insanely fanatical."

"Fanatical! That's what I always say about him…"

I looked at her and thought: Maybe it's true… maybe she is a "partner in crime", in her thoughts… Perhaps this act of revenge fulfilled some of her own wishes, of which she herself was unaware… What do I know about what goes on between her and him?

"A critic is entitled to massacre a book, of course," I said. "But that review…it seemed to be written with a lot of hatred…"

"Yes, he sure knows how to hate," she said sadly. "He hates many, many people. About half the world."

"Well, then he doesn't hate the other half, so that's some consolation," I joked.

"Consolation for whom?" she laughed.

"He never says hello to me… I have no idea why…"

She looked at me and smiled. Smiled as if she were weighing something in her mind. And blushed a little. Finally she said:

"Once, a long time ago, after I had read your book *The Flying Camel* and said how much I liked it, he looked at me angrily and said… never mind…" She hid her blush with her hands.

"Tell me…if you've already started…"

"There's a character in the book, pretty ugly," she laughed between the fingers covering her face, "a bitter intellectual, nasty… named Lifschitz…"

"Yes…"

"He thought you were aiming at him…"

"WHAT?!" A cry escaped my lips.

"He said 'Lifschitz' is a combination of 'Naphtali' and 'Schatz'…"

"God!"

"Absurd, of course!"

"But what's the connection?! How could he…"

"He thought that the whole book was sort of an allegory about literature and criticism."

"No!!"

I was so surprised, so shaken, so excited, that I couldn't even laugh. I got up and said, "I've got to drink to this!"

I went to the living room, brought back a bottle of cognac and two glasses, poured, clinked my glass to hers and said:

"To allegory!"

"And he just hates allegories, as you very well know!" She sipped from the glass.

"Yes. I read his book. But… How could he even imagine that it was an allegory about…"

Naomi, between sips, explained:

"In his interpretation, the camel's wings are the wings of Literary Creativity, yearning to fly, free, unbounded, lawless; and the hump laden with gold is Criticism riding on the back of Creativity, laden with intellectualism and scholarship, weighing down the flying beast, pulling it down, earthwards, until it overcomes and destroys it. A constant battle between the wings and the hump…"

When she pooh-poohed his interpretation and said that, in her opinion, if it was an allegory, it was an allegory about the country in general, about Zionism, which began as a dream with wings, and then later came the race after gold, materialism, and knocked it down from the heights—he said that was true as well, but that it was an allegory on two levels: the surface level, or the obvious one, which is the one she had pointed out, whereas the deep level, the hidden one…

"Is he paranoid?" I refilled the two glasses, which had been emptied.

Naomi smiled, looked into my eyes and said:

"Critically!"

We laughed. I wanted to kiss her.

"He's very vulnerable," she gulped down about half the glass. "If he finds out that anybody said, or wrote, a word against him—he's shocked. He goes completely out of his mind!"

"La Fontaine—who by the way learned a lot from his contemporary, Rabelais—has a fable about that." And I told her the fable of the lark and the falcon: there was a farmer who hunted birds with a trap he would lay for them in the field, with a mirror lying upon it. One time a lark was attracted by the mirror and began flying towards it, but before she got to the trap a falcon caught her and sunk his talons into her. At that very moment the trap closed on the falcon. The falcon wept and begged the trap to let him go, for he had done it no evil. Said the trap: And what evil has the lark done thee?

"A mirror? Naphtali has three mirrors!" she laughed.

"Yes, I read the second book too. What's it like to live in a room with three mirrors?"

"Hard," she emptied her glass.

"How many years have you been married?" I poured again for the two of us.

"Five. No, six. Yes, six already! Hard to believe."

And after she'd sipped a bit:

"And he doesn't want any children. Doesn't like children."

"Women?"

"He tolerates them."

"Tolerates?"

"Suffers."

"And you?"

"I suffer."

Then she poured for the two of us, drank a bit, and said:

"He's very jealous about me. If he knew that I was sitting here right now…and with you!"

"He would push me down the stairs!"

"He would punish me!"

"Push you down the stairs?"

"With silence! Me he punishes with silence!"

Then she said:

"Tell me, am I crazy? What am I doing sitting here badmouthing him to you, when he's lying there with a broken arm… What kind of cognac is this?" She turned the bottle around to read the label.

"Superior!" I refilled her glass. "My mother's husband is a vintner, in Zikhron Ya'akov. He supplies me with forty-year-old wines."

"Whenever I sin—he just excommunicates me, with silence."

"You sin?"

After she had sipped a bit, she told me about her "sins":

Sometimes she gets up late and doesn't prepare his breakfast. In the evening, he might find the sink full of dishes she had not washed. She forgets to buy things that he asked for in the store. Once she lost the key, once a wallet with money in it… For such things he doesn't forgive her. He punishes her with silence.

Our faces were close to one another, on either side of the narrow table, like mirror facing mirror, and from the ceiling a third mirror did not look down upon us. I had never felt so near to the sunny green valley of Jezreel as I felt then, opposite her tanned, warm face. I could hardly refrain from kissing her.

"He likes to make me feel guilty, you understand? He enjoys it."

We were silent.

"Well, I've talked too much," she rose. "And now I'm going to feel guilty again…"

I accompanied her to the door. As we stood on the threshold she lay her head on my shoulder, and with her eyes closed she said: "I shouldn't have been drinking."

I embraced her shoulders with my right arm, and as my lips touched her hair, I said to myself: No, it can't happen like this! Now life itself is turning into an allegory! And a simplistic one! The writer's manly chest a refuge for the head of the critic's wife! The nest of her repressed desires! And love shall yet bloom here for her and for him! No, it can't happen like this! Because what I am doing now takes on literary significance! And in a little while I will cease to be alive, and turn into an allegorical figure! No!…

Chapter thirty-one

Snakes and Scorpions

The building was quiet. No typing was heard, nor echoing pings. Tranquility reigned on the staircase.

Schatz had not yet returned from the hospital.

One of those mornings, when I'd gone up to the roof to feed the rabbits, I went into the room next to the hutch where I stored the books that had belonged to my late father to have a look at the works of Avraham Uri Kovner, which I hadn't opened for years.

In a stack that included several volumes of *Hashiloach* and *Hatzfirah*, a volume of *Moznayim* from 1932, books by Yehudah Leib Gordon (Yalag) and Micha Joseph Lebensohn (Michal), Reuben Brainin, and Gottlober, I found his *Investigation of a Question* (Warsaw, 1865), *A Bouquet of Flowers* (Odessa, 1868), and under them Paperna's memoirs, Zitron's *Behind the Screen* and other pamphlets from the same period. I dusted them off, got rid of the cobwebs and took them downstairs with me, to my study.

I was completely absorbed in reading until three in the afternoon. I neither ate nor drank.

Ah, what a world was revealed to me! Such rivalries, such quarrels! Such annihilation's, such devastations! At one another's throat, to choke and destroy! And such brilliant, explosive language! And such holy fire burning in the bones, to purify the temple from all the outlaws defiling it!

Here I found an article of Kovner's criticizing a certain poet named David Moshe Mitzkon, who had brought out a book of poems in the Hebrew language, *David's Harp.* Kovner wrote:

"And now forgive me, dear reader, if I guide you and lead you to Mitzkon's poems, and together we shall peruse them until we cast them aside in disgust and breathe fresh air, relieved of the heavy burden that had been weighing us down…

"Upon my life! For indeed, before a poet so great, who recognizes the righteousness and purity of the sun, all the poets of the world must kneel…

"Why did he not take pity on the years and the days to have written such idiotic verses? …Can you understand, dear reader? Nor can I!

"After a poem like this, which demonstrates neither sense nor sensibility, but only insolence and stupidity, my prayer wafted heavenward a moment and vanished, only to be replaced by tremendous laughter issuing forth from my mouth, and I truly hope, dear reader, that wherever you may be, you hear this laughter and your face lights up like my own…"

And in another article:

"Latterly there has arisen a humble and very holy man, the great saint, righteous and abstinent, religious scholar, light of the universe and its glory, singular in his generation, the celestial exegete, our leader, our teacher and our rabbi Avraham Baer ben Haim Hacohen Gottlober whose name shall be forever remembered…

"And along comes the eminent wise man, the famous raconteur, the most magnificent of the giants, the awesome saint, wondrous ritual slaughterer, foundation of the universe, light of Israel, pillar of wisdom, and mighty hammer whose great and sanctified name is known from one end of the universe to the other, our teacher and rabbi and guardian of our purity, Eliezer Lipman Silbermann and says in all his great modesty…"

And you should see what the writers he scourged wrote about him! Gottlober, Lerner, Harkavy, Tsederbaum even Paperna, even Mendele Mocher Seforim!

"His wings were singed in heathen flames. He crept on his belly. He fawned, and went from bad to worse... The slave of slaves sold his God like he sold his soul... That was the end of the singed fly."

"He betrayed his people in his Russian articles, counterfeited, stole and apostasized. A pathological type, in his eyes Hebrew literature was a 'heap of vanities'..."

"An egotist from his youth until his death. For money he changed his religion and betrayed his people, stole for his own benefit. And about all these vile deeds he was not ashamed to speak, and in speaking of them he felt no pangs of conscience, no shame, and displayed not a shadow of remorse..."

"To seal up this well, which has no water in it, but only snakes and scorpions..."

But as I read his writings and what others had written about him, it was not the polemics and the exchanges of vitriol that gripped and fascinated me so much as the man himself. The man full of contradictions, who attacked others so rabidly and destroyed himself! The educated man, of good taste, crusading against hypocrisy and falsification and hollowness in literature who fell lower and lower until he himself became a counterfeiter and embezzler of money! The man who "shares the sorrow of his people and suffers from its sicknesses," who wrote letters to Dostoevsky and Tolstoy demanding that they speak out against anti-Semitism—and who ultimately "betrayed" the Talmud and the Jews in his writings in the Russian language, and finally changed his religion! The man who caused great storms in the Hebrew Enlightenment, dedicating himself to the struggle against ignorance, provincialism, empty rhetoric, flattery and insincerity—and died like a dog, mourned only by anti-Semites, and who for twenty years after his death went completely unremembered!

What a drama! What a subject for a great novel!

I saw him in my mind's eye, a man of thirty-three; eight, ten years after the appearance of his books that had raised such a storm—

persecuted, shunned, banished from "the seat of Hebrew Literature", bitter, hating, jealous—sitting hunched over the account books in the banking house of the wealthy, vulgar, arrogant supporter of the Hebrew Enlightenment, Moshe Zack, in Vilna; sitting and plotting revenge for the insults he had suffered, for his degradation, his isolation, trying to work out how to escape the pit into which he had fallen. An illusive spark glitters in the darkness of his thoughts: To get rich! At a single blow! Thus he would break free of his lowly status as a miserable clerk, and thus he would be able to marry the young girl to whom he was betrothed, the sickly Sofia Kannengisser, and turn over a new leaf—far from the murky swamps of the Hebrew Enlightenment. He reveals his plan to his uncle, Naphtali Herz Boyarin, and brings him into a conspiracy. He forges the signature of Zack the banker on a check for the sum of 168,000 rubles. Boyarin cashes the check at the Moscow Merchants' Bank. Kovner takes his fiancée and journeys to Moscow. He gives 45,000 rubles to his uncle Boyarin— who hastens to flee abroad—and keeps 123,000 for himself. The daring of it all! Going after the big prize! He purchases a forged passport, in the name of Baruch Soleveichek, and travels with Sofia to Mohilev, where her family lives. At one of the stations he leaves the train with her, and performs the marriage ceremony in the presence of Jewish witnesses. He sends an insulting letter to Zack, who "had not taken cognizance of him and his worth", and calls him an "egotist, despicable, proud, thirsty for fame and void of wisdom, alienated from his people and from humanity, a little Jew in the grip of folly", and signs it with his full name. Upon his arrival in Kiev he is arrested and imprisoned. He tries to commit suicide with three shots from a pistol, but misses. He is brought to trial—in his speech in his own defense he expresses no remorse for his deeds—and is sentenced to four years imprisonment with hard labor and loss of all his rights. Four years that, because of his poor health, the authorities commute to exile to Siberia. He spends sixteen years in Siberia as a minor official of "The Office of the Inspector"—in Tobolsk, Tomsk, Omsk—and at the age of fifty-two, fourteen days before his marriage to a Christian schoolgirl, he converts.

And the women in his life! His first wife, the mother of his son, who worked in her father's shop, whom he hated, abandoned and divorced. And Sofia, who fled with him, whom he also divorced. And the schoolgirl in Siberia...

What a life! What contradictions! Beginning with his youth, in the house of his father—a poor cantor and teacher—through his days as a student in a yeshiva, where he was beaten when he was caught reading secular books, through the turbulent years of his struggles, when he did battle with the greats of Hebrew writing, when he corresponded with the geniuses of Russian literature, when he fought against ignorance and religious fanaticism, and raised high the banners of Yehudah Leib Gordon and Avraham Mapu until his fall to the lowest most despicable depths in his own eyes as well as the eyes of his People.

What a subject for a great novel!—I thought as I lay the books down on the table. What wonderful chapters, rich in dramatic incident, external and internal, "Dostoyevskian" chapters, it would be possible to weave here—in his meetings and conflicts with respected, 'established' writers honored by the Jewish people, whom he flayed mercilessly, without fear or favor, about their vanities and their hollowness; what gripping scenes, piercing the depths of the soul, it would be possible to draw here, with a fine pen—as he sat in the office of the bank, in his flight on the train, standing before his judges, sitting in prison, in his Siberian exile, in his return from Siberia and his tragi-comic meeting with the critic Paperna... Was he a wrathful prophet "zealous for the word of God", or a villain? A fearless defender of the truth—or a seeker after honor, sick for publicity and fame? Was he a misanthrope? A megalomaniac? Paranoid? Devoured by feelings of inferiority? What did he look like? The way he looks in his photograph in the book—robust, proud and sure of himself, dandified in his trimmed mustache, his handsomely combed hair—or was he something finer, more delicate than that? How tall was he? A meter sixty? A meter seventy?

And Schatz?—I said to myself on my way back up to the roof, to return the books to their place—isn't he a subject for a novel? And if not a novel, then a forty-page novella? Is it from an excess of self-satisfaction that he attacks the young writers of his own generation so fiercely? Is it only "the love of truth" which pushes him to rip his erstwhile companions to shreds? What demon drives him? The lust for power? A persecution complex? Bitterness deriving from failure? Perhaps self-hatred? And perhaps the root of the evil metastasizing within him is in the cystic kidney? In the anuria?

When I peeked into the rabbit hutch, my eyes lit up at the sight of five babies under Ada's curves! Five white babies, all damp and licked clean, lying on the straw, nursing and suckling, blind and blinking, sprawling on their tiny legs and snuffling with their snouts... So, she's finally given birth, the plump pink-nosed little one! During the very hours I was brooding over Avraham Uri Kovner—she was bringing her offspring into the light of the world.

Chapter thirty-two

To Soothe a Savage Breast

When I left my house that evening to visit Michael, Mr. Ben Ze'ev left at the same time and we walked together for a while.

"How is our friend the professor?" he asked.

I said that the professor's right arm was bandaged, and that he was still in the hospital for tests of his internal organs.

"A war casualty!" he grinned. "Well, whoever sets out to make war has to accept the risks. But I'm sure he'll recover. Recover, and his right arm shall be mighty!"

I told him that the entire morning I had been absorbed in reading the exploits of another man of war—Avraham Uri Kovner.

"Ah, the apostate! What an ugly type!" he wrinkled his face in disgust. "That he attacked Mendele Mocher Seforim for translating 'Beinen Würmer' as 'bee worms' rather than 'internal worms' and made such a big deal out of it, so what? He can be forgiven that. But that he wrote such fawning letters to the anti-Semite Rozanov and defamatory articles in *Golos* about all the crimes and trespasses of the Jewish people, and recommended that the study of Talmud be forbidden—it's absolutely disgusting! He's condemned to burn in hell—there's no doubt of that!"

I said that Kovner had been a very complex man, full of contradictions, and that I was surprised that a great biographical novel hadn't yet been written about him.

"About Kovner? He doesn't deserve it! He himself prophesied that he would be called 'the Jewish Haman'. Do you know who should really have a novel written about him?—Feitelson! Have you heard of Menachem Mendel Feitelson?"

I said that I had come across his name reading about Kovner and Paperna, that he was of their generation, but that I knew very little about him.

"Ah, now *there* was a human being! A tragic figure! A fine critic, with a gentle soul."

And he told me all about him: that he was a man ugly to look upon, short of stature, poor as a begger, who suffered only disappointments in life. He taught Hebrew in the villages of southern Russia, tried to get accepted to the university but failed the entrance examinations, journeyed to Warsaw to try his luck there, but happened, unfortunately, onto a street riot where he was wounded by an errant bullet, became ill, and went back to be a teacher in Yekatrinoslav… and even though he was far from the centers of Hebrew culture, he wrote articles in good taste, clean and clear, free of rhetoric, about writers and books…

One time he came to Odessa, hoping to find a job in a Jewish institution, and went to the home of Mendele Mocher Seforim. Mendele came out to meet him in the hall. At the sight of the short-statured critic, who so impudently had dared to write in one of his articles that he, Mendele, had been influenced by such and such Russian writers—the author measured him with a disdainful glance, rested one of his legs on the seat of a chair that was standing there, and said: "So, you're Zelig the dwarf bath-house attendant, who in order to rinse off the body of the notable Alter the Tall has to stand on a chair. And you thought you could pour a bucket of cold water on Mendele!" Then he turned his back and returned to the room, leaving Feitelson in the hall.

Feitelson, who admired Mendele, went back to Yekatrinoslav,

and shortly thereafter swallowed poison, and died. And in his will he asked that the following be written on his tombstone: "Before noble patrons you did not stand / Among tranquil spirits you had no seat / The life of bitter souls was yours / From the table of Life you did not eat."

"Committed suicide, my friend!" Ben Ze'ev thumped me on the shoulder before he took leave. "Forty-two years old! Because from the trauma of his meeting with Mendele, he couldn't recover!... You know what it means, 'For in their anger they slew a man'?—Even by turning your nose up you can kill a man! Especially a nose as big as Mendele's! Yes indeed, there have been writers who have killed themselves because of what critics had written about them, and here you have the story of a critic who killed himself because of a writer turning his nose up at him! Now that's a subject for a novel!"

Michael, to my great surprise, greeted me as if nothing had happened, as if that lambaste had never been published, as if he had never yelled at me over the telephone and hadn't slammed down the receiver, as if he had never—

Maybe it wasn't he?

"Come in! Come in!" he cried happily, red-faced, excited, opening his door wide for me.

He's blooming!—I said to myself.

Upon entering his room I saw a girl and a fellow with whom I was not acquainted.

"This is Ayanna, the singer, and this is Julian Milosz—am I pronouncing your name correctly?"

The man—about thirty years old, with big glasses behind which were smiling eyes that radiated intelligence, and a face strewn with freckles—nodded his head in my direction.

Julian is a composer, Michael told me, and he wants to write music to several of the poems in *I Said No*.

"Great!" I said, somewhat disappointed. I had expected to find him in a different emotional state. And I asked whether I was disturbing them.

"No! Why? Come join the consultation!"

Ayanna, who sat on the floor, her legs folded beneath her, leaning her back and arms on the sofa where Julian sat, was beautiful. Fairytale beautiful. Like a fairy princess. Her golden hair cascaded to one side of her face, like a splendid waterfall. Over her round face played a silent smile that beamed benevolence upon the entire world. It shone upon me as I walked in there—and she didn't even need to bother to return my greeting—it shone upon Michael as he spoke, and it shone upon Julian as she listened to him.

Julian Milosz read words from one of the poems and accompanied them with movements of his hand which drew a sort of a sketch of a tune.

"Dar-arkness driz-zles on the moss-y rocks, ta-ta, ta-ta-ta…" He accompanied his falsetto singing with wave-like hand motions.

"A-a-an-dro-me-da's ref-lec-tion," his voice and his hand rose way up, to the high notes of the scale, "di-i-i-ving like At-lan-tis," his voice dove all at once to the bass clef, and with it his arm went down almost to the floor. "Ta-ta-ta, ta-ta. How does it sound to you?"

Michael, a soft smile on his face, as if he couldn't decide: Nice? Not nice? He looked over at me, as if asking my impressions. I gave him a smile of approval: Yes… yes…—I smiled. The tune was not melodic. It didn't travel along a smooth path, but wound its way over the potholes. It was in the spirit of the times.

"Yes… yes…" said Michael slowly, as if echoing my silent approbation. "It's nice… yes… I only wonder: will the audience get it?"

"The words?" asked Julian.

"The tune…"

"With Ayanna's voice?!"

Ayanna smiled in gracious acknowledgement.

"A-a-an-dro-me-da's re-flec-tion…" She sang the short phrase in a wonderful soprano, clear, celestial, which echoed through the room like the trill of a nightingale inside a vast temple.

Michael laughed in evident delight: "Yes… yes…"

And then a second line, and a third.

Michael's small room turned into something of a temple. The notes flew on the wings of the words. Beautiful Ayanna was a Muse. Happy is the man whom the Muses love—as Hesiod said—even if pain and suffering are in his heart. If he but hears their singing, he instantly forgets his gloomy thoughts and will remember his sorrows no more. Yes, Michael too, before my very eyes, his pain and suffering ebbed, his anger and his bitterness of soul, all his rough edges slipped away, and his face was bathed in pure spirituality.

Ayanna's celestial smile shone upon us when her voice was silent.

She turned her head towards me and her smile rested upon me.

I blushed. And brought a soft smile to my own face, too.

Our smiles met.

Her smile touched my smile like a ray of light on spiderwebs.

As if something wonderful had happened and both of us were amazed by it.

I saw that Michael was smiling at me too, and Julian.

I didn't know what to do with my smile, so I said: "Those songs… They have a wave-like movement of opposing forces…"

Ayanna did not take her gaze from me. Her eyes shone as if I had said something very profound.

Michael smiled as if to confirm my analysis.

"Yes…" Julian broke the divine silence. "Shall I do another one?"

Michael nodded with a smile of pure joy.

Julian sketched three more songs.

The idea is—he said—that Ayanna would appear with a complete cycle of eleven poems.

"I adore them!" said Ayanna fervently.

Michael smiled. He lit a cigarette with trembling hands and smoked.

Then they spoke about conditions, a contract, an advance, percentages. There was no argument between them. Michael agreed to everything Milosz offered. Ayanna said: You can trust him, if he weren't so honest he would be a very rich man by now; and Michael said that he was sure of it, because if Julian wanted to get rich he wouldn't have chosen his poems. Ayanna rested her hand on Milosz's thigh and said that he was so totally committed to his principles that he wasn't prepared to make any compromises for the sake of popularity; and Michael said that only with people like that was he ready and willing to work.

I was entranced.

Julian rose from the armchair. Ayanna rose from where she sat on the floor, and the two of them, satisfied, headed for the door. They bid farewell to Michael, and Ayanna graced me with that same radiant, benevolent smile promising blessing to all who are pure of heart that she had smiled when I had come in.

"Congratulations!" I said to Michael after they had gone out.

He lit another cigarette, nervously, and it trembled in his mouth.

"An extraordinary human being, that Julian! Extraordinary!" he said.

I asked him how Julian had come to his poems.

He went over to the desk, pulled open the drawer, took out a letter and handed it to me.

It was a letter from Ayanna. Ayanna Melamed.

Dear Michael Hochhauser,

> For the past two weeks I have been living with your poems from *I Said No.* I go to bed with them, I sleep with them, I wake up in the morning with them…

She had picked up the book by chance, in a bookstore, and "it grabbed her instantly," "a real discovery." She hadn't been familiar with his poems before then… At the end of the letter, Ayanna asks if he would be kind enough to meet with her and with the composer Julian Milosz, who, like herself, also…

"I got this the day before yesterday," he took the letter from my hand and put it back in the drawer.

"Great!" I said.

"Let's hope… Let's hope…" he said, and went silent. Sank into melancholy.

"You should be happy!" I said. "Why are you so sad?"

He lit a cigarette from the butt of the previous one and continued to smoke in silence.

"You know, sometimes I ask myself…" he said finally with a modest smile. He stopped, and began again: "I read a few chapters of Tishbi's *The Zohar*. Wonderful, marvelous! There's a story there about Rabbi Shimon Bar Yochai in the cave, who spent the whole night reading the Hidden Book, which was like a fortress surrounded by birds of fire, and at daybreak—the book flew out of his hands, and was no more. And he was happy: he had achieved the ultimate end! Think about it. There's a very profound meaning here: books are written in darkness. In letters ringed with fire. When day breaks, it all disappears. That which is hidden disappears. And it's then that you have to be happy! When the letters disappear! …What's the real purpose of poetry, Kalman? You know what?—The annihilation of itself. That's the ultimate end! To write in such a way, to achieve such refinement, such concision, such abstraction—that the word itself becomes light! That is to say, the non-word! Shall I ever achieve that? Never! And you ask why I'm unhappy…"

We were silent for a long time.

I didn't mention Schatz. He didn't mention leaving the country.

Chapter thirty-three

Caveat Lector

The reader whose heart is set not merely on pleasure—unlike those boors who become enslaved to the thrilling plot and whose eyes are plastered over so they cannot see that which is hidden beyond it—but rather wishes to plumb the depths of the books he reads, to dive down to their meanings and their sub-meanings, to excavate their strata, layer after layer, to understand not only the text, but also the sub-text, would do well to pause in this book, too, between chapter and chapter and contemplate. And having read the preceding two chapters, he would do well to think about the significance of the hero's relationship with the two other men in the story who are his age: Schatz and Michael. Does he indeed feel only hatred towards the former and only love towards the latter? Perhaps his relationship to each of them—although it is not obvious on the surface—is more complex? And perhaps—and this is altogether a more daring hypothesis—there is in his relationship to both of them a hint of...

It is worth contemplating, for any such contemplation is its own reward.

Chapter thirty-four

Intermezzo

Schatz had not yet come home from the hospital. Naomi was by herself.

That evening, at nine, she rang my doorbell, wrapped in a dressing gown, and apologized for asking my help: she was scared—terribly scared!—of roaches, and a roach had flown into her kitchen—she had nearly passed out—and now it was running around among her dishes. She had closed the door on it and she couldn't go in there. Would it be too difficult for me…?

I went up to her apartment, I went into her kitchen—she watched from outside—and after an energetic chase and much ado, with me moving furniture and dishes from place to place, my shoe in hand—I caught him, crushed him, and threw his corpse down from the balcony.

Then——When I opened my eyes—and opposite me, on the wall, in the weak light coming from the living room, hangs the poster of *The Taming of the Shrew*, Petruchio kicking

Katherine's exposed bottom, her back bent almost to the ground—I thought about the man who lives downstairs, under this floor, upon which this bed stands. I crossed my arms under my head and thought: Who is that quiet Romanian, hiding out in his apartment there, like a mouse in its hole, like a mole in its tunnel, who calls himself a writer? What does he do down there, night and day?—He writes. Yes, writes. Plows lines in secret. The squeak of his pen is not heard, nor a voice nor a rustle. Like a thief in the underworld he writes, a story, and another story, and another, and another. What does he write for, and for whom?

And what ambition, what corny claims! To create characters! To breathe life into them! Heaven and earth and all the inhabitants thereof! Poor thing! Doesn't he realize, in his stupid hubris, that the characters he creates wander like hollow spirits through the vastness of the universe?!

Float through it like ghosts and maleficent imps!

He describes a house and thinks that it is a house. He describes a camel and thinks that he has created a camel. He describes a man smoking a cigarette and thinks that the man is thinking and that the cigarette is smoking. And he doesn't sense at all that if his house is an imitation of a house and his man is an imitation of a man, both of them are not the Truth, because Truth expressed in an imitation is no longer Truth—as the hassidim say. And if onto his camel he fits, capriciously, a pair of wings—then the fate of this camel, who barely rises off the ground, is that it plunges back to earth, with splayed limbs like a mechanical doll. He is as foolish as a clown, and struts like one—that writer!

Sure, sure, a decent man. He speaks but little, and goes calmly about his business. Lives in peace with his neighbors. Walks down the stairs, walks up the stairs, his expression blank. But behind that innocent facade—I know—writhes a nest of vipers. Hatreds and jealousies. Hatching schemes. He plots and undermines. Under this very room, too. Treacherous! He cannot be trusted!—

Thus I lay and thought, my arms beneath my head, and I sensed the hatred swelling within me. Swelling and rising. Yes, I hate him!

I don't know why I hate him so much—but I cannot live under one roof with him! I would like to wipe him out! Roll him down all the stairs until his head breaks open

I was so greatly delighted with this hatred of mine that I rolled over on my side, embraced the woman lying to the left of me and thrust my horn of plenty into her.

Chapter thirty-five

On the Advisability of Marriage

In Chapter 9 of Book 3 of *Gargantua and Pantagruel*—a chapter which I will get around to translating three years from now, if I ever get around to translating it at all, seeing that I've been stuck for two weeks now in Chapter 13 of Book 1—which deals mostly with matters of excretion, secretion, cacation and evacuation—going crazy trying to figure out how to get various vulgarities like the following to rhyme in the Holy Tongue:

Chiart
Foirars
Petart
Brenous
Ton lard
Chappart
Sèspart
Sous nous—
etc.

We are told about the scoundrel Panurge, who asks the opinion of Pantagruel his master regarding the advisability of marriage. An exact translation into Hebrew, even of Pantagruel's short answers to his interlocutor, as he replies alternately in the affirmative *Marriez vous donc* and in the negative *Poinct doncques ne vous marriez*, with all the puns contained therein, would cost me five days of hard labor. For the nonce then, dear reader, here is the major part of the dialogue between them when Panurge asketh counsel of Pantagruel whether he should marry, yea, or no, in the English translation by Sir Thomas Urquhart that was first published in 1653:

"My lord and master, you have heard the design I am upon, which is to marry, if by some disastrous mischance all the holes in the world be not shut up, stopped, closed, and bushed. I humbly beseech you, for the affection which of a long time you have borne me, to give me your best advice therein."

"Then," answered Pantagruel, "seeing you have so decreed, ... what need is there of any further talk thereof, but forthwith to put it into execution what you have resolved?"

"Yea but," quoth Panurge, "I would be loth to act anything therein without your counsel had thereto."

"It is my judgment also," quoth Pantagruel, "and I advise you to it."

"Nevertheless," quoth Panurge, "if I understood aright that it were much better for me to remain a bachelor as I am, than to run headlong upon new hairbrained undertakings of conjugal adventure, I would rather choose not to marry."

Quoth Pantagruel, "Then do not marry.

"Yea but," quoth Panurge, "would you have me so solitarily drive out the whole course of my life, without the comfort of a matrimonial consort? You know it is written, *Vae soli!* and a single person is never seen to reap the joy and solace that is found with married folks."

"Then marry, in the name of God," quoth Pantagruel.

"But if," quoth Panurge, "my wife should make me a cuckold—as it is not unknown unto you, how this hath been a very plentiful year in the production of that kind of cattle—I would fly out, and grow impatient beyond all measure and mean. I love cuckolds with my heart...and I truly do very willingly frequent their company; but should I die for it, I would not be one of their number. That is a point for me of a too sore prickling point."

"Then do not marry," quoth Pantagruel, "for without all controversy this sentence of Seneca is infallibly true, What thou to others shalt have done, others will do the like to thee."

"Do you," quoth Panurge, "aver that without all exception?"

"Yes, truly," quoth Pantagruel, "without all exception."

"Ho, ho," says Panurge, "by the wrath of a little devil, his meaning is, either in this world or in the other which is to come.

"Yet seeing I can no more want a wife than a blind man his staff—(for) the funnel must be in agitation, without which manner of occupation I cannot live—were it not a great deal better for me to apply and associate myself to some one honest, lovely, and virtuous woman, than as I do, by a new change of females every day, run a hazard of being bastinadoed, or, which is worse, of the great pox, if not of both together. For never—be it spoken by their husbands' leave and favor—had I enjoyment yet of an honest woman."

"Marry then, in God's name," quoth Pantagruel.

"But if," quoth Panurge, "it were the will of God, and that my destiny did unluckily lead me to marry an honest woman who should beat me, I would be stored with more than two third parts of the patience of Job, if I were not stark mad by it, and quite distracted with such rugged dealings. For it hath been told me that those exceeding honest women have ordinarily very wicked head-pieces; therefore is it that their family lacketh not for good vinegar. Yet in that case should it go worse with me, if I did not then in such sort bang her back and breast, so thumpingly bethwack her gillets, to wit, her arms, legs, head, lights, liver, and milt, with her other entrails, and mangle, jag, and slash her coats so after the cross-billet fashion that the greatest devil of hell should wait at the gate for the reception of her damned soul. I could make a shift for this year to waive such molestation and disquiet, and be content to lay aside that trouble, and not to be engaged in it."

"Do not marry then," answered Pantagruel.

"Yea but," quoth Panurge, "considering the condition wherein I now am, out of debt and unmarried; mark what I say, free from all debt, in an ill hour, for, were I deeply on the score, my creditors would be but too careful of my paternity, but being quit, and not married, nobody will be so regardful of me, or carry towards me a love like that which is said to be in a conjugal affection. And if by some mishap I should fall sick, I would be looked to very waywardly. The wise man saith, Where there is no woman—I mean the mother of a family and wife in the union of a lawful wedlock—the crazy and diseased are in danger of being ill used and of having much brabbling and strife about them; as by clear experience hath been made apparent in the persons of popes, legates, cardinals, bishops, abbots, priors, priests, and monks; but there, assure yourself, you shall not find me."

"Marry then, in the name of God," answered Pantagruel.

"But if," quoth Panurge, "being ill at ease, and possibly through that distemper made unable to discharge the matrimonial duty that is incumbent to an active husband, my wife, impatient of that drooping sickness and faint-fits of a pining languishment, should abandon and prostitute herself to the embraces of another man, and not only then not help and assist me in my extremity and need, but withal flout at and make sport of that my grievous distress and calamity; or peradventure, which is worse, embezzle my goods and steal from me, as I have seen it oftentimes befall unto the lot of many other men, it were enough to undo me utterly, to fill brimful the cup of my misfortune, and make me play the mad-pate reeks of Bedlam."

"Do not marry then," quoth Pantagruel.

"Yea but," said Panurge, "I shall never by any other means come to have lawful sons and daughters, in whom I may harbor some hope of perpetuating my name and arms, and to whom also I may leave and bequeath my inheritances and purchased goods (of which latter sort you need not doubt but that in some one or other of these mornings I will make a fair and goodly show), that so I may cheer up and make merry when otherwise I should be plunged into a peevish sullen mood of pensive sullenness, as I do perceive daily by the gentle and loving carriage of your kind and gracious father towards you; as all honest folks use to do at their own homes and private dwelling-houses. For being free from debt, and yet not married, if casually I should fret and be angry, although the cause of my grief and displeasure were never so just, I am afraid, instead of consolation, that I should meet with nothing else but scoffs, frumps, gibes, and mocks at my disastrous fortune."

"Marry then, in the name of God," quoth Pantagruel.

Chapter thirty-six

Hedva's Son

Yaron, Hedva's son, was killed in a helicopter accident, a crash in Sinai.

His picture stood on the dresser next to her bed, pressed between two sheets of glass without a frame: a boy of about seventeen, with arched dark eyebrows, a faint mustache, a mouth that broadens into a forced, almost painful smile, narrow eyes smiling ironically, or suspiciously.

Victoria, on the staircase, said to me accusingly: Don't you know that Hedva is ill? It's been ten days already! And she reproved me for being "like all those writers and artists," interested only in themselves, those whose neighbors could be dead as far as they're concerned.

Her expression isn't like it used to be. Hostile towards me, for some reason.

Schatz came home from the hospital three days ago, his arm in a cast that hung from his neck in a sling. I saw him through the peephole of my door, more sour-faced than ever, going up the stairs with Naomi, who carried his briefcase. In the evening he tried to type with one hand, and that sound is as nerve-wracking as the thumping of a cripple's crutch on the sidewalk.

In any case I couldn't write. I went in to see Hedva and found her in bed. When I came in, she sat up and propped her head on the pillow. I asked her how she was doing, and she said she had piercing pains in the heart. Difficulty breathing. They had examined her and hadn't found a thing. "You know how it is with doctors," she said. "Whenever they don't find anything they say it's psychosomatic. But that doesn't stop the pains."

"Now too?" I asked. She placed her hand over her heart, breathed deeply, and I saw that it was hard for her. I said it happened to me too sometimes, maybe because of the weather, maybe nerves.

"So I'm not a hypochondriac," she smiled.

I looked at the picture on the dresser and asked if it was her son. Yes, she said, she had been thinking about him a lot these past few days, when she was by herself, with no distractions except for the books she read—and it's in the nature of reading that you pause every few pages and think about what you have on your mind. For example, she was in the middle of the diary of an Egyptian soldier who had been killed in Sinai during the Yom Kippur War. Very moving, bearing witness to the fact that when a person is alone in the face of death, all that remains is that he is created in God's image and it doesn't matter what race he is from, or what religion: longing for a mother, a father, a native village; worrying about brothers; fear; the painful question of whether there is life after death… She remembered his words: Mother, I am tormented when I think about your tears as death enfolds me… If I die, I hope that I will not live on only in the memory of my brother Khaled, who died in battle… She read and thought: Yaron lives on only in her memories. He left nothing after him. He was buried in a mass grave, because his body was not found—only bones scattered with the bones of the rest of the victims. When she leaves this world…not even the memory will stay behind… Is it possible that a person meets his end and he has no immortal soul? As if he had never been?

Then she told me about her son. I will put down what she said the way it has been preserved in my memory. Although she told it bit by bit, pausing from time to time due to the difficulties she had breathing, I shall put it down in one piece.

Yaron was a nervous and restless boy. Even when still in his mother's womb, he would kick so much that she had to lay both her hands on her abdomen to calm him down. When he was nursing, he would thrust the nipple from his mouth from time to time and burst out crying, and in his crib, when he lay on his back, he would pedal his feet in the air very energetically, as though riding a bicycle fast. Once he learned to walk he never stayed in one place for two minutes at a time, but would run around the room of the tiny apartment in which they then lived and escape from it whenever the door opened, rushing off down the stairs. If she didn't catch up with him and grab him, he would run into the street. When she took him out in the stroller, she had to strap him in, because all he wanted was to get away from her and run free. All the years of his childhood she was pursued by the fear that he would rush across the street and get run over.

When he was four years old, after some teasing by children in the nursery school—that is, Hedva's nursery school—he asked her for the first time why he didn't have a father like all the other children. She had long been prepared for this question and had decided to reply to it courageously—not "Your father went on a long, long trip" or evasions of that sort—but: There are some mothers who are not married and who do not know where the fathers of their children are. He listened to her answer, thought whatever he thought, and didn't ask any more. But the children continued to tease him from time to time, and he found a stratagem to use against them: he would "make faces". Every time one of the children would ask about his father, he wouldn't answer, but would pull a funny face instead: press his lips together and pull them to the sides, narrow his eyes and squeeze the muscles of his face into a mask that aroused laughter and revulsion at once. As he kept doing this time and again, the children stopped bothering him.

When he was five, Hedva took him to visit Merhavim, the

kibbutz in the Negev which she had left several years earlier along with her young husband, Shlomik.

All those years they had held a grudge against her in the kibbutz—she said—not forgiving her for leaving, and for causing Shlomik, whom everyone had liked, to leave. For that reason, and for fear of the wagging tongues and the evil eyes, she had never gone back to visit, not even once. But her good friend Adinah, who would come to visit whenever she was in town, and sit and relate all the news from the kibbutz, and even sleep over sometimes—begged Hedva to come again and again, promising that "Time cures all ills" and that no one remembered her "sin" any more. A few days after Yaron turned five, Hedva gathered her courage and decided to go there for a weekend, in order to treat him to a trip as a birthday present.

"And that was the most wonderful thing that had happened to Yaron since he was born," said Hedva. "Adinah had a son his age, and when we got to the kibbutz she brought him over to her son's kindergarten. He ate there, played there, slept there with all the children. Because he had come from the city, the children were very curious about him and he immediately found himself the center of attention. The teacher asked him to tell them all about Tel Aviv, and he did. He told them about how things really were in the city, and about totally imaginary things as well. As he had such a good audience, attentive, alert, and responsive, he got enthusiastic about his own stories and flew off on the wings of his imagination! He told them about flying fish in the sea, and chariots with white horses, and elephants in a circus that never even existed, and all about movies that he had seen and movies that he hadn't seen, and he kept on talking even when they had gone to bed, until the night-attendant had to make him be quiet.

"The next day, on Saturday, the children took him to the shelter, which they used as a sort of clubhouse. When they had all sat down, in the dimness, and their teacher wasn't with them, they became very quiet in order to impress him, or maybe to create a feeling of mystery—and he suddenly had an idea—maybe out of a fear that he wanted to get rid of—and he started to make faces for them!

Adinah's son told us afterwards how he made animal faces—a monkey, a camel, a bulldog, a Siamese cat, a fish—and also assorted human faces—an old man, and an old woman, and someone afraid of the dark, and a man who has lost his hat, and a mother who thinks her child has been run over…and they all had laughed and admired him, and he was the hero of the day! He had never before earned such an honor! How happy he was…

"After we returned to the city, he didn't stop talking about the kibbutz, and every Friday he would ask me to take him back there. He remembered the names of all the children, and the nurse and the kindergarten teacher, and he talked about the children's menagerie, and the grove, and the swimming pool… Memories of Eden! We went there two more times—for the Passover Seder and the festival of the first fruit. That Shavuot, with its parade of tractors and combines, the ceremony of reaping the wheat, and the dances in the fields—he never forgot it, all his life. When he grew up, he would talk about it as one of the greatest experiences of his childhood. Adinah, and a few of my other friends among the kibbutz members, tried to convince me to come back to the kibbutz, but I… No, no, I didn't feel right there…and maybe… maybe because I didn't want to take such an easy way out… I wanted to raise my child by myself."

Thus—after his success at the kibbutz—Yaron discovered his talent for acting. And so did his mother. And when he started school, she begged the teachers to include him in plays.

He was an undisciplined and scatter-brained student. He was careless in doing his homework, often came late to school, absented himself from classes he didn't like, and disrupted lessons by making the children laugh at his jokes and his funny faces. He was not expelled only because the school authorities made allowances for his special situation.

It was not until he entered the fourth grade that he was allowed, for the first time, to participate in rehearsals for the Hannukah play. He got the part of Jason, the Hellenist high-priest, in *The Revolt of the Maccabees*; and even though he would disturb the rehearsals by inventing his own lines—which were usually very funny—when he forgot the text he was supposed to have memorized, the director "suffered" his nonsense because of his acting ability.

During the actual performance, which took place in the big auditorium, he made a mistake that aroused thunderous laughter in the audience of pupils and their parents. In a long priest's robe, with a scepter in his hand, he stood next to the statue of Zeus, and conducted the ritual. When the moment came for him to command Hannah with her seven sons to prostrate themselves before the idol, he cried out in a loud voice, pointing his scepter at her heart: "If you don't prostitute yourself—you are condemned to die!"

The curtain was lowered at once, to roaring laughter in the auditorium. In the ensuing confusion, his teacher hurried backstage, grabbed Yaron by the arm, pulled him off the stage and sent him out. When quiet reigned, they skipped half an act, and continued without him.

And the sentence "If you don't prostitute yourself—you are condemned to die!" became a by-word in the school, and accompanied him, followed by laughter, that whole year.

He was eleven years old when he met his father. His mother, who knew how much he loved acting, would take him to the theater from time to time. One night, in the intermission between two acts at Habimah, as they stood in the lobby, she saw his father, the artist, coming towards her. Panicked to the point of stupefaction, she attempted to grab her son's hand and escape, but was rooted to the spot. With measured and confident steps, a smile on his face, he approached her, held out his hand, and said hello. He then offered his hand to Yaron, asked how he was, what grade he was in, what his favorite subject was... And, still holding onto his hand, he turned to look at Hedva and said: "Do you like the stage set?'

"'Oh yes!'—I said. 'Do you?' He didn't answer. He looked at me with that smile I knew so well, which he reserved for 'simple folk' who don't understand art, but must be forgiven, or ignored...that same distracted look on his face when he doesn't see you any more, when you don't matter to him any more, when you don't exist for him any more... Only when I asked what was new with him did his usual, alert look return... He would be having an exhibition in Amsterdam in the spring, he told me, maybe also in New York; Then he immediately asked Yaron if he wanted anything from the refreshment bar, juice, chocolate...and he was, of course, pleased when Yaron refused, because to spend a single *prutah* on anyone cost him tremendous effort... And when the warning bell rang, he shook hands again with a slight, polite, gentlemanly bow... God!—I thought—no shame! No shame at all!... Afterwards, when we were back in our seats, Yaron said to me, 'Who is that lousy guy?'—'Why lousy?'—'Sort of phony, thinks he's God-knows-what!... Were you ever in love with him?' he asks me—'What makes you think so?' I say to him, and am silently grateful for the darkness which hides my face. 'Because you blushed terribly when you saw him, and you were sort of confused...'— 'Really? I didn't notice... He's an artist, a famous artist...' For weeks afterward I couldn't sleep at night. Again and again and again the scene in the lobby played itself out before my eyes, and I would think: the universe runs without any rules of reward and punishment... That man goes around serene, successful, pleased with himself, while I..."

A few weeks before his bar mitzvah, Hedva found out that in rabbinical law Yaron was a 'bastard'. She had wanted him to learn his haftarah and be called up to the Torah for his bar mitzvah ceremony, like the rest of his classmates, so she approached the rabbi of the nearest synagogue. When the rabbi asked who the boy's father was, she said "unknown", and when he asked whether she was single, she admitted that she had been married to a man, many years ago, and had not been divorced from him. "You must know," the rabbi told her, "that according to the laws of the Torah, if you have a child by a man who is not your husband while you are still married—the child is a bastard. Although he is obligated to fulfill all the commandments, including being called up to the Torah, when it comes time for him to marry..."

She was so hurt by this that she decided she would never again set foot either in the rabbi's office or in the synagogue.

That evening she spoke with Yaron and revealed to him a bit

of her life story. She told him that years before she had given birth to him, when she was a member of Kibbutz Merhavim, she had been married to a man named Shlomo Porat; that two years after they were married, they left the kibbutz, and two years after that he left her and disappeared, and she still didn't know where he was; that when she was alone she had a brief love affair with a certain man, by whom she became pregnant with him…

"Was it that artist we met that time?" smiled Yaron.

Hedva replied that it didn't make any difference who the man was, because he had spurned her and she didn't want any connection with him either; if a father doesn't acknowledge his paternity, there is no sense in the son knowing the father, right?

Yaron, instead of answering, responded reflexively and "made a face" at her. A face that was both funny and horrifying, like those he used to make as a child—wide-mouthed, slit-eyed, wrinkled facial muscles. And he didn't say a word. She laughed. "A ghost laughed inside me."

Then she told him that she had been to see the rabbi, and asked Yaron if he wanted to be called up to the Torah anyway.

"No!" Yaron snickered, and got up, preparing to leave. "In any case I didn't want the whole bother! I hate the synagogue!"

His bar mitzvah party was modest—they already lived in this apartment, on Avigdor Street—and only a few of Yaron's friends were invited, as well as several of Hedva's friends, including Victoria Azoulai and Adinah and her family, who came in from Merhavim for the occasion. Instead of "delivering a sermon" or making a speech—as is customary for bar mitzvah boys to do, and as some of Hedva's friends begged him—Yaron brought a big tin basin from the kitchen, and two wooden spoons, and opened the Bible to Chapter 16 of Jeremiah, the chapter he would have read had he been called up to the Torah in the synagogue, and began to read it, accompanying every line by drumming on the inverted basin:

"The word of the Lord came also unto me saying"—tatatatum-tatatatum—"Thou shalt not take thee a wife, neither shalt thou have sons nor daughters in this place"—tatatatum-tatatatum—"For thus saith the Lord concerning the sons"—tatatatum—"and concerning the daughters"—tatatatum—"that are born in this place"—tatatatum—"and concerning their mothers that bare them"—tatatatum—"and concerning their fathers that begat them in this land"—tatatatum-tatatatum…

"Everyone was silent," Hedva told me. "No one laughed. I didn't know whether he was doing this to amuse the audience, or as a protest. Against me? Against his father who didn't recognize him? Against religion, which seemed to exclude him? I don't know how the party would have ended if it hadn't been for Adinah, who began to sing in the middle of his reading. Several of the other adults joined in at once, and then everyone else, and then there was a good atmosphere again. At the end of the party, when just the two of us were left, I asked him why he had done that, and he said: 'Because I've got an idea, to read the whole Bible in jazz rhythm, accompanied by drums, a trumpet, a saxophone…'"

At the farewell party at the end of eighth grade—which took place in the big auditorium—Yaron appeared in a "solo performance". He went on stage with a sketch of impersonations. He did imitations of the principal, some of the teachers, some famous politicians making speeches… He won gales of laughter and applause. At the end of the party, when refreshments were served and everybody was mingling—the students, the parents and the teachers—Hedva lost sight of him. She looked for him in the auditorium and in the schoolyard, and she couldn't find him. His friends didn't know where he was either. When she got home, she found him in his room, sitting on his bed and listening to a record of quiet jazz. When she asked him why he had run away so fast, especially after his great success, he said: "I was nauseated by those imitations. I wanted to throw up." Then he looked up at her and said: "So I'm a bastard, hmm?" and laughed.

"When I heard his imitations," said Hedva, "the thought came to me that this art was a way for him to defend himself against life's calamities."

During all his years in high school, Yaron never asked any questions about his father. But when he was sixteen, in the tenth grade—Hedva heard about this from him only three years later, when he was already serving in the army—he tracked down the name of the artist they had met at the theatre so long ago, whom he was sure was his father, and went to an opening of an exhibition of his at one of the galleries. He stood some distance away and watched the artist as he spoke with the people surrounding him, waiting until he would be free, and when he was left on his own for a moment, he went up to him, held out his hand, and said: "My name is Yaron. Do you remember me?" The artist looked at him, pulling his head back a bit, as if he were examining a picture, and said: "No. Remind me."—"Years ago, in Habimah, don't you remember?" The painter did not remember. "But you were a child then, of course!" he said. "You children change so rapidly, not like us! And your last name is?"—"Porat." "Oh, of course!" said the artist as he shook Yaron's hand and laid his other hand on top of it as well. "Of course! Hedva's son, right? How is she?" he inquired. Someone came up to congratulate the painter, who immediately turned towards him, and Yaron hurried to leave the hall.

That was about two weeks before Passover. During the Passover break he announced to his mother that he was going, with two of his friends to Nuweibeh, way down the Sinai coast and would spend the vacation there, amongst the hippies from all over the world.

He didn't get to Nuweibeh. In the evening the three of them arrived in Eilat after a long day of hitch-hiking, stretch by stretch, and they organized themselves to spend the night on the beach in sleeping bags. Yaron didn't sleep the whole night, and in the morning he told his two friends that he wasn't feeling very well and that he had decided to go back home. He parted from them and traveled north. He did not go home, but to Kibbutz Merhavim.

When he got there, he found Adinah's son Meir and asked him if he could stay at the kibbutz for ten days and work to pay for his room and board. Meir was happy to see him, found him a room in an old shack, and organized work for him in the peach orchard.

When he came home—suntanned, tired, a strange glitter in his eyes—he told her that he had spent "ten days of total happiness."

He had enjoyed the work, and in the evenings he would meet with the kids his age, who would pass the time talking, playing musical instruments and telling tall tales.

He did not tell her that he had fallen in love there with a girl named Nira. That only became known to Hedva in the summer. She had suspected something of the sort earlier, because he had visited Merhavim several times for weekends, and she wondered what the great attraction was. But in the summer he told her about it.

"I thought how strange it was," said Hedva, "that he was attracted to the same kibbutz I had left…as if he were looking for his father there… I never spoke to him about missing Merhavim, and I never told him anything about the man who was my husband then. He himself, on his visits there, tried to find out about him, and pieced together bits of information, until he had formed some picture of him… Did he identify with him? One time he told me jokingly: 'I'm called by his name—Porat! And what if he ever meets me?' …And how strange that he fell in love with a kibbutz girl…as if some circle were closing…"

The following year, Nira came to their house several times. A quiet, small, modest girl—Hedva liked her. She wished Yaron that she would be his wife. And she wouldn't have minded if he followed her to the kibbutz. When she thought about it, she even felt a hidden satisfaction, as if she could make amends for something that way. That things would return to their rightful order.

Then Nira stopped coming. And Hedva didn't know why, and she couldn't drag any information from her son about the reason for it.

Yaron went to Merhavim a few more times, and each time he returned more and more depressed, and enveloped himself in silence.

The last time he went there was during summer vacation, and when he came back—after three days—his face was covered with small blisters, which exuded a yellowish liquid.

He said that it was because he had come into contact with some plant or other. He had lain in the grass. Nettles, maybe. When she asked him to tell her what was happening between him and Nira, he said: "There are better men than I am."

He needed medical attention, and he was given a white ointment to apply to his skin. His face was a white mask, in which only his eyes made windows.

And then, when he was shut up in the house, long hours by himself, every day—he would stand before the mirror and contort the mask of his face. Stretch it, wrinkle it…

"One day, when I came home," Hedva said, "he imposed silence on himself. He replied to all my questions only with facial contortions and hand gestures. I asked what he had done during the day, and he, with grimaces and gestures, showed me how he had read a book, how he had made himself an omelet, how he had washed the dishes, how he had been bored, how he had sat and thought… I was entranced and afraid. He did it with great talent. His faces expressed more than words could have expressed. And at the same time…something frightening, God…he himself wasn't even here! He himself had died! A ghostly spirit was speaking from inside him without words… Only at the end of that long show, when I was sitting there wide-eyed, recognizing him and not recognizing him—he burst out laughing and said: 'I finally know what I want to do with my life'…"

To be a pantomime artist. That is what he wanted.

In his final year of high school he announced to his mother that he didn't want to live at her expense any more and that he had decided to earn money: he would appear evenings in pantomime shows. He had already tried his talents before a limited audience, and he saw that it "works"! Succeeds! They enjoy it! They laugh! …All her protests, all her explanations, about how he should be devoting all his time to his studies, to preparing for the matriculation exams, didn't help. He had already come to an agreement with a certain jazz group that between their sets he would come on with pantomime acts—five acts that he called "Moods"—and his salary, for two evenings a week, would almost equal her pay as a nursery school teacher…

He neglected his studies. He would come home from school,

eat, and start practicing. At first by himself, in front of a mirror, and later with a director he had chosen for himself.

"I would watch him from the side, mesmerized: he would play types…no, not imitate them…he would create them! The essence! …A simple-minded person crosses the street, gets caught up in traffic and can't find his way between the wheels of the car… A conceited lover, taking advantage of girls, strewing around false promises, seducing this one and that one, and not giving up on a single one of them… A man who decides to commit suicide, tries one way, another way, and hasn't the courage to do it, until he accepts his fate and lives on in humiliation… A child with an introverted personality, playing with his toys all by himself and the other children pestering him, teasing him, and he defends himself, fighting for his life… A young man searching for his beloved who has disappeared, calling after her on every wind and his voice is like someone lost in the desert… He would tell me that the audience would laugh, would roll with laughter… I, I would stand there with tears in my eyes…"

He didn't take the matriculation exams. At the end of the summer he was conscripted into the army. After three months of basic training and two months in the Tank Corps, he was seconded to an army entertainment troupe that went around from base to base, and he appeared with it in his pantomime acts.

Of her last meeting with her son Hedva told me:

"He had come home for one night. The next day he had to fly to Rephidim, and continue from there, by helicopter, to a performance at one of the bases. We had a few 'hours of grace'. Yes, grace. We sat in the kitchen, and he was in the mood—rare for him—to talk about what was on his mind. Usually he would make light of his successes. When I would tell him that I had heard from people how good he was, he would dismiss the praise and say, Nonsense! What were they enjoying so much? The talent? Every clown has talent!—But that time he told me about a performance in the Jordan Valley that had given him great satisfaction: no one had laughed! There was total silence during the entire act, and at its conclusion they didn't even applaud! And it was wonderful!—he said. And then he told me that he had prepared a new piece, and that he would perform it for the first time the following day, and the name of the piece was—'The Bastard'. What!? The cry escaped from me. Why do you get so upset?—he smiled—What's so bad about being a bastard? Not such a miserable bastard! There are happy bastards, and there are bastards who don't even know they are bastards… And anyway, it's only some religious label, or legal…

"And he described the piece to me, 'A Miserable Bastard': a boy looks for his father, sees him from afar, tries to get close to him, but the father eludes him. He pursues him, implores him on bended knee, prostrates himself, wants to kiss his feet—and the father kicks him. He remains alone in a field, and suddenly they begin to stone him. Stones are thrown at him from all directions. He covers his head with his hands, hunches over, becomes very tiny… Then, slowly, he straightens his back, his eyes light up, as if the whole world looks beautiful to him, and he is king of the world… I sat there in shock. I couldn't get a sound out of my mouth. He smiled and said: I see this is depressing you, but this is my most optimistic piece! You don't understand that it's optimistic?—It's a victory! We were silent. Then he told me about his meeting with his father, in the gallery. And he said that all those years, since he was eleven, he had known that the artist was his father, and he knew that one day he would meet him again. And it was actually *because* he had impressed him that time as such a 'lousy guy' that he had aroused his curiosity so much. He wanted to touch him. As if to understand himself. The blood flowing in his veins. After the meeting in the gallery he had felt terrible loathing, and wanted to cleanse himself from the handshake. From the defilement. To escape to the desert. When he decided to go to Nuweibeh, it was because he wanted to be as far away from his father as possible, far, even, from the city he lived in. To purify himself in the clear waters. But he went to Merhavim instead. Maybe because he was looking for human innocence… Ran away from his father and found love…

"I asked him what had happened between him and Nira. Why they broke up. He hesitated for a few moments. Then he said: She got pregnant. And I suspected not by me. I didn't believe her. Maybe I suspected her for no reason, I don't know. In her third month she had an abortion. But I couldn't see her any more. Trust was broken. Mine, that is. I'm also a 'lousy guy' apparently…

"That's it. We didn't say anything more, and before he went off to sleep he kissed me. Said I should wish him luck with his 'Bastard'. The next day I received word that his helicopter had crashed."

I looked again at the photograph on the dresser: a forced, painful smile; a troubled look, suspicious, oppressed.

"And now I think," said Hedva, "what will remain after my memory, too, is no longer?"

"His laughter, the sadness… They live on," I said.

Chapter thirty-seven

Notification

The following morning, as I left the house, I found this letter in my mailbox:

> To:
> Mr. Kalman Keren
> 39 Avigdor Street
> Tel Aviv
>
> Re: Nuisance
>
> Dear Sir,
>
> I hereby address you on behalf of my client, Mr. Naphtali Schatz, as follows:
>
> My client is the owner, proprietor and tenant of apartment number 8 on the fourth floor of the building located at 39 Avigdor Street, Tel Aviv.
>
> On the roof of said building, the co-operative apartment building in which my client resides, which

includes on its premises a structure the area of which is six square meters, said structure having served formerly as a laundry facility for residents of the building, you keep and raise six hares of which you are the sole proprietor.

I hereby inform you that the raising of said hares on said premises constitutes a nuisance to my client, twenty-four hours a day, which manifests itself in part as follows: noises, the spreading of unpleasant odors, the causing of dirt on the roof and on the staircase, as well as the prevention of the enjoyment and utilization of the roof on the part of my client.

I am instructed to inform you in particular that the matter causes grievous material loss to my client, in addition to the damages enumerated in the paragraph above, as my client works for the most part in his place of residence during the evening hours, and said noises and odors prevent him from concentrating and doing his work, which is also his source of income.

I deeply regret to inform you that since you have not, to the best of my knowledge, responded to my client's personal requests to remove said nuisance, this letter of notification is being sent to you.

I hereby inform you that if said nuisance is not removed within fourteen days of this notification, and if you have not removed said hares from the roof—upon the day following the end of the aforementioned period a complaint against you will be lodged in court, and all the expenses, court costs and legal fees will be your sole responsibility.

I remain, Sir,
Respectfully yours

Yoav Mengler, Attorney

I folded the letter and put it in my pocket. On my way to the French library I said to myself that in court I would claim that the plaintiff, the hare-brained critic, has sorely libeled me: "I deeply regret to inform you" that I have never raised hares on the roof of said co-operative apartment building in which he resides.

Chapter thirty-eight

The Abduction

On the way to Zikhron Ya'akov, in the bus, I told Naomi how my first story, "The Outcast", had appeared in print when I was twenty-four years old.

At that time, I had not been personally acquainted with any writers or editors, I told her. What was more, I had spent two years in France, and I knew that if I were to send my story to one of the newspapers through the mail, the editor wouldn't even bother to flick it a glance before throwing it into the wastebasket, as he surely did with the dozens of manuscripts he received from authors he did not know. And then, as I was trying to plot my way into that lofty citadel, enveloped in a cloud of glory—that "Young Israeli Literature"—it came to my attention that the very same writer who had visited our home in Bucharest when I was a boy was the editor of a respected literary supplement, in the shadows of whose battlements were assembled many young writers. I gathered up my courage, and decided to call on him and put my story directly into his hands.

I went up to the second floor of the building, which looked to me like a quiet regional health clinic, except for the regular thumpings of printing presses echoing through it from the basement. The door of the literary editor's office was open. I walked past it and recognized the writer, who sat behind a desk loaded with manuscripts, with the telephone receiver to his ear. He had not changed much since our first meeting: a shock of black hair, one lock of which angled across his forehead, sharp eyes with a shrewd or amused twinkle in them, two or three horizontal wrinkles across his forehead, like a forty-year-old man. I walked up and down the corridor, peeking into the room every time I passed it, but I could not find the courage to go in. I hadn't tried to make an appointment with him on the telephone, for fear of being rejected, for fear that he would say to me, as he probably said to so many people who contacted him: Mail it to me and I'll read it… And right now, he's probably busy… Somebody walked past me and asked who I was looking for, and when I told him, he pointed towards the editor and said, Go on in!

I said to the editor: "You probably don't remember me, but many years ago you visited our house, in Bucharest… 'Oh, of course!' His face lit up. 'Korngold, right?' And he acted glad to see me, and told me to sit down opposite him, and reminisced about details of that encounter, which had made a great impression on him, he said, and the big festival… 'And you're the little boy who sat there off to the side and listened, and asked his father what the words meant?' he smiled at me in a friendly way; and he asked, with genuine interest, when did we immigrate here, and how was my father… I said that my father was no longer alive, and he expressed his regrets, and asked what I was doing.

"When I lay the manuscript down before him, six typewritten pages—I had gotten the story copied in an office—he said: 'So my prophecy has come true then, you write!' When he saw the title of the story he said that Agnon has a story called 'The Outcast'. I said I hadn't known that, and if necessary I could change it. 'No, it's not important,' he assured me. 'If the story is good…' and he ran his glance down the first page, and turned it over… I saw that a sort of cloud passed over his face. As if he was saying to himself: Oh, one more pest! And how can I send him away empty-handed? After all, I owe him something for that memory, and to a young immigrant from

Romania just starting out and writing in Hebrew...and in addition to everything else he has lost his father...

Naomi laughed. She sat by the window, watching the changing landscape, giving me a warm and affectionate look from time to time.

"A beginning writer," I said, "submitting his first story to an editor with awe and trembling, is sharply, almost pathologically, sensitive to every bead of sweat on the editor's face, to every blink of his eyelids, to every nuance of his voice. He searches his face for affirmation, encouragement, and is terribly afraid of any hint of negation, or even of doubt. And I, in those moments, felt as if he, who had so much experience, from the very first lines over which his eyes flickered, had sighed inwardly and said to himself: No, it doesn't make it. I'm very sorry. But so as not to hurt him... And when he said, 'Fine, leave it and I'll read it. Call me back in another ten days or so'—I discerned that his voice fell, that the note of happiness which had been there when I had introduced myself to him was gone. And also when he got up and shook my hand and said 'I was very glad to see you' and the like, I saw the cloud on his face."

I waited for twelve days, days in which I couldn't do a thing. I read the story over and over again, and I read it with his eyes; and like a love-struck adolescent pulling petals off a daisy and guessing the fate of his love, yes, no, yes, no—I asked myself from morning till night about the fate of the story. When I phoned him and waited for his answer with my heart beating so hard it would burst—he said he was sorry, he hadn't yet managed to read it, he had been preparing a special holiday issue and been loaded down with work, and he apologized, and ask me to call again in a week.

When I called a week later some secretary answered me, asked me my name, let me wait on the line for two minutes—very long minutes—and then said that the editor was in a meeting that would last several hours, and would I be kind enough to call back in a few days.

"Poor thing..." Naomi smiled at me.

"Agony!" I said. "I called two more times, and got the secretary again, with various excuses. I started to loathe that writer-editor! I saw him sitting there, behind his desk, confident, established, like the lord of the manor, enjoying his power to wreak havoc upon people whose lives depended on his slightest word, on the flick of his pen…"

"Poor thing…" Naomi hugged my arm and pressed against my shoulder.

When I telephoned for the fourth time—I told her—it was he himself who answered the phone, and he couldn't avoid me. "Yes, I read it…" he said, and apologized for having put me off for so long. "Look, the story is sensitively written, but…"

I kept quiet. He mumbled, blurted out a few confused sentences, and I kept quiet. When he had finished, and said, "Try again—in any case I'll always be glad to read whatever you write"—I said thank you and hung up.

"I was terribly heartbroken. I sat there defeated and said to myself: That's it. The beginning is also the end. I haven't got a hope, I was just wrong about myself. I thought I had written something wonderful, unique—but I haven't, it seems, any judgment about myself. I sat there like that, drained, low-spirited, despairing… And suddenly a suspicion gleamed in my mind: maybe he hadn't read the story at all! Maybe because he hadn't wanted to turn me away yet again, and was embarrassed about it, he felt constrained to say that he had read it, and invented some shortcomings in it…maybe he had gambled! Because from his experience he knows that only one out of ten manuscripts is worth printing—he gambled on a refusal! I was suspicious, because when I reconstructed what he had said on the telephone I saw that nothing had really been to the point! General things, abstract… 'The characters aren't sufficiently clear, not alive…' But what 'characters' are there in this story, damn it? There's only one character, and he narrates the story in the first person! And maybe he had read it but didn't remember what he had read? Just remembered his general impression?

"A person who has the true urge to write—he doesn't give up so easily. Even if he is just a beginning writer, whose confidence is shaken by the sentence passed by a well-known, veteran editor.

He enlists spiritual antibodies against anyone who threatens to choke off his talents. And I, when I had recovered a bit from the first blow, said to myself: Who is this author judging me anyway? What do I know about him? Maybe he's an editor with conservative taste, who can't relate at all to innovations? And maybe what he writes himself…"

"…is donkey dung and asses' bray?" smiled Naomi.

I paused a moment, and continued:

"I went to the library and borrowed two of his books. I read them…"

"…and you didn't like them."

"You—have you ever read him?"

"Years ago! At one time he was very popular! Yes, I pretty much liked what he wrote…but it's been years… I don't know…"

"After I read those two novels," I told her, "I said to myself: He isn't capable of liking my story! It's too remote from him! Two different worlds! Because 'The Outcast'—the story of a man wandering in a strange city—is a non-realistic story, set in an imaginary place and time! And when I understood this, I calmed down. My self-confidence returned. I decided to swallow the insult and try my luck with another editor. To trust only the power of the story, and not to count on any doubtful friendships or charity."

"And you tried."

"I had spoken to him on the telephone on a Monday. On Thursday I took another copy of the story out of the drawer and sent it, by mail, to another newspaper. On Friday—I opened the literary supplement edited by my acquaintance the writer, who had rejected me so politely, and I couldn't believe my eyes at the sight of the caption: 'THE OUTCAST' in big letters right there in the center of the top of the page—'A Story by Kalman Keren'!—four wide columns that take up nearly the whole page! I had won the jackpot! I, the beggar, starving for a morsel of bread, open the newspaper—and Rothschild! Can you imagine it? A kid of twenty-four, pretty much alone, unknown, without any literary connections—sees his name in large print at the top of the page of a respected newspaper?!"

"He hadn't even read the story when he spoke to you..." said Naomi.

"I called the newspaper to thank him. He wasn't there. I found his home number in the telephone book. I was so excited I could barely speak. I stuttered: 'You said to me when we spoke...' 'Yes, yes,' he said. 'I owe you an apology. On a second reading I realized I'd been mistaken. A wonderful story! Congratulations!'"

As the bus turned onto the winding road that led to the village, both of us sank into our own silent thoughts. It was already five o'clock. On either side of the road was a grove of oak trees, and the cliffs gleamed in the sunlight. I thought about how I always came back to the same places. Go around in the same circles and never get out of them. Why didn't I go to Safed with her? Eilat? What drew me to bring her to my mother's house, in Zikhron Ya'akov?

The previous night, at half-past eleven, I had been sitting in my room and reading, when the doorbell rang. When I opened it, there was Naomi. Her hair was disheveled, her face was flushed and she was wearing a bathrobe and house-slippers. "I am seeking refuge," she said with a bitter smile.

I led her into the living room and asked her what had happened. She sat in the armchair, face hidden in her hands, and didn't answer. For about a quarter of an hour she sat like that, hunched over, not lifting her face, and I sat opposite her in silence. Then she uncovered her face, straightened her hair, and said:

"Since the day he came home, he has been punishing me with silence. The minute he walked into the apartment, he caught sight of the book you lent me, *Butterflies*, and asked how it had come to be there. I said that I had gotten it from you. I saw his eyes go black with hatred. I know that look. It's dangerous. 'What else did you get from him?' he asked. I laughed. 'Was he here?' He pointed a long finger at the book lying on the table. I said yes, I asked him to come up here one evening because there was a cockroach in the room and I wanted him to kill it. Naphtali knows how afraid I am of cockroaches—I really get hysterical. 'To chase away the cockroach he brought you butterflies!' he said. I didn't answer. Then, in a voice choked with anger and loathing, he said: 'You brought him here? Him? While I was lying in the hospital? Like the lowest kind of whore?!' And since then he hasn't spoken to me. I would talk to him and he wouldn't answer. I waited on him, because with his one hand he can't do very much. I sliced the bread for him, served him his food, helped him dress and undress himself. He didn't speak at all. Not a word of thanks. As if to say: this is how you will do penance for your sins. With the sweat of your brow. By serving me. You will be my slave! Not only did I not earn a look of gratitude from him, but he would look at me with loathing, as if I were unclean. This morning I woke up feeling so disgusted with myself, with this whole humiliating situation, that I decided to put an end to it. I said to him: If you don't start speaking to me again, I'm not doing anything in the house. If you have something to discuss with me—we'll discuss it. I am prepared to listen to whatever you have to say, and I also have some things to say to you. But you will not shut me out with silence. You will not humiliate me. I am not your servant. He didn't answer, of course. In the morning, he took himself a few things from the refrigerator and ate, without me serving him. At noon—he left for an hour and came back. Ate in a restaurant, apparently. Just now, when he was getting ready for bed, I saw that he was having a hard time getting his shirt off. He was struggling to pull his arm out of his sleeve, without much success. I felt sorry for him. I got out of bed and went over to help him. And then—with his good hand he pushed me hard away from him, and I fell over backwards. I got up, put my robe on, and left."

I sat opposite her, and as I recalled our first meeting, on the roof, when she was revealed to my eyes, and everything that had happened since then—I was flooded by a wave of excitement: Remediation!—I said to myself—finally the remediation! It was only by mistake that Fate had come between us. She had been a prisoner, and now she has fled from her imprisonment and come back to me, to her rightful place, to dwell with me. Yes, thus it has been decreed on high, that we shall be one heart and one flesh!

"Come make me feel better," she said.

I made her feel better.

Before dawn, when the first twitterings of the bulbul were heard in the courtyard, she fell asleep. And she woke up only at ten. "What's going to happen?" she asked. And then: "I'm not going back there. I can't." And then: "He'll murder me." And ten minutes later: "It's over. I've burnt my bridge."

About an hour later, when I heard the door slam upstairs, I went over to the peephole and saw Schatz going down the stairs, black briefcase in hand.

"What shall we do?" asked Naomi.

"We'll get out of here. Go away for a few days. Then we'll see."

I phoned my mother. I asked her if I could come for a few days, not by myself. With a girl.

"Who is she?" she asked.

"A friend," I said.

"Normal?"

"Very!" I laughed.

"I hope she's not another one from the milieu of Lili F...."

"No," I laughed, "she was born in Ein Harod."

"Ein Harod is alright. Bring her."

Naomi, who had taken her keys when she left the apartment, went upstairs to get dressed and to pack a few things. I went up to feed the rabbits. There were twelve of them now, five babies.

When we left, carrying two small suitcases, I asked Naomi to go down ahead of me. I rang Victoria's doorbell, to ask her to feed the rabbits in my absence. There was no answer. I wrote a note: "Dear Mrs. Azoulai, I have had to leave town for a few days, unexpectedly. I would be very grateful to you if you would be kind enough to put food in the rabbits' mangers on the mornings when I am not home. I hope this will not be too great a bother for you. The feed is in the two barrels. Thanking you in advance, and with best wishes—Kalman." I slipped the note through the crack under her door.

Naomi was waiting for me downstairs. We went to the central bus station.

The four of us—my mother, Nuriel Jacobson, Naomi and I—sat on the verandah of the villa and watched the sunset. The sun, golden, huge, slipped down towards the sea, and on the plain below glittered the fishponds, square by square, surrounded by thickets of reeds and tamarisks, with a few solitary herons fluttering low above them, like paper gliders. When the wheel of the sun, reddening, touched the horizon and began to sink slowly into the sea, as if bitten by an invisible fish—Naomi said that it was too bad she hadn't brought her camera with her. I told my mother and Nuriel that Naomi worked with photography, and her pictures appeared on book jackets and in children's books. "She's in books too?" laughed my mother. Naomi, who didn't realize that my mother was referring to someone who had sold books, said modestly that she only served those who actually wrote books, and I, well, I had the thought that unconsciously she had just admitted that she had indeed been the servant of someone who wrote books, as opposed to me, who is now engaged in not writing books. Nuriel asked what she photographed, and Naomi said mostly nature, plants, animals; and stretching her hand out towards the plain and the sea below, she said: "I really love water. Streams, pools, the sea..." My mother, picking up her words, recited the "Water Riddle" which I remembered from my childhood:

Je suis dans les airs
On m'attend sur la terre
Quand gronde le tonnerre
Quand brillent les éclairs
L' ètè je suis liquide
L"hiver, blanche et solide
En toute saisons
Une douce boisson.

I translated for Naomi: In the air I am found / Awaited on

the ground / When thunder crashes / When lightning flashes / In summer I'm liquid / In winter white and solid / In every season, I am a sweet drink.

My mother, wearing her expression of "noble weariness"—as I defined it privately to myself—on her pale face, and a string of pearls around her neck, asked Nuriel to bring some wine to the table, for nothing suits a clear evening hour like this better than a bottle of "choice vintage" wine. Nuriel, who looked like Dr. Albert Schweitzer, with his silver mane of hair and his mustache, rose with alacrity, as if he had been waiting for just this moment, and said, making a ring in front of his eye with his thumb and forefinger: "Something that will surprise you!" After he'd gone, my mother asked Naomi if she liked opera, and when Naomi replied that she liked any good music and wasn't fussy, my mother said that in the setting of a landscape like this, serene and enchanted, it would be lovely to play Mozart's *Magic Flute*. Should she put a record on the phonograph? Naomi laughed: "Perhaps Kalman would be interested in *Madame Butterfly*, he's written a book called *Butterflies*..." My mother laughed too and said: "Maybe it's *The Bartered Bride* that he's interested in..." I said: "Maybe C*osi Fan Tutti*..."—and all three of us laughed.

Nuriel returned balancing in his two hands a bottle of dark wine with no label, corked and sealed, as if he were holding a heavy artillery shell from the days of the Turks, and displayed it to us: "One of my last three bottles! Vintage 1905! This is what they call a truly great wine!" Naomi and I whistled appreciatively, and while he broke the seal and began pulling the cork with great ceremony, he said: "My father laid down twenty-one bottles like this in the cellar. The first time the baron visited here in 1887..."

"Nuriel," pleaded my mother.

"They haven't heard it yet..." grinned Nuriel as he pulled the cork.

"They're not interested!" and turning to Naomi, she said: "I've heard that story about the *phylloxera* infestation thirty times!" And to Nuriel: "What makes you think that every guest for whom you pour a glass of wine needs to pay for it by listening to your stories about the time of the Turks!"

"History of the country!" laughed Nuriel as he poured the wine—heavy and dark—slowly and carefully, into the goblets.

"Let them enjoy the wine!" and raising her goblet towards us, she toasted us: "Many happy returns!"

"Many happy returns?" laughed Naomi.

"It feels like a birthday, doesn't it?" There was a mirthful glint in her tired eyes.

The bitter-sweet taste of the wine was like the taste of ancient oak wood—if such wood has any taste—and a tiny sip of it sent the senses spinning at once. Naomi said that when she was a child, in Ein Harod, she had worked at picking grapes, but they drank wine there only on Passover and at weddings.

"I knew Sturmann from Ein Harod," said Nuriel. "In 1939, when I was regional commander of the Haganah, we chased three Arab marauders through Wadi Milkh..."

"Nuriel..." begged my mother.

"I'm shutting up!" Nuriel wiped his lips and mustache.

"Nuriel decided that I must learn to ride," smiled my mother.

"You ride?" asked Naomi

"I even enjoy it!"

"Rides like a duchess," said Nuriel.

"Terrific! At your age!" Naomi complimented her.

"At my age?" My mother took umbrage.

Nuriel, who had looked up to my mother as a representative of a cultured and aristocratic world ever since the day he met her, told us how the two of them had ridden to Dalyat-El-Carmel, and an aged Druze had been so impressed with my mother's straight-backed, "noble," riding that he had presented her with an embroidered saddlebag as a gift. My mother, who meanwhile had drunk her glass of wine down to the dregs, laughed and said: "What does Rabelais have to say about wine, Kalman? I believe he praises it, no?" I said that if I were to quote his praises of wine from chapter five of the first book alone, we would finish the whole bottle and sit here until the cock crowed. "I'd gladly sit here with the cock and the coquette, *au chant du coq,*" said my mother, with veiled eyes that bore witness to her having reached the highest rung of spiritual elevation, "but since you can't remember a single line by heart, I really must leave you and go to my room." Nuriel, who treated her like a fragile porcelain vessel, got up too and supported her elbow. As she reached the threshold, she looked back, raised her hand towards the eastern sky, and said: "Look at the moon they've prepared in your honor! *Lune pour les amoureux!* Go forth to the bosom of nature, young people!"

The moon was full, big and orange like a pumpkin, and we got up and went forth.

Arm around waist, light of foot, we climbed up to the pine grove. We found a bench made of woven branches, in a hidden corner, and the moment we sat down we fell into one another's arms. I whispered to her: "I have a confession to make to you. One morning when you were lying on the roof…" Naomi kissed me and laughed: "I know, I know…"

How shall I describe what happened between us in the grove as the light of the moon filtered through the pine needles, without overstepping the bounds of modesty? Perhaps thus:

Another part of the forest.
Lysander: We'll rest us, Hermia, if you think it good,
  And tarry till the break of day.
Hermia: Be it so, Lysander: we have found a bed
  For upon this bank will I rest my head.
Lysander: One turf shall serve as pillow for us both,
  One heart, one bed, two bosoms and one troth.
Hermia: Yes, good Lysander, for my sake, my dear,
  Lie closer yet; thy place is here…

And so, beneath the pine tree, our cradle sweet, her love was better than wine.

The next day we got up late. Naomi, wrapped in my arms, mumbled with closed eyes: "I could lie here like this the whole day." The bedroom was on the second floor of the villa, which had been put entirely at our disposal, and through the lace curtains that fluttered in the light morning breeze the crown of a carob tree swayed in the clear air.

Then she shook herself, sat up, and propped herself on the head of the bed.

"Look, he always wanted to humiliate me!" she said, as if she were seeking to justify herself, in her own eyes, and in mine. "At every step he wanted to prove to me that I wasn't worthy of him, that I..."

On the opposite wall hung a large, elliptical mirror in a gilded frame, supported by the wings of two cherubs, one on either side, and in it were our reflections, leaning on the head of the wide bedstead, the two *chinoiserie* table lamps, the pink painted walls, the pictures hanging on them, which I recognized from childhood—*The Gypsy* by Theodore Aman, and *Farmers Eating Their Meal in the Fields* by Stefan Popescu.

Naomi told me how her husband would humiliate her by imposing "punishments". He had various "degrees of punishment"—she said—according to the seriousness of the "crime".

When she made a mistake, for example, in the identification of the name of a place, or a famous person, or a historical date (once she said Guinea was in South America, because she had mixed up Guinea and Guyana; once she thought Levi was Strauss's first name, and she didn't know that Levi-Strauss was a surname) he would merely curl his lip to express utter contempt: such ignorance is not even worthy of being corrected.

If she mispronounced a name, or a technical term, when they were in the presence of other people (she once had blurted out "omonatopoeia" instead of "onomatopoeia"), he would estrange himself from her the whole evening, and when they got home he would scold her harshly and warn her never to dare to use expressions of which she was not completely certain...

Suddenly she became silent and her face clouded over.

I asked what happened.

"Nothing. I just remembered something."

"What?"

"That the electrician was supposed to come today. To fix the washing machine..."

"So..." I trailed.

"There won't be anyone home..." she said anxiously.

But right away, as if she had caught herself in error, she fell upon my neck and kissed me: "Forgive me, I'm still terribly confused!"

Then she straightened up and continued:

"I couldn't argue with him. He has such closed logic, organized, like a lawyer's arguments. Not a loophole! I would listen to what he was saying and cry inside from hopelessness! I knew that he wasn't right, but I simply wasn't able to prove that he wasn't right! Can you understand what it's like? Let's say that one evening he didn't find his house slippers in their place, under the bed—he has velvet house slippers that he pampers himself with—and he asks me if I've seen them. I say I haven't seen them, that I don't know where they are. After looking for a while, he finds them in the drawer at the bottom of the wardrobe. He takes them out and holds them up to me: Did you put them there?—I admit that I had.—Why did you say you didn't know where they were? —I forgot, I say. —No! You didn't forget! You couldn't possibly have forgotten, because you put them in there when you cleaned the house! After I, the accused, am exposed as a liar, the long lecture begins, which I have to listen to as punishment: a psychological dissection of my behavior, the whole purpose of which is to demonstrate how corrupt I am, how low: I consciously tell lies! And why?—Because I'm a coward! Because I haven't the courage to face the truth! To face my weaknesses! Instead of confronting them and struggling to pull them out by their roots! And because I lack courage, I live with inner falsehood! And therefore I fail at every move! Get snarled up in tangles of lies! ...And I listen to this learned disquisition and I say to myself: none of this is right! I am not corrupt! I'm just scatter-brained, and maybe a little careless, and it's not myself I'm afraid of, but his reactions... But I can't contradict his logic! I'm not a lawyer! So I keep quiet, let him talk on and on, and sit there like a scolded schoolgirl before the teacher who has caught her cheating on an exam..."

Once—she told me—when Schatz went into the bank to deposit some money, the clerk pulled out a check that had been returned. The check, which was signed by Naomi and made out to herself, had not been countersigned on the back, so it had not cleared. As she had given it to pay a debt that they owed, their account had been charged both a service fee and additional interest on the debt. When he got home, Schatz laid the check before her and demanded that she tell him why it had been returned. His gaze pinned her down, hurt her, waited for an answer, and she looked at the check, thought about it, and didn't know what to say. Only when he turned the check over so she could see did she grasp her mistake and apologize. He demanded an explanation about how a failure like this could have happened to her, which cost them blood! And when she didn't know how to explain, he punished her with an entire day of silence.

Another time they decided to go to a concert at the museum. He was supposed to go there from the university, and she from their home. He arrived first and bought the tickets. She was late. He stood and waited for her at the entrance until five minutes after the concert started. When she arrived, out of breath, he said, pale with fury: "It's all over between us! This is the end!" and tore up the tickets in her face. Then, when they got home—

I said to Naomi that he was coming across like a person with absolutely no sense of humor. "Absolutely, absolutely!" she cried. "No sense of humor at all. He never smiles at a weakness or a mistake that he discovers on the part of anyone else! Does a crow have a sense of humor?"

"A crow..." I laughed.

"But if you discover a weakness in him, or a mistake—he'll never admit it! Like the pope, he's eternally infallible! And he's so sensitive! God! You just touch his skin, or dare to say a critical word to him—he prickles like a hedgehog! Blushes like a turkey ready for battle!"

"A veritable zoo!" I chuckled. I asked her if he loved her at all.

"Very much!" she giggled.

"He's insanely jealous about me!" she said. "He doesn't let me leave the house at night. And if I do go out, he has to know exactly where, and exactly when I'll get home. And God help me if I'm late! He slapped me once!"

"What for?"

"I lied. He caught me in a tiny lie."

"You dared?!"

"And he's also very jealous if he sees me reading a book by someone he doesn't like, and enjoying it.... And by someone he does like as well," she added, laughing.

Then she told me how he had courted her when she was a student at the university. When his class was over, he would, from time to time, invite her for a conversation, discussions that would commence in the lecture hall and continue along the paths through the gardens of the campus. He would lecture her about literary matters as she walked along beside him and listened. And then one day, in the middle of one of these disquisitions, he said to her: "You understand of course that the purpose of our conversations is marriage." She was astounded. Didn't understand, didn't believe it. It hadn't occurred to her that such intentions had been slithering around under the rocks of his detailed explanations, well-phrased and precise, about the distinctions Ortega y Gasset makes between aesthetics and human content in art. She had never imagined that a young man, in this permissive age, in this free country, would court a girl like this, and propose marriage to her like this, after the fashion of previous generations, before he had even tried to touch her. Because she didn't know what to say—she laughed. Schatz said: "You're laughing, but when I set a goal for myself, I usually attain it." How dare he!—she protested inwardly—and why isn't he ashamed to think of me as a 'goal'! And where does he get all that confidence from?...

"He had incredible self-confidence!" she said. "He was persistent, diligent. He 'kept his eye on the target' as they say in the army. When I avoided him, it didn't put him off at all. When I'd refuse, almost explicitly, to meet with him, he wouldn't get insulted. He kept after me as if I were only pretending to refuse him. As if he knew what I wanted better than I did. And on those long walks, 'in the paths of Academe,' he demonstrated to me, with his rhetorical ability, that he also knew better than I did what was good for me. He has incredible powers of persuasion! He...he convinced me that I loved him!" She buried her laughter in my chest.

"I'll get even with him for everything he's done to you!" I said.

"Yes? How?"

"I'll write a satire about him!"

"Is it worth it?" she laughed.

"Why not? Didn't Voltaire write a satire about Leibniz?"

"Leibniz was a great man!"

"Alright, so I'll write a mini-satire..."

"He'll see it as a parable, an allegory..."

"I don't care. You will be the Land of Israel. He...the cruel conqueror? The conqueror who rapes the beautiful land and brutalizes it..."

We laughed. We made love.

When I lifted my head, I saw the double of our image in the mirror opposite: lovers between whom even Parable will not come.

Chapter thirty-nine

My Well-Beloved Hath a Vineyard

We left the village with Nuriel—my mother stayed home because her head ached—and we turned onto the dirt road that runs eastward, in the direction of Bat Shlomo. Naomi, as if she had returned to the days of her childhood, flitted about like a butterfly among the grasses and the bushes, plucking a flower here, a tendril there, and bringing them to me so I could admire and smell them. To teach me a nature lesson about our country, she explained the difference between heath and thicket, thicket and copse, copse and forest. Look, this one, which releases a sharp, minty fragrance when you crush one of its leaves, is the mastic tree. And this one with the stem that's fuzzy and sticky and the tiny little yellow flowers is called sticky elecampane. And this one with the dark wrinkled-up leaves that has such a fresh and sharp smell is—

I was like an urban tourist in the midst of all this lush and abundant flora; and Naomi, who sensed this, waggled a stem of rue or primrose at my nose and said:

"You, as a writer, really ought to know the names of plants! Of every single one of them. Par-tic-u-lar-i-ty in literature, that's what's important, isn't it?" She laughed and sprinkled the pollen from the flower over my nose.

Sage. Stock. Globe thistle. Syrian acanthus. Hairy cassia. Arbutus. Medlar. Thyme...

Nuriel said that even he, a native of this place, didn't know all those names; and Naomi said that when she was a child, in Ein Harod, she would gather wildflowers and dry them. She still had her album of dried flowers, and under each one she had written its name and characteristics, as she had found them in the field guide, and as she had learned from her nature studies teacher. All of a sudden she noticed a flower peeping out from between some rocks: "Golden henbane!" and she leapt into the bushes. Nuriel, who had noticed, from afar, an Arab lad shepherding three goats on the hillside, called out something in Arabic and climbed up the hill towards him. I followed Naomi into the thicket or copse, and she came towards me, in her hand a sticky, fuzzy plant, with yellow, funnel-shaped blossoms intermingled with prickly, long yellow leaves. Pointing out the different parts of the plant, she explained to me how an insect reached the nectar hidden deep at the base of the cone: it is attracted by the crimson color of the throat, which draws it in, it goes deeper...

"Are you worried?" she whispered.

"No, why?"

"I thought..."

I saw sadness and anxiety in her eyes.

"It'll be alright?" She gazed into my eyes expectantly.

"It'll be alright," I encouraged her.

"The two of us?"

Nuriel—I saw—stood at the top of the hill, waving his hands at the Arab boy.

I hugged her around the neck and kissed her.

We got to the vineyard at the foot of the mountain. Nuriel, who was now beyond the reach of my mother's supervision, felt free to talk to his heart's content, and told us the history of this very old vineyard, which his father had planted in the year 1887, the year of Baron Rothschild's first visit to Zikhron Ya'akov.

I am setting down the essence of what he had to say, because of its importance for the history of Jewish settlement here:

Twelve years after the planting there was a major crisis in the wine grape industry. The baron, who always bought the wine at prices higher than the market price in France in order to subsidize the farmers, transferred the supervision of the vineyards to the Jewish Colonization Association, which paid the farmers half the price that he had paid. Many uprooted their vineyards, but not Nuriel's father. And because he believed that the power of wine would never wane, he labored for three years at a loss, and improved the vineyards by adding to his *vinifera* stock the *labrusca* grape, or the 'fox vine', which is more productive and has a stronger structure, and ended up making good profits. In 1910, the year which saw the birth of Nuriel, who was a child of his father's old age, the vineyard was stricken with *phylloxera*, the infestation that had destroyed more than half the vineyards of France. It wiped out almost his entire holding. His father did not give up. From Aharonson's farm and from the German colony in Haifa he obtained cuttings of an American vine that was immune to the leaf-lice, planted them in place of his infested stock, and grafted onto them a strain of the Rheinhesse vine, which is known for its transparent, bluish, thin-skinned and nearly seedless grapes. Once these began to bear fruit, their grapes were accorded great respect in the winery for their excellent wine; their quality determined their price. When Nuriel grew up and became the owner of the vineyard, after his father died, and after his two older brothers had left the village, he uprooted the vines that had gotten too old and less fertile, and planted new ones in their stead, which he cultivated not by the goblet method, but by the cordon method in which you spread the branches out on wires stretched between posts—as you can see right here—

Naomi didn't take her eyes off him as he spoke, as if she were thirstily drinking in his words. Is she so interested in what he has to say?—I wondered—is she really so knowledgeable about these things, strains of grapevines and their diseases? Maybe she's fascinated by his appearance? Or by the way he speaks, in a somewhat archaic Hebrew, with his Arabicized gutturals?—At any rate, her sparkling, admiring gaze made his words more spirited, like an actor who senses that he has conquered his audience.

"...Now if this young man had any brains in his head," he pointed Naomi's gaze towards me, "he would beat his pen into a pruning hook, leave his books, and move here to manage the vineyard and cultivate it! What does he get out of books?—Books get read, get ripped, and the vine renews itself year after year, giving wine to renew the heart of man!"

"And what would you do?" asked Naomi.

"I would get my rest and he would get his inheritance!" laughed Nuriel. "I'd give it to him free! For nothing! Here, take it! It's yours!" He waved his arm over the vineyard which spread along the foot of the mountain. "I'll even transfer the deed to your name!"

Millions!—I thought—Millions!

"*Asfur bilyad, walla ashra 'ala shajera*!"—he let loose an Arabic proverb, and translated: "A bird in the hand is worth ten on the bush!"

An assured lifetime income! Millions!—I said to myself—His sons had abandoned agriculture long ago, one a contractor in Haifa, the other the manager of a bank in Binyamina; his daughter had married a lawyer in Netanya and now he's ready for me to inherit the vineyard because of my mother!

The fly in the ointment—that from morning till night I'd have to be running back and forth among those cordons...

"I'll lease it out!" The idea popped into my head.

"Oh no, my friend! No no no! On one condition: that you manage it yourself! I will teach you everything, and you will live here, in Zikhron, and supervise the work—the harrowing and the pruning and the fertilizing and the vintage—all of it!"

"And put an end to books!

"It's hard for him to let them go!" laughed Nuriel. "Good. So if that's the case, let's head for the winery!" He swept us along with his arm.

What happened in the winery I remember only vaguely. First of all—this stage is still clear in my memory—Nuriel showed us the trucks unloading the grapes they brought from the vineyards, dumping them into the receiving pits. Then he showed us how the load was pressed, squeezed and swept along on its way up to the separation apparatus, which divided the fruit from the stalks of the bunches. From there he led us along the "Via Dolorosa" of the fruit—as he called this long route with many stations—from the separation apparatus to the inspection stations, and from them to the fermentation vats, filtering, mixing…

As we went down to the aging vats and from there to the dimly-lit cellar where the huge oaken barrels were stored, we were accompanied by a hefty and ruddy-faced man named Ezra—one of the supervisors in the winery, apparently—and at every station of this Via Dolorosa he offered me glassfuls "to taste" so that I could offer my opinions on the various wines, and so I could distinguish between Claret and Sauternes, Sauvignon blanc and Cabernet Sauvignon, Alicante and Malaga, Bourgogne and Côtés du Rhône, Port and Madeira…

The winery and everything in it—the barrels, the vats, the bottles, the flasks—spun around like a wheel in my head. Through a warm, pleasurable fog I saw the blurred faces of Naomi, Nuriel, the supervisor—were they laughing? Or did I just imagine it?—whirling round and round and seeming to float.

I remember that when we went back up into the light of day—and the sun struck my eyes—I was supported under the arms by Nuriel and Naomi, one on either side, and thus I was carried—floating, as it were—from the winery to the house, which was to the west of the village.

"What were you reciting down there in French?" laughed Naomi, when I woke up after two hours of deep sleep.

I tried to recall. Had my floodgates opened when the wine went in? Had I declaimed lines from *Gargantua*?

"What did I say?"

"I didn't understand the French, but when we got upstairs you spewed out verses in Hebrew, very funny… 'from goblet to gullet the wine doth gallop'…'if my sins turn wine red, then my books I'll forget…'"

Yes, this was from the drinking scene at Grangousier's inn. Now I remembered a great many lines from it. I recited:

'Tis drink made Jacques Cueur rich,
'Tis drink makes tree trunks tall and thick,
With drink did Bacchus conquer India,
With drink philosophy took Melinda.

"And you, my dear knight, turned from a satirist into a satyr," laughed Naomi, and kissed me.

Chapter forty

Caveat Lector

After having read the two preceding chapters, an interpreter of literature, his eyes darting back and forth among and between the lines of this book, will undoubtedly assert that our author, by depicting the pastoral idyll on a spur of Mount Carmel in colors verdant as the vine and rosy as the wine, wishes to demonstrate the superiority of the simple life, as lived by those who till the earth and toil in the woods, over life in the city, as lived by those who spill the dirt and spoil the goods, so that it may be seen and taken to heart. Therefore—it will be claimed—he has presented these things—not by chance!—near the end of his tale, as did Voltaire, who sent Candide, at the end of all his journeys, to cultivate his garden together with his Cunegonde.

Wrong. Unlike that writer and editor from Tel Aviv who had been godfather to my first story, and whom several exegetes credited with exhortations to "return to Nature", this author has no such intentions. He does not see 'Nature' as an exemplum of perfection, nor does he view urban life as a mosquito-infested swamp of corruption, and he has neither advice nor counsel to give.

And you too, reading this bona fide, pray do not hasten to

conclude from those chapters that the author wishes to set forth a lesson in the ways of the world. It might appear that through this tale of the triangle of which Naomi is one side he proves that evil is punished and virtue rewarded. He has no such didactic intentions. He is not righteous in his own eyes, nor does his rival have horns... What does he know about him, anyway? Everything he knows is from but a single angle of vision, two-dimensional knowledge, sufficient to create a flat character, but not a rounded one, as the theory of literature dictates.

And indeed it is impossible to know whether the reward is truly a reward and the punishment truly a punishment; for whence the certainty that the writer's good fortune will profit him? Perhaps it will divert him from the path of his destiny. Perhaps it will distract him from his Art—which is the purpose and center of his life—to the pleasures of Love and its delights, until, addled by caresses, his writing hand forgetteth its cunning. And withal, it is not impossible that it is the critic, rather, who will come out ahead in this incident; for henceforth, all his hours, night and day, will be available for tap-tap-tapping on the typewriter, and his fury shall be wasted neither upon the vanities of housekeeping nor upon the sins of the housekeeper, but will be dedicated wholly to the great wars of the Spirit!

Chapter forty-one

The Cart of Naphtha

I wake up in the morning at eight—and Naomi is gone. Had she gone downstairs to eat without me? Had she risen at dawn to wander in the woods?

I get out of bed, and through the window, I see her walking along the path which cuts through the thicket, or copse, to the west of the house. She stops, looks out to sea, stands thus for several long minutes—

What is she thinking about?

Then she continues to walk along slowly, breaks a twig off a shrub—a mastic tree?—beside the path, halts again and gazes northwards—

Is she having second thoughts?

In the afternoon we explore the environs of the village. We get to Ramat HaNadiv, the baron's gravesite, which is a large, pleasant and well-cared for park. Hundreds of varieties of plants grow there, while stone porticos and small pools afford it a regal air. As we walk along the paved path between the rows of flowers, a bird flies out of one of the treetops. Naomi stops, says "Song thrush," and for another long moment after the bird disappears she gazes in the direction of its flight, and says nothing.

When Naomi is silent, what is she thinking?

Does she regret having left home? Is she remorseful about her husband, whom she left so suddenly, in the middle of the night, without leaving a trace? Is she worried about him? Six years aren't just a passing fancy! And maybe now that she's so far away from him, she herself realizes—

When she wraps herself around me, cradled in my arms, it seems to me that she's wrapping herself around me not only because she's in love, but also because she's afraid.

I say to her: Naomi, if you think…

Don't speak!—She blocks my mouth with her hand.

And in the dark, in our room, she tells me that even then… Even then, when she was hanging out the laundry on the roof, and when we knelt next to each other and watched the rabbits…even then.

But all of a sudden, in the morning or at twilight, she disappears. Nobody knows where she's gone. Two hours go by—and she returns with a bouquet of wildflowers in her hand.

Does she miss him?

A woman of the Hebrews. Married. Hadst thou known the man whom thou didst wed? Didst thou love him? Hast thou seen with him eye to eye?

I am curious, very curious to know how her life with Schatz had been. Six years! Surely it hadn't all been quarrels and disagreements!

We walk along the road to Shfeya. We go through a dense wood. Rays of afternoon light dance through the branches of the oak trees, casting a grid on her face. I dare to ask: And didn't you have some good times? 'Moments of grace'?

She turns her smiling face to me, stripes of light and shadow, light and shadow.

After twelve paces she says: "Of course there were."

And doesn't elaborate.

I wait. No comment. No contest.

When we reach a clearing in the woods—a ring of sooty stones encircling a pile of ashes, the remains of a campfire—she says: The best times were when he would read to her. Read passages from a rare book that he admired and share his admiration with her, or read poems to her that he would translate, for his own pleasure, not for publication. Blake, Hölderlein, Scottish ballads…

I feel a twinge in my heart. I see the two of them sitting opposite one another in the evening, his face glowing, intellectual excitement, her eyes shining as she listens to him… He knows German?—I ask in a faltering voice, almost inaudible.

Taught himself, she says. Even learned Greek by himself. Translated a few elegies. Theogonis?

A man of many talents!—I say to myself—Maybe he translates Rabelais as well?

"Sometimes I feel sorry for him," she says.

And a few steps later.

"He suffers. Since his childhood."

Suffers? I wonder.

I don't ask. No comment. No contest.

She sits down on a boulder, and I sit down beside her. With a dry stick she scratches the letters in the dust: N, A, P, H, T…—and hastens to blur and erase them.

"Imagine that right up until the wedding he hid from me the fact that his father had a naphtha cart," she says. "By the way, a hasty ceremony. Pretty sad. A dozen people maybe, in the courtyard of the rabbinate building."

I prick up my ears. I wait.

"Are his parents alive?" I ask.

"His father. His mother died when he was fourteen or fifteen."

"Peddles naphtha? Still?"

"Still. Naphtali doesn't speak to him. Cut all his ties."

"A quarrel?"

"Because of the naphtha cart. Naphtali demanded that he sell it and open some small business. He didn't want to. Traded the horse for a motor," she raises an amused smile to me.

I burst out laughing: "For that he doesn't speak to him?"

"He's vicious!" She rose and shook the sand off her hands. "Believe me, vicious!"

All the way to Shfeya, with Naomi every now and then uttering remarks about the flowers of the field and the birds of the air, I compose the story "The Naphtha Cart."

The story is about Naphtali Schatz's childhood and youth.

He was not called Naphtali by the children of the neighborhood—a poor neighborhood in the southern part of the city—but "Naphti", after his father's naphtha cart. This naphtha cart, harnessed to an emaciated white horse which his father leads through the streets, ringing a bell and pouring out the fuel from its keg into the tins and jars of the housewives—fills him with great bitterness. At school he is ashamed of it, at home he suffers from it. The smell of naphtha emanates from his father's hands and clothing, he thinks that he too is contaminated by it, and it is compounded by the smell of horse droppings and straw, rising from the stable in the courtyard. In the evenings—as from the bedroom are heard his father's snores, stinking of naphtha fumes, and the feeble sighs of his mother, that sickly and humble woman—he shuts himself into the kitchen of the low-ceilinged house, and does his schoolwork, studying, always studying.

The children in school do not like him. He has a rather mustardy expression, closed, and sharp eyes that never laugh. He does not take part in games. Keeps to himself during recess. At the top of his class. Once—was it in sixth grade, or seventh?—he tells on a classmate who had stolen the questions for the geometry exam from the teachers' common room. During recess they attack him, throw him to the ground, straddle his back, he nearly suffocates. When he gets up, he does not cry, and he doesn't complain to the teacher or the headmaster either: he keeps it to himself. One day he'll get even with the pack of them.

The poverty, the revolt, the rancor forge his character. All his spare time is devoted to reading. He's read—by the age of ten or twelve—books on electronics, cybernetics, astrophysics, Einstein's theory of relativity. Dreams of glory illuminate his bleak heart: he will be a scientist. A world-famous scientist. He will invent a method for measuring electronic speeds that will astound the world. The first money that he earns as a scientist—he vows—he will give to his father, so he can get rid of the naphtha cart. He'll open a little store for building supplies or household goods, and then he won't need to be ashamed of his father any more.

When he is fifteen, and an outstanding student in the high school, his mother dies of a malignant disease.

— And then—

Then comes a turning point in this life.

His aunt—

Yes, his aunt, his father's sister, who lives in the city center (Sheinkin Street? Nachmani?) takes him under her wing. Every afternoon he has lunch at her house, and sometimes he stays there to do his homework until the evening. There, in the quiet apartment, glowing with cleanliness, unpolluted by the smells of naphtha and horse piss—a new world is revealed to him: there is a big bookcase in the house, and in it, row upon row of books—philosophy, history, social theory, statecraft, biography. His aunt's husband, a thin man with a wrinkled face, but a vessel full of learning (formerly a construction worker and today a medical insurance official or a member of the Oversight Committee of the Labor Federation) opens before him the portals of Kant, Hegel, Marx and Engels, Lenin…

Is he a Communist, this uncle of his?

Yes. A fervent Communist, fanatic, bitter. But Naphtali is not smitten by Marx, nor by Lenin either, but by Bakunin! The figure of this son of the nobility who turned against religion and the state, who was arrested, condemned to death, exiled, who wandered from country to country, stood at the head of revolts, founded the World Revolutionary Covenant—it is he who excites Naphtali's imagination! Like him, and like Nichayev his disciple—he too will one day write a "revolutionary catechism", an underground guide to seizing power! Here!

He completes his studies—with honors—and is drafted into the army. The first year—in basic training and the infantry—is a year of terrible agony for him, agonies of body and soul. They abuse him. They humiliate him. His thin body, his delicate, long-fingered hands are not up to it. He drags along feebly on marches, fails his target shooting, is punished often. He cannot bear the coarseness of the soldiers, the insolent arrogance of the commanders; the bondage of discipline crushes his flesh. At the end of that year, his officers realize that he will not succeed in combat missions in any case and they transfer him to the command of the Chief Education Officer at Army Headquarters. There they give him the task of editing information leaflets.

The first leaflet he is given to edit is called: "Sources of Petroleum in the Middle East."

In the evenings, after his tiring and dull day at headquarters (Stupidity! Stupidity all around! Girl-soldier clerks with tight little skirts and narrow little minds, haughty officers, ambitious and vain) he goes home to his father's house. Once again the smell of naphtha in the rooms constricts his nostrils. But there, now, he writes his first literary piece—

The name of the piece is—

The name of the piece is—"Bakunin in Schlisselburg."

Yes, "Bakunin in Schlisselburg"—not quite a story, not quite an essay.

A composition about Bakunin's meditations and spiritual condition during the course of his imprisonment in the fortress at Schlisselburg; a sort of diary, including the false confession that the anarchist wrote after Czar Nikolai I offered to release him from prison if he would confess his crimes, declare that he had recanted his beliefs and reveal everything he knew about revolutionary organizations in Europe. Cramped handwriting, cramped thoughts, in long sentences with little punctuation.

He keeps the notebook—about a hundred pages—in a drawer.

Decides that one day, after he has organized the first cells of the revolutionary organization, he will publish it.

Upon the completion of his military service, he commences his studies at the university: major—philosophy; minor—comparative literature.

In his first years there (his father continues to roam through the streets with his naphtha cart, ringing the bell), he writes "Principles of the Israeli Anarchistic Covenant"—a five-page leaflet, peremptory, aggressive, written in an angry and sarcastic style, calling for the overthrow of the corrupt, oligarchic-theocratic regime in the country, the seizure of power, and the establishment of a supra-national society as part of a Mediterranean federation, in which all natural resources—above all, sources of petroleum—will be common property. Several hundred copies of the leaflet, which he has published at his own expense at a printshop belonging to his uncle's good friend, in the commercial center—get distributed among the student population.

Bitter disappointment: nobody responds. Nobody argues with him. Not a voice, not an echo. He is all alone, alone with his daring thoughts. A prophet unto a generation that had not been readied to receive his prophecy.

In the third year of his studies he casts aside all his involvements with matters of society and politics, and devotes himself solely to literature. If he hasn't managed to undermine the foundations of society, he will bring the walls of its uppermost story crashing down—the conventions of literature! He devours two or three books a day; with great pleasure he discovers thinkers in aesthetics and poetics who are known only to a select few, like Quintilian from the first century, Longinus from the second or third century, Antonio Minturno from the sixteenth century, Thomas Peacock from the nineteenth century. At this point—embryonic, as yet, but taking shape—the ideas that he will later crystallize, and express lucidly and brilliantly in *Against Allegory* are already sprouting in his brain.

When this first book of his appears, he redeems an old vow: he adds the royalties he receives for it to his savings and presents this respectable sum—several hundred lira—to his father, so that he can sell his naphtha cart and horse and buy a small shop for electrical appliances.

The father takes the money, sells the cart and the horse, and buys a mechanized naphtha wagon. He continues to ring his bell in the city's streets and pour the clear, oily liquid into the tins and jars of the housewives.

"So keep your naphtha cart," says Naphtali to his father on his way out the door. And once out, he decides that he will never again set foot across this threshold.—

Vanities!—I say to myself as we arrive at the entrance to Shfeya—this so prevalent tendency to 'explain' a person's bad character as if it were the result of 'a difficult childhood'—poverty, desperation… Both Cain and Abel had 'a difficult childhood'; both Ivan and Alyosha grew up in Fyodor Karamazov's household! All sorts of people spring forth from poverty's stony soil, the righteous and the wicked, saints and sinners, geniuses and fools! Good is good and evil is evil! That's how it is! Genes! You can't change 'em! And Schatz is "a very vicious man," like Naomi said!

"Did he ever write any stories?" I ask her.

"No, I don't think so. Or maybe he did… Maybe he wrote some and didn't show me…"

"He could have written a good story, about his childhood, and his father's naphtha cart…"

"He?" she cried. "About himself? Expose himself?!"

"'The Cart of Naphtha' would be a good name for a story," I joke. "Like 'The Chariots of Fire'…"

"Never. And besides… He's afraid of the critic Naphtali Schatz."

"Especially since naphtha fuels the flame…"

"And you'd be his interpreter! You'll switch roles…"

"We're switching," I said.

Chapter forty-two

Last Chapter

For eight days we "plucked the flowers of love"—in the house, in the vineyard and under every green tree, and on the ninth we decided, with the help and encouragement of our gracious hosts, to remain at their house until the end of the summer. Both Nuriel and my mother liked Naomi, and she liked them. Her escape with me from her husband, which Nuriel called *hattef* in Arabic, or 'the abduction', and which aroused mythological associations in my mother's imagination, won the approval of both of them. Nuriel, who would sprinkle his speech with Arabic and Yiddish aphorisms, said: "*Min hafer hofratin la'ahihi, waqaa fiha,*" which means: He who digs a pit for his brother will surely fall into it. We sat for hours around the table on the verandah, sipping excellent wine, looking out over the fishponds and the sea below and telling stories. Nuriel Jacobson would tell about his heroic adventures, from his youth up until a few years ago, in his encounters with the local Arabs, with Beduin, robbers, raiders; my mother would tell about the days of her girlhood in Cernowitz, when she dreamt of being an actress and a singer; I told about what had happened to me in Lyon—the city where Rabelais had lived for a few years, serving as physician to the Cardinal Jean du Bellay—about my arguments with Jesuit priests in the old city, about the wild parties that we, the students, would have in our nightly excursions to the region of Beaujolais.

On the ninth day of our stay there, in the morning, we decided—in the council of four—that I would go back to Tel Aviv, bring Naomi some clothes and other possessions, as well as her camera—which I would smuggle out of their apartment—and bring for myself the books I needed for my translation, notebooks, and also the twenty-three pages of the novel I had begun; I would return well-equipped for a lengthy stay in this peaceful habitation. And as for the rabbits—

"What's the problem?" said Nuriel. "I'll send Abed tomorrow morning, with the truck, he'll take them, with the cages, and he'll also take you and the suitcases... They'll have the time of their lives here! We'll water them with Beaujolais, if you want!"

Abed, from the Arab village of Faradis, was the vineyard foreman.

And in the afternoon, Naomi's bunch of keys in my pocket, I took the bus to Tel Aviv.

The minute I walked into the courtyard I met Mr. Ben-Ze'ev, who came towards me as he walked out of the building.

"You've been away for a few days, I believe," he said.

"Yes," I said. "I was visiting my mother, in Zikhron Ya'akov."

"The professor isn't here either," he said. "His mailbox is overflowing, from which I conclude that he and his wife have gone on a trip..."

"Yes?" I glanced over at the mailbox. The edges of newspapers and large envelopes stuck out of its slit. Strange! Very strange!—I thought—Has he gone off to look for her?

"When a just man departeth from a house, so departeth its splendor and its glory," joked Ben-Ze'ev. "And really, the building is very quiet now. The Bzhizovskis are off in Switzerland, Hedva Porat, I heard, was taken to the hospital..."

"To the hospital?!" I cried. Hedva's pale face, as she breathed deeply and lay her hand across her heart, rose before my eyes. "Something about her heart. Cardiac insufficiency. That's what Victoria said, and she visits her every day. She's a saint, Victoria. Well, we should live and be well..." and he went on his way.

I took the mail out of my box and went upstairs to my apartment. The silence of an empty building prevailed on the staircase. So Schatz had left!—I thought wonderingly. Didn't have the strength to withstand the insult, the blow to his pride! Or maybe he just couldn't manage by himself with his one arm out of commission, and went to stay temporarily with relatives?

Or maybe he's confined to bed, and no one in the building is aware of that?

I went into my study, set the letters down on the table, and like in the days of "the war of attrition" I turned to the telephone and dialed his number. The ringing echoed into empty space. For about five minutes I listened to their recurrent, rhythmic bleat bouncing off the walls.

Suddenly it occurred to me: maybe he died. Committed suicide. After his wife left him—eloped with his enemy!—he lay down, swallowed poison, and never got up. Drank naphtha. "For what remains to the man of darkness, who still cries out, My wife, my wife!"

I went up to the fourth floor, opened the door with Naomi's key, and rushed to the bedroom.

The bedclothes were disheveled, and on the pillow lay an inadvertently dropped pajama top. Over the back of a chair were thrown two pairs of pants, and on the seat an undershirt. On the dresser by the bed—small change, crumpled bus tickets, and receipts. The door of the closet hung open.

On the armchair in the living room, lay a man's dressing gown, and at its feet—velvet slippers. Pages of an old afternoon paper were spread over the round, low table. Paper napkins rolled on the dusty floor. A used, crumpled handkerchief was lying on one of the bookshelves. The books stood there, row after row, as ever.

In the kitchen, in a basket on the table, was a quarter of a loaf of moldy bread, and around it were strewn crumbs, bits of vegetables, and a container of yoghurt that had turned green. On the stove stood a pot, the bottom of which was scorched. The tap wasn't shut right and it dripped with a rapid beat. In a corner lay two dead roaches, flipped on their backs.

What a sorry sight, an apartment hastily abandoned by its owners! All the signs pointed to a precipitous, unplanned exit.

And maybe he meant to punish her?—I thought—Perhaps he left so that when she came back she would find the apartment like this and he gone?

I went over to the corner where Schatz worked to see if he had left a note for Naomi on his table, if he expected her to come back.

The typewriter was covered with a grey shroud, and to one side of it was a pile of books. On the other side of it, next to Bakunin's picture, were several sheets of paper, and from the uppermost of them, typewritten, sprang the alarming title: Naomi's End. I went over and read:

<u>Naomi's End</u>

> "...and she crawled on all fours and her voice was like a beast's, accursed of God!"
>
> —Micha Joseph Berdichevsky: "Kalonymos and Naomi."

> Her filthy shift ripped her thighs bloated and fresh blue bruises dripping pus she crawls on all fours on the floor of the filthy pigpen her shame shameless and itching like a piercing wound towards the heap of peelings in the stinking manger snorting kalonymos kalonymos her voice grunting from hunger a dim memory of a wild meadow studded with star thistles supine under seven suns in the vale of splendor flickering in the dimness of her malfunctioning mind prick pricks up her ears hears the bleat of a beast a beast licking the dust tonguing the

feet of her humping master masturbate master ate the slops of whoring opens her legs to anyone who kicks her only last night your hair grew breasts ready lips pink asking me for it bow wow and again barks kalonymos kalonymos concealed in his mildewed room do do do it hollow words stumble around an empty room curse cursed lies on the shitted floor waiting for someone to save her from the solitary confinement of her cunt mind find her on all fours crawling to the corner of the freezing pigsty mewling kalonymos kalonymos digs five fingers into the foul mess of peelings stuffs peelings in her full mouth slopping out gums peelings tongues peel-ings swallows peelings to her shitting gut swollen belly to the trough hiccupping kalonymos kalonymos sits on the other side of the wall calm comes casting crapulent concupiscent call man her man harm man mangle the slave beast end animal end foul whore's peeling soul foul soul curse

I stood amazed and agitated before this page and I couldn't take my eyes off it.

The thought crossed my mind: Schatz has gone insane.

Yes, he's gone insane. Naomi's flight has caused him to lose his mind. The terrible fury, the jealousy, the impotence.

Yes, he's gone mad. Wandering the streets, wild-haired, spittle dribbling from his lips, and shouting curses.

Or maybe he's been transmogrified to a black cat. A street cat.

Or a mosquito, flying about among people, going up their noses and biting their brains

I stood there amazed and agitated.

Then I set about carrying out Naomi's instructions, which she had written down for me:

I took down a suitcase from the crawl space in the bathroom.

I went to the closet and took out four dresses, two skirts, three blouses, a sweater, underclothing and stockings.

Two pairs of shoes from the drawer of the closet. A leather handbag.

The camera from the dresser drawer.

The album of dried flowers from a compartment of the bookcase.

Cosmetics from the bathroom cupboard.

Cat and Mouse by Günter Grass.

A packet of letters and personal photographs. It was in a locked compartment in the upper part of the cupboard on the kitchen balcony. The key to the compartment was in the very bottom of a drawer of the dresser next to her bed, under an old checkbook.

I packed everything into the suitcase.

I surveyed the apartment again. Schatz has gone mad, I said again.

I picked up the suitcase and went out. On the way to my apartment, I glanced over at the seaman's empty apartment, and a shudder passed through me.

About a quarter of an hour later I went up to the roof to see how the rabbits were doing.

A scene of horror met my eyes:

All twelve rabbits were dead.

Amalia, Amira, Adina, Aliza, Atara, Ada, Zebulun and the five babies—all of them were lying in their cages, without a spark of life in them.

They lay shriveled, on their backs, on their sides, on their bellies, one with her legs stretched out beside each other, one with her legs curled upwards, frozen, one with her head covered with straw, and one with her neck bared, and the babies lying defeated around their mother. Swollen, their fur stiff, their ears limp.

And the eyes! Pupils frozen like sapphires. Like rubies!

He has poisoned them!—the words escaped me—Poisoned them, the villain! This was his revenge!

The mangers were empty. The water troughs were dry.

I fled from there. I ran down two flights and rang Victoria's doorbell.

There was no response.

I went back up to my apartment and fell into a chair. The monstrous scene wouldn't leave my eyes. A sadist's revenge! To spend his fury upon innocent helpless creatures, who had never done anyone any harm!

In my imagination I saw him step out of his apartment, a bottle of poison in hand, go up to the roof, pour the fatal liquid—naphtha? No, naphtha wouldn't kill them—into the drinking troughs, sneak away like a thief, return to his apartment, pick up his briefcase and leave the apartment—

When did it happen? The day we left? The following day?

I saw the rabbits twitching, fluttering in extended death throes, moaning, wailing—

And not one of the neighbors heard anything? Saw? Noticed it until now? Where was Victoria?

I got up and phoned Zikhron Ya'akov. I asked for Naomi.

"All the rabbits are dead," I announced. "He poisoned them."

"What?!!"

"He poisoned them. Dead. All of them."

Silence.

"Where is he?"

"He's not here. Left the house. Several days ago. Your mailbox is full. A few days' worth."

"I can't believe it! I can't…"

"It's his revenge."

"He's gone mad!"

"Looks like it."

"Do you want me to come?"

"No. I'll be back tomorrow. I'll take the bus. Tell Nuriel not to send Abed."

"Frightening."

"Yes."

I paced like a leopard in a cage. The fires of vengeance burned within me.

Murderer!

"Oh! you carping critics, from the root of Zoilus!" Lines from *Gargantua and Pantagruel* rang in my ears. "Envious rivals! Go hang yourselves, I say; go choose your own trees to hang from. Rope shall not be lacking! Oh you biting-bitches, lusters for money and glory! I declare that I shall provide the rope in plenty! With an open hand, free, without money! I'll save the hangman's fee!

"Oh you brazen faced blazers, crop-cocks! All your books shall be as naught! No hand will desire to touch them! No eye to see! This will be their end and their predestined fate."

When I had calmed down a bit, I went over to the table to look through the mail I had taken out of my mailbox. Among the bills, reminders, invitations, advertisements, and bank statements was an unstamped envelope. I opened it and recognized the round, childish handwriting. Victoria's. On a sheet of pink paper were written these words:

Dear Mr. Keren!

You snuck out of the house like a thief
And cuckolded Mr. N.
If you prefer married women to bunnies
I won't take care of them.

I'm not an intellectual like you are,
Nor even as smart as she
But you'd better not forget:
I'm a woman of dignity!

And I'm not a household servant
So don't you dare get in the habit
Of leaving me little notes
Telling me to feed your rabbits!

Oh no, you big-shot writer!

Riding on the camel's wings!
You may have gotten the critic upstairs,
but you can't get me!

Beware the evil eye,
Victoria Azoulai.

I set down the paper, completely overwhelmed. She?!

Keeping food from their mouths? The entire eight days? Starving them to death?

She had the heart to do this? To know that they, upstairs there, are suffering agonies of hunger, the suffering worsening hourly, dying—and to sit quietly in her apartment?

She, the merciful, the "saint"?

She, who would bring them scraps from her table, and coo at them as if they were babies?

She is that consumed by jealousy?

He wasn't the murderer? She?!

Evening fell. I didn't turn on the light. I sat and pondered the fate of the rabbits, who had fallen on the battlefield of an inane literary war. If Schatz had not come to live in this building—Victoria would not have been jealous, my friend Michael would not have done him bodily injury, he would not have been taken to the hospital, Naomi would not have fled in the face of his anger, the two of us would not have left town—and the rabbits would have lived on for a long, long time, unto the third and the fourth generation.

Tears stood in my eyes as I recalled the many beautiful moments I had spent with them, moments of calm serenity, when I would watch them and see how they twittered their sensitive whiskers, ceaselessly twitched their fleshy mouths, pricked up their pink, transparent ears, the veins of which looked like the traceries of leaves, hopped with sharp turns over the straw, hungrily mouthed their food, or stood before me and gazed up with their bright eyes shining like precious stones, with an expression of innocence and gratitude. My gut churned when I remembered Ada's pregnancy, how her pretty belly swelled, and an expression of joy added grace to her lovely face. And the soft, cuddly babies that lay on her shiny belly and suckled at her nipples; the noble-spirited Zebulun, as he so swiftly and deftly mated Amalia or Atara, slipping his thin and charming member towards their wombs, unerringly and unimpeachably—

Ah, senseless victims of fierce literary rivalry, or of untrammeled female jealousy! I am distressed for you, Amira, Adina, Aliza, I am distressed for thee, Zebulun, very pleasant have ye been unto me; your love to me was wonderful—

It was silent in the building. Not a sound was heard. Not the sound of speech, not the sound of the typewriter, not the sound of footsteps on the stairs. It seemed to me as if the building had been emptied of its inhabitants. And as I listened to this silence, the fearful thought struck me that by writing about the tenants of the building, I had put them to death, as it were. They had ceased to exist and had become names, words, letters. Like the flowers Naomi would pluck and identify, and dry between the pages of her album. Even I myself—

Turning on the light, I was startled by the sight of two roaches skittering across the floor. I went after them with my foot, attempting to crush them, but failed. They scuttled zig-zag to the kitchen, escaped from under my heels and hid under the cupboard and the stove. While I was still looking for the broom to get at them in their hiding place, a third one appeared, from the direction of the refrigerator niche. I stamped my foot with all my strength, here, and here, and there, and there and missed again. It fled like one drugged towards the front door and escaped through the crack of the threshold. I opened the door, sprang after it onto the landing, and with a mighty blow of my heel crushed its head until his marrow sprayed over the tiles.

At the same moment the door opposite me opened, and Heinz appeared.

"By you as well?" he said.

"I don't understand how all of a sudden…"

"It's from there!" He pointed upwards, towards Schatz's apartment. "*Herr* Professor went away and left all his *Schmutz.* We need to break into his apartment and exterminate there!"

On one of the steps going down from the fourth floor skulked a fat roach. We watched as it moved spasmodically towards a corner, and froze to the spot.

Heinz jumped on it furiously, crushing it with his shoe.

"*Schwein!*" he muttered.

And when he came back down to where I was, he said that if Schatz didn't come back tomorrow he would call the municipal inspectors to enter his apartment and fumigate it. "I don't care if they burn all the books in there!" he said.

Late that night I sat down at my desk. From the drawer, I took the twenty-three pages of the book I had begun writing several months ago, the one intended to be the *ultimus liber*, the one that would include within itself plot and its interpretation, and lay them before me. I reread what I had written—twenty-two and a half pages telling about the first five minutes of the family gathering on the eve of the Seder—and I was pleased with them. The last sentence, which had been cut off in the middle, was:

"The dining room was like a temple of splendor, and light was sown in his eyes, but when he saw her at the set Passover table, beneath the bronze bird, and the pallor of death on her face—"

I picked up my pen and added:

"he bowed to her, offered her the bouquet of poppies red as blood, and passing his glance over the twenty-two place-settings of gleaming silver and china, he inquired with a sad smile: And the cup for Elijah the prophet ?"

Finis. June 22, 1982.

Glossary

Afikoman— the final piece of matza eaten in the Passover Seder. After the *afikoman* is eaten, one may not consume any other food for the rest of the night.

Aharonson, Aharon— (1876-1919) A famous agronomist and a pioneer of botanical research in Palestine and Transjordan. His discovery of the earliest ancestor of the wheat plant garnered him fame in France and England. At Atlit, near Zikhron Ya'akov, he established an experimental farm where he grew many varieties of grape. He is best known as the founder of NILI, a controversial organization that supplied intelligence information to the British at the end of World War I.

Ari *or* HaAri— appellation for Rabbi Isaac Luria (1534-1572), kabbalist and poet. Ha'Ari, 'The Lion', is an anagram for 'The Divine Rabbi Isaac'.

Ba'al Peor— an idol, whose place of worship was a mountain. Balaam stands on the "top of Peor" as he prepares to curse the Israelites in Numbers 23:28.

Bar mitzvah— a coming-of-age ceremony, admitting a boy of thirteen as an adult member of the Jewish community. Often, on the Sabbath following the week of his birthday, the boy will publicly read the weekly Torah portion as well as the HAFTARAH. The equivalent for a female is a bat mitzvah, which takes place at the age of twelve.

Bat Mitzvah— a coming-of-age ceremony, admitting a girl of twelve as an adult member of the Jewish community.

Brainin, Reuben— (1862-1939) a Hebrew and Yiddish author born in Byelorussia. One of his primary interests was Hebrew literature in the context of world literature. He settled in the United States, and in later life alienated himself from the Zionists and Hebrew literature by writing mostly in Yiddish and supporting an autonomous Jewish province in Birobidzhan rather than a Jewish state in what was then Palestine.

Gottlober, Abraham Baer—(1810-1899) a prolific and active figure in nineteenth-century Hebrew and Yiddish letters. A poet, editor, writer, translator, and patron of young talents, notably Mendele Mocher Seforim. Considered by Kovner—and some more recent critics—to be among the worst of the Enlightenment windbags.

Haaretz— an Israeli daily newspaper, founded in 1919. It is generally more affiliated with the left.

Haftarah— a portion of the Prophets read in the synagogue on the Shabbat and holidays immediately after the weekly Torah reading. Its theme usually amplifies the themes of the Torah reading.

Haggadah— lit., 'the telling'. A compendium dealing with issues of freedom and the Exodus, used at the Seder on Passover.

Haman— the biblical villain of the Book of Esther. The vizier of King Ahasuerus, (generally identified as Xerxes I), he plotted the genocide of the entire Jewish people.

Harkavy, Abraham— (1835-1919). Also known as Albert Sarkavi, a publicist and distinguished Orientalist. His theories concerning the origins of Russian Jewry in the conversion of the Khazars were taken up and popularized by Arthur Koestler in *The Thirteenth Tribe* (Random House, 1976).

Haskalah— the Hebrew Enlightenment. A movement among European Jews in the late eighteenth century that advocated adopting Enlightenment values, pressing for better integration into European society, and increasing education in secular studies, Hebrew, and Jewish history. Haskalah in this sense marked the beginning of the wider engagement of European Jews with the secular world, resulting, ultimately, in the first Jewish political movements and the struggle for Jewish emancipation.

Hatzfirah— one of the most respected and sophisticated

of the early Hebrew journals, founded 1896 and printed in Eastern Europe until 1920, after which it was published for another six years in Jerusalem.

Jabotinsky, Vladimir Ze'ev— (1880-1940) founder of the Zionist Revisionist Movement, (forerunner of the right-wing modern Likud Party). He was not only a military and political figure but also an accomplished linguist and translator as well as a writer of essays, fiction, drama and songs. In 1910 he translated Edgar Allen Poe's "The Raven" into Hebrew. This translation is inventive with respect to Hebrew locutions, florid, portentous and in every way worthy of the original.

Kabbala— Jewish mysticism.

Kaddish— from the Aramaic 'holy'. An important and central prayer in the Jewish services. The central theme of the Kaddish is the magnification and sanctification of God's name. In the liturgy, several variations of the Kaddish are used functionally as separators between various sections of the service. However, the term 'Kaddish' is often used to refer specifically to 'The Mourners' Kaddish', declaimed as part of the mourning rituals in Judaism in all prayer services as well as at funerals and memorials.

Kibbutz— an Israeli community settlement, usually agricultural, organized under collectivist principles.

Kibbutznik— a member of a kibbutz.

Kovner, Avraham Uri— (1842-1909) poison-pen critic of the period of the Hebrew Enlightenment and pioneer of an anti-conventional, anti-traditional trend in Hebrew criticism. After a tempestuous, checkered career, he eventually converted to Christianity.

Lerner, Chaim Tzvi— grammarian, pedagogue and editor, who was considered by Kovner to have been one of the worst violators of the Hebrew language.

Mapu, Abraham— (1808-1868) an early Hebrew Enlightenment writer, who wrote biblical adventure novels and love stories. He was one of the members of the generation against which Kovner revolted. Nevertheless, his historical novels set in an independent ancient Israel earned Kovner's high praise because they awakened useful and exalted feelings in their readers.

Mendele Mocher Seforim— (1836-1908) lit., 'Mendele the Bookseller'. A pen-name of Shalom Jacob Abramowitz, who became one of the pillars of modern Jewish literature with his critical and satirical novels of Eastern European Jewish life.

Mezuzah/mezuzot (pl.)— lit., 'doorpost'. A parchment placed in the doorway of rooms in Jewish homes, upon which the first two paragraphs of the Shema prayer are written.

Michal— an acronym for the 'Micha Joseph Lebensohn poets' of the Hebrew Enlightenment *(Haskalah)*, who attempted to emulate the gentle lyricism of poets such as Micah Joseph Lebensohn (1828-1852).

Midrash— lit., 'exposition'. Early Jewish interpretation of, or commentary on, a Biblical text. Also used as the name of a collection of such commentaries.

Midrash Tanhuma— one the main compellations of midrash.

Minyan— lit., 'count, number'. The quorum of ten adult Jewish males required by Jewish law to be present for communal prayers. Loosely used for any communal prayer service.

Mishnah— a collection of oral laws compiled about 200 C.E. and forming the basis of the Talmud. It is the foundation of Jewish law (halakha).

Moshav— a cooperative community in Israel made up of small farm units.

Moznayim— literary organ of the Hebrew Writers' Association in Israel, founded 1929.

Paperna, Abraham Jacob— (1840-1919) Russian-born Hebrew writer and critic who is credited with having diverted Hebrew criticism from shrill *ad hominem* attacks to the righteous paths of systematic literary analysis. At the outset of his career, his ideas ran parallel to those of Kovner, with whom he corresponded, but were expressed more calmly and judiciously. In his 1909 memoirs, he denounced Kovner as "a slanderer and a traitor to his people."

Seder— ceremonial dinner held on the first night of Passover that includes the reading of the Haggadah and the eating of foods symbolic of the Israelites' slavery and the Exodus from Egypt.

Shavuot— the holiday of Pentecost. Lit. 'weeks', after the seven weeks counted from the second day of Passover in preparation for the holiday. A harvest holiday that also celebrates the giving of the Torah on Mount Sinai.

Shulkhan Arukh— lit., 'the laid table'. The authoritative code of Jewish law and custom, composed by Rabbi Joseph Caro and published in 1565.

Silbermann, Eliezer Lipman — founder, in 1856, of one of the earliest newspapers for Russian-Polish Jewry.

Torah— lit., 'the teaching, law'. The Pentateuch, as well as the parchment scroll on which the Pentateuch is written, used in the synagogue. Also an inclusive term for the entire body of Jewish religious literature, law, and tradition.

Tsederbaum, Alexander O.— (1816-1893) founder and editor of journals in Russian, Yiddish and Hebrew, including *HaMelitz*, the first Hebrew journal to be published within Russia. As editor, Tsederbaum allowed Kovner to air his views in its columns, until the attacks became too much for him to tolerate. Tsederbaum eventually adopted the view that the Russian language should be the chief means of secular communication for Russian Jewry.

Vogel, David— (1891-1944) Russian-born Hebrew poet who spent a brief period in Palestine between 1929 and 1930, after which he returned to Europe and finally settled in France. He perished at the hands of the Nazis. During the 1950s, he became popular among the Israeli modernist poets.

Yalag— an acronym of the revered Hebrew epic poet, Judah Leib Gordon (1830-93), considered the founding father of HASKALAH-period poetry.

Yishuv— lit., 'the settlement'. Term used before the establishment of the State of Israel to refer to the body of Jewish residents in Palestine.

Zitron, Samuel Leib— (1860-1930). Lithuanian Hebrew and Yiddish writer and journalist.

About the Author

Aharon Megged

Aharon Megged was born in Poland and came to Palestine at the age of six. He was a member of Kibbutz Sdot Yam from 1938–1950, and later, a literary editor and journalist. He has been a pivotal figure in Israeli letters since the 1950s. His many novels, short stories, and plays reflect the complexities of Israeli society over the past fifty years.

The president of the Israel PEN Center from 1980–1987, and the cultural attaché at the Israel Embassy in London from 1968–1971, Aharon Megged is also a long-standing member of the Hebrew Academy. He has won many literary awards, among them the Bialik Award, the Brenner Award, the Agnon Award, and the much-coveted Israel Prize for Literature, 2003.

He has two sons, Eyal, also a writer, and Amos, who teaches history at the University of Haifa. He is married to the writer Eda Zoritte.

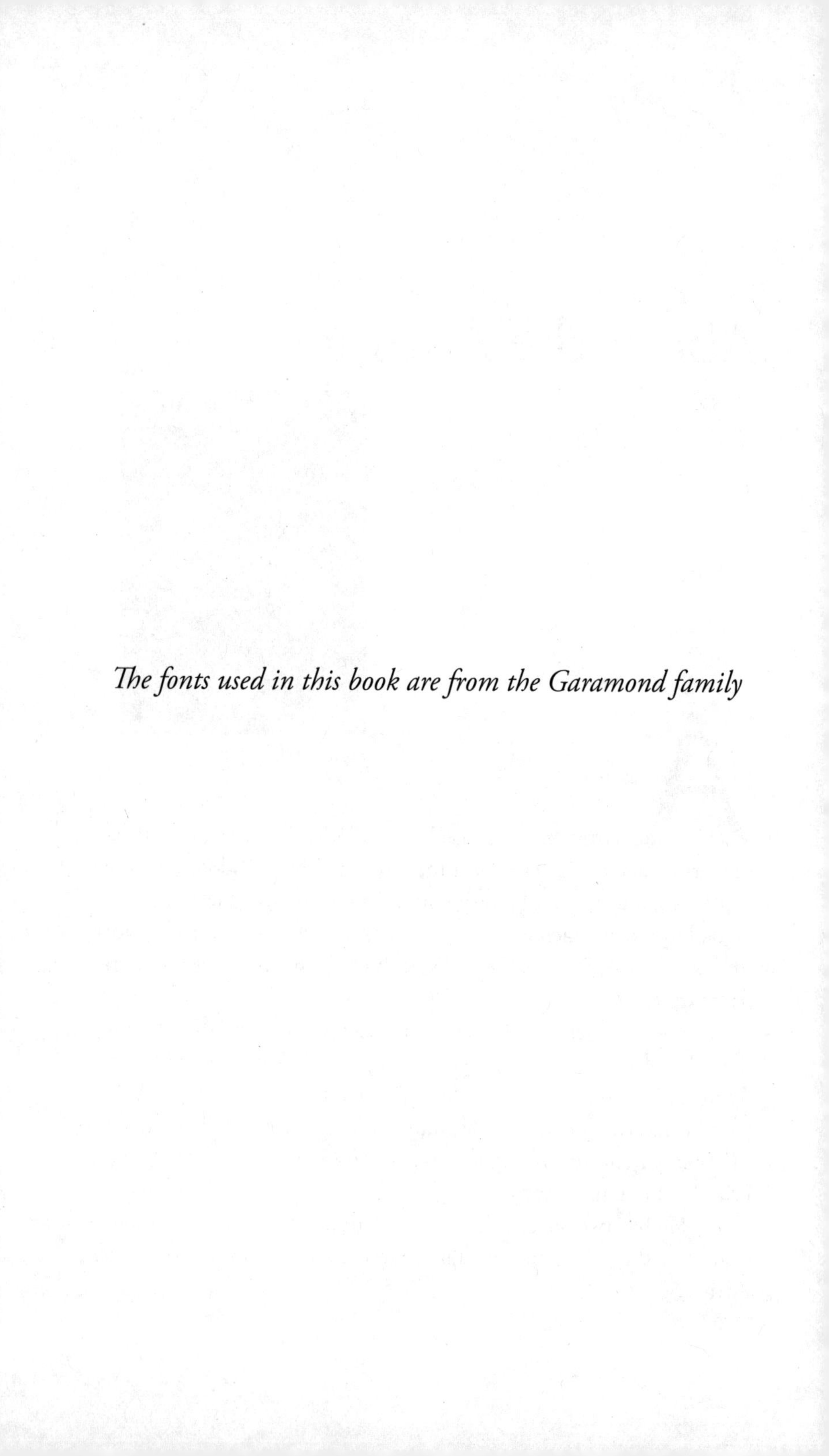

The fonts used in this book are from the Garamond family

Other works by Aharon Megged available from *The* Toby Press

Foiglman
The Living on the Dead
Mandrakes from the Holy Land